CW01647725

RAZR

THE OUTLAW CHESS SERIES

HARLEY DIAMOND

Published by House of Books Press

www.harleydiamond.com

Edited by Karen Sanders Editing

https://www.karensandersediting.com/

PA Services by Arcane and Reverie

contact@arcaneandreverie.com

Proofreading Services by Proofreading by Mich

https://www.instagram.com/proofreadingbymichx/

PR Services by Peachy Keen Author Services

https://www.peachykeenauthorservices.com/

Cover Design by Vicious Desires Design

https://www.instagram.com/viciousdesires/

Cover Model is Josh Mario John via Wander Aguiar Photography

https://www.instagram.com/spizoiky/

http://wanderaguiar.com/

Created with Vellum

Blurb

JEKYLL OR HYDE.
The Scorpions need me. I'm their prez.
But I'm losing control of my sanity, making rash decisions, and costing lives.
Two personalities. Inner conflicts.
Good versus evil.
Right now, my demon is winning, and he's waiting impatiently.
What's he chasing?
My condemned biker soul.
Two women. One unchaste. One pure.
One is the angel of death, the other my saving grace.
But which is which?
Because only one can save me from my nemesis.
Only one can save me from me.

Playlist

Paint it Black by The Rolling Stones

Cover Design by Vicious Desires Design

https://www.instagram.com/viciousdesires/

Cover Model is Josh Mario John via Wander Aguiar Photography

https://www.instagram.com/spizoiky/

http://wanderaguiar.com/

Created with Vellum

Blurb

JEKYLL OR HYDE.

The Scorpions need me. I'm their prez.

But I'm losing control of my sanity, making rash decisions, and costing lives.

Two personalities. Inner conflicts.

Good versus evil.

Right now, my demon is winning, and he's waiting impatiently.

What's he chasing?

My condemned biker soul.

Two women. One unchaste. One pure.

One is the angel of death, the other my saving grace.

But which is which?

Because only one can save me from my nemesis.

Only one can save me from me.

Trigger Warning

This book contains mature content, violence, swearing, and other potentially triggering situations that some readers may find offensive.

Please do not read this story if you are uncomfortable with any of the above.

Thank you.

Author's Note

RAZR'S story starts from where CILLIAN's ends (EXCLUDING the epilogue).

RAZR is NOT standalone.
RAZR is BOOK 3 of a SERIES, which contains an ONGOING STORYLINE that CONCLUDES in BOOK 6, DIRTY PADRAIG.

These books contain MULTIPLE POVs from characters across the entire series.

Due to the nature of the CONTINUING STORYLINE, these books MUST be
READ IN ORDER.

ACE
DIRTY CILLIAN
RAZR
DIRTY DYLAN
DIRTY EOIN
DIRTY PADRAIG

CHAPTER ONE

RAZR

The Iron Scorpions' Clubhouse, Brightling, New York

TICK TOCK.

Is it a clock, or is the sound in my screwed-up head? I'm not sure why I'm even asking myself the question. I know it's the latter. There's no timepiece in here. My life's already passing me by, so why the fuck would I want a constant audible reminder of the swiftness of its progression? It would drive me insane.

Well, even more insane than I already am.

I lie there and stare up at the ceiling. It's the middle of the night. Around two a.m., I reckon, considering how dark it is and the chill in the air. I've only slept for a couple of hours, but I'm already restless. My hand is twitching, itching for the comfort of my blade. It's craving the familiarity of flicking that smooth piece of metal back and forth like some sort of murderer's soother. The silent sound the repetitive movement makes is like a pacifying lullaby trying to appease my condemned soul.

An undercurrent of rage flows through my veins, the same as it always does. Red hot. Molten. Bubbling away just under the surface, threatening to erupt like a volcano with a burning need to scorch every damn thing and every damn fucker in its path. It's just waiting for an excuse. Any reason will do. It doesn't matter how trivial. I'm sure I can taste it, even though rage doesn't have a recognizable flavor.

It's all in my head. I know it is. In that fucked-up space, like a boiling kettle that constantly needs to let off steam. If I don't release the pressure, it will explode, and the demon clawing away at the base of my skull will escape. He'll have won.

Every day it's an endless battle for control. Every hour. Every minute. Every second.

I breathe in the blackness of night. The bedroom stinks of sex, tequila, and cheap perfume. It's an unpleasant pleasant smell. It encapsulates vague memories from a short time ago, from when I was temporarily able to silence the demon screaming out for attention in my head. Like a siren singing their song of enchantment trying to lure me onto the rocks of fucked up memories and evil thoughts. The voice echoes, spawning more until they form a cacophony of deafening sound, all screaming the same thing.

Telling me what to do. Telling me how to react. Encouraging me to do bad things. My head throbs with the relentless torture of it all.

I need a release. A temporary fix. A respite from loud thoughts filled with chaotic madness. Thoughts that are even more deafening when it's silent and still.

I let my mind drift to a pair of green eyes and a pair of perfect, pouty lips. Lips made for sinning but have never even uttered so much as a damn cuss word. Shit, the things I want to do to that mouth. Unthinkable. Unspeakable. Downright degrading.

I'm a selfish fucker. I never feel remorse. I seldom feel guilt.

With her, I do.

I will not go there. I will not fucking touch her. Not ever. She's too good for the likes of me. Too pure. I will not condemn her soul to hell with mine either in this life or the next.

I need to stop thinking about those plump lips of hers wrapped around my cock and her hands gripping my length and squeezing my heavy balls.

Pushing the bedsheets down, I palm my now rock-hard shaft, rubbing the pre-cum across the tip before slowly stroking myself.

Turning my head, I take in the outline of the sleeping form beside me. Bailey. I fucked her hard last night while trying to find some mental reprieve. I even let her stay in my bed in the hope that having another presence here would help me sleep. That maybe it was the cure for this chronic insomnia. It wasn't. I'm still lying here wide awake, same as every other goddamn night.

I turn on my side and grip her hip, rocking my hard dick up the cleft of her ass. She's used to my constant demands now. Or at least, she should be. I've been fucking her most days for months. Since Jaine told me she didn't want to be with me anymore.

Since my demon came back with a vengeance.

I've been using Bailey for self-gratifying purposes, and while she's got the attention of my dick, she's mine. The brothers know not to lay a finger on her. That is unless they want their fucking hands sliced off.

They may be okay with sharing pussy, but I don't do sloppy seconds.

She presses her ass against my cock in silent acceptance.

BAILEY

Razr's restless. I know the only reason he asked me to stay with him last night was in the hope it would help him sleep. It didn't. He's been awake. I've been awake.

All night long.

He's fighting his demon. I'm fighting mine.

Him.

The moment I laid eyes on Paul Delaney, I knew I was a goner. A lean, mean fighting machine, looking every inch the tall Celtic god with his long strawberry blonde hair, angled features, and piercing green eyes. They sink into your soul. Seeing everything, missing nothing.

It was only when I became involved I realized how fucked up he was.

How beautifully broken.

Would knowing that have made a difference? Nope. See, I wanted him from the moment I saw him, and I was determined to get him. I needed him to be mine, even if only for a short while. Even if just for a second. Just for a taste.

He could have any woman he wants with his striking looks and unparalleled wealth. What would a thirty-two-year-old somebody like him ever see in a twenty-one-year-old nobody like me? But when he and Jaine finally split up after four years together, he did see something in me. Out of all the cum sluts, he chose me, much to the disappointment of all the others. But then again, I was doing everything in my power to attract his attention to the extent where I was pretty much sticking my pussy in his face.

It worked.

It probably helped that I never let any of the brothers touch me. Not like the other girls did. Razr doesn't share.

So, he's mine. For now, at least. We're as close to exclusive as we're ever going to be. I know he's not fucking anyone else. As much as he doesn't do relationships, he's not promiscuous.

The bed dips, and he grips my hip, pressing his hard dick

against my ass. He needs to get out of his own headspace. He can only do that by drifting into a disturbed sleep or by fucking. Given that the first option is evading him, he's silently asking for the latter. I hadn't slept with many men before him—only one, in truth. But I doubt I'll ever come across another man who knows how to handle his dick the way Razr can. Who knows how to pleasure a woman as well as he can.

My stomach coils in anticipation as the pre-cum from his cock wets my skin, the dampness instantly cooling in the frigid night air. He growls in appreciation when I push back against him. Wanting him. Needing him.

His hand drops from my hip to cup my pussy. I'm wet. No foreplay necessary. Using the heel of his hand, he presses against my clit while slipping two fingers inside me before pumping deliciously in and out in slow, steady thrusts. He knows my body so well now. He could make me come in seconds.

He removes his hand, and I know he's reaching for a condom. Moments later, he positions my leg over his hip, and he sinks into me.

I groan in pleasure as he fills me, my inner walls stretching to accommodate his thick length. His cock hits every pleasure point as he fucks me. Hard. Slow. Steady. I come. Then come again. And again. See, a man like Razr will never leave any woman unsatisfied. In his eyes, even a lowly cum slut like me deserves fulfillment. It's a macho pride thing, I guess. He likes to be the best at everything he does. That's probably why he's so successful in all areas of life.

A man to be admired. Envied. Feared.

His shaft swells inside me as he nears his own end. Impossibly thick. Impossibly long. He fucks me faster, his once precise movements now becoming more erratic.

He roars his appreciation as he claims his release, his climax silencing the demon in his head, at least for now.

One final thrust. Deep. So fucking deep. Deep enough to touch my heart from the inside.

See, I love Paul Delaney. Manhattan's most eligible male and prez of one of the largest charters in the U.S.

Stupid Bailey. Silly girl.

I ran away from shit only to wind up in more, and this time, it's like quicksand. See, I'm with him. Right here. Right now. But he's not with me. I'm not being fucked by the man. I'm being fucked by the monster.

There's no shared intimacy. No conversation. No kissing. No tender caresses or whispered sweet nothings. I'm easy and convenient. I require zero effort except for making sure that I'm up for it, my pussy is wet, and I reach orgasm.

Will the man ever see me? The truth is, I don't know. Still, I like a challenge. My daddy didn't raise a quitter.

Meanwhile, I'll take anything I can get, and right now, I have one half of Paul Delaney. Then again, when Razr finds out who I really am, he may just slit my throat.

Problem solved.

CHAPTER TWO

LAILA

The Iron Scorpions' Clubhouse, Brightling, New York

"BUT I THOUGHT *I* WAS YOUR BEST FRIEND," I COMPLAIN AS I RIDE shotgun in the SUV she's borrowed from Cherry.

"We've already been through all of this. You *are* my best friend, Laila, but Cillian and I could only have two witnesses, and we chose Jaine and Eoin as, without them, we'd never have met in the first place."

Sarah's trying to make me feel better. She got married around four weeks ago to the second eldest son of Roisin and Fergal O'Connell. I haven't seen much of her since she moved into his apartment.

She didn't even tell me she was getting married, let alone invite me along. I know it was last minute. I understand it was rushed. But all our lives, we promised we'd be each other's bridesmaid when we took our vows in front of God. Now she's gotten in with the

Irish mob and Jaine Jones, sadly any sense of friendship or loyalty she ever had for me seems to have fallen by the wayside.

"Anyway, we're doing it all over again in front of a huge congregation, and this time, you get to be my chief bridesmaid." She offers the same olive branch she has ever since, but they're not having a do-over because she feels terrible about excluding me from the first event. It's because Ma and Da Duster are insisting on it. So they can invite all of Manhattan's elite and keep up their outlaw appearances.

"It's because you think I don't fit in, isn't it? That's why you didn't want me there. You think we shouldn't be friends anymore. That's what this is all about." I sound needy and pathetic. I know I do.

Her hand covers mine, and she turns her head briefly, so I can see her rolling her eyes. My gaze scans over my slim best friend with her model looks, strawberry blonde hair, and beautiful hazel eyes. Her olive skin has a pregnancy glow. She's ten weeks or so now and looks so happy and radiant. I envy her contentment. The fact that she's found her happily ever after. Not that I'd want to be married to an Irish mobster.

"No, I'm not saying that, Laila. Don't put words in my mouth. But one of the witnesses was Eoin O'Connell, and he even scares the crap out of me."

I huff. That's just an excuse. I don't fit in. Why not just admit it? I'm not from the life. Just because I've lived next door to bikers. Just because my best friend is one, it doesn't make me one.

We pull up at the clubhouse gates. From the outside, the building looks like a prison. It's so ugly. It's set in around sixty acres of nothingness, and the exterior of the two-story property is depressingly grey with windows covered in sheet metal and bars over the top. To keep people in or out? Who knows. Both, most likely. Metal railings surround the perimeter, and the top of the fencing is electrified and finished with barbed wire.

There are security cameras everywhere. I wonder what system they use. Maybe I could offer to take a look at their setup. Computers are my thing, after all. If I can't kill anyone in cold blood—which seems to be a prerequisite to fitting in around here—then maybe I can make myself useful in other ways

Jamie, the prospect, swaggers on over like he's ten men. He's cute, I have to say. All tall and lean, with long black hair and crystal blue eyes, but he's arrogant and cocky with it. Sarah lowers the window, and he leans his arm against the doorframe, his gaze running slowly over me from top to bottom. He's undressing me with his eyes, I know he is. He's also wearing a smug grin. They're probably all still laughing at the way I ran off crying after witnessing that blonde girl, Bailey, give Paul oral sex. He smirks at me knowingly. It's like he can read my mind.

Yup, they are. Still laughing.

Why am I such a freak? And why do I fly the flag so fudging high?

"Sarah." He nods at her, and she winks at him. "Laila, you're looking mighty fine today."

Feeling self-conscious at the compliment, my cheeks heat. Do I like him talking to me like *that*? Looking at me like *that?* I'm not sure that I don't.

Why is it everything about this place, about these bikers, screams sinning and debauchery? And why does it feel so natural and acceptable here? Like there's something wrong with you for not wanting to take part rather than them. I stand out like a sore thumb with my seemingly outdated views and belief that you should save yourself for marriage.

Jamie opens the gates, and we drive into the compound.

I can hear him laughing out loud, and I know it's directed at me. He's not even trying to be discrete about it.

Still, coming here and tolerating the snickering at my expense is worth it if it means I get to see Sarah's brother, Paul Delaney. My childhood crush.

We open the door to the building, and everyone immediately turns to stare at us. Well, at me. Why would they stare at Sarah? She's one of them.

My cheeks burn even more. The last time I was here, I didn't stop to look around, I just went searching for Paul, and what did I find?

Him receiving fellatio.

My eyes scan around the Iron Scorpions' clubhouse. The white walls contrast against the grey tables, chairs, and bar. The floor is black and shiny. Is it sticky? I'll bet it is. I lift my foot discreetly to check. Yup, it is. I don't want to imagine what with.

I sniff the air as discreetly as I can. This place has a smell. I'm sure it's sex. Not that I'd know what sex smells like, but it's most likely ingrained on the walls of this place.

It's then I see him. Paul. He's sitting at the bar with the biker with the long blonde wavy hair who's dating Cherry Avery. The girl Sarah and I went to convent school with and the lawyer running Jaine Jones's legal firm in her absence. I frown when I see Paul's hair—reminded of the fact that, not so long ago, he shaved its sides and hacked off its length. I watch as the top falls down into his green eyes.

My gaze then drifts to her. Sitting in his lap and almost grinding herself against him. Bailey. The giver of the oral and God knows what else. I mean, she's pretty, with her long blonde hair and tall, slim body, but Paul deserves better than someone slutty. Someone who's no doubt slept with half the bikers in here.

She turns, her cool blue gaze taking me in. I stare at her. She stares at me. I'm guessing we're seeing each other as competition for the man she's currently sitting on.

She smirks at me, and I lift my chin defiantly in response.

She might be the one sleeping with him, but we'll see who wins Paul Delaney in the end.

RAZR

"Here comes your sweet little virgin crybaby." Blaze grins as Sarah and Laila make their way inside the clubhouse.

I push Bailey off my lap, and she shoots me a warning glare before storming off. If looks could kill, I'd be dead right now. She'd do well to remember her place.

"She's not mine. Leave that shit alone if you know what's good for you," I warn him as I sip on a beer.

"Leave what shit alone?" Sarah presses a kiss to my cheek as she looks between Blaze and me.

I need to be more careful. My sister misses nothing, and as much as she's a Delaney, she's also an O'Connell now. A Duster. Not that anyone else knows that yet.

"Just Blaze being an asshole, Sarah."

"About?"

Blaze's gaze drifts to Laila, and his grin widens.

"You were talking about me, weren't you? About what happened last time I was in here?"

Laila's standing with her arms crossed defensively in front of her, the chin on her heart-shaped face raised so high she's pretty much staring at the goddamn ceiling. She's so tiny I could almost fit her in my pocket.

My eyes drift over her. A plain white t-shirt, some tiny denim shorts with cute lace trim, and a pair of flat, sensible sandals. Her mousy brown hair is tied up in a messy bun, and her round spectacles are perched on the edge of her nose, drawing attention to green eyes that spit fury. Well, as much outrage as Laila could ever spit. She pushes her glasses back and continues to glare at Blaze.

It's like David meets Goliath.

On the surface, the overall package that is Laila shouldn't be attractive to someone like me, let alone have any sex appeal whatsoever. But my dick? Try telling him that. Who the fuck knew I'd like her pure and innocent look? He's rising to attention at the thought of touching any inch of her. Inside or out. Preferably in, and currently, he's not picky about which orifice either.

Blaze raises his hands in mock surrender, snickering as he does. "I'm saying nothing, little Laila."

"Don't call me little!"

"Well, sorry, but you are little."

"I'm five-one, and well, you're… you're… big!"

"Why, thank you, princess. It's nice to know Cherry's been bragging to her friends about the size of my dick."

"I wasn't talking about your penis!"

Jesus Christ, I could sit back and watch this shit all day long.

I hold my hand up to silence them before pulling her to me and placing a kiss on the top of her head just to let everyone in here know she's important to me. Almost as important as my sister.

"Calm the fuck down, baby girl."

I inhale the smell of her strawberry shampoo and bury my face briefly in her hair. She stiffens in my hold then relaxes against me. I know she wants to be here. In my arms. I know I want her to be here too, or at least, I think I do. I'm just not sure any of that shit's wise. Living this life isn't for many, and it could swallow an innocent like her up whole and never spit her back out.

"Prez, we've got a problem."

Blaze and I turn to look at Ripper.

I nod.

"Let's take this to the meeting room." I motion my head towards the door. "Excuse us, ladies."

BAILEY

I watch them from across the room. He dotes on her, holding her close before breathing her in. She smells of strawberries. She must bathe in that shit then spray it on just for good measure. It surrounds her like some sort of invisible cloud. Unlike me, the innocent little Laila, who I've nicknamed Strawberry Shortcake in my head, gets fussed over by the man, not the monster. Right now, she controls one half. I lead the other around by his dick. I'm aware the only reason I get to do that is because she's a bonafide virgin. If she let him fuck her, she'd win hands down. Then again, I'm not sure his conscience would let him. She tosses a glance in my direction from over her shoulder, her expression smug. So, she thinks she's got this in the bag, does she?

Well, let's just see who winds up with both halves of Paul Delaney.

She's asking for a fight. Who am I to refuse? Bring. It. On. I need to speak to one person. Probably a kindred spirit more than she knows. Definitely more than she knows. Still. My truth will come out in due course.

Until it does, I need to speak to Jaine Jones.

CHAPTER THREE

RAZR

The Iron Scorpions' Clubhouse, Brightling, New York

Closing the door behind me, I take my seat at the head of the walnut councilors' table and switch on the grey banker's light. Staring at the surface, I run my fingers across the Iron Scorpions' insignia, a scorpion and a dagger, as I do every time like my daddy and his daddy before him. The others are already present. One seat remains vacant.

Since Bomb's betrayal and subsequent dispatch at my hand, Blaze has been made VP. His promotion leaves the role of enforcer unoccupied. It's currently being held open for Jefferson. Has been for months. He's an Angels' council member, but he's not too sure he wants to leave Rising. I need to have a word with Cherry about that situation. The council can't continue to operate with a man down. As much as she's doing us a favor acting as our legal representation while Jaine's out of town, we can't keep the post open indefinitely for her on-off spare boyfriend.

"So, does someone want to fill me in on what the urgent problem is? Is it another trafficking situation?" I take out my switchblade and start flicking at the thought of what my sister went through all those months ago when she and Laila were abducted in Mexico to be sold on as sex slaves.

"No, Prez. It's all quiet on that front." I take in our road captain, Knight. He wouldn't look out of place on a high school football team with his short blonde hair and blue eyes. He's definitely a favorite with the cum sluts and several of the old ladies, from what I hear.

"Well? What is it?" It's like pulling goddamn teeth at times with them.

He cracks his knuckles, and the irritating sound makes me want to slice his goddamn fingers off one by one.

"On the last run, we bumped into a couple of brothers in a bar who were supposedly from another MC. The loose-lipped fuckers accidentally let it slip that they were looking at undercutting the Mexican's supplier and poaching some of their gun business. Ripper and me thought they were full of shit, and it was all bravado. Well, it turns out that may not be the case. The order the Mexicans placed today has dropped by around twenty-five percent. We can only assume it's because they're purchasing from this other MC."

"Where are they based?"

'Rumor has it they're a Nevada-based charter."

"Which one?" It may be a relatively new alliance with La eMe but it's still ours and we've invested time setting things up. I can already feel my blood boiling in my veins at another club daring to step on my toes. Do the fuckers have a death wish? I'll raze their goddamn place with them inside.

"Which fucking MC?" I growl at him when he doesn't give me an immediate response.

He noticeably swallows as he takes in my twitching fingers, which are still messing around with my blade. He's nervous. He should be.

"We're not sure. They weren't wearing cuts."

"Next time you come to this table with serious accusations of this nature, you bring all the goddamn facts. You hear me?" Anger pulses through my veins, and I embrace it almost like a welcome high. Using my blade, I slice through the thick scarring at the tip of my pointer finger to try to keep the demon under control.

"I hear you, Prez."

"I want a list of all the MCs in that area. Let's flush these fuckers out from whatever stone they're hiding under, and then let's show them what happens when they mess with the Scorpions. Agreed?"

All the brothers pound on the table as *agreed* is hollered in unison.

"Meanwhile, I'll have a word with Jaine to see if she can shed any light on this. She's on the west coast. We meet back here as soon as there's news."

They stand to leave, and I point my blade at each of them in turn as they pass.

"This goes no further than this room. The Irish will find out about this shitshow imminently if they don't already know, and they'll expect us to have all the answers with it being another MC."

Each brother nods as they file past. They realize this is serious shit. During a year, a reduction of twenty-five percent overall represents millions of dollars in weaponry sales.

Nope. We need to nip this situation in the bud and show these fuckers who they're messing with.

SHE ANSWERS THE PHONE WITHIN THREE RINGS SAME AS ALWAYS.

"Jaine."

"Delaney."

There's a pause. Things have changed between us since she announced she was pregnant. In my own way, I'm happy for her and Ace. She knows that.

"How are you?"

"Well, aside from feeling like I've got a watermelon resting on my goddamn bladder twenty-four-seven, I feel fine. Anyway, I'm guessing you're not calling to enquire after the state of my health."

"I do care, Jaine."

"I know you do. But I also realize how this must look to you. This baby wasn't planned."

"You're marrying him."

"Yes, because my baby needs a daddy."

"I…"

"Delaney, don't even go there or I'm hanging up right now. We've been through this a million times. Going over it again isn't going to change anything. It makes you feel shit. It makes me feel shit. So, please. Just don't."

I hear the guilt in her voice. She loves me. Would die for me. I know that. She just doesn't love me in *that* way. Not like she loves him. Ace. Prez of the Angels. Even though the kid's his, I'd still marry her. Raise it as my own. Love it like it was. Why would she want that, though? She loves Ace. He loves her. Perfect ending. Meanwhile, I have all the wealth and success I could ever need, but what the fuck else do I have? At thirty-two years old, I have nothing. No one. Apart from my baby sister, who went AWOL from my life for seven years because, by her own admission, I was such an asshole to her. On her return, she married one of the Dusters and is now expecting a baby of her own. Perfect ending for her too.

"You'll find someone, Delaney. I promise you that."

We sit in silence for a few moments. Reminiscing. Contemplating. Fuck knows. What I do know is that my demon is almost purring at the sound of her voice. Jaine is the only person who can keep him calm and control him. Then again, she had four years of practice.

"There's a charter your way that's offering weapons to the Mexicans."

"I heard. Ace mentioned it."

"Any idea who it could be?"

"I have one or two. I need to make a few calls."

"The Irish know?"

"They're aware, yes. Ace told Cill. In fairness, it's best never to keep that sort of shit hidden from anyone in the chain. Given they're the supplier, it's only right they know."

"You'll keep me posted?"

"I will. I'll call with an update as soon as I find out anything."

"We'll be going to war as soon as I know who the fuckers are."

"We'll be doing no such thing. We'll talk about it like adults beforehand. You forget the Angels are local to this problem. We don't need to be shitting on our own doorstep if it can be avoided."

"Tomorrow, Jaine." My tone is firm. We need to know before it spirals. She realises that.

"I'll do my best, but I may need more time. Nevada has several clubs, as you know."

I put the phone down. Half of me tells me she's right. This doesn't necessarily call for a war. The other half is itching for a fight. Doesn't matter who with. Doesn't matter what about. Doesn't matter who gets hurt.

I need to purge. And to do that, I need to spill some fucker's blood.

CHAPTER FOUR

BAILEY

The Iron Scorpions' Clubhouse, Brightling, New York

I DIAL THE NUMBER, AND IT'S IMMEDIATELY ANSWERED. THEN silence. Several seconds pass. I know there's no way she'll speak first.

"Is that Jaine Jones?"

"Who is this?"

Shit. It seemed like a good idea at the time, and now I'm lost for words with my life flashing in front of my eyes. I quite clearly have a death wish. Razr's insanity is obviously rubbing off on me. What the fuck was I thinking? What the fuck am I doing?

"If you don't tell me who you are, I'm putting a tracer on this number. Trust me. I'll know within seconds your exact location, and then I'll hunt you down. That's a promise, not a threat. Now tell me who you goddamn are."

"It's Bailey."

"Bailey who?"

"Bailey from New York. You know, the Scorpions."

"How the fuck did you get my number?" she hisses. She's probably pissed off, not only that I have her number, but that I've dared to use it.

"Cherry's phone."

"You went through her phone?"

"It was open on your number."

"Don't fucking lie to me. Jesus Christ, Bailey. You know what happens to liars in this life."

I pause, weighing up my options, then decide just to come clean. She's right. Lying will just see me wind up dead.

"I went through her phone."

"If Delaney finds that out, he'll slit your throat."

"I know."

"You're not going to ask me not to tell him?"

"You'll do what you want to regardless of what I say or ask."

"You're right. I will."

"And I don't think you'll tell him."

"Whether I do or don't will depend on why you're calling me."

"I'm sorry about before."

I may as well start by trying to get into her good books since I'm about to ask her a favor. The single interaction we've had to date wasn't one of my finest moments. Girl code went right out the window. I figure she'll realize I'm talking about the time in the Scorpions' clubhouse. When I pretty much offered my pussy on a plate to Razr right in front of her and while they were still together. She broke my nose that day. I'm lucky that's all she fucked up.

"You disrespected me."

"I did. And I'd like to apologize for that."

"I over-reacted. I don't usually fly off the handle the way I did.

I'm sorry for that too. So, now we've both gotten that off our chests, what do you want?"

"Razr. You've heard about him and me?"

"That you've been fucking him since he and I split up. Yes, I've heard."

"I'm in love with him." I just come right out with it.

She exhales loudly. Then there's a pause before she speaks. "Well, that's not going to end well, is it?"

"Why not?"

"He's eleven years older than you, for one thing. He's also a very successful businessman who attends many functions and mixes with a lot of like-minded people, most of whom are either Manhattan's elite society or New York's highest-ranking outlaws. No disrespect, but I'm not sure you fit the mold of what he needs in an old lady."

Well, I've got to respect her for not pulling her punches and just saying it how it is. I guess I never figured we'd be seen as such a poor match.

"Listen, I'm not trying to be unkind, Bailey. I'm just stating facts. Delaney's also not the type of man to share his woman."

"He's not sharing. Razr's only the second man I've ever slept with." I admit, feeling and no doubt sounding deflated at her hard-hitting responses.

There's a pause.

"But you were a cum slut for another MC before?"

"I never said those words. When I applied, I just said I'd worked for another MC."

I'm conscious I need to change the subject, and quickly.

"Surely I've got to be a better option than Laila."

She laughs out loud—no doubt at my brazenness.

"I'll be honest, I don't think either of you is a good match for

Paul Delaney. Anyway, you've never told me what you want. Why are you calling me?"

"At the moment, he's just using me for sex."

"Yup. Figures. You've been brought in as a cum slut. Go on."

"I know he has two sides, and the one I see is the unfeeling and uncaring one. I'd say unkind, but he's not. Not really."

"Razr's emotionally detached is all."

"Yes, that's it."

"Is there a point to all this?"

"I want the other side of him to see me. To recognize I exist. The good side. The side that sees her. Laila."

"So, you want Delaney, the man, to notice you?"

"Yes."

"And what do you want from me." She sounds curious now more than anything.

"You know him better than anyone. What he likes. What he doesn't like."

"I do."

"Will you share it with me?"

"Why the hell would I do that?" She snort-laughs.

"Because you've been there. You loved the prez of the Angels, and he didn't love you back."

"He did, though."

"Yeah. But you still know the pain of what it felt like when you thought he didn't."

She pauses once more. No doubt reflecting over how it felt when she was in my shoes.

"Listen, Bailey. I'd love to help you. Really, I would, but Sarah's a good friend of mine, and in turn, Laila is a friend by association. I don't want to tread on any toes."

"I realize that. I'm not asking for any intervention. I'm just asking for some advice. Woman to woman."

There's a pause while she deliberates. She wants to help. I know she does. I realise I've put her in a difficult position. Needs must.

"Listen, I'm going to give you a few suggestions."

I close my eyes in relief and say a silent prayer of gratitude. "Thank you."

"You're welcome, and good luck. Because you're sure as hell going to need it."

JAINE

Jaine's House, Rising, California

Jaine: *Bailey called me today.*

Sarah: *Cum slut Bailey?*

Jaine: *Yup. It turns out she's not much of a cum slut.*

Sarah: *She's fucking my brother, and he hasn't had to wine and dine her beforehand to gain access to her pussy. She willingly spread her legs for him. She's a cum slut.*

Jaine: *You and I both know there are a lot of women who would happily forfeit dinner and just offer it up on a plate to your brother. Plus, I don't recall Cillian O'Connell having to court you before he took you willingly to his bed. Blindfolded, I might add. At least Bailey knows who the hell she's fucking.*

Sarah: *Touché. Bitch.*

Jaine: *Good to know I haven't lost my touch. Anyway, it turns out he's only the second man she's ever slept with.*

Sarah: *So she never fucked any brothers at the last MC she worked for?*

Jaine: *Only one it would seem.*

Sarah: *How did she get your number?*

Jaine: *Best not to go there.*

Sarah: *Noted. What did she want?*

Jaine: *It turns out the silly girl's fallen head over heels in love with him.*

Sarah: *And?*

Jaine: *She wanted my advice on how best to secure his affections.*

Sarah: *What did you say?*

Jaine: *I gave her my advice.*

Sarah: *She's way too young and way too stupid for Paul.*

Jaine: *Young, I agree. Stupid, I also agree. She found my number, and she called me, knowing the trouble her actions could land her in. But what she did, while insane, also shows grit and determination. That girl has balls bigger than most bikers if you ask me.*

Sarah: *But what about Laila?*

Jaine: *That's why I'm telling you. I wanted you to know that I gave Bailey advice.*

Sarah: *All's fair in love and war?*

Jaine: *Exactly. They're both big girls, so may the best woman win.*

CHAPTER FIVE

PADRAIG

Padraig's Apartment, Hudson Yards, New York

My phone vibrates, and I smirk. I know exactly who it is without looking.

Jaine: *You there, Dyl?*
Padraig: *Always here for you, darlin'. How are you feeling today?*

She may be pregnant with another man's child. She may be marrying him and not me. Our lives may be going in different directions, but while my heart still beats in my chest and I still have air in my lungs, I will never lose hope that she's it for me. That Jaine Jones is still my end game.

Jaine: *Aside from needing to pee every five minutes, I'm* *fine. I've forgotten what it feels like to have an undisturbed night's sleep.*

Padraig: *Not much longer now.*

Jaine: *Don't remind me. I'm still not sure if I'm equipped to take care of a small human.*

Padraig: *Is Ace nervous?*

Jaine: *Are you kidding me? He's the most laid-back person I know.*

Padraig: *You'll be the best, ma. I know you will. Thought about godparents yet?*

Jaine: *Not sure I'll bother with any of that. I'm not a practicing Catholic, as you know.*

Padraig: *Your wee one deserves to receive The Almighty's blessing regardless of whether you have faith or not, darlin'.*

Jaine: *Sarah keeps asking me to be a godparent.*

Padraig: *It's an honor to be asked. We Dusters are very selective about who we invite to join our immediate family.*

Jaine: *Not that selective, obviously.*

Padraig: *Now, now, Jaine.*

Jaine: *Well. You really are scraping the barrel with the Ruoccos.*

Padraig: *The decision's been made.*

Jaine: *I know.*

Padraig: *So, stop being a mardy arse about it.*

I can't understand why she's so bothered. She doesn't love me. She claims she never has. She must just feel aggrieved that my family has made what she considers to be a poor choice on my behalf. She obviously still cares, and that gives me hope.

Jaine: *Can if I want to be.*

Padraig: *Stop being childish.*

Jaine: *Yes, Daddy.*
Padraig: *Any more of your cheek and I'll put you over my knee.*
Jaine: *Lowering the tone again, Dyl. Next, you'll be telling me you're into all the kinky shit.*
Padraig: *I'm game if you are.*
Jaine: *I'm pregnant and soon to be married!*
Padraig: *I'm still game. Anyway, I'm waiting for you to tell me what went down between you and my big brother. He gets very reactive whenever your name's mentioned these days, although he does his best to hide it.*
Jaine: *Nothing happened.*
Padraig: *You expect me to believe that?*
Jaine: *It's the truth. He asked me to do something. I didn't do it. Nothing happened. That's the problem.*
Padraig: *What did he ask?*
Jaine: *It's not my story to tell.*
Padraig: *Fair enough.*
Jaine: *Do you want to be a godparent?*

I pause. What to say to that? I'm not sure our Dyl would appreciate me volunteering him for that duty. Then again, I'm not sure the offer would still be on the table if Jaine knew exactly who she was asking and the lies we're currently spinning her.

Jaine: *I'm going to start calling you Indecisive Dylan.*
Padraig: *That's me. So to your wee one?*
Jaine: *No, to Jesus himself at the second coming of Christ. Of course to my wee one.*
Padraig: *I'm not sure if that's such a good idea.*
Jaine: *Fine.*
Padraig: *Have I offended you?*

Jaine: *A little.*
Padraig: *Will you be coming back to Manhattan?*
Jaine: *Yes.*
Padraig: *Really?*
Jaine: *Yes. What made you think I wouldn't be returning?*
Padraig: *I didn't think there was anything here for you anymore.*
Jaine: *Anything or anyone specifically?*
Padraig: *Anyone.*
Jaine: *There will always be someone for me in Manhattan. You, for one.*
Padraig: *Anyone else?*
Jaine: *Dyl.*

It's a warning. She doesn't want to go there. And I want to know why.

Padraig: *Well, let's cut a deal. When you return to Manhattan, I'll think about signing up for godparent duties.*

I won't. Or at least Dyl won't. I'm hoping she'll have forgotten by the time she returns, but I know it's unlikely. All I'm doing is spinning the web of lies that bit further and, at some point, it's all going to unravel and get me hung.

Padraig: *Anyway, you have to speak to our Eoin. He's insisting on talking to you direct. I'll bet you can't wait.*
Jaine: *What's it about?*
Padraig: *There are some professional services he needs access to. Cill and Sarah suggested you may be best placed to assist, given your plethora of contacts.*

Jaine: *Nice of them to volunteer me and throw me under a bus.*
Padraig: *Now, now, Jaine.*
Jaine: *Surely he's got several women he could utilize for that sort of thing, his PA being one of them. From what I hear from Sarah, he fucks Candice over his desk most lunchtimes.*
Padraig: *LOL. It's not that sort of professional service he needs.*
Jaine: *Ask him to call me, Batman. I'll see what I can do.*
Padraig: *Will do, Robin.*

JAINE

Jaine's House, Rising, California

My phone rings a few minutes later. As is the norm, I let him speak first. Will he or won't he mention my standing him up before I skipped town for Rising? Do I try to suggest it was accidental? It was always a given he'd be furious.

I'm glad. Fuck him.

I suspect his ma and da were furious too. I'm only sorry they were casualties, caught up in the crosshairs in this battle of wills between me and their eldest. Again, Eoin O'Connell underestimated me and overestimated his ability to control and manipulate me. If he thinks he can have me jumping through hoops, he can think again. I'm nobody's fool. Nobody's goddamn puppet either.

If I've made an enemy of him and his folks, then so be it. I've got a boatload of the fuckers as both Jaine Jones and as The Exterminator, so they can just join a never-ending queue, take a goddamn ticket, and wait their turn.

"Jaine."

“Eoin.”

“I hear congratulations are in order.” He sounds almost cheerful. Almost. I know it’s an act to lull me into a false sense of security. Well, it won’t work.

“Am I to accept that statement as you congratulating me?”

“Of course.”

He’s a goddamn liar. I can hear the underlying tone of just how pissed off he is. *About my no-show or about my personal situation*? There’s a lengthy pause. Both of us are considering which chess piece to move next. He won’t want to come across as overly bothered by my behavior, even though he’s clearly fucked off. But then he won’t want to be seen to be just brushing it under the carpet either.

I deliberately flicked the bird at the O’Connells. We both know that’s the case, even if I choose to plead momentary memory loss or complete insanity. I threw down the gauntlet after I slapped him hard across the face with it. I’ll be made to pay, I’m sure. I’ve done something not many would dare to do. Insulted a Duster. And not just one of them. Three of them.

All I’ve achieved by returning to California is to buy myself some time before I have to face the consequences of my actions.

“Why did you do it?”

Here we go.

“Do what?”

“You know exactly what I’m referring to, Jaine.”

I smile to myself. I shouldn’t. I mean, it’s a dangerous game I’m playing. I threw caution to the wind, and now it’s time for the blowback.

“It slipped my mind.”

“Don‘t lie to me.” His voice is quiet. I can feel the tsunami effect of it coming all the way from Manhattan to California.

I don’t reply.

"I asked you why." He's borderline hissing now. I rejoice in the fact that he's struggling to rein in his rage.

"I never agreed to meet with them, Eoin."

"I told you where and when."

"I acknowledged both, but I never said I'd be there."

"You deliberately misled me."

"I refute that claim. You interpreted our communications in a manner that suited your own purposes."

"You knew I would. That's the point."

He's right. I can't deny it.

I can hear a crashing sound in the background. It's my guess he's just cleared his desktop in his apparent hissy fit.

I exhale loud enough for him to hear.

"Listen, Eoin, I realize I'll be held to task over this… miscommunication. Might I suggest, however, that we shelve this matter until I return to Manhattan? The Dusters can punish me how they see fit then."

"As you wish. As long as you're aware that my da will not forget that blatant show of disrespect. He has a long memory."

"I look forward to receiving my well-deserved penance from the mighty Da Duster in due course. In the meantime, I'm sure you can both use my absence to conjure up a worthy punishment. Anyway, what is it you needed to speak to me about so urgently?"

"The IRS is sniffing around some of our smaller companies. Unfortunately, the head of our accountancy team isn't equipped to deal with their interrogating questions. We need access to someone of a suitable caliber that can handle the situation on our behalf. We'll pay handsomely for their expertise, of course."

"By suitable caliber, you mean an outlaw accountant."

"Correct."

"Is this a short-term contract or a long-term career move for the individual concerned? What exactly are you offering? As you will appreciate, these people are scarce. I'll have to call in a few favors, and even then, I may still come back empty-handed."

"We have a lot of new business in the pipeline, so we need someone who can handle our affairs long-term."

"Is location an issue?"

"Ideally, Manhattan. They'll be working alongside our Paddy and me."

"Sex?"

"Employee with benefits?"

"That wasn't what I meant, but then again, that's what you normally employ, so I guess that's high on your list of priorities. I've heard all about your daily shenanigans with Candice."

"Careful, Jaine. Your jealousy is showing."

"Maybe when it comes to your brother. Definitely not when it comes to you."

"You're getting wed. You shouldn't be thinking about my brother."

"I'll always think of him. Just because you split us up doesn't mean I don't still love him."

"Does Ace know?"

"That's none of your goddamn business," I hiss.

"Temper, temper, Miss Jones."

"Fuck you," I whisper.

"I heard that."

Good. Asshole. I ignore the arrogant prick and continue.

"So, as I was asking, male or female?"

"Males won't be considered. They have to be female."

"Jesus Christ. Hair color? Bra size? Any goddamn preference?"

"I just work better with women, that's all."

"Really? You could have fooled me. Anyway, just make sure you keep your hands to yourself."

"And if I don't?"

"The business professionals I associate with don't come with a mattress attached to their backs."

"What if she wants me to fuck her?"

"Why would any sane woman want you to fuck her?"

"Has the thought of me fucking you ever crossed your mind, Jaine? Be completely honest now."

I disconnect the call with the sound of his laughter ringing in my ears.

Asshole.

CHAPTER SIX

LAILA

The Delaney Home, Brightling, New York

Sarah: *I'm just setting off. I'll be there soon.*
Laila: *I'll pop the pizza in the oven.*
Sarah: *Pepperoni with double cheese?*
Laila: *Vegan vegetable supreme.*
Sarah: *Yummy. I can hardly wait.*
Laila: *They say sarcasm is the lowest form of wit.*
Sarah: *I'm not trying to be funny.*
Laila: *Your baby will thank me one day for looking after your health and well-being.*

With a small smile, I slip the phone into the back pocket of my jean shorts. Standing at the entrance to the kitchen, I look around the all-white space that's brimming with out-of-date mod-cons. There's no point in replacing any of them now Sarah's all but moved out. There are just the last few items to shift. Once they're gone, I'm sure things will just revert to how they were before. To a paid stranger just stopping by every once in a while to check up on a house that will quickly become unlived in and unloved once more.

My smile fades as quickly as it appeared. My best friend is moving on with her life. Am I jealous? Yes. It's a curse, I know, but it's all I've ever wanted. Marriage, a husband, children. You know. The simple things.

I realize I'm a disappointment to my folks. When I left high school, I went to Columbia, majoring in computer sciences, much to their dismay. They're both world-renowned surgeons, and they wanted their only child to follow in their footsteps—a pretty tall order for a girl who quite often passes out at the first sign of blood. They saw my lack of ambition for what it was when I went off to visit Sarah in Bolivia. I told them I'd be gone for a month. I didn't return for two years.

Sarah's always been a bad influence in their eyes. They probably rue the day I ever met her. Their perfect daughter, tarnished and led astray by the daughter of the president of a motorcycle club. And her brother, of course. Paul. The bad boy I've been obsessed with since I was five years old.

Twenty-Three Years Earlier (Age Five)

"Please, Momma. Another little girl is playing outside. Look." Pointing my finger towards her, I stare at the girl with the long red hair.

My momma leans down beside me to look out the window, and I use the opportunity to gaze up at her. My momma's so beautiful with her long black hair and dark eyes. She looks just like my Pocahontas doll, and she smells like sunshine and flowers.

"Okay. You can go outside and say hello, Laila, but only for a little while." She smiles down at me.

I run to the front door before she can change her mind, stepping outside and quickly closing it behind me. I then stop still.

What if the pretty girl doesn't want to be my friend? What if she doesn't want to talk to me? I walk slowly towards her. She's wearing a summer dress, the same as me. Mine is blue, but hers is yellow like the color of daffodils, and she has a matching ribbon in her hair.

"What are you doing?" I ask, watching as she plays with two little dollhouse figures.

"Nothing." She looks at me, and I can see the sadness in her eyes.

"My momma let me come out to say hello. I'm Laila." I run my hand down the front of my dress, then hold it out to her.

She stares down at it then looks back at me.

"I'm Sarah." She takes my hand in hers and shakes it gently.

"What you got there?" I motion my head towards the two little figures she's holding tightly in one hand. It's like they're the most precious things in the whole wide world going by the way she's hidden them from view as though someone is going to try to steal them from her.

She unclenches her fingers and shows me. They're worn and chipped, and the paint is missing in places like they've been played with a lot. Like they've been loved a lot.

"It's a daddy and a daughter." Her voice is a whisper, like she's telling me her deepest darkest secret and doesn't want anyone else to hear.

"Where's the momma?"

"I killed her," she whispers. I watch as her brown eyes fill with tears and a fat one rolls down her cheek.

I don't notice him at first. The boy behind her. He's so silent he's like her shadow.

"That's right, Sarah. You killed her."

His voice is nasty, and he scowls at the pretty girl with the red hair like he hates her. His shoulder-length hair matches hers in color, but his eyes are green like mine. His are darker, though, like the color of the evil forests in my storybook. The one that gives me nightmares.

I look between them. The boy stares down at her, his fists clenched. His pale cheeks are blotchy and red with anger. The girl sobs silently.

"That's a really mean thing to say," I whisper.

The boy turns his attention to me, and I can see the rage in his eyes. Anger that is now all directed at me. I swallow nervously. Why did I open my mouth? I don't like this boy. Not at all. He walks over to me slowly, the same way my old lady neighbor's cat stalks a mouse. He's scary like a monster. He's wearing shorts and a wifebeater, and his hands and knees are all covered in dirt like he's just killed something and then buried it.

"Mind your own business, four eyes."

I push my glasses up my nose. Momma says I do that a lot when I'm feeling defensive.

"You shouldn't say nasty things just to make people cry." I hold my chin up, trying to pretend I'm not scared.

"I said mind your own business!" He scowls before reaching across to tug really hard on my pigtail. So hard it feels like he's going to pull it clean off my head.

I yelp in pain and tears prick my eyes. Turning, I start to run home.

"You're a nasty, horrible boy," I yell over my shoulder, tripping and falling as I do. Getting back to my feet, I rub the grit from my hands and take in my bloodied knee. "I hate you."

All he does is laugh in response like that's exactly what he wanted to hear.

Present Day

My moment of reflection is interrupted by the sound of a motorcycle pulling up in the driveway.

"Fudge, I forgot to put the pizza in." Switching on the oven, I pop it inside just as the front door opens. Without turning around, I take a clear bowl from the cupboard and fill it with a packet of vegan chips.

"I thought we'd decided you wouldn't be riding that hog of yours anymore, Sarah O'Connell. I agree with Cillian, not that I'm proud to be siding with your Irish mobster husband, but riding two wheels is way too dangerous for a girl in your condition."

I lecture her. I know I do. Too much. I try not to, but I can't seem to help myself. It's hard trying to break the habit of a lifetime.

"You need to stop flying through life by the seat of your pants now. That was all fine when you only had yourself to think…"

I spin around, only to be confronted by a wall of steeled muscle. The smell of sandalwood cologne, leather, and pure, undiluted testosterone wraps itself around my olfactory senses as I look up into the dark green eyes of Paul Delaney. The man from my dreams and the boy from my nightmares. Every inch of him screams male dominance and authority. But then, it always has, right from that very first day.

My traitorous eyes drift slowly down his tight-fitting white Henley to the snug dark blue jeans gripping his thighs before landing on his crotch. I've seen what's hidden underneath. How big he is. A penis shouldn't be beautiful, but his is. My cheeks burn at the memory. Even more so knowing this is the first time he and I have been alone since I walked into his office and found Bailey with her lips wrapped around his male hardness, his release dripping down her chin. My cheeks redden further, knowing he's just witnessed me ogling him, crotch and all. He'll also know exactly where my thoughts have just been.

"Paul… I… I thought you were Sarah."

"Nope. Definitely a man last I looked. And last you looked too." He snickers. Placing his hands on the counter on either side of me so I can't escape, he leans forward and presses his nose to my hair before inhaling deeply. "You always smell so good, little Laila. I'll bet you taste real good too." He places a lingering kiss on the top of my head before pushing himself back from the counter, freeing me from his caged arms.

I close my eyes, instantly missing his closeness. Wanting it back again so I can suffocate in it and drown.

Opening my eyes, I find him staring at me with a smirk on his face. He's laughing at me. At my infatuated expression. At my pathetic crush, which is only too apparent.

Get a grip, Laila.

"Sarah's on her way." I state the obvious, then silently curse myself. Why else would I be in their home surrounded by packing boxes?

"I kind of figured that one out for myself." He reaches across and takes a handful of chips. Salted flavor. Not that it matters. I watch as he pops one in his mouth before licking the taste from his bottom lip. Rightly or wrongly, I've decided I want that mouth on me. Lips. Tongue. Teeth. I want him to suck on me. Bite on me. Lick every inch of me. I'll even let him sprinkle me with salt first.

Holy hell, Laila.

With heated cheeks I drag my gaze back up to his eyes. They're darker than they were. His own drop from my eyes to my chest. I'm braless, and the stupid white tank top I'm wearing will be displaying my aroused nipples for the world to see. For him to see.

I bite my bottom lip as he throws the last of the chips he's holding into his mouth. I watch every single movement so closely I can almost feel their rough texture and taste their salty flavor on the tip of my tongue. More than anything, I want to taste them second-hand. On his mouth. Right. Now.

I raise my eyes to meet his, my tongue darting out to lick my lips. It's a come-on, I think. Or at least that's what I've read in books and magazines. What would inexperienced me know?

Am I doing it deliberately? Yes. Am I asking for trouble? Yes. Do I care right now? No.

He swears silently, then reaches me in two strides. I gasp as his hand fists my hair so he can tilt my head back to where he wants me. His grip hurts. It's almost as painful as the hand on my hip, the fingers digging into my flesh and bruising my skin. It's a good pain. A welcome one. It's letting me know I'm affecting him as much as he's affecting me. I stare up at him. I'm so close I can see the gold flecks in the depths of his green eyes. My eyes scan his features. He's beautiful. He always has been. He lowers his head, and his warm breath mingles with mine. He's battling with himself over whether to kiss me or not. I can see the war raging within.

I dart my tongue out to lick my bottom lip once more, and he growls before dropping his mouth to mine.

I've been kissed. Not a lot, and I found the whole swapping of saliva experience pretty uneventful. But this? Holy hell. Paul's mouth is as hard as it is demanding, his tongue running across my bottom lip before pushing past to stroke deep inside my mouth and suck out my very soul.

I can't breathe. I can't think. He tastes of salt and raw masculinity. I groan, and he growls like a wild animal before deepening the kiss further and swallowing the sound possessively. His mouth is exquisite torture.

Yanking my head back further, the flat of his tongue trails the length of my throat. He drops both hands to grab my ass and jerk my front roughly against his. He's hard. Paul Delaney is hard. For me.

Lifting me, he places me on the kitchen worktop, and my legs instinctively wrap around his waist as he sucks on my neck, bruising my skin.

"Tell me to stop, Laila." His voice is husky, his breath hot on my ear as he bites down on the lobe. I groan at the almost overwhelming combination of pain and pleasure. "You feel what you're doing to me, baby girl? Hmm? You fucking feel that?" He grinds his erection against me before yanking my top from my shorts and sliding his calloused hand up my naked flesh to cup my breast. Tweaking my nipple hard, my core responds with a gush of wetness. "You're soaked for me, sweetheart. I can almost smell your arousal. Your pussy is screaming out for my cock."

My cheeks flush at his dirty talk. He knows exactly what to do. What to say. All the right buttons to press. I grip onto his shoulders as his hand drops to cup my pussy, massaging my clit through my shorts. I can feel the material dampening with every experienced stroke.

"You want me to make you come, baby girl? Would you like that?" He increases the pressure, and my core tightens in response.

"Please…"

Lifting my top, he lowers his head to suck my nipple into his mouth. The combination pushes me over the edge, and I gasp as the waves of pleasure shoot through me, drowning me in everything that is Paul Delaney.

It's then we both hear the sound of a vehicle parking outside.

He steps back and wipes his mouth with the back of his hand. I watch as realization crosses his face. At what we've done. At what he's done. At what I've done. There's no coming back from this. We've both given in to temptation.

"Fuck, Laila. Shit, I need to go."

Running his hands up the side of his shaved head, he storms out of the house, slamming the door behind him.

I hop down from the counter and try my best to straighten my appearance just as Sarah walks in.

"Pizza will be ready in five." My tone is too bright. Too cheerful. Too fake.

I turn to face her with an exaggerated smile on my face. She stares at me, then looks at my neck. Have I got a hickey?

Yes. No. Maybe. Fudge.

"Laila, did you just have a make-out session with my brother?"

My fingertips trace my bruised lips, which I'm sure are also a dead giveaway to what's just taken place. I'm tempted to lie, but lying's a sin, so all I can do is nod. Then again, I've just danced with the devil, and he definitely won, so maybe my soul is already condemned.

CHAPTER SEVEN

BAILEY

The Iron Scorpions' Clubhouse, Brightling, New York

"She thinks she's better than us because she's fucking the prez."

I smirk as Chanel and Dee Dee whisper about me. They're not actually whispering, though. They're deliberately talking at a level to make sure I can hear every word. They're also both standing at my open bedroom door.

I'm wrapped in a towel, having just showered. There's no real privacy around here, even though we each have our individual spaces on the first floor of the clubhouse. It's nothing much. Just enough to hold a bed, some shelves, a lockable tallboy, and a movable rack for hanging the small number of clothes each of us owns. You don't need many when you're a cum slut. The walls are white, and the floor is coated in the same black wipeable surface as everywhere else. Except for some pale grey furnishings, the room is as it was when I first arrived.

I didn't expect to stay for over six months. My time here was meant to be brief. An escape. A distraction. Some short-term freedom while I let off steam.

Until I met Razr, that is.

"You're just a cum slut like everyone else."

I glance at Chanel as I brush out my wet hair. She must only be in her late twenties, but she looks ten years older, likely due to the volume of cigarettes she chain-smokes daily. Even now, she has one dangling from her lips, the poisonous smoke curling up into her eyes, causing them to water and her to blink repeatedly. She's hourglass-shaped, and her hair is dyed bright red with added extensions in the same color, so it reaches her ass. Maybe she was going for the Jessica Rabbit look. It hasn't worked. I feel sorry for her. She's also one of those people who, through the day, agrees with everyone else just to fit in before spending her evenings on her back being fucked in every hole, sometimes all three simultaneously, by hairy bikers.

Then again, so does her friend, Dee Dee. A perfect pair. My attention switches to her. She's bleached blonde. See, with fake, you need to have your dark roots tended to constantly. She doesn't, so her hair always looks greasy. Dee Dee's not much older than me. She's a pretty girl. Surely she must have had other choices on the table.

I wonder what attracts them to a life where they're constantly fucked. But, I guess that's true no matter what you do for a living. I'm partaking in their life right now, but mine is more of a social experiment, or maybe a fleeting moment of rebellion.

Plus, I'm only letting one man dick me.

"I don't think I'm better than anyone. I've never said that. You said that."

They both look at each other. They know it's true. I don't think

I'm better than anyone else. We're all here for our own unique reasons. We come into this life the same way and leave it the same way. We are all born equals. And we all die alone.

"Anyway, if you'll excuse me, ladies."

I motion my head for them to leave, then close the door. Sitting on the edge of my bed, I think about my conversation with Jaine. The first piece of advice she gave me.

Ditch the cheap perfume and those shitty hair extensions.

I see her point. Razr may be a biker, but he's also a man of excellent taste. He's a billionaire, after all. In truth, I started wearing cheap scents to fit in around here. To make sure I didn't stand out. I'm sure I'd have raised eyebrows if I were wearing the Louis Vuitton fragrance I did before I signed up for this temporary lifestyle of debauchery.

I stand up, discard my towel, and look at my naked reflection in the mirror attached to the back of the door. I'm grateful for how I look. I fully realize I'm a walking cliché—tall, around five-nine, and slim with above-average looks. I'm not vain, but I'm not blind either. Jaine was surprised when I told her my hair color is natural. I run my hand through my mid-back honey blonde tresses, grimacing when my fingers snag on the hair extensions. Tomorrow, they'll be gone.

Removing one of my suitcases from the tallboy, I unlock it and take out my expensive lotions and perfume. I smile as I inhale the ginger and citrus notes. It screams luxury, and from now on, it's what I'll be wearing. I'm not going to be pretending much longer. If Paul Delaney chooses me over Strawberry Shortcake, I'll need to tell him the truth. If he doesn't, then I'll be heading back home and taking my lie with me. That's if he doesn't find out who I am beforehand and slit my throat.

Taking out my phone, I look at the last message. It's time to let my family know I'm still alive and kicking. Not that they deserve it.

Was it spiteful to disappear for so long and not make contact? Maybe, but they deserved it. They're the ones who forced me to run by trying to back me into a corner. No one will ever tell me what to do.

> **Jay:** *I know you need your space, Bee, but just let us know you're safe and well.*
> **Bailey:** *I'm fine.*

There. That's all they're getting. Finally, after months with no communication, they get two words.

I'm. Fine.

They need to own their shit.

I proceed to rub the luxury lotion into my skin before getting dressed. Rather than wearing my default hot pants and crop top, I put on a little black dress. It cost a fortune, but on the surface, it doesn't scream designer, or at least not to the untrained eye. A pair of strappy heels finish the look. The second piece of advice from Jaine?

Delaney's a chauvinist. He's also vain. He wants to be envied. That applies to the woman on his arm. He'll want you to turn heads and for other men to want what he has.

Having locked all my things away. I take a final look in the mirror before switching off my room light and making my way down to the communal area.

"WELL, WOULD YOU LOOK AT WHAT WE HAVE HERE? BAILEY, YOU look good enough to eat, sweetheart."

I smile gratefully at Dollar, the club treasurer, as he looks me up and down the moment I enter the communal area. He's not ogling, merely appreciating. Out of all the council members, he's by far the sweetest.

"Why, thank you, Mr. Money Man. You're not looking too bad yourself."

He snickers as he runs his hand through his shaggy brown hair, showing off the cutest pair of dimples.

"Where's everyone at?"

Dollar knows what I'm really asking is where Razr is.

"The prez went to the house. He's on his way back now," Flame answers as he passes me a bottle of water from behind the bar. I'm smiling my thanks just as Razr storms into the clubhouse.

My eyes drift over him as he pauses briefly before running one hand through his hair. He's agitated. His demon is gnawing away at his brain for some reason. Has he done something he shouldn't have, maybe? His eyes connect with mine and his nostrils flare.

Seems I'm the cure.

He strides towards me. "Come with me, sweetheart." Grabbing me by the wrist, he yanks me after him, causing me to almost topple over on my heels. I'm conscious everyone is watching as I reach down to adjust the strap. My cheeks redden when I hear someone snicker. They all know he's dragging me behind him because he wants to fuck me. Not because he cares. Just because he's got a hard-on, and he needs somewhere to empty his balls.

My eyes drift across his familiar bedroom, and I inhale the smell of sandalwood cologne that always lingers in the air. The bed and furniture are all black leather and scream quality. There's a bookcase filled with first editions and books on business and economics. The man, not the monster, put the space together. The person I never see. The one who doesn't even know I exist.

He glances at me briefly, tucking my hair behind my ear in an attempt to display at least some form of tactility and intimacy before he uses me as a vessel. There's no real tenderness. No kissing. No soft words. No eye contact beforehand. It's an act. I'm simply a means to an end.

A living, breathing, two-legged means of release.

That's when I smell her on him. The scent of strawberries. He's been with Laila. Did he kiss her? Whisper sweet nothings in her ear? All the things he doesn't do with me. Tears prick my eyes, but I blink them back. Tears don't help when you're from the life. You won't garner sympathy. You'll just be seen as lily-livered and weak —someone who can be easily manipulated. My daddy didn't raise a coward. He didn't raise any fool either.

"Get on your knees." His voice is gruff, the moment of tenderness over, not that it ever really began.

I do as I'm told in a ten-thousand-dollar designer dress that contrasts against the cum slut he sees me as. You see, I am just like all the rest to him. I'm sure they think I get preferential treatment because I'm being dicked by the prez. I don't. It's the opposite, in fact.

He makes me feel totally fucking worthless.

He unzips himself and pulls out his thick cock. It's rock hard, the swollen tip purple and leaking, the veins throbbing. He rubs the pre-cum over my lips using the blunt head like some sort of fucked-up lipstick. I wouldn't mind, but this erection isn't on account of me. Nope. It's for her. It's her mouth he wants to be painting his pre-cum on. And he's going to be thinking of her as he finds his release through me.

"Open your mouth."

I part my lips and he thrusts deep, throwing his head back and growling in satisfaction as his dick connects with the back of my throat. For once, I don't gag. I refuse to. For once, I don't fist his shaft to stop him from going too deep. Instead, I grip his muscular thighs, and every time he thrusts down my throat, I sink my nails into his flesh, making sure I'm piercing his skin. The fucker caused me emotional pain. Well, I'll do the same physically. Twice fucking over.

Fair's fair.

After tonight, I'm done. I'll suck, and I'll fuck, then I'll blow this place off. Razr's had enough of my valuable time. If he wants to dick my mouth with his eyes closed while smelling and thinking of her, well… that's not acceptable. It's downright disrespectful. I'm worth more than that. Way more.

I get to my feet and push him backward angrily, wiping my mouth exaggeratedly on the back of my hand.

He grabs my hair. "I didn't say you could stop, sweetheart."

"Is that right, Prez?" I laugh dryly. "Well, I fucking did." My gaze connects with his, and for once, I hold it. Menacing green eyes silently demand that I stand down. Do as I'm told. Before today, I would have. Now? There's not a chance. I slip down the straps of my dress and let it fall to the floor, leaving only my sandals in place.

His eyes trail slowly down my outside nakedness. He may not want or even see the person inside, but he sure as hell wants to find his release using the holes on this body. Reaching down with his other hand, he grips his thick cock and starts to stroke himself. His movements are rough. Almost aggressive. Like he's annoyed with his dick for getting hard and making him show weakness in front of me.

I smirk confidently, but my body is screaming out for his, my arousal already coating my thighs. This man is lust. The carnal sin itself in human form, and I'm more than ready to serve my penance.

"You see, right now, my thinking is, if we don't do things my way, Prez, then I'll walk out of this room and one of the other girls will have to finish you off. So, if you want me to do the honors, I suggest you take off your clothes and lie on the bed."

His grip on my hair tightens, and he pulls my head back. I almost cry out, but I stop myself. He doesn't deserve a reaction. He doesn't deserve anything from me.

"Are you fucking threatening me?" he hisses, his eyes switching between my gaze and my lips. I pray to God the fucker doesn't throw a last-minute curveball and try to kiss me.

"I'm not stupid enough to threaten you, Razr. I'm simply telling you how it is."

There's a pause. A battle of wills. He releases my hair and starts to remove his clothes. The vision as he slowly unwraps himself is like no other. He's inked perfection on a body that was made for sinning. A body that's begging for my mouth to lick, suck, and bite every inch of it.

He moves to the bed and sheaths his hard-on before lying back and putting his hands behind his head.

"Show me what you got then, Bailey."

I'll show him all right. I stand at the foot of the bed, and smirk up at him. Then, parting my legs, I drop my hand to my swollen folds. Running my finger through my slick pussy, I lift it to my mouth and suck it in before releasing it with a pop. The sound that leaves him is barely human. He's staring at me like a wild animal ready to pounce. I know he's itching to grab me, but he knows this is on my terms. I've made it so. He'll wait. He won't want to show weakness. He won't want to lose control.

I crawl up the bed towards him and stop when my mouth hovers over his, my knees on either side of his hips. For the first time ever, his breath mingles with mine. He fists my hair, pulling my head down in an attempt to connect our mouths, but I pull back. It's too little too late for that emotional shit. Way too late. Leaning back, I lower myself over the blunt head of his cock. I'm soaked as usual. No foreplay necessary.

As I start to sink onto him, he thrusts upwards, spearing me, deliberately trying to hurt me. Is this payback for not doing as I was told? For defying him? Does he think this is punishment? On the contrary; I view it as a reward. I've got his attention. For him to react like this shows I've gotten under his skin. Finally.

All eyes on fucking Bailey.

For the first time ever, we're playing the game as equals as we get each other off. I cry out at the mixture of pain and pleasure as he fills me to the hilt. I'll be fucking sore tomorrow.

Rotating my hips, I lean forward and suck on his nipple before biting down, causing him to curse under his breath.

He grips my hips so I can't move, and he fucks me. Hard. Fast. Deep. The sound of skin slapping against skin fills the silence. He pulls down my head to kiss me, but I pull back, pressing my mouth to his neck instead. I suck and bite on him as he ruthlessly fucks me from below, the position letting his cock connect perfectly with my sweet spot.

I can feel the orgasm claw at the base of my spine just before it spirals through my core and unleashes hell. I cry out as my walls clench around him, and he growls in appreciation as my wetness coats his dick before I milk him dry.

I'm fucked. More importantly, he's fucked. And I will fuck him all night long. The third piece of advice from Jaine?

Fuck him so good his dick will never want to let you go.

That letting go part? Well, I'm taking that decision out of his hands. If he wants Strawberry Shortcake, he can damn well have her.

I play second fiddle to no one.

CHAPTER EIGHT

RAZR

The Iron Scorpions' Clubhouse, Brightling, New York

I WAKE TO THE SOUND OF MY PHONE VIBRATING. STANDING, I WALK to the window and take in the solitary tree in the backyard. Behind it, the morning skyline glows red and orange as the sun shows itself on the horizon.

I feel rested. It's an alien feeling, having not felt it for so long.

I glance back at my bed, at the twisted grey sheets. Bailey's already gone. My dick twitches when I think of how hard I fucked her last night. Of how hard we fucked each other.

"Delaney."

"Jaine, it's the middle of the night in California." I rub my hand across my beard. My fingers smell of pussy.

"I know. I can't sleep. Getting comfortable these days is practically impossible. Folks that say pregnancy is a great experience lied through their teeth. It's shit. Pretty soon, it's going to be easier for me to roll around rather than walk."

I snicker—more out of politeness than anything else. I still haven't come to terms with the fact that Jaine's moved on with her life without me after four years together. The familiar rage starts to billow inside me. Frustration. Jealousy. Regret. It doesn't take much to trigger it.

Picking up my jeans from the floor, I pull them on, then reach for the blade in the back pocket. The familiarity of the flicking movement immediately soothes my alter ego.

"Any news?" I ask. She's calling me for one of two reasons. She's either got an update on the Nevada club that's been stepping on our toes, or she's going to bitch about me making an appointment with a shrink. The latter I'm not interested in doing.

"I've narrowed it down to one of two charters."

"I'm waiting."

"Sons of Satan, and the Undertakers."

"Motherfuckers."

She ignores me and continues. "I've got a feeling it's the latter. Rumor has it they've started supplying weaponry. Smaller handguns in the main, so they're not going to be able to compete on every level, at least not for now. I only mention the Sons as they've recently had a drive to increase numbers, maybe to take on more runs. Both clubs may even be working in tandem as they're based in the same town. I'm still looking into that."

"So, what do we do in the meantime?"

"I suggest we look at the order the Mexicans placed. Find out if the reduction is related to handguns. If it was, then we may have found our guilty party."

"Then what?"

"Then we take stock."

"You told the Dusters yet?"

"I'll be advising them today."

She hangs up.

My mind immediately flicks back to yesterday. At home. When I kissed Laila. I can feel the fucker inside my head laughing at me. For being weak. For giving in to temptation and tasting that sweet, innocent mouth of hers.

I slice the blade into the tip of my finger to silence him. Then, gathering the resultant liquid in my clenched fist, I let it drip to the floor.

That shit must never happen again.

"WHERE'S BAILEY?"

Flame stares at me from across the bar, raising an eyebrow at my question as he hands me a bottle of chilled water. He's probably wondering why I'm asking. I never have to ask where she is. She's always here. Just hanging around and waiting for me to give her some attention.

"She borrowed a hog. Needed to go somewhere, apparently."

"What the fuck do you mean she's borrowed a hog? She's a cum slut." I never even realized Bailey could ride.

He shrugs. "Well, she rode out of the compound handling a Fat Boy as well as any of the brothers can, Prez."

I stare at him. Why does it matter, and why the fuck do I care where she is or what she's doing?

"Council meeting in an hour. Let the others know."

Knight goes through the order from the Mexicans line by line. He's wearing glasses. Shit, are we all getting that old? I went to school with all the Scorpion council members. I've known every one of them my whole life, pretty much.

"Jaine may have hit the nail on the head, Razr. It looks like the reduction was mainly on handguns."

I nod. Jaine's seldom wrong, so his response is what I expected.

"So, what's the next step?" I stare at Flame as he voices the question, taking in his transparent albinism look. He usually doesn't talk much, hence why everyone's staring at him, in surprise more than anything else.

"Since Jaine has dealings with us all, I'm going to toss this back to her. We need to be led by the Irish on this one. While the Scorpions and the Angels stand to lose money, as the supplier, the Dusters stand to lose way more."

"They'll expect us to act, though, when the decision's made. They won't want to get their expensive business suits dirty interacting with another MC." Ripper snickers, and the others join in. It's not a question. It's a fact. They won't want to involve themselves with unknown bikers. They only tolerate the Scorpions and the Angels because we're a necessary evil. My eyes scan over our sergeant at arms. He's a huge fucker. He used to have black hair down to his waist until recently but shaved it all off when I did mine.

"Yup. I reckon so," I reply finally, flicking my blade.

"Surely it should fall to Ace and his guys. They're local to the problem." This time it's Blaze. It seems they all want to throw their two cents worth in today.

I shrug. "Depends on the size of the problem. Plus, Jaine has a point. They don't need to be shitting on their own doorstep. That would see the Angels having to look over their shoulder twenty-four-seven, and we all know if you're looking backward, you can't look forward. Shit like that's not good for business."

"You sure that's the real reason, or is it because you don't want anything happening to Jaine?"

I point my blade at Blaze. If he's not mindful of his words, I'll cut him ear to ear. He knows I'll never let anyone harm a hair on her goddamn head. If they did, they'd have to answer to my blade. Then again, she's more than capable of looking after herself.

"Watch your mouth, VP. Jaine does a lot for this club. More than you know. She's also got your ass off the hook with the NYPD more times than I can count. Let's not forget, last time they collared you, you had to spend the night in custody because your posh lady friend couldn't sweet-talk Detective Prescott in to letting you go."

I watch as he sinks down in his seat. Jaine's friend Cherry may be a lawyer, but she's not cut out for operating in this world of ours. We really do need to work on that. She's not a long-term solution, and this problem will never disappear. It's a fact of our life. The pigs are always looking to pin any shit on us they can. If one of the brothers ends up on a vacation to Rikers Island, it'll be an automatic death sentence guaranteed.

I don't mention the fact that a lot of our club wealth comes from Jaine's extra-curricular activities. The fact that as well as being a lawyer, she's also a vigilante sniper in her spare time. Shooting two-legged vermin in the head for obscene amounts of money with half of her share going straight into the Scorpions' coffers.

"Bailey's back." Flame nods towards the compound entrance. I watch on the security screen located behind the bar as Jamie makes his way across the yard to open the gates.

Standing, I walk to the door. I want to see the way she handles the hog. We don't have any female riders aside from my sister, Jaine, and Cherry. All the other women ride bitch.

It's mid-afternoon, and the sun's out. The other cum sluts are outside, wearing as little as possible and taking advantage of the weather while the brothers spend their time inside with their old ladies. The women don't cross paths often. Only if there's a celebration like a wedding. Everyone knows what goes on inside the clubhouse walls. The old ladies will head home usually before seven p.m., and the cum sluts will remove most of their clothes and get prepared for a boning by the brothers. Out of sight, out of mind. If they don't witness it, it's not happening. Any woman who becomes an old lady knows her old man will likely fuck around on her. It's the norm in this life.

I don't follow that rule. I don't stick my cock in a snatch that's been owned by any of my brothers. Blaze is the same. Chances are, if the thought even crossed his mind, his posh pussy Cherry would cut his dick off and stick it up his ass. I know he was my sister's first. I also know he fucked a cum slut while dating her. He has a scar on his stomach as a result. The asshole's lucky to be alive. Not that Sarah knows that. Disrespect my sister, you disrespect me. He learned his lesson the hard way.

A group of kids runs past playing tag, causing a cloud of dust to greet the air. I smile at their innocence. An innocence I was never able to fully embrace, at least not since I lost my mom at four years old.

I raise my gaze to where Bailey's sitting astride the hog, chatting to Jamie. She's got her visor up, and she's flirting with him, likely for my benefit. He's clearly enjoying the attention as he's running his hands up and down the seams of his cut, which is what he does when he chats to pretty women. The cocky little asshole's been patched in now, and he's dicking his way through the cum sluts like nobody's business. He's angling for a taste of Bailey's pussy, but she knows if she lets him, I won't go near her. I'll also slice his tongue and his dick clean off before cutting his throat.

"Jamie." My tone's authoritative. He knows to let the hog in and close the damn gates. We're in the middle of nowhere, but I still feel calmer with the locks in place. Plus, I don't want him talking to her. She's mine. For now, at least.

He salutes me with a smirk, and Bailey revs up the hog. In response, the shiny straight metal pipes vibrate with exhaust fumes. Kicking up the stand, she rides it into the compound with ease. Flame's right. She handles the Fat Boy like she was born riding. Like the one percent blood is running through her veins, same as the rest of us condemned fuckers.

I watch as she dismounts the ride. She does it slowly. She knows exactly what she's doing. I do too. She's doing it for maximum effect and to get my dick hard. Her little trick works. My eyes scan over her as she slips the full helmet off, releasing her blonde hair. She looks different somehow. Her hair's straight down her back and sleek looking.

She steps off the bike and brushes the dust off herself before removing the fringed leather jacket that Jaine left behind. Underneath, she's wearing a tank top and a pair of khaki combats.

I frown at the image. If Jaine had a doppelganger, then right now, I'm looking at her.

Why have I never noticed her before? Why have I never actually seen her before? Likely because she was parading around in way too high heels, portraying herself as a cum slut by wearing fake nails, fake hair, too much make-up, all finished off with a layer of cheap perfume.

Now, with nothing fake going on. Well, Jesus Christ, Bailey's goddamn beautiful.

She walks over to me, her chin raised in defiance, then stops.

My gaze runs over her slowly, top to bottom, taking in her slim shape and the face and hair now free of any cosmetics or products.

"We need to talk, Razr."

She moves past me and heads into the clubhouse. It's then I notice the subtle trace of expensive perfume.

Raising one eyebrow, I follow her inside.

CHAPTER NINE

JAINE

Jaine's House, Rising, California

Jaine: *Four months maybe five.*
Padraig: *No sooner?*
Jaine: *I can't, Dyl. Have you forgotten that I'm pregnant?*
Padraig: *So, that's the earliest normal activities will resume? Can we only book things in from then?*
Jaine: *You can book things in from now, but that's the earliest they'll be dealt with. Not before.*
Padraig: *My da's going to wonder why The Exterminator's been out of action for so long. I can't say it's maternity leave given that he thinks he's male.*
Jaine: *Chauvinist much? Tell him he's gone away to pray for his own salvation and to cleanse his condemned soul. You know? To wipe the mortuary slab clean so he can start committing atrocities all over again.*

Padraig: *Like sniper rehab?*
Jaine: *Exactly. You know your da's more than welcome to use an alternative. I'm not the only sniper, and it's also not like I need the business. The last I heard, the Scorpions are getting plenty of inquiries for my alter-ego's services. I'm not going to give preferential treatment to the Dusters, so I suggest you compile a list of names for me to run through before passing them to Delaney.*
Padraig: *Will do. We used an alternative last week. The eejit missed.*
Jaine: *Jesus. That's my worst nightmare right there. What happened?*
Padraig: *Thankfully, he was shot and killed outright, so he didn't live to tattletale. We book other snipers via an intermediary, though. Never direct. Eoin won't allow it. So, it's not likely it would ever have been traced back.*
Jaine: *So, it's just me you have a hotline to?*
Padraig: *Yes. Well, not that Eoin knows it's you.*
Jaine: *I can only imagine his reaction if he did.*
Padraig: '*Turns out that pretty biker chick with the mouth of a sailor is the deadliest sniper in the US.' That's what he'd say.*
Jaine: *Mouth of a sailor. He actually used those exact words?*
Padraig: *He did, darlin'. He's not a fan of ladies cussing.*
Jaine: *I'm a biker, not a lady.*
Padraig: *I told him that.*
Jaine: *Jesus Christ, you O'Connells really are full of compliments when it comes to little old Jaine Jones, aren't you?*
Padraig: *Well, Paddy always defends you.*

Jaine: *Does he now? Well, it's good to know I've got someone on my side.*

Padraig: *He does, and I'm sure he always will, darlin'.*

Padraig: *You've gone quiet. Would you rather I didn't mention him?*

Jaine: *Yes and no.*

Padraig: *Melancholy moment?*

Jaine: *Hormonal is all. I get emotional. Can I ask a favor?*

Padraig: *Sure thing, darlin'. Anything.*

Jaine: *Can you send me a pic of him? A current one?*

Padraig: *Why?*

Jaine: *Let's just call it curiosity.*

Padraig: *Sends pic.*

Jaine: *When was this taken?*

Padraig: *A couple of days ago. You know how he is. He likes to remind us that he's the best-looking of us all, so he sends us regular images so we don't forget.*

Jaine: *Yup. Sounds like Irish. He's cut his long hair off.*

Padraig: *Last week. He was fed up with listening to Da telling him he looked like a girl.*

Jaine: *His hair is how it was when I first met him. Anyway, listen, Dyl. I need to go as I need to call your big brother.*

Padraig: *About the professional services?*

Jaine: *Exactly that. Later, Batman.*

Padraig: *Later, Robin.*

I STARE AT PADRAIG'S IMAGE ON THE SCREEN. HIS HAIR IS LIKE IT was when we studied at Yale together. Familiar sparkling blue eyes stare back at me, and he has his cheeky chappy smirk on his face. He looks happy. In many ways, I'm glad. It shows he's moving on with his life without me in it. Finally accepting things for what they are.

In other ways, I'm sad. It's proof paramount that he doesn't miss me. Definitely not like I miss him. Maybe it's just as well. Maybe it's turned out for the best that all this happened. Perhaps I was just some sort of infatuation. That once he fucked me, he got me out of his system. I smile sadly at the image as tears roll down my cheeks.

I hate Eoin O'Connell regardless. So he doesn't like women cussing? Well, fuck him. I'm just going to do it all the more.

"Jaine."

"I've got an update on the rival club. How do you want things handled, Eoin?"

"Good morning."

He exhales. It's the type that generally goes hand in hand with an eye roll. I can't help but smile to myself. I ignore his pleasantries. When he realizes I'm not going to play nice by acknowledging what he's just said, he exhales again.

"What do you suggest is the answer, Jaine?"

"You're the supplier. You tell me."

"A civilized conversation initially. If they wish to sell their weapons, we can't stop them, but they find their own customer base."

"Sensible decision."

"Why wouldn't it be? I'm not going to start a war unless I have to."

"Will the Dusters handle it?"

"No. The MCs will have to handle matters between themselves."

"You don't want to get dirt under your perfectly manicured nails?"

"Not at all, Miss Jones. I just think it's best handled biker to biker. You speak the same language, after all."

"Back to being Miss Jones again. Is that title reserved for when I fuck you off?"

"Yes."

"Good to know."

"Don't pretend you don't enjoy getting a reaction from me."

"I'm not. It's the highlight of my day, actually."

"Careful, Jaine. You've just admitted to thinking about me at least once every twenty-four hours."

"Just ways in which to fuck you off." I hiss.

"I'm still resident in your headspace." He sounds smug.

"Which MC would you like to take care of business? The Angels or the Scorpions?" I change the subject. The asshole has a point. He is taking up way too much room in my head these days, and he doesn't deserve any.

"Not the Angels. It's too close to home, plus, you're there. It's way too dangerous."

"Are you concerned for my safety, Eoin?"

"Yes."

There's a pause while we both take stock of that confession-like response. He cares. About me. I'm not sure how I feel about that. Going by the silence, I don't think he knows how he feels about it either.

"I'll speak with Razr and ask him to take care of things."

"Thank you."

"The other matter. The accountant. I haven't been able to source anyone suitable that can be employed, unfortunately, so I have a proposition for you."

"Go on."

"JAL has been in negotiations for some time with an individual who may be suitable for your needs. We want to create a separate professional arm that we can offer to our existing client base. The lady in question is currently operating out of Vegas, but a move to New York is imminent now we've agreed terms."

"So, we would access her services through your law firm?"

"Well, not exactly. A new firm would be created which would be shared ownership with JAL holding the controlling interest."

"She's trustworthy?"

"Watertight."

"Recommended?"

"By Rodolfo."

"Background?"

"MC."

"Another biker."

"We multiply like Gremlins. Didn't you know?"

"If we refuse?"

"Feel free to source an alternative solution yourself. I'm trying to help you, not the other way around."

"So, effectively, we'd employ your services. You'd work for me."

"Not sure I like where this is going, but in a roundabout way, yes." I admit.

"Send the paperwork to me direct. I'll have Paddy go through it. Then, provided it's all in order, we'll have it returned today."

"It will all be in order. Do you not trust me, Eoin?"

"No."

"Good to know." I sound smug. I know I do.

CHAPTER TEN

BAILEY

The Iron Scorpions' Clubhouse, Brightling, New York

I WALK INTO HIS OFFICE, AND HE FOLLOWS, CLOSING THE DOOR behind him. After the night we shared, the air between us is charged with sexual tension. But I won't give in. I can't. I'm always destined to become invisible again.

My mind is made up.

I'm not stupid. I realize nothing will ever change. Not while he's still fawning over Miss Goody Two Shoes.

For the first time ever, Paul Delaney can see me. Bailey. It's probably only temporary, though. Like the switch of a light, I'll be plunged straight back into darkness again once the smell of strawberries fills the air.

I glance around. The desk he apparently flipped over and destroyed recently has now been replaced. Like his bedroom, everything is black or dark wood in here and with no expense spared. He's currently staring at me like he's never seen me before. Then again, he never has. The fourth piece of advice Jaine gave me?

Delaney likes simple and natural. When he doesn't need you to dress up, dress down. The only extravagance you need to wear is a subtle perfume. It will see you stand out.

That's easy to take on board. Before I signed up for this cum slut shit, it's me being me. Still, none of that matters now.

He sits behind his desk and motions for me to sit opposite him. I don't. I remain standing. I won't be in here long enough to even warm the seat. His eyes bore into mine—green on blue. My gaze sweeps over his face and at hair that's now way shorter after he hacked off its length. Frustratingly, it makes him look even sexier, his neat facial hair perfectly displaying those angular features, that full mouth, and those kissable lips.

Lips that have never once touched mine. And now never will. I'll bet he's kissed her, though. Strawberry fucking Shortcake. Then proceeded to dick me wearing her scent all over him. Jaine's fifth piece of advice?

Speak your mind. Always. Delaney will respect that. The majority won't stand up to him. Be in the minority.

"I'm leaving."

I come right out with it. No point beating about the bush. I want to fold my arms in front of me, but that will just make me look defensive and weak, so instead, I stick my hands in my pockets.

He frowns at me. Confused. Shocked. Those two words I dared utter were unexpected going by the frown he's now wearing. He probably thinks I've got a death wish speaking to him the way I am. Maybe I have. Got nothing to lose now, have I?

"What the fuck do you mean you're leaving?"

"I don't want to be a cum slut anymore. I want out," I say firmly.

We both know what I'm actually saying is that I no longer wish to be his personal fuck toy. I guess it's the equivalent of slapping him in the face with his own dick and turning down his biker advances.

He runs his hands up the sides of his head. When he reaches for his hair, it's always a sure-fire sign that his alter-ego is about to join the party. The red mist will descend if that happens, and Delaney won't see me anymore.

He leans back in his chair and sticks his hand in his front jeans pocket to reach for his blade. My eyes follow the movement until I'm staring at his crotch. Way to fucking go, Bailey. My cheeks redden, and with not an ounce of make-up on my face, there's no way he won't notice. He's an observant fucker.

He smirks at my blatant ogling and then proceeds to flick the piece of metal back and forth. He's borderline now.

Razr. Delaney. Razr. Delaney.

You can almost see the contrasting personalities fighting for control behind his penetrating gaze. Which one will triumph? Who the fuck knows? It really doesn't matter to me anymore.

"You can't just leave."

I raise my chin. "Why can't I?"

He stretches his legs out in front of him and crosses one ankle over the other while continuing to flick the blade. "You signed a contract if you recall."

"I'm aware of that."

"There'll be a notice period you'll have to abide by."

"Unless you just let me go."

"If I don't apply the rules to you, then I may as well rip them up."

"So rip them up. It's not like this is paid employment where we should have to give notice anyway. And it's not like I'll need a reference."

"No cum slut's ever left before. We normally have to drag them kicking and screaming out the door. Why do you want to leave?"

"I don't have to give a reason."

"No, you don't, but I want to know."

"I'd rather not say."

I can hardly admit it's because I'm in love with him. Or that him coming back stinking of Laila then fucking me while imagining I'm her was the straw that broke the camel's back. I'm not telling him any of that shit. I'm just getting the fuck out of here as soon as I damn well can.

"I'll find out from Jaine what the contractual situation is." He turns to face his laptop.

"Thank you."

"You can go." He motions his head towards the door to dismiss me without making eye contact.

I guess I'm invisible once more.

"So, you're leaving because you've fallen in love with the prez?" We're standing at the bar, which is currently unmanned.

Mojo is my favorite of all the cum sluts, and we've become good friends. She's not a beauty by any means, but she does have a fabulous figure, which is currently sporting the tiniest hot pink bra top and a pair of pale blue Daisy Dukes so tight her camel toe is showing. That's all the brothers are interested in anyway. Stick a paper bag over her head and have at it is their attitude. Better still, flip her over and dick her from behind. That way, you don't have to look at her face or try to source a suitable bag.

She's due to retire this year as she'll reach her thirtieth birthday. Once a cum slut reaches that ripe old age, they're retired out to pasture while they still have their teeth so they can chew on the outside world's cud. If I were staying, I'd have missed her, but I'm not, so it's no big deal. For Mojo, leaving is a huge deal, though. I feel for her. This is her family. Her life. The only one she's ever truly known. But they make no exceptions. The rules are the rules.

She's been here for eleven years. She's probably seen every dick in this place several times over. She's never once been fucked by Razr, though, despite trying to get his attention through the years. Her only hope of staying is that one of the brothers makes her his old lady. Time's ticking, though, and, with no disrespect to her, who'd want a woman who's been dicked by every brother in here, even if she is a gem of a human being?

"I just want to go home is all."

I'm lying and she knows it. She shakes her head at me, partially loosening her peroxide blonde hair, which is tied up in a messy bun.

Here we go. I know what's coming.

"Rule number one. Never kiss them on the mouth."

I roll my eyes at her, given I've heard all her rules before, many times over. I wet my fingertip and draw a check mark in the air. I've never kissed Razr on the mouth. I don't add that it's not because I didn't want to. It's because he's never tried. Well, at least not until last night, and by then, the damage was already done.

"Rule number two. Always wear a condom."

I draw another check mark in the air.

"Rule number three. Never fall in love with them."

I pause and then draw a cross in the air. There's no point in lying about it. She'd see right through my bullshit anyway.

"Damn it, Bailey. Did I not teach you anything?"

My lips twitch. "You taught me everything you know, Mo."

We both snicker. She leans her elbows on the bar top. It's just her and me, except for a few brothers playing a game of poker at one of the tables.

"I saw him dragging you off last night."

I nod and frown. "That was the final straw. The one that broke the camel's back. He dicked me while stinking of her."

She lowers her voice.

"Speaking of stinky camels, guess who just walked in."

CHAPTER ELEVEN

BAILEY

The Iron Scorpions' Clubhouse, Brightling, New York

I DON'T EVEN NEED TO TURN TO LOOK. I CAN SMELL STRAWBERRIES the moment she enters the place.

"Bailey, Mojo. You both okay?"

My gaze meets Sarah's the moment she steps up to the bar. She sweeps hers over me before narrowing her eyes. Razr's sister has a unique beauty. She's tall and slim, with a great rack. Her skin is olive, unlike her brother's. She has the same strawberry blonde hair, but her eyes are hazel. I hear she looks just like her mom. Not that many here ever had the good fortune of meeting the former prez's old lady. She died giving birth to Sarah. Rumor has it that's when Razr first made an appearance. Paul Delaney's never been the same since.

Her gaze is penetrating. She knows how I feel about her brother. I can see it in her eyes. Sarah's quietly assessing me. I wonder what she sees. I know she's trying to gauge if I'm good enough for her brother. Not that it matters now.

I nip her silent scrutiny in the bud.

"I'm leaving."

Her eyes bore into mine, much like her brother's did earlier at my utterance of the same two words. Yup. She's a Delaney, alright.

"Is that right?"

"That's right." I don't break eye contact.

"And why is that?"

"That's my business. Razr's speaking with Jaine to find out how much notice I need to give."

"How did he take it?"

I shrug. "I'm invisible to him most of the time, so it barely caused a ripple of a reaction. He's just making me follow the rules as he's doesn't want me to be flouting them and setting a precedent for others."

"So, you're leaving?" Laila pipes up having overheard.

My eyes scan over who was my competition until now—the one who returned from Bolivia and screwed everything up for me. But then again, did she? Before she came back, I was still invisible where Delaney was concerned.

"Yup."

She smiles saccharinely sweetly.

"No need to look so smug, Laila."

"What do you mean?" She tries to look confused but fails miserably.

"I mean, he's all yours."

"Who's all whose?"

The masculine voice is right behind me. When Paul Delaney speaks, it makes my ovaries contract and I immediately want to offer to have his babies. A hundred of the screaming little fuckers if that's how many he wants. I'd even consider more.

"Bailey was just telling us that she's leaving."

There's no need to sound quite so pleased about it, Laila.

"Three months."

He confirms my worst fear. I was hoping for one. Shit. I turn to look at him then wish I hadn't as his green gaze immediately connects with mine, trying to penetrate my soul. To dig for shit he has no right searching for.

"Seriously?"

"Seriously."

I smirk at him, even though I feel deflated inside, and nod my head. "Then consider my notice given and consider me on gardening leave with immediate effect."

All eyes are on me. They all know I've effectively just told Paul Delaney that he can't fuck me from hereon in. That I'm now in control. That he'll need to find someone else to dick while he's dreaming of his precious Laila. Better still, he can cut out the middle person and just fuck her. Save wasting anyone else's time.

"Excuse me, but I need some air."

Four pairs of eyes drill into my back as I walk away.

Some folks opt for a gun as their weapon of choice. The Delaneys use a blade. Me? I'm a bit more culturally diverse than that. I can kill a person with just one throw of a shuriken, having studied the art of ninjutsu and aikido for several years alongside my sister. My daddy instilled in my siblings and me that we should always be able to defend ourselves. So, all of us were pretty much forced to take up one form or another of self-defense. I guess me and my katana-loving sister watched too much *Power Rangers* to choose anything else.

I always used to dream of being the pink one.

I would never admit that I throw stars to anyone here. Why would I? To them, I'm just a lowly cum slut. Only good for a dicking and not much else. Well, little do they know.

I gather my shuriken from my locked suitcase. Razr needs a blade for emotional respite? Well, I need my stars. A dozen of them. I run my finger across their razor-sharp edges, careful not to slice myself open. I place them back in the safety of their pouch and make my way outside.

IT'S ANOTHER SCORCHING DAY. HAVING GONE WITHOUT RAIN FOR SO long, the compound surface resembles a desert. It reminds me of home. I smile politely as I pass the other cum sluts sun-bathing outside in suits that offer little to no coverage whatsoever. I wonder if they know yet that I'm leaving. If the gossip mill rumors have already started spouting their Chinese whispers. Then I wonder which one Razr will move on to in my absence. Chanel? Dee Dee? There are a few new girls who've recently joined the ranks. Eager eighteen-year-olds who've heard tall tales of how wonderful it is to be fucked by bikers and have their cum spill into their willing and waiting mouths. Razr obviously likes his women young, so maybe one of the new recruits will be the lucky recipient of his advances. It's none of my business anymore. Not that it ever was. I'll be leaving and heading back to the west coast in three months.

I walk around to the rear of the clubhouse. It's safer to throw back there as no one ventures behind the building too often. The only thing you can see for miles on the horizon is land. Nothingness. That shit suits me just fine. It's something else that reminds me of home.

I lean a piece of discarded wood crudely against the only tree in the backyard. It's not a very broad piece, maybe around twelve inches or so, but it's a decent height. I don't want to be throwing my stars at the tree itself. Be at one with nature and all that. The tree didn't do me any harm.

Moving back as far as I can, I start to throw my stars. My mood lifts. I get a buzz each time one connects. Not that any will miss. I've got my technique down to a fine art, having practiced for many years.

"You know they're banned in New York, right? Those ninja stars."

My gaze drifts to Sarah Delaney. Why she's come back here looking for me, I don't know. Hopefully, she hasn't come to pick a fight. I don't want to be shooting any stars in her direction. That won't go down well with her older brother.

"I realize that."

Jogging to the piece of wood, I pull all twelve from the surface, then jog back and start all over again. It's a discipline. I'll do it all day long until exhaustion takes over and my arm starts to ache. Then I'll switch to the other arm. Let's face it. I haven't got anything better to do to fill my time.

Sarah sits on a rickety old bench, which is the only piece of furniture out here, so it's clear she's not going anywhere anytime soon. She watches, and we sort of fall into a comfortable silence as I practice and hone my craft.

"You're good."

"Yup. I am."

"Modest too."

I snicker. "Yup, I'm that too."

"You love my brother?"

"We're not going there."

"You running away because of it?"

I don't reply. That's the only answer she needs. She can decipher and interpret the lack of response and jump to her own conclusions. Let's face it. She will anyway.

"You know, running doesn't make the problem disappear. I tried that with Cillian. It didn't make me love him any less. Probably had the opposite effect."

"There's a difference. He loved you back."

She doesn't reply to that. What's there to say?

I'm not sure if she sends a message or if they all decide just to wander around here, but pretty soon, a small crowd starts to form, all of them watching me throw my stars, collect them, and then repeat the process all over again.

"Those are banned. You do know that, right?"

I nod in silent response. I don't look at Dollar. I just keep right on throwing.

"How far can you throw and still hit the target?"

I recognize the voice. Deep, menacing, and instantly making my panties wet.

I shrug, trying to maintain an air of indifference. "The target's around ten meters now. I can do farther, but there's nothing to lean it against."

"I can hold it."

I stop what I'm doing for the first time, though I still don't look at him. "You know what one of these will do to you if it connects with your flesh, right?"

"Yes."

I turn and stare at Razr as he tosses me the challenge, then nod slowly. There's not a chance I'm backing down. If he wants me to throw farther, that's what I'll do.

"Fifteen meters is the farthest I've ever thrown, but that's with a fresh, untired arm."

"Fifteen meters it is."

He walks off, and my eyes automatically drop to his ass. I'm sure everyone can see where I'm looking, but no one says a word. Everyone knows I've seen way more of him than just that these past months.

I look at Razr in the distance. Suddenly, the target seems way too small. Matchstick-sized. At least compared to the brute of a man currently holding the piece of wood between his arms.

"Hold the wood out from your body as the stars will puncture it," I yell across.

He does as he's asked, and then he waits.

I stare at him. I can't read his expression as he's too far away, but I know this is a moment of trust. I could easily kill him with one of my shuriken.

"Fingertips only please, and on the very edge of the wood."

Again, he does as he's told. Something passes between us. Trust. Understanding. I don't know what the fuck it is, but it just cements my love for the prez of the Iron Scorpions even more.

"Ready?"

He nods.

"Use your words, Prez." I'm firm. He needs to be sure. I need to be sure.

The others snicker at how ballsy I'm being.

"Ready, sweetheart." I'm sure I can hear a smirk in his voice.

"Bailey's just fine, Prez," I reply with a wry smile.

Again, even more snickering.

I hold my hand up to quieten them down. I need to focus. Taking my first star, I feel its weight in my hand. My mind instantly connects with the lethal piece of metal like it's an extension of me.

I can still feel beads of sweat form on my brow.

"Treat it as a life and death situation, Bailey. One day it might be," I mumble to myself.

I throw the first star and watch as it cuts through the air before connecting with the wood. Relief flows through me: one down, eleven to go.

When I throw the final one and it connects with the target, I almost want to sink to my knees in relief.

Challenge accepted. Challenge won.

Razr walks across, holding the wood with all twelve stars jutting from its surface. His eyes never leave mine. Is he impressed? It's hard to tell. He never gives anything anyway. At least not to me.

He holds on to it as I start to pull the shuriken from the surface, placing them one by one in their pouch.

"Are they really sharp?"

"Very. So don't touch…" I answer Laila, who's appeared from nowhere, and who's now reaching out to do just that. Fool. The moment she does, blood pools on the surface of her finger as one of the sharp metal points pierces her skin.

"Jesus Christ, Laila," I hiss at her.

She stares at her bleeding finger for just one second then sinks to the floor in a faint.

For the past fifteen minutes, Delaney saw me once more. Now, his eyes are on Laila, and I'm forgotten about all over again.

My heart stings with the pain. Like one of my own stars has sliced it open.

This is going to be the longest three months of my life.

CHAPTER TWELVE

LAILA

The Iron Scorpions' Clubhouse, Brightling, New York

I fainted at the sight of blood. Well, I think it was that combined with the stinging pain.

Now, I'm lying on Paul Delaney's bed. I can smell his addictive sandalwood cologne on the sheets. The Almighty definitely works in mysterious ways.

I'm tempted to roll around and cover myself in his scent. I don't, as that would be silly. He'd also think I was weird.

I open my eyes, and he's sitting on the edge of the bed, looking down at me, his green gaze full of concern.

"You okay, baby girl?"

I love that he always calls me that. I've never once heard him call her that. Bailey. I smile shyly up at him as he pushes my loose hair gently behind my ear.

"Yeah. Sorry for being such a wuss."

"It doesn't matter."

"And I'm also sorry that I'm not really good with blood or pain." I bite my lip nervously. Two things that are pretty much essential for being part of his life, and I can't handle either very well.

Figures.

"We're all good with different things, Laila."

I pause for a second, then sit up.

"Bailey was good at throwing those metal things, wasn't she?"

"Yup. She was."

He turns his gaze out the window. Not so long ago, there was a buzz of excitement back there. That was until I collapsed. Now? The backyard is empty once more. Everyone must have filtered back inside.

Well, I refuse to feel guilty. I'm not sorry it happened because now I have his undivided attention.

"Are you upset that she's leaving?" I watch for a reaction.

Turning to look at me, he shrugs. "In this life, people come and go every day, Laila. Some things are under your control, and some aren't. Some folks you want to leave, others you don't. You learn to accept both for what they are. People are entitled to live their lives how they see fit, even if the choices they make mean they can no longer be part of yours."

He didn't answer the question. Was that intentional? Or did he not realize he was doing that? Will he miss her? Or won't he?

Well, I'm going to make sure he doesn't.

Leaning forward, I press my lips gently against his. I don't want him thinking about her. Not now. Not ever. I want him thinking about me.

Only me.

"You're playing with fire, baby girl, you know that?" His whispered breath is hot against my lips.

"Am I? Well, maybe I want to burn, Paul."

His questioning eyes search mine.

What am I saying? What am I asking? Would he take me up on it if I offered myself to him right now?

Cupping my face in his hands, his mouth covers mine. His lips are soft and warm. His tongue trails along my bottom lip, nipping it gently with his teeth, and I part my lips with a sigh, allowing him in. He strokes deep, tasting me, but he does so slowly this time, allowing me the chance to explore him in return. With each experienced sweep, he encourages my tongue to dance with his, breaking down my nervous barriers one by one.

Does he kiss her like this? I don't want him kissing her or touching her. I want him to be mine.

I want Bailey to leave and never come back. I'm only frustrated that I have to wait three months for that to happen.

Snaking my arms around his neck, I pull him towards me before moving one hand down to press it against his chest. He's solid. A wall of steeled muscle. I want to feel his bare skin under my fingertips. As if he can read my mind, he yanks his Henley over his head in one movement, giving me the access I crave. His skin is hot to the touch. His smooth flesh feels like it's scorching the very tips of my inexperienced fingers.

My hand moves to trail across the Sarah tattoo inked across his heart. Would he get one for me? One that says Laila?

Yanking my top free from my shorts, he reaches up to stroke my breasts through my cotton bra, his calloused fingers causing my nipples to pebble. I groan against his mouth as a jolt of desire travels straight to my core.

I'm wet. I know I am. But I dare any woman alive not to immediately fall in lust with Paul Delaney.

He's not acting like a man possessed this time. He's gentle. It's like he cares about me. Like he doesn't want to rush anything. To rush me. I know he's holding himself back for my benefit. To make sure I'm one hundred percent certain about what I want so I have no regrets if we take things further.

We're disturbed by a knock on the door.

"Paul. Is Sleeping Beauty back in the land of the living yet?"

It's Sarah.

He pulls back immediately, his guilty hands running through his hair. Yanking his Henley back over his head, he waits until I'm decent before he opens the door.

Sarah walks in, stopping in the middle of the room to look between us. She knows what we've been doing, what she's just interrupted. Would she be happy for us if we became a couple? If her brother and I moved forward together? It's difficult to tell. She has a great poker face, and she's wearing it right now.

"We need to go, Laila. I'm meeting Cillian in an hour." Her head motions towards the door, silently indicating for me to leave.

She remains standing where she is as I walk past. As soon as I exit the room, the bedroom door closes behind me, shutting me out.

SARAH

"You need to make the right choices, Paul, and for the right reasons."

I look at my brother. It's clear he and Laila have been kissing again, and God knows what else. He runs his hands through his hair before tucking his white Henley back in his jeans. He's agitated, and he's struggling to stay in control because of it.

"I'm trying to, Sarah." He's staring out the window, his hand rubbing across his mouth.

Instantly feeling guilty, I walk in front of him and poke him in the chest, trying to lighten the mood.

"Listen, I'm not saying you can't be with Laila, but only venture down that path if you really do want to be with her. Don't do it because you feel obligated to because she has a crush on you."

He stares at me, but I can see that I've lost him. He's deep in thought. I know it's because he's unsure of what he's doing with her. She's not from the life. She's different from anyone he's ever been with. I know he loves her but is he *in* love with her. And is she in love with him, or is this just the remnants of her childhood crush?

I have to approach each of them separately on this.

"Don't take something from Laila that you can't ever give her back, Paul. Not unless you're one hundred percent certain," I warn him gently.

He knows what I'm talking about. That virginity of hers that she's meant to be saving until she gets married. Despite what was preached to us at school, I was glad to be rid of mine. But Laila's is important to her. She's held onto it for twenty-eight years. For her, it means something—her first time. It's meant for the man she'll spend the rest of her life with.

He nods at me distractedly, and I kiss him on the cheek. I can tell he's not listening. Right now, he's trapped inside his head and fighting his demon, so there's no point in saying anything further.

"Later, brother."

When I close the bedroom door, he's staring out the window, his attention fixed on the single tree that's standing there.

LAILA

"You're not happy for us, are you?"

Sarah's focusing on the road. She seldom takes her eyes off it when she's driving these days. Not after what happened when she was handling the trafficking vehicle and took out a road sign.

"I never said that, Laila."

"You don't need to. It's written all over your face."

"I just want you to be sure. Both of you."

"What did Paul say?"

She spent several minutes with him before she came to find me. I was the topic of conversation, that much is obvious.

"Just that he's trying to figure things out. Make the right decisions. Make the right choices."

"And you don't think I'm the right choice?"

"Jesus Christ, Laila. Stop with all the peppering and negativity. I haven't said that. I've told him he needs to be sure before taking things any further. I'm saying the same to you."

She's gripping the steering wheel. I've clearly pushed her too far. I wait for her to speak rather than just continue with my tirade as I usually would.

She sighs. "Laila, this isn't just about you. This isn't just about what you want or need. My brother has issues. Serious issues. I'm sure you can see that. I mean, it's pretty obvious to most people."

Her voice is calm, her words spoken slowly. She's thinking about what she's saying and taking her time with how she's saying it so as not to upset or offend me. She also needs to be able to say her piece and get whatever this is off her chest without me interrupting. I need to allow her the opportunity to do that.

"Paul's not in his right mind a lot of the time. I know it looks the opposite when he's in Razr mode, but that headspace makes him weak, not strong. That mindset causes him to do reckless things and make stupid decisions. Decisions that could see him get himself or someone else hurt or worse."

She exhales again, and I know it's because she's struggling with her emotions.

"Laila, I don't want to see my brother losing his mind any more than he already has. I don't want to see him cut his hair off because he's pulling it out in clumps or watch him constantly flick a blade to try to retain some control over his life. You know how it was between him and me in the past. You know that better than anyone. But no matter what he did back then, he's still my brother. My blood. I love him so much, and I'm so scared for him. I can feel myself losing a little bit more of him with each passing day, and I'm terrified that pretty soon, there'll be nothing left. I'd really like for my big brother to be part of my future too, you know?" Her voice breaks, and she sobs.

I wait before I answer.

"I realize he has issues, Sarah, but maybe I can help bring some stability and normality to his life." I speak quietly.

"Do you love him? Because you have to want Paul for the right reasons. Not because you see him as some broken biker bad boy you want to tame and fix. This isn't some fucking romance novel that's going to have a fairytale ending. Shit like that doesn't happen when you live this life."

"I realize that, and yes. I love him."

She nods. "Fine. I won't get involved if you love him, and if it turns out he loves you too."

She pauses before she goes on, and I prepare myself for the 'but' moment because I know that's what's coming next.

"But I'm warning you, Laila. You mess with his feelings? You break my brother's heart? You make his condition deteriorate? Those are things I will never forgive you for. You won't just lose him. You'll lose us both."

"I won't." My voice is quiet.

Paul Delaney will be mine, and I will fix him.

CHAPTER THIRTEEN

BAILEY

The Iron Scorpions' Clubhouse, Brightling, New York

My daddy always tells me that life's what you make of it. You put in the effort, and you reap the rewards. It's an old cliché, I realize that. Is it true? In part, I guess. Sometimes you can put a whole heap of effort in, and the rewards bear no relation.

That's how I feel about the time I've spent at the Scorpions' clubhouse. Since handing in my notice, all I've done is help Mojo and Abigail, one of the new girls, with the cooking and cleaning. Now I'm not being used as a fuck toy, there isn't much else for me to do. In the evenings, I just stay in my room and read. I avoid the communal area. I don't want to witness which cum slut Razr's fucking these days. I'm not sure my heart could take it.

So, lots of effort but no rewards. Zero.

"It's my birthday, Bailey. You need to come downstairs and celebrate with the rest of us tonight." I'm lying on my bed staring up at Mojo, who's sitting on the edge. She's wearing a happy, sad face. She's pleased it's her birthday, but not so pleased it's her thirtieth. It means she's got three months or so to find someplace else to live.

You get a gold watch in some walks of life when you reach retirement age. Here? The club rewards you with fifty thousand dollars to start afresh in the outside world. A sizeable deposit for a modest property. Not that Mo has to worry about that. Apparently, Razr's already got an apartment lined up for her, so she doesn't have to rush to find her feet.

As much as there's never been anything physical between them, he's known her most of his adult life. They're family in a way. Well, as much as you ever can be in this life.

"I don't know, Mo." I shake my head to decline, although deep down, I know if she begs me, I won't be able to say no. How can I? She's been my best friend these past months, and I've never really had a girlfriend before now. A female I can chat with about girlie stuff. Well, apart from my sister.

"Please? For me? And can you do my hair? You do it so much nicer than me."

She grabs my hand in both of hers and flutters her eyelashes exaggeratedly. I roll my eyes in silent response, a smirk crossing my face.

"Okay, but if you were anyone else, I'd be sticking to my guns."

"Promise me you'll always keep in touch, Bailey. You know, when we both have to leave." The mood shifts to one that's way too morose and melancholy.

I sit up, drape my arms around her neck, and rest my chin on her shoulder.

"I promise," I whisper as tears prick my eyes. I blink them back before she can see them. Me throwing myself a pity party won't do either of us any good.

"Hey, I got you a birthday gift."

I hand her the plain black bag that's been laying on the opposite side of the bed. The bag she's been glancing at continually since she walked into the room. I threw away the original packaging from the shop where I had the item made as it would highlight how expensive it was. I'm hoping that way she won't guess the exorbitant price tag attached. It's a small price to pay for someone who's been a good friend.

"You shouldn't have, Bailey, but I won't turn it down. You know me. I can't resist presents." She laugh-sobs as she takes the gift from my hands.

I watch as she pulls the navy velvet box out of the bag and clicks it open.

"I thought you may change your name back to Carly once you're on the outside world, and I didn't want you to forget us. Forget me."

We both chuckle at her real name.

She lifts out the platinum necklace. The pendant says Mojo, and the dot above the j has a diamond pressed into it.

She stares at it open-mouthed.

"Is it real?" Her finger runs over the stone.

"As real as our friendship, so I'd say so."

She hands it to me, turning so I can fasten it around her neck. Then she turns back and almost squishes me to death in a vicelike hug.

"Thank you. I love you, Bailey."

"I love you too, Mo."

"Oh, and can I borrow that little black dress of yours for tonight? Maybe wearing that I can still bag myself an old man."

By old man, I know she means Dollar. I smirk at her. I also know she's talking about the dress I was wearing when I got down on my knees in front of Razr and took his dick in my mouth.

"Of course you can. It's your birthday, after all. So, today, what's mine is yours. We need to have you looking a million bucks."

AND SHE REALLY DOES LOOK LIKE A MILLION DOLLARS.

My dress fits her like a glove, and her new necklace glints when any lights hit it. Its shine is nothing compared to her beaming smile, though, as all the bikers bombard her with gifts and well wishes. Mo's positively glowing and is constantly blinking back tears. Even some of the old ladies have stayed behind to help her celebrate, although they'll be ushered out soon enough. Before the sexual shenanigans begin that they're not allowed to witness.

We might be the scum of society. We might be blood-thirsty killers. We might be a group of nasty fuck-ups in the eyes of the world and deemed the lowest of the low by our outlaw peers. But bikers look after each other. We're there for each other always.

Loyal. Trustworthy. Honest. Family.

We're brothers and sisters, regardless of blood. It's times like these I embrace my biker roots and feel thankful for them. I'm proud of who I am and where I come from. Grateful that I was pretty much born riding a hog and wearing leathers.

I fucking belong here. This life is in my DNA.

She raises a glass to me from the bar area, and I smile warmly back at her from where I'm standing alone at a distant table. I'd raise one in response, but I'm not drinking. That would be way too dangerous and way too stupid. I need to keep my wits about me for the rest of my time here with the Scorpions. Two months down. One to go. I don't need to find myself under the influence of alcohol then find myself under a certain prez as a result. Or worse still, confessing my undying, unrequited love to him. Then again, it's not like he's paid me any attention since I announced I was leaving, so it's not like I'm having to go out of my way to avoid him.

"Beautiful dress, Bailey. It comes with a hefty price tag attached."

I side glance at Cherry, casting my eyes over her long crimson hair and her minute but perfect hourglass shape. Cherry comes from money. Old money. There are some people you look at, and you just know as it's evident in their features and mannerisms. They wear an air of entitlement like the rest of us wear a scarf.

Cherry's fucking Blaze, the new VP who replaced Bomb. The latter disappeared a few months back. He took a sabbatical if I recall. In truth, I can't remember what bullshit line we were all fed. My guessing is Razr killed him for a blatant betrayal. He always did look like a shifty fucker, so it was probably deserved.

"It wasn't cheap."

I run my hand down the silver sequins. There's no point trying to deny that it was expensive. Everything Cherry wears is designer, including the short sparkly red number she's wearing right now. Four figures, minimum. She'll know where I got my dress, which designer, how much it cost, and even possibly which season it debuted.

"How did you manage to afford it?"

I turn and stare at her. Her face is impassive. She's a lawyer. Not a very good one from what I hear, or at least not when it comes to representing outlaws. She's studying me, trying to figure out precisely what I'm hiding.

"Just because I associate with MCs doesn't mean my family doesn't have money, Cherry. You, for one, should know that."

"Touché." She smirks, raising her flute glass at me.

It's champagne, and my guess is it won't be the cheap stuff they stock behind the bar here at the clubhouse. She'll have brought her own. She'll have expensive tastes. Apart from when it comes to men, that is. Then again, there aren't many women who aren't turned on by a bad boy biker wearing a cut and sitting on his hog, his scent made up of raw masculinity mixed with leather, engine oil, and grease.

"So, you're leaving."

"That's the rumor."

And I'm guessing I don't need to explain why. Everyone must know about my unrequited love situation. I find myself wondering if Razr knows. Even if he did, what the fuck would he care? He's too busy fawning over Laila.

"I say leaving, but you're running."

"Yup. I am." I don't even try to deny it.

"Why not fight for him if you want him that badly?"

"Because he's chasing someone else, and I have way too much respect for myself to put up with any more of his bullshit. Anyway, why do you care?"

"Because Jaine does. For some reason, she's rooting for you."

"It's the biker background."

"What do you mean?"

"She's showing me loyalty because I'm MC. Nothing more. She hates my guts."

"I wouldn't be too sure about that. Jaine doesn't do hate. She's not one for holding grudges either unless it's deserved. You're a determined little thing. I think she sees a lot of herself in you at the same age, and that's high praise indeed."

"Little?" I look down at her.

"Young, then." She chuckles.

"I'm honored she thinks so highly of me since she broke my nose."

"That was deserved, and you know it. That was for disrespecting her. I'm one of her closest friends, and my nose wouldn't have been safe either if I did what you did."

I smile. She's right. I regret my actions. Jaine didn't deserve that.

"How are my two favorite ladies!"

A tipsy Mojo almost trips over her own two feet and has to wrap her arms around my shoulders to steady herself. "I love you, Bailey."

I screw up my nose at her breath, which stinks of tequila. "You're drunk, Mo." I grimace.

"Yup. Drunk on love right now, and later, I'll be drunk on cum." She snickers. "I'll miss all this." She throws one arm wide to take in the whole room and everyone in it before letting out a sigh. "I'll miss you two the most. And Razr. You know…" She wags a finger in my face. "…You shouldn't just give up on him, Bailey."

"I've just told her the same thing," Cherry murmurs.

"You see? Posh pussy over there thinks you're in with a chance. I didn't take you as a quitter."

I grimace at how loud she's being. I'm pretty sure most of the folks in the room can hear her.

"I'm not a quitter, Mo, but I'm no one's doormat either."

"Cherry, baby."

I watch as Cherry smiles up at Blaze just before he sticks his tongue down her throat. He's a brute of a man. A devil disguised as an angel with that long blonde hair he has hanging way past his shoulders. His hands drop to her perky ass as he drags her front against his noticeable erection. It's all sex and debauchery in this place, and it doesn't matter who sees. In most cases, there's an unwritten invitation for you to join in if that's what floats your boat.

Same shit. Different MC.

"You ladies care to dance?"

A drunken Mo immediately snakes her arms around Dollar's shoulder. I guess that's all the response she thinks is needed. She has a thing for Mr. Money Man, as I like to call him. She has done for a while. I think she was secretly hoping he would ask her to be his old lady. I guess there's still time.

"Sure." I look towards Knight, who's standing beside Dollar, wearing the biggest smirk and holding his hand out to me. Swinging my long, now extension-free, blonde hair around my shoulders and sashaying my slim hips, I walk towards him and take his hand. He immediately spins me around, letting out a low wolf whistle as he does.

He probably thinks his luck's in. It isn't.

Knight is unruly short blonde hair and blue-eyed handsomeness wrapped in ink and topped with a leather cut. As a result of his good looks, he's fucked pretty much all of the cum sluts in here and, from what I hear on the clubhouse grapevine, also serviced most of the old ladies. With the blessing of their old men, of course. There's no cheating involved.

Knight wouldn't have dared approach me if I'd still been Razr's fuck toy. Not if he didn't want to end up with his throat on a plate and his well-used appendage sliced off then stuffed up his ass.

He pulls my body close to his.

"Man, you look and smell good enough to eat, Bailey." His breath is hot against my ear.

I smirk up at him. "Use that line a lot?"

"Only when it's deserved. You look like a different woman now you're wearing dresses. You look like posh pussy. Like Cherry."

"Maybe I am."

"I reckon you are. I reckon you've been slumming it here with us, and now you're going to high tail it back to wherever the hell it is you came from."

I smile up at him. He doesn't know how right he is.

"Before you go. How's about you and I create some lasting memories, starting with me having a little taste."

His hands drop to my ass as he pulls me tighter against him, his lips grazing my neck.

"I do believe I have all the memories I'll ever need of this place, but thank you for your very kind offer," I whisper in his ear as I snake my arms around his neck.

It's then I see him. Out of the corner of my eye. Razr. He's standing at the bar talking to Ripper and Flame and facing in the opposite direction. He must have just come from the back as he wasn't there when we took to the floor.

"I'll sweet talk you around before the evening's out, don't you worry your pretty little head about that." Knight nuzzles against my ear. He smells good. All aromatic cologne and leather. In truth, if he hadn't fucked pretty much every woman in here and if I wasn't in love with Razr, I might have been tempted.

I laugh exaggeratedly and deliberately press my tits against his chest. It won't do any harm to let Razr see me having a good time. He's quick enough to wrap his arms around Laila when she's here, pretending I don't even exist.

"Well, I'm all ears, hotshot." I whisper the challenge back.

Moving one hand from my ass, he fists my hair, his eyes scanning my face. I know he's going to kiss me. At least Knight's trying to woo me before trying to fuck me, as opposed to an emotionless Razr who thinks he can just stick his dick in me because he's an entitled asshole.

Our breaths mingle. I feel the temperature in the room drop even before I hear his voice.

"I wouldn't do that unless you want me to cut your goddamn throat out."

CHAPTER FOURTEEN

RAZR

The Iron Scorpions' Clubhouse, Brightling, New York

THEY BOTH TURN TO STARE AT ME. KNIGHT LOOKS SHEEPISH AS HE releases her. He knows he shouldn't have gone anywhere near her. I may not be fucking her, but she's mine until she leaves. Everyone knows that.

He was just trying his luck, and I can't say I blame him given how good she looks. Still, the asshole should be grateful I didn't decide that it had run out. It was disrespectful, and he knows it. I curse him silently. If he'd stayed the fuck away from her, I wouldn't be reacting right now or be standing in front of her.

For the past two months, she's been keeping out of my way, and I've been keeping out of hers. The avoidance has been intentional on both our parts. It's just easier that way.

No temptation.

She's looking at me defiantly. Is she deliberately trying to stir up trouble? Trying to get a reaction? If she is, then it's worked.

She's got my full attention. And my dick's.

I grab her wrist to pull her away from him, but she jerks it from my grasp.

"Fuck you."

Two words. Spoken loudly. Words that very few people have ever dared say to me. And for those who ever did? Well, most didn't live to tell the goddamn tale. I've been known to kill folks for way less.

You could hear a pin drop as everyone watches our interaction. I glare at her, but she doesn't stand down.

"We can do this the easy way or the hard way, Bailey."

"The hard way."

"You got it, sweetheart."

With her screams of protest ringing loudly in my ears, I pick her up and throw her over my shoulder.

"I'm not wearing any panties, you neanderthal."

"Good to fucking know."

I stride towards my bedroom as she punches at my back.

"Put me the fuck down."

I throw her on the bed before locking the door behind me. She leaps up, all claws and teeth and hissing like a wild thing.

"Let me the fuck out of here, you asshole. You have no right to do this. I'm fucking leaving, or had you forgotten?"

She flies at me, her nails raking down the side of my face. I can feel the blood instantly rise to the surface.

"You little fucking hellcat." Spinning her around, I push her hard against the bedroom wall, pinning her hands above her head. She grimaces in pain. I've hurt her and winded her. I know I have. Not that it matters to her as in an instant she's recovered, immediately whipping her head from side to side, trying to bite me anywhere she can while throwing her body around, trying to free herself from my grip.

"Calm the fuck down."

"Fuck you, asshole."

I restrain her until she's physically exhausted herself, then, adjusting my hands so one grips both her wrists, I use the other to push her hair back from her face. She's panting, her chest heaving with exertion at the effort she's gone to to try to free herself from my hold.

Does she hate me that much?

She knows she never had any chance of escaping, but she persevered all the same.

She glares at me. Her chin tilted and her cheeks flushed pink. I can see anger in her eyes, but I can also see pain. Not physical pain. Emotional pain.

I frown. Have I hurt her in the past? Because it's right there. I can see it clear as day, just like I can see the quiver in her bottom lip and the tears that threaten to spill from her blue eyes.

She bites her lip to stop it from trembling before raising her chin in a last show of defiance, but my attention has already switched to her mouth. I run my finger across where she's just bitten. She shakes her head, struggling once more to free herself from my grip.

"Please don't, Razr. Please." Her voice is barely a whimper.

But it's too late. I'm a selfish, inconsiderate fucker, and I'm going to possess the one thing that, for whatever reason, she desperately doesn't want me to have.

Her mouth.

I run my tongue across her lips, and she sighs her pleasure. Raising my head, I look down at her again. Her face is flushed, but now it's with desire, and my dick twitches in response. Pressing my mouth to hers, I suck on her bottom lip, then bite down hard. She groans, and I can almost taste the need that floods her. Her lips part, and I thrust my tongue into her waiting mouth. She tastes how I'd expect. Sweet and all things Bailey. Why have I never kissed her before now? Her mouth is addictive. My tongue strokes deep, missing nothing, and hers responds, dancing with mine, her quiet moans of appreciation a clear sign of her increasing arousal.

Pushing my knee between her thighs, I feel her heat through my jeans, and she automatically grinds her pussy against the rough material in silent invitation.

Pulling her arms free from my hold, she snakes them around my neck as I deepen the kiss and plunder her soft mouth. Lifting her dress to her waist, my hands drop to cup her ass. Her naked skin is so damn smooth, and she smells so fucking good.

Clean and citrusy. Subtle and expensive.

Her mouth leaves mine only for the time it takes for her to yank her dress over her head.

She's naked. She's offering herself to me. Is it for the last time? Or for a fresh start? My mouth drops to cover a pink nipple, and I tug on it with my teeth, causing her to fist my hair in both hands and smash her tits against my face.

Wanting more. Needing more. Demanding more.

I suck hard on both tips as my hand drops to cup her pussy.

"You're soaking, sweetheart."

"So, fuck me, Prez."

She's not afraid to speak her mind and ask for her own pleasure. I like that about her. I like it a lot.

She unfastens my jeans, then frees my dick. I'm rock hard. It's been two months. There's been no one since her. I groan as she rubs the pre-cum across the crown before fisting my cock and stroking my length.

"Condom?"

"Back pocket."

"Feeling lucky?"

"Always."

She tears open the packaging before sheathing my dick with it. I lift her, her legs anchor around my waist, and I sink into her wet, welcoming warmth, groaning as she tightens that little pussy of hers around my thick length.

"Fuck me hard, Razr."

"You got it, sweetheart."

I pull out almost completely, then thrust straight back in, watching as her eyes close in pleasure.

"You like that, don't you?"

"Yeah. Don't stop."

My movements are precise. Her nails dig into my shoulders as I fuck her hard against the wall. Then, positioning her knees over my arms, I lean back so we can both look down and watch as my dick drills into her, its length sheened with her juices.

"Your pussy feels so fucking good. Hot and tight and gripping my dick just right."

I can already feel my release clawing at the base of my spine. I angle her hips, and my cock connects with her sweet spot.

"Razr."

She's almost there, so I thrust deeper.

"Fuck." It's barely audible; she's too far gone.

"Take your pleasure first, sweetheart, and then I'll take mine."

I drive into her, fucking her hard. The sound of my flesh slapping against hers and our mutual growls of appreciation fill the room.

"Look at me, Bailey. Look at me as you come all over my cock, sweetheart."

Green on blue, her gaze meets mine. Her legs shake, her walls clench around me, and she cries out as her wetness floods my shaft. I thrust into her, my movements now selfish and erratic, seeking my own end.

Her mouth connects with my neck, and she sucks on my skin, then bites down. I hiss at the pain just as my balls tighten and explode, my cum filling the condom as I continue to thrust into her. Panting, I lean against her, pinning her slightness to the wall with my weight.

Seconds pass—or is it minutes—before I say one word.

"Stay."

CHAPTER FIFTEEN

BAILEY

The Iron Scorpions' Clubhouse, Brightling, New York

"So, Razr asked you to stay?"

I look at Mo, who's lying on my bed.

"Well, I'm not sure if he meant to stay the night or stay indefinitely."

I did the first, and we fucked the entire time. Who needs sleep anyway? It's over-rated. The latter? Stay indefinitely? Well, I may reconsider. The jury's still out. I examine the hickeys on my neck in the door mirror. Now Razr's been let loose with that mouth of his, he's been continually licking, sucking, and biting every part of me like I'm some sort of human buffet. Not that I'm complaining. And I did return the favor several times over.

"So, what are you going to do?"

I shrug. "I've still got one month of my contract left to run. I'm not going to retract my notice, so I've got that timeframe to make a final decision. Anyway, enough about the prez and me. What about you and Mr. Money Man?"

She sighs and stares at the ceiling. "I think he's real close to committing, Bailey. I just wish I had a little more time."

We're both silent as we contemplate our shared reality. That over the next month, I may leave, and Mo may follow. It's the end of an era for us both. More so for her. I walk over and sit on the edge of the bed, and she moves across to fling her arms around me. There's nothing to be said. There's no point in either of us filling the other's head with that rose-tinted spectacle bullshit that's unlikely to happen. Still, I'd be lying if I said I wasn't feeling a tad more optimistic after last night. See, it's the first time I've been fucked by Delaney the man and not Razr the monster. Made love to, even. Yes, it was still downright dirty sex. I doubt Delaney knows how to fuck any other way. But it was mixed with a tenderness this time that has never been there before.

"See you downstairs in ten, Bailey?"

"Sure thing."

SARAH

Laila and I walk into the clubhouse. All the cum sluts are still clearing up the aftermath of Mojo's thirtieth party. No sooner are we in the door than the woman herself comes running across the floor, throwing her arms around me in one of her familiar tactile embraces.

I wish she didn't have to leave. There aren't many people who remember my daddy, especially the women. Mojo's one of the last remaining few.

"I'm so sorry I couldn't make it last night, Mo. The pregnancy gurus lied. Morning sickness is an all-day event, and I'm struggling to keep anything down."

She tsks at me. "You don't have to apologize, Sarah. I knew you were here in spirit the same as King was. I'm just glad that Irish mobster of yours is looking after you so well and making sure you're resting up."

Unexpected tears roll down my cheeks at the mention of my daddy's road name.

Mojo wipes them away, then pushes my hair back from my face in a motherly fashion. "King would be so proud of you, Sarah."

I nod, not trusting myself to reply straight away.

"I got you a gift." I shoot her a watery smile eventually as I hold out the package. I watch as she unwraps it before removing the little silver charm bracelet from its black velvet box.

"It's beautiful, Sarah." She holds it up and smiles at the little hog and helmet charms already in place. I spot the necklace as I fasten the bracelet to her wrist.

She notices me looking and reaches to touch the sparkling pendant.

"It's my gift from Bailey." She smiles brightly as she does every time she mentions her friend.

"It's beautiful," I whisper as I touch the diamond. I know who the designer is. I have a few of his pieces myself. Each one is individually hand-made. This necklace wasn't cheap. Four figures at the very least as the expert craftsman would never lower himself to use anything fake, so the stone glinting at me is the real deal. Just who the hell is this Bailey chick? I make a mental note to prize it out of her next time I get her alone. Something isn't stacking up. I mean, I know she and Mojo are close, but that's a lot to spend on a gift.

Unless, of course, money is no object.

My attention drifts to my brother, who's propping up the bar with Flame. He's laughing out loud, which is a rare sight and sound these days. Leaving Laila to chat with Mojo, I walk across, curious to know what or who is behind one of his rare moments of happiness.

"Sister." He places a soft kiss on the top of my head as he always does, and my eyes are immediately drawn to the hickey on his neck.

"You grinning like a fool because you got your dick wet, Paul?"

He snickers. "Something like that."

"Anyone I know?"

"Maybe." His grin widens. Who the fuck's put a smile on my brother's face that's making him look ten years younger? Maybe it's one of the new cum sluts.

"Laila." He smiles down at my little friend before kissing her on the top of the head, the same as he did with me. I can't help but wonder if that's a sign. Does that greeting mean he really sees her as more of a sister? Laila's eyes are immediately drawn to the bruising on his neck, as mine were only moments before. It's clear evidence that he's been making out with someone at the very least. She frowns.

My brother's smile leaves his face as he witnesses Laila's adverse reaction to the mark on his neck. He's gone from cheerful back to withdrawn in the time it takes to flick a switch.

Is it guilt?

I know he won't want to hurt Laila intentionally, but it's not like they're exclusive or anything. As far as I know, they haven't spoken to or seen each other since the time Laila fainted. According to her, they're being careful not to rush things, but secretly, I think she's just biding her time until Bailey leaves so she has a clear path and a captive audience.

Tears prick my eyes as I watch him emotionally shut down, his rare carefree moment gone so fast it's like it never happened in the first place.

"Bailey, look at the new bracelet Sarah got me."

Mojo's shriek is loud enough to be heard from across the room. She jangles the piece of jewelry I affixed to her wrist only moments before in her friend's face.

Bailey's wearing dark blue Daisy Dukes and a white tank top. A pair of worn high tops finish her look. Jesus Christ, my brother really does have a type.

She laughs at Mojo's barely contained excitement, then hugs her with genuine affection. She turns, and our eyes connect. She smiles warmly. It matches Paul's. That smile. She's literally glowing from the inside out. My eyes drift to her neck, at the telltale bruising on the skin. I know I'm now taking in the girl who brought a smile to my brother's face today.

Is he falling for her? For Bailey?

It's clear how she feels about him. She's never admitted it freely, but when questioned, she's never denied it. She loves him. The look she's giving him now is reminiscent of how I look at Cillian.

The problem is, I don't think Paul even realizes.

I smile back at her. I'm grateful she's brought a little bit of sunshine to my brother's life, even if it turns out only to be temporary.

I then watch as her smile fades and slips from her face entirely. I glance across to where she's looking. Beside me, Laila is throwing her a look so malicious, if it were a weapon, Bailey would be toast. I've never seen my little friend act this way, but she's staked a claim on my brother, and the bruising on Bailey's neck is clear evidence of who he spent last night with.

Is Bailey still leaving?

Turning my attention to Paul, I watch him frown as he takes in their exchange. If he cares for Bailey, he won't want to hurt her, but he won't want to hurt Laila either. The latter will take priority, I'm sure.

Time stands still. What happens next is not something I expected. And definitely not from Laila.

She looks at Bailey determinedly, then turns and walks across to Paul. Snaking her arms around his neck, she raises on tippy-toes and kisses him full on the mouth. I watch as he tenses briefly before he slides his inked arm around her waist and kisses her back. Does he want to kiss her? Is he kissing her because he has to? I just don't know anymore.

The bikers erupt in hollers at the scene. At this public declaration of whatever the fuck this is.

Wrong.

It's the first word that comes into my head and my gut. It's a very public declaration of wrong.

Swinging my attention back to Bailey, I watch as her expression fleetingly fills with pain. She tries her best to hide it, but I catch it and recognize it straight away. You can't hide that shit from someone who's been there and got the t-shirt. I wore that look myself not so long ago. I've felt that very same expression implode, destroying my heart and soul and leaving behind a vacant shell. A shell that still had to smile and act normal on the outside like everything was still A-okay in the outlaw world.

My situation was only temporary. I'm not sure Bailey will be that fortunate.

I stand there and watch her witness the man she's in love with kissing another woman. There's no pain quite like it.

Mojo walks over to her, her expression full of concern as she takes in her friend. She didn't miss it either—Bailey's fleeting moment of devastation.

Unlike the bikers, the cum sluts seldom have a camaraderie. They see each other as competition. All of them pushing, jostling, and vying for the same men's attention, their end game to secure a biker who will make them their old lady. It's not like that with those two. I'm glad Mojo has finally found a real friend. Then again, going by what we've all just witnessed, she's about to lose her. Is it better to never have something if you're only going to lose it in the end? Who knows? I guess I should ask Bailey the same question when it comes to my brother.

Bailey continues to watch the heart-shattering visual. She's strong, though. She won't let on just how affected she is. She's a biker. We don't show weakness. Not if we can help it. We just dust ourselves down and carry on.

I have so much fucking respect for her right now as she takes this shitshow on the chin. I watch as Laila turns and smiles smugly at her.

My determined best friend is standing her ground and refusing to back down. She wants my brother, and she will have him. Nothing and no one is going to stand in her way.

Bailey nods at her. A sign of defeat. A sign of acceptance that Laila's won. She then walks away. I turn my attention to my brother. He has his arm around Laila's shoulder, but his gaze is fixed on the retreating back of Bailey, his face expressionless. What's it hiding?

Regret? Frustration?

I'm not sure he even knows.

Laila put him in a position, and he had to make a spur-of-the-moment decision. I pray to God it was the right choice for his sake, as I've got a feeling Bailey will never forgive him for this very public act of betrayal and humiliation.

CHAPTER SIXTEEN

BAILEY

The Iron Scorpions' Clubhouse, Brightling, New York

THERE'S NOTHING QUITE LIKE THE FEEL OF A HOG'S ENGINE humming between your thighs, the wind whipping through your hair, or the smell of sunshine and fresh air mixing with grease and exhaust fumes. They should bottle the latter up and sell it. Then again, would I always associate that scent with pain, regret, and all the other shit I've fought my way through today?

I left.

After the scene went down in the clubhouse. The one that was acted out exclusively for my viewing pleasure, I switched into jeans, borrowed Jaine's fringed leather jacket, and got the fuck out of Dodge.

Pronto.

Bailey has now left the building. I assured Mojo I was one hundred percent fine and that I was just heading out for a pre-booked appointment. I convinced myself the last part wasn't a lie. That I was just doing what I always intended to do, just one month earlier than planned.

But I did lie about one thing.

I wasn't fine. I'm not fine. I will never be fucking fine.

But do you know what? I'll survive.

I regurgitated to Jamie the same shit I spouted to Mo as he opened the gates wearing that annoyingly familiar smirk of his. Running his hands up and down the seams of his cut, he flirted with me the entire time. I'll miss him.

Jamie didn't ask any pertinent questions and waved me off as I rode out of the compound on the spare Fat Boy one last time. Why would he suspect anything? It's not like I haven't borrowed this ride before.

I'm glad he didn't pry. I wouldn't have wanted to lie any more than I had to. Lying's a fool's game. The truth will always out, no matter what. When he's interrogated, which he most definitely will be, he can hand on heart say that he knew nothing about my plans. That he suspected nothing. That I told him nothing.

I wouldn't want him to end up being served his own throat on a plate.

The heavy clunk of the gates closing behind me signaled the end of my time with the Iron Scorpions and with Paul 'Razr' Delaney.

I will carry that unforgettable sound with me always.

My one regret is that I didn't get to say a proper goodbye, especially to Mo. But I know if I had, she'd have alerted Razr. Her loyalty is to him first and foremost, which is as it should be. He's her prez. Even though she's leaving, he will always be her prez. Call me lily-livered, but I just didn't want to hear his excuses or his apologies or be served up a heaped plate of stone-cold pity.

He made his choice loud and clear in front of an audience, publicly humiliating me in the process.

Then again, what did I expect? He's never considered my feelings before, so why the hell would he start now?

In the end, I only took what I needed. My stars. My phone. My wallet. Anything else I figured I could just buy on the way.

Razr asked me to stay. I guess in the end, he only wanted me to stay the night to keep his bed warm and his demon at bay while he was waiting for her to arrive the very next morning. The rest was just wishful thinking on my part.

Fool. That's precisely what I am—a fool.

Anyway, I'm free. Well, with one month remaining on my contract, I've gone AWOL. I'll take my chances that the Scorpions won't come after me for some sort of recompense. I doubt they will. Razr will let me go. Gladly, I'm sure. He'll be relieved to see the back of me. We shared one last hurrah, and now he has Laila. He doesn't need me hanging around like a bad smell making things awkward for them. Not now they've officially declared themselves a couple in front of the entire clubhouse.

Poor little Bailey sitting on the sidelines, pining for the life she'll never have as her love is unrequited. I don't want their pity. I especially don't need Strawberry Shortcake looking down her smug little nose at me again, all because she's won.

The man I love is in love with her. Go figure.

Fuck him. And her. Fuck them both.

I travel over two hundred miles before I stop at a gas station. After purchasing a bottle of water and a sandwich, I lay the leather jacket on the damp grass beside the hog, then I sit and eat. Taking out my phone, I lie back on the grass.

Bailey: *I'm on my way home.*

Jay: *No more running?*

Bailey: *No more running.*

Jay: *Do you want to talk about it? Or should I say him? Whoever he is? Or was?*

Bailey: *Nope. He's an asshole. No point.*

Jay: *I've been called away on business, but Daddy, Tadgh, and Conor are home.*

Bailey: *Good to know.*

Jay: *Raf's been asking after you. He's been very patient, Bee.*

Bailey: *Not so good to know.*

Jay: *I'm surprised he waited.*

Bailey: *I wish he hadn't. He should have run too while he had the chance.*

Jay: *Don't be like that.*

Bailey: *Easy for you to say.*

Jay: *Hey, I offered his older brother, but he doesn't like blondes. Guess he's not a gentleman. You know. They're meant to prefer blondes.*

Bailey: *You're hilarious. Anyway, what about what I want?*

Jay: *You know us womenfolk never get a say in such matters. Our lives are dictated to us by others.*

Bailey: *Apart from your mom. She got out.*

Jay: *And look what happened to her.*

Bailey: *That was natural causes.*

Jay: *Not according to Daddy. That was her penance for asking for a divorce.*

Bailey: *He's an asshole*

Jay: *Watch your mouth. He's still our daddy.*

Bailey: *He's a dictator. And blood isn't always thicker than water, you know.*

Jay: *When you're Irish Catholic, it is.*

Bailey: *I'm not.*

Jay: *Baptized and confirmed.*

Bailey: *If I can't remember then it didn't happen.*
Jay: *Careful, your immaturity's showing. Anyway, I was there and witnessed the whole thing.*
Bailey: *Well, I'm eight years younger than you, Jay, and always will be.*
Jay: *Age is just a number.*
Bailey: *Tell that to your wrinkles and everything that's starting to head south.*
Jay: *If I said I miss you, I take it back. I don't.*
Bailey: *Noted, and you didn't.*
Jay: *Good. Go away. I hate you.*
Bailey: *I'm going. And no, you don't. I'm your favorite person in the world.*
Jay: *In your dreams.*
Bailey: *Let Daddy know I'll be there in a couple of weeks. I'm going to take the scenic route.*
Jay: *Will do. Love you, Bee.*
Bailey: *Love you too, Jay.*

Bailey: *This is my number. Bailey.*
Mojo: *You're not coming back, are you?*
Bailey: *No.*
Mojo: *I'm sorry about what happened.*
Bailey: *It wasn't your fault. It's what I fully expected to happen. Strawberry Shortcake was always going to get her man in the end.*
Mojo: *So where to now?*
Bailey: *Back home. Tell Razr I'll transfer the monies for the hog if he tells me what I owe. If he needs it back, I can arrange for a transporter to return it.*

Mojo: *Won't that cost a fortune?*
Bailey: *I'm not poor.*
Mojo: *Then why do all this?*
Bailey: *I needed to get away. New York seemed as good a place as any, even better that it was on the opposite coast.*
Mojo: *Why become a cum slut, though?*
Bailey: *I'm a biker. The MC life is all I know. I was only going to stay away for a month or so. I wasn't intending on sleeping with anyone. One month just turned into almost nine.*
Mojo: *Because you fell in love with the prez?*
Bailey: *It's in the past now.*
Mojo: *You can't just switch feelings like that off.*
Bailey: *Watch me. Anyway, I'm getting back on the bike. I'll give you progress updates on my journey.*
Mojo: *I'll pin each destination on a map.*
Bailey: *You do that. And when I reach home, make sure you come to visit. Miss you already.*
Mojo: *I will, and I miss you too.*

Just as I'm putting my phone in my pocket, it vibrates. I shake my head and smile, thinking it's just Mojo again.

Jaine: *I've just spoken to Sarah. Mojo called her. You did right to walk away. Leave the ball in his court now. Delaney always goes after what he wants in life. No exceptions. If he wants you, he will move heaven and earth to find you.*
Bailey: *You think he will?*
Jaine: *Only you know the answer to that.*

I guess this is Jaine's final piece of advice. I also think I'll never see Paul Delaney again after what I witnessed today.

Bailey: *Thank you. For everything.*
Jaine: *You're welcome. And from one biker chick to another, the moment of disrespect aside, if ever you need anything, then just let me know.*
Bailey: *I borrowed your fringed jacket.*
Jaine: *Keep it.*

I smile to myself. Even if I never got the guy in the end, I met some good people.

"Damn you to hell, Paul Delaney," I whisper under my breath as I blink back tears, wishing for once I could have had it all.

CHAPTER SEVENTEEN

JAINE

Jaine's House, Rising, California

Padraig: *Eoin's asking when we can expect to meet the new accountant. He's convinced you've been avoiding him.*
Jaine: *Yup. Every opportunity I can, Dyl. You'll meet her the day after tomorrow. She's popping along for an informal chat to see if you all click.*
Padraig: *What's she like?*
Jaine: *Tall, blonde, and has a really good sense of humor.*
Padraig: *You're lying. Accountants don't have a sense of humor.*
Jaine: *This one does. She'll need it to put up with you guys.*
Padraig: *Single?*
Jaine: *You interested?*
Padraig: *Not at all. Our Eoin might be, though.*

Jaine: *He's interested in any female with a pulse. He's already asked me if I thought she'd be up for desk sex.*
Padraig: *He said that?*
Jaine: *He implied it. He suggested that she might not be able to help herself.*
Padraig: *Not be able to resist Eoin's manly charms?*
Jaine: *You can't say Eoin and charm in the same sentence. I can think of several other words that are way more suitable. Anyway, fucking someone over a desk is a business low. Who even does that?*
Padraig: *How do you know he has desk sex?*
Jaine: *Sarah's been subjected to the unbusinesslike noises coming from his office when he and Candice are in there.*
Padraig: *You think the new girl would be up for it?*
Jaine: *I doubt she's Eoin's type. You'll know what I mean when you meet her. She's very forward. She also tends to say what's in her head without thinking. Her mouth has zero filter and no zip. I'm not sure he'll appreciate that, given she speaks with a smirk on her face most of the time. He'll probably find her annoying and want to kill her from the get-go. She's maybe better suited to you, Dyl.*
Padraig: *I'm not interested, darlin'.*
Jaine: *Still hung up on cliché girl?*
Padraig: *Always.*
Jaine: *Just sex then, maybe?*
Padraig: *There's no such thing as just sex. At least not for me. Not anymore.*
Jaine: *So, you're not… you know?*
Padraig: *No, I'm not.*
Padraig: *Don't you ever get lonely?*
Padraig: *Having sex with someone just for the sake of it doesn't make you less lonely. It makes you more lonely.*

Jaine: *Dyl. I wish I could make everything right for you.*
Padraig: *The power is in your hands, darlin'.*
Jaine: *Only if I had a magic wand.*
Padraig: *Then until you turn into the biker equivalent of Tinkerbell, I'll just keep fucking my hand in the shower every morning.*
Jaine: *Thanks for that. Now I can't get that visual out of my head. No offense, but I'd sooner not have imagined you naked, Dyl.*
Padraig: *You're not even a teeny-tiny bit curious?*
Jaine: *No. Your Irish's brother. You're also Batman. No one should ever get to see Batman naked.*
Padraig: *Apart from Robin.*
Jaine: *Especially Robin*
Padraig: *I'll report back to the rest of the family, darlin'.*
Jaine: *Send Eoin my love.*
Padraig: *LOL. Will do.*

Eoin: *I've heard we've to expect the accountant the day after tomorrow. That's not a lot of notice, Jaine.*
Jaine: *No? Here was me thinking the future Irish king would be sitting with his Italian-leather-clad feet on his desk while twiddling his thumbs and staring at an empty calendar. You know, as he lets his toy soldiers do all the real work.*
Eoin: *That shows how little you know me. A resume would be good.*
Jaine: *My goddamn word not enough?*
Eoin: *Stop trying to antagonize me.*
Jaine: *Where's the fun in that?*
Eoin: *I prefer a different kind of fun with women.*

Jaine: *Careful. Someone may accuse you of being a chauvinist. Thinking women are only useful for one thing. Anyway, you're not dicking my accountant.*

Eoin: *Jealous at the thought?*

Jaine: *Not at all. I don't want anything to do with your dick.*

Eoin: *Are you coming along with her?*

Jaine: *You know I'm not. You know fine well I'm in Rising. Is this another attempt to get me to meet your folks?*

Eoin: *No, that can wait.*

Jaine: *Until never.*

Eoin: *Until you return to Manhattan.*

Jaine: *I might not bother then.*

Eoin: *Immature.*

Jaine: *What can I say? You bring out the worst in me.*

Eoin: *Maybe I'd bring out the best in you too. What's her name?*

Jaine: *Jessie.*

Eoin: *Nice name.*

Jaine: *Glad you goddamn approve.*

Eoin: *Do you ever not cuss?*

Jaine: *Nope. I'm a pretty biker chick with a mouth like a sailor.*

Eoin: *Has someone been quoting me.*

Jaine: *Yup. Apparently, you talk about me all the time.*

Eoin: *Not all the time.*

Jaine: *All. The. Time. So, who's taking up space in whose head, Mr. O'Connell?*

Eoin: *Send me the resume.*

Jaine: *What's the magic word.*

Eoin: *Please.*

CHAPTER EIGHTEEN

JESSIE

The Hudson Duster's HQ, Manhattan, New York

"Any last-minute requests or advice before I walk into the lion's den, partner?"

I stand on the sidewalk, looking up at the imposing skyscraper, the sun reflecting off the glass-covered building. It's one of many owned by The Hudson Dusters, but this one boasts their HQ. They own most of Hell's Kitchen and Hudson Yards. An impressive property portfolio and a plethora of businesses running from within their confines. Some legal. Many not.

That's why they need me. No one wants the IRS sniffing around, and that's precisely what the organization is doing. The Dusters have too many new business ventures, too much money going through their accounts, and all in too short a space of time. Their laundering technique is all wrong. It's outdated. Pertinent questions are being asked.

And rightly so.

If I did everything by the book, I'd be asking the same. So how do I know the Dusters are a hot topic of conversation behind the IRS's closed doors? There's not much I don't know about the Internal Revenue Service and who's currently under their forensic microscope. I have a plethora of people on the inside, and all are handsomely rewarded for the tasty tidbits of information they feed me. Not directly, of course. No, sirree. That shit is diluted through so many bent professionals beforehand. Not a crumb of wrongdoing will ever land on me.

I'm squeaky clean on the outside. I'm also the best. Far from modest, I know. And expensive. Let's not forget that—worth every dime.

To be head-hunted by the most successful outlaw lawyer in the business confirms my second-to-none reputation. An offer to join ranks and work together? Well, that's not something I could ever have turned down, even if it meant having to relocate to New York.

Inhaling the smell of trash, I take in the black bags lining up on the sidewalk. Smells like Vegas. At least something's familiar.

"Make your own mind up and just play them to our best advantage, Jessie. These boys are sharp. Razor-sharp. If you're going to toy with them, make sure you have your poker face firmly in place."

I chuckle. "Don't worry. I'll be myself, Jaine. I'll just have a little fun with your boys along the way. And I promise I won't even look at the youngest."

She laughs.

Falling out with other women over men is a fool's game. I had more than enough bitching and backstabbing at high school to last me a lifetime. Most of it was on account of how I looked, which is not something I was in control of. My folks made me. It's their gene pool I was birthed from. Blame them. None of the girls ever bothered to get to know who lay under the surface. I was judged.

Harshly and unfairly. I had very few friends due to my appearance as no one trusted me with their boyfriends.

So, I dated the quarterback and became the head cheerleader. It's what they expected, and it just made them hate me more—living the high school dream that they all wanted for themselves. The perfect life.

On the surface, at least.

Little did they know all I ever wanted was to be accepted for me.

"And you are?"

"They're expecting me."

"I'd like a name."

"Jessie."

"Jessie?" She's wanting me to give her my full name. I can see my name right there on the desk calendar. It's the only name on the damn thing. She's just being a bitch.

Story of my life.

"Well, they're not going to be expecting anyone else since I have an appointment at this time, which is written right there in black ink. See, I like to be punctual. What's your name?"

"Candice."

"See, I like to be punctual, Candice. I don't like to keep people waiting, and I don't like to be kept waiting either. Right now? You're keeping me waiting. In turn, I'm keeping them waiting."

"I need your name."

"Why? Don't you have one of your own?"

Immature, I know.

"Is there a problem?" The door is yanked open, and a GQ model walks out. I mean, Jaine told me these guys were fine. She didn't mention that they were *fine* fine. This one's tall, dark, and handsome and then some. I'd guess he's in his late thirties. His hissing voice is almost as deadly as his gaze, and he's looking at me like I'm the most annoying person in the world.

Another story of my life.

He probably heard the whole ruckus going down between the lovely Candice and me.

They share a look. Yup. They're fucking.

I grin. They both know I've just clocked their dirty secret. I may not be a lawyer, but I'm as observant as one. I see everything. I'm a shark at scanning desks and reading shit upside down. It's the auditor in me. Always looking for and finding what folks are trying their best to hide.

"No problem. Candice wants my name. I told her she already has one of her own, so if it's all right with her, I'd like to keep mine." I smile at him. I can tell he's rolling his eyes inwardly.

It's a look I'm used to. Did I already mention the story of my life? Reckon I did.

"Jessie O'Brien, I presume."

I hold up a single finger in acknowledgment and smile. "Guilty as charged, Your Honor."

He glares at me and motions with his head for me to enter the lion's den.

First impressions matter, and I really do like to make sure I stand out from the crowd. Love me or loathe me?

My aim in life is never to be forgotten

I TAKE IN THE FACES OF THE PEOPLE SITTING AROUND THE TABLE. Jaine told me in advance who I'd be meeting. The four O'Connell brothers and their daddy. There's also a strikingly beautiful red-haired girl.

I place my briefcase on the leather-covered circular top, then lean against it briefly as they all stare at me.

I let them have their fill before walking to the window and staring out at the skyline. I fully appreciate that having the opportunity to represent an empire such as this is something most accountants can only ever dream of. I also fully understand that my association with Jaine means this gig is pretty much in the bag. But I still want them to see me as an individual in my own right all the same.

"Great view." I compose myself before I turn around, choosing to remain standing. "So, let me guess. You must be Eoin O'Connell." I look at the GQ model who opened the door earlier. He nods, his expression impassive. "You must be Cillian O'Connell. That red hair of yours is a dead giveaway." I smile at him, and he grins back. "You must be the one and only Irish." I screw up my face jokingly. "Sorry, Padraig O'Connell. Shit, Jaine told me over and over to make sure I got that one right."

The eldest one frowns, but Padraig laughs heartily. "Paddy will do just fine, Jessie."

"And you must be Dylan O'Connell." I turn to look at him, and he blushes. I swear to The Almighty it's the sweetest thing I've ever seen. A murderous Irish mobster blushing.

"Are you hot, Dylan? I know I am." I wave my hand exaggeratedly in front of my face, pretending to cool myself. "There sure is a lot of testosterone flying around this room. That'll be the reason why." I then turn my attention to the smiling girl. "You must be Sarah. Cillian's wife." I mouth *wife* silently as it's meant to be a secret. She chuckles at me and looks at her husband, who smiles and shakes his head. The love between them is almost tangible.

I'd like some of that for myself one day.

"And last but not least, you must be Fergal O'Connell, the one and only Da Duster himself."

My gaze connects with that of the patriarch of the O'Connell clan. His eyes are like deep blue wells. Bottomless.

Understanding passes between us. That I'm completely trustworthy and offer no threat. That what goes on behind these four walls will remain here. Always.

I now stand quietly as they all take me in once more. They'll have moved past my physical appearance. Now they'll be searching for any chinks in my armor.

Sorry to disappoint, but there are none.

"Now, as you may know, my name is Jessie O'Brien, and I work alongside Jaine Jones, who you've all met, save for your good self, Fergal."

I immediately feel tension radiate from Eoin. Jaine filled me in on the standing-up matter. I want the future Irish King to understand that as her bonafide business partner, I know absolutely *everything* there is to know.

"I never give out business cards. There's no point. Most people tend to find me unforgettable. Compliment or not, I'll take it. Plus, not handing out pieces of paper helps conserve the planet."

"What's your background, Jessie?"

I turn to look at Fergal O'Connell. "MC."

"With a surname like O'Brien, are you Irish?"

"Irish daddy, west coast mother who's now sadly passed." I cross myself.

"Catholic?"

"I'm baptized and confirmed."

He smiles at me. "Welcome to the Duster family, Jessie."

"Not so fast."

I turn to look at Eoin as he rudely interrupts my bonding session with his da.

“What do you know about our situation?”

“It would be easier to answer what I don’t know.”

“Meaning?”

“If we don’t get a move on, the IRS will be sending out their troops next week to begin their investigations into several of your new business ventures, all on suspicion of money laundering.”

“You know this how?”

“I know this because it’s my business to know this.”

“You’ll be able to prevent this from happening?”

“I’ll do my best.”

“How confident are you?”

I shrug. “99.9%”

“You have a person on the inside?”

“I have a team on the inside and one person currently ranking in their top three.”

“When can you start?”

I remove my jacket and hang it over the back of my chair. “Now.”

Eoin nods. He’s looks impressed. I smile around the table before finishing at Dylan. He blushes again, and I can’t help but smirk. I open my briefcase and pull my laptop out as I take him in. The invisible O’Connell. The one no one ever talks about. The one no one can ever recall the name of.

“You’re cute.” I mumble it like I’m unintentionally speaking out loud while deliberately saying it just loud enough for everyone to hear.

“Thank you,” he mumbles in response, his face reddening further as he pushes his glasses up his nose. I can’t help but smirk again as Paddy snickers and elbows him in the ribs.

DYLAN

I don't often come into contact with people who aren't family. I never come into contact with members of the opposite sex, and when I do, and if all my siblings are present, the woman in question seldom looks at me once, let alone twice. Instead, she vies for their attention.

Never mine.

I'm the forgettable brother. The geeky nerd. The social pariah. I even shave my own hair off as I don't want to interact with strangers. Aside from my ma, and Sarah on occasion, the only woman I ever really speak to is Jaine.

This girl. This Jessie. She stormed into the meeting today like a whirling dervish, and I can't take my eyes off her.

She's tall. She must be almost six feet without her shoes as she's not far off Eoin's height in the four-inch heels she's wearing. She's got the face and figure of a goddess. All long blonde hair and beautifully carved features. She doesn't look like an accountant, even dressed professionally as she is. I look like more of a stereotypical number cruncher than she does. Jessie looks like she should be a contestant on *America's Next Top Model*. And she'd win for sure.

When she looked at me, I could feel my cheeks go red. I was sure she could read my mind. When she remarked about the heat, they went redder.

Then she said I was cute. Loud enough for everyone to hear.

"Thank you."

Well, what else could I say? I'm not convinced it's a genuine compliment, but it doesn't stop our Paddy from snickering and elbowing me in the ribs like we're two high schoolers being winked at by a cheerleader.

Does she really think that, or is she just making fun of me? That's all girls have ever done in the past. Laughed and joked at my expense while using me as a stepping stone to get to one of my brothers.

Maybe she's going after Eoin or Paddy. Then again, given what she knows about the family and how well she seems to know Jaine, she'll probably know all about Paddy's arranged marriage situation.

I look at her again. She catches me and smirks.

"I'm booked into a hotel for a few nights, but the apartment I'm taking on won't be ready for a few months. Ideally, I need somewhere to stay and work out of until my place is ready. Given the systems I invite myself into without their owners' knowledge or consent, and also the sensitivity of the information I'm analyzing, I need somewhere I can lockdown at a moment's notice. You boys know of anywhere suitable?"

"You can stay at our Dylan's. He has an annex attached to his place, which has top-of-the-range security. Plus, you can keep him company. He's just rattling around in that huge apartment all on his lonesome."

I glare at Paddy. I don't want to share my apartment, and it's not like she'll want to share it either.

"You okay with that, Dylan?" She's asking the question, and I don't quite know what to say. I was pretty sure she'd decline. Politely, of course.

Say no, you eejit. "Yes, of course."

"I'm a mean cook, so I can pay you that way, unless you have other ways in mind." She smiles at me innocently.

Paddy snickers, and I can feel my cheeks redden once again as my mind, unfortunately, goes down the same path as his.

"That's a good offer, Dyl. Just think, as you'll have company, there'll be no more dining on ramen noodles or sitting around in your y-fronts playing sudoku."

I roll my eyes at him. Paddy thinks he's hilarious. I'm only glad he's never made any references to sex.

"You could always share a bedroom and save on laundry."

There we go. It's never too late for our Paddy to lower the tone.

"I don't think that will be necessary." My tone is sharper than I intended.

"Dylan O'Connell, a girl could be quite insulted by how quickly you shot that suggestion down in flames." She smiles at me again, and I just swallow. I can't even think of a suitable response.

Paddy laughs out loud, but I'm not finding it funny. Always being the butt of everyone's jokes gets tiresome.

Jessie and I make eye contact, and her expression shows understanding. I think she realizes I don't really enjoy being the center of attention.

"Cooked meals it is, then. You like football?"

"Yes, of course." I don't, but I say yes anyway.

She points at her own chest proudly. "Numero uno Rams fan. Maybe we can catch a game together."

She then stands up like she's noticed something. Everyone watches as she makes her way across the room and stops behind Da's chair. She's made herself quite at home, as she's now barefoot.

"Is that a Newton's Cradle?" She points at Da's new toy and looks at us all. "May I?" She doesn't wait for a response. She simply pulls the silver ball back and lets it go.

Yes, Jessie O'Brien has crashed into our lives.

My concern is where will it all end.

CHAPTER NINETEEN

RAZR

The Iron Scorpions' Clubhouse, Brightling, New York

"PAUL, WHAT THE HELL ARE YOU DOING?"

Sarah's pacing my room as I lie on my bed with my hands behind my head. I've hacked more at the length and also shaved the sides again to make sure there's nothing to grip on to as the need to pull on it is increasing daily. If Sarah witnesses me doing shit like that, she'll go off on one even more than she is right now.

"Just say what you mean, Sarah."

She stops dead and glares at me.

"You know exactly what I mean. What are you doing with Laila?" She points at the closed bedroom door like her small friend is on the other side. She's not. Last I heard, she was in the communal area suggesting alternative clothing choices to the cum sluts. Stuff that leaves more to the imagination is what they need to consider wearing, apparently. Like the brothers haven't seen all of them naked on more than one occasion.

I stare back at my sister. Only when she's sure she has my full attention does she continue.

"Are you leading her on?"

"No, I'm not doing that."

"Do you love her?"

"It's a bit too soon for that word, don't you think?

"Okay, let me rephrase that. Do you think you could ever love her?"

"I don't know. Maybe?" I shrug.

"What the hell do you mean *maybe*? What sort of response is that?"

I rub my hands up the side of my head, frustrated at the situation I find myself in.

"And Bailey? What about her?"

I shrug again. "I asked her to stay. She left."

"After you stuck your tongue down Laila's throat right in front of her."

"Laila gave me no choice." I'm growling now. Reaching into my pocket, I pull out my blade. I breathe in time with the flicking motion. In. Out. In. Out.

"We all have choices, Paul."

"She left me with none. What was I supposed to do? Turn down her advances? Humiliate her in front of everyone?"

"Like you did Bailey, you mean?"

"Why do you care so much about Bailey? She's a cum slut."

"She's a person, Paul. A human being with feelings."

"And what would you have done?"

She doesn't reply. Deep down, she knows she would have done the same thing. It was hurt one or the other. We both know that.

They couldn't both walk away from that situation unscathed. Sarah knows I'd always protect Laila first and foremost. She's an innocent. We both also know Bailey can take care of herself if she needs to. She's wired differently. She's MC.

"I like both of them in different ways, Sarah."

"You say like. But which one has the potential to turn into something more? Who could you see yourself spending the rest of your life with?"

I frown, and she reads me like a book. She knows the name on the tip of my tongue.

"Don't you dare say it. You need to move the fuck on from Jaine. She loves you, but not like that. So, let her fucking go, Paul."

"I'm trying to."

She sits on the bed beside me and takes my hand in hers. "I get why you love her. I do. I love her too. But she's your past, Paul. You need to be looking to the future. You need to move on with your life and start thinking of Jaine as just a friend."

"So why are you against Laila and me? I thought you of all people would be pleased."

She squeezes my hand. "Laila is my best friend. I don't want her getting dragged into this life if either of you isn't one hundred percent sure. You have a lot of enemies, Paul. As your old lady, she would be in the firing line with you. Having to live a life where you constantly have to look over your shoulder? I'm just not sure she's cut out for that. Her glasses are rose-tinted when she looks at the life we live. The life she would live. We didn't have the choice. We were born into this shit. But Laila? She does.

"Both of you need to go into this with your eyes wide-open because once she's in, she's in. There's no going back. Not for her. Not for any of us. She'll never be able to leave once she's part of the inner circle. Secrets will have been shared. Not just Scorpion ones, but Duster ones too. If she decides two or three months down the line that this isn't for her after she's witnessed this life for what it really is, then what do we do? Slit her throat to keep her silent? Plus, we both know it's hit or miss on whether she'll remain upright whenever she sees blood and that there would be a major problem."

She lightens the mood, and we both smile.

"Listen, if you're telling me you see a future with her, if you're falling in love with her, then I'll accept it for what it is. Is she right for you? I'm not too sure she is. But it's your choice. The bottom line is, as much as I love Laila, you're my brother. I love you more. You will always be my number one priority in this." She smiles again, leaning over to kiss me on the cheek.

My sister has deliberately given me a whole banquet of food for thought. I need to digest that and make a choice when it comes to Laila. The decision's already been made when it comes to Bailey. Laila made that for me when she staked her claim in front of the brothers. There's no point in seeking forgiveness where there's none to be found.

It's over with Bailey. She's gone.

I'm conscious I've been quiet for some time and that the only sound is the repetitive flicking of my blade.

I make eye contact again with Sarah, and her gaze immediately drops to the weapon in my hand. She's got something on her mind, and I know exactly what it is.

"Jaine's passed me the details of a doctor. Highly recommended. I made the appointment for you."

"I'm not going." I hiss. I don't need help. I don't want help.

"You are."

"I said I'm not fucking going." I'm grinding my teeth, and I watch my knuckles whiten as my hand clenches around the blade.

Sarah leans close, so she's inches from my face.

"If you want to spend time with your niece or nephew, then you will go, and you will sort yourself out, Paul. I'm sorry, but I refuse to allow my child to be subjected to the same crazy shit I had to deal with."

She stares into my eyes—green on hazel. I see a lot of myself in the gaze directed back at me. I know she won't budge on what she's just said. We both know the emotional damage I inflicted on her through the years. She's going to be a mom. It's inbuilt in her to protect her young, even if it's from her own brother. More so when I could inflict the same emotional damage on them. History must not be allowed to repeat itself. That's something we both agree on.

"Where and when?"

"I'll email you the details. Jaine's going to be involved in any initial discussions but only because she knows both sides of you so she may be best equipped to answer any additional questions. Let's face it. In many ways she knows Paul 'Razr' Delaney better than the man himself."

She's right. I know she is. I'm a fuck up. Broken in so many ways. Into multiple pieces that only Jaine's ever been able to put back together. I look at my sister's face. At the hope there. That I'm finally going to rid myself of my demon and be fixed.

My concern? That I'm not fixable, and what I really need in my life is another Jaine.

BAILEY

Bailey's Family Home, Colton, Nevada

Pulling off the helmet, I shake my hair free then inhale the smell of desert and not much else. The air is hot and dry already. It's only eleven a.m., and I can already feel the moisture being sucked through my pores.

I stare up at the cloudless blue sky, too bone-tired to move from the hog. From New York to Nevada in fifteen days. My eyes drift over our family home. It's a white-painted property with a cream-tiled roof. Custom built, single-story, with ten bedrooms, all ensuite and with loads of other living spaces. There are no gardens. Nothing grows in Nevada except for professional gamblers' bank balances. Everything else just turns to dust, the same as the bodies we live in eventually will. The driveway is gravel, and the landscaping is rocks.

The views are to die for, though. On one side, it's nothing but open space, and on the other, breathtaking, beautiful mountains.

Home. Where the heart is, or so they say. Well, if that's true, then I guess my home's still in New York. And it always will be.

This is now simply the place I grew up. Where my daddy and my siblings raised me after my momma ran off when I was six months old. By all accounts, she was an addict. At least that's what I'm told. Addicted to what I'm not sure. Never asked. Don't want to know. If she wasn't bothered about me, why should I bother about her? I'm sure one day she'll show up with an armful of excuses. It's not difficult to fall into that life, though. Addiction. Not when you live just over sixty miles outside of Sin City itself.

Then again, rumor has it she ran because she could no longer tolerate my daddy. That he mistreated her on account of his not loving her. Not physically. Emotionally.

His heart broke when his first wife left him for someone else. Maybe she couldn't tolerate his dictator-like ass either. She divorced him in the end. Something that doesn't ever happen either in the life or in our religion. Marriage is a lifetime commitment. No exceptions.

Usually.

He boasts that she got her comeuppance when she died some years later, but on the inside, it destroyed him as with her died the only woman he ever truly loved. Still, he has Tadgh and Jay to remind him of her, though. My half-siblings.

"Hey, Little Bee."

When you have brothers, you get no peace whatsoever. It's like they have an inbuilt sixth sense to know when you're in their immediate vicinity. To know when you're close enough for them to become the bane of your life once more and to get on your last damn nerve. I think it's something boys are just born with.

I step off the Fat Boy, laying the helmet on the seat. Conor immediately grabs my head and gives me a noogie.

"Fuck off, you annoying asshole." I punch at him, but he steps back so it barely connects.

"Still useless and feeble, I see, sis." He smirks at me while jogging backward.

Despite my physical exhaustion, I run at him, screaming at the top of my lungs before lunging at his middle, causing both of us to fall to the ground. He noogies me again before jumping up and laughing down at me. I lie there and stare up at my brother with a smile on my face.

Two years older than me, Conor's coloring is exactly like our momma's, with his unruly black hair and eyes the color of chocolate molasses framed by the longest lashes I have ever seen on a man or a woman. I used to hate him as a child. They're wasted on him.

He's not gangly anymore. At twenty-three, my brother has grown to way over six feet and filled out at the same time. He's a handsome brute with his tanned, inked skin, and a face that wears just the right amount of stubble. He's also a cocky fucker. He knows he makes the girls giggle and whisper behind their hands when he parades that masculine beauty of his, which he does at every opportunity. His smile widens, displaying white teeth as perfect as the rest of him. We're the complete contrast from each other.

I'm blonde like my daddy. My daddy's little angel.

"Little Bee."

And speaking of the devil.

His voice is as deep and dangerous as the man himself. I stay lying on the ground and cross my leg over my knee like I'm making myself comfortable and planning to stay here the rest of the day.

"Daddy."

"Where you been, angel?"

"East Coast."

"Spending time with anyone we know?"

"Nope."

"You sure?" Despite being his daughter, I can hear the warning in his tone. He's the president of an MC. What do I expect? I leave one male chauvinist prez behind to turn around, come back, and be immediately confronted by another. It must be a requirement that goes with the title—that and being an asshole.

"You sure about that, angel?"

"Yup."

"Get off the ground. You're not a child anymore." His tone is authoritative.

I roll my eyes inwardly, then do as I'm told. Exhaling in a juvenile huff, I raise myself to my feet before wiping the dirt off my ass.

"Now, give your old man a hug."

I stare at my daddy. I always thought he was a Viking when I was growing up, with his long, light blonde, now greying, hair and pale blue eyes. He's chiseled as opposed to being outright handsome. All sharp lines and angular features with a well-kept beard to finish the look. He's not Scandinavian, though. He's a Celt. He was born on the Emerald Isle and moved to Nevada when he was sixteen. I never met my grandparents. Both died in a car wreck when my daddy was eighteen. He was embraced by the local MC then made his way through the ranks to become prez at the age of twenty-two. He's held that position ever since, so some thirty-three years now.

His real name is Liam. His road name? Lucifer.

It's fitting.

I walk over, and he pulls me to him. He's a mountain of a man. Not fat. Every inch is toned, deadly muscle. He's never let himself go. He instilled that in all of us. Treat your body like a temple. We all do.

I inhale his woodsy cologne and the smell that makes up everything representing my daddy.

He holds me at arm's length, and I look up at him. His eyes are searching my face. Not because he's missed me. Because he wants to figure out if I'm lying.

"You been sewing those wild oats of yours?"

"Something like that."

"You got it all out of your system?"

"I guess so."

"You ready to do what's expected of you now? For your family? For our future?"

I nod. I can feel tears prick my eyes as I think of Razr. So what if I love him? So what if I miss him? So what if I spent most of the journey home wiping tears from my eyes while telling myself they were watering because of the road dust thrown up by the hog? So what if my shattered heart is rattling around like loose shrapnel in my hollowed-out chest cavity?

None of that matters. That shit's for losers. You reap what you sow? Bullshit. For almost nine months, I invested every part of myself in Paul Delaney. What did I get back in return?

Rejection. Humiliation. Pain.

"Good girl. I told Raf you were on your way back."

I nod as we walk towards the house. I'm aware I'm dragging my feet. My daddy's fully aware I am too. Not that he cares. The sword of Damocles has fallen, and he's the reason why.

The reason I ran in the first place hasn't changed. Both sides are obviously willing to overlook my apparent reluctance to enter into a union and my subsequent anarchic dalliances as a result.

So, it looks like my arranged marriage to Rafael Flores will still be going ahead after all.

CHAPTER TWENTY

RAZR

Twenty Eight Years Earlier (Age Four)
The Delaney Home, Brightling, New York

"Now you be a good boy while Momma and Daddy go fetch your baby sister."

"But you already have her, Momma. Why do you need to go away?" I rest my hand on her belly. She says my little sister is in there cooking, the same as she cooked me. I don't remember being cooked.

"It's safer to be in the hospital just in case there are any complications when they deliver her, Paulie."

"How did she get in there anyway? And why couldn't the mailman just deliver her like he does everything else?"

My daddy snickers and my momma frowns at him, shakes her head, and then smiles.

I stare at my momma. She's so pretty with her brown hair and eyes, and with skin that goes an even prettier color when the sun's out. Not like my daddy and me. Our skin is pale, and our hair is red. Daddy says it's because our family is Irish.

"God decided that it was the safest place for your baby sister to be, Paulie. With your momma. And that it was easier for her to be carried around this way." My dad kisses my mom on her head like he does a million times a day, maybe even more.

"Did you have to eat her to get her in there?"

Momma laughs and rubs her hand over her tummy. "We'll explain all that when you're a big boy, Paulie."

"I'm a big boy now, Momma. I'm four." I frown at her.

"When you're a bigger boy, then."

I cross my arms and huff, and she ruffles my hair and smiles at me in response.

"Time to go, Ella."

I step back and watch as Daddy helps Momma up from the chair she's sitting in. She grunts and groans like old Mrs. Princeton across the street does when she's leaning on her stick and walking down her path to get her mail.

"You be good for Aunt Amy while we're away, Paulie."

I glance at my always smiling aunt who's in the kitchen. She's watching us out the corner of her eye as she hums along to the radio while making me a peanut butter and jelly sandwich. Uncle Wolf says Aunt Amy makes the best PBJ, and he's right. My tummy growls just thinking about it.

I watch as Momma stands with her hand resting on her tummy as Daddy picks up her bags.

"Give your momma a hug now, little man, and tell me you love me."

I run at her. My arms try to stretch around her, but they're way too short to reach now. I breathe in the smell of cherry blossoms. My momma always smells just like cherry blossoms.

"I love you, Paulie."

"I love you too, Momma." I close my eyes and rest my head against her tummy just as the baby moves. "Oww, she just kicked me." I rub my cheek exaggeratedly, even though it doesn't hurt.

"She's just letting her big brother know she loves him too." Momma ruffles my hair again before bending down to kiss me on the top of my head, just like my daddy does with her.

"You behave now. Pinkie promise?"

"I will, Momma. Pinkie promise." I hook my smallest finger around hers, then watch as they make their way to the car. I wave from the window, and Momma blows me kisses. I don't stop until the car's out of sight because I know she won't stop until she can't see the house.

"Bye, Momma. I love you," I whisper, even though I know she can't hear me.

"My momma says it's rude to whisper."

Their low voices woke me. I walk into the kitchen. I don't know what time it is, but it's still dark, so it mustn't be morning yet. Uncle Wolf is hugging Aunt Amy, and even though she's trying to hide them, I can see her wet cheeks and red eyes.

I walk over and wrap my arms around her too. Closing my eyes, I breathe in her familiar smell of cookies and cupcakes. She's always baking something for my uncles at the big house. I squeeze her tight. My momma always says if you don't know what to say, then a hug says it all for you. That when you hug, you don't need to find any words.

"Why are you crying, Aunt Amy?"

"I've just got something in my eye, little Paulie." She kisses my head. "Let's get you a glass of warm milk and get you back into bed."

"Can I have chocolate in it?"

"Of course you can, little man."

"Daddy." I rub my sleepy eyes and stare up at him. "Is my baby sister here yet?"

"Yeah, she's here, Paulie."

"Can I see her?"

Pushing back my bed covers, he lifts me into his arms, his grip tightening almost painfully around me. Holding me, we walk through to the littlest bedroom. The one that's been painted pink and that has a little white rocking bed in the corner. Momma told me it used to be mine. I told her I didn't want to share, but she asked if my baby sister could have it because I've moved up to a big boy bed. I said yes in the end, even though I didn't want to. Momma says it's important to share.

"This is Sarah, Paulie."

From my daddy's arms, I look down at the smallest person I've ever seen. She's all wrapped up in a white blanket, and she's sound asleep, even though it's morning now. She looks exactly like the dolls some of the little girls play with at the big house. Her hair's the same color as mine.

"Is she real?" I stare at my daddy.

"She's real alright."

"You love her, Daddy?"

He sobs, and I wrap my arms around his neck. "I sure do, buddy."

"Does Momma love her? Where is Momma?" I look around. Maybe she's still sleeping too.

"Here's the thing, Paulie. Your momma loved your baby sister so much that when God decided he needed another angel by his side, your momma decided that it should be her that should be that angel, and that me and you… well, we should get to keep Sarah with us."

I frown at him. "Is Momma not coming back now that she's God's angel?"

Daddy shakes his head, his face sad. I don't like to see my Daddy looking sad. I can feel tears gathering, but I'm a big boy, and big boys don't cry.

"Because she loved Sarah too much?"

"Yup, that's right, Paulie."

"But I want her to come back." I know the tears are running down my face now. Because I don't understand how my momma could leave me.

His tears match my own. "I'm so sorry, Paulie."

Using my small fists, I pummel my daddy across the face and the chest. Anywhere I can reach. I want to hurt him the way I'm hurting.

"Momma loved Sarah more than me. She left when I wanted her to stay. She didn't even say goodbye."

My daddy grips my flailing fists as I cry and lash out. Eventually, I stop struggling. I stare down at the crib, at the baby who's still sleeping soundly despite all my yelling and crying.

I hate you, Sarah.

I WATCH AS MY DADDY HUGS UNCLE WOLF AND AUNT AMY. They're all crying, and when they're not, they're all fussing over my baby sister.

I clench my teeth to stop myself from running across the room, yelling, and lashing out. I want them to hurt like I'm hurting. I don't want them to be fussing over the baby. I hate the baby. She made my momma leave.

But I don't do anything. I just sit there and stare at them, digging my nail into my fingertip over and over until it starts to bleed.

When it does, it's only then that I start to feel better.

"Bye, Momma. I love you," I whisper, even though I know she can't hear me.

CHAPTER TWENTY-ONE

JAINE

Jaine's House, Rising, California

"Dissociative Identity Disorder, or DID as it's more commonly known." Dr. Nesbitt's voice is pompous, nasally, and very English. I've never met him, but according to Delaney, he looks how he sounds. He's tall and thin with grey hair to match his complexion, a long face, and large black spectacles. All of this topped off with a white doctor's coat.

"What is that exactly?" Delaney sounds calm, but I can hear the underlying worry in his tone. That this is all going to be too much for him. That whatever is wrong with him, he won't be able to cope with or fix. That's why Sarah and I came on this conference call with him. To offer our support. To show him that he has us. That he will always have us. That we will be by his side no matter what.

"It's a mental health condition. People with DID typically have two or more separate identities. These personalities control their behavior at different times. Each has its own traits, likes, dislikes…."

"So, like a split personality disorder? With Paul being one and Razr being his alter-ego?" Sarah interrupts

"Exactly. As well as exhibiting two personalities, Mr. Delaney also displays several of the classic symptoms. Anxiety, violence, self-harming…."

"Self-harming? What the fuck do you mean?" Having inwardly chided Sarah for doing so, I now rudely interrupt, suddenly worried that Delaney has deteriorated even further than we had first suspected.

"Mr. Delaney cuts his fingertips. Sometimes all of them, but usually one in particular. It's a form of self-harm. He does it to reduce his anxiety levels in an attempt to keep his alter-ego under control."

"And the trigger for all this was our momma's death, right?" I can hear the pain in Sarah's voice. The regret. The guilt.

"Yes, unfortunately. Exacerbated by the passing of your father."

"Is it curable? Will it go away in time?" I ask.

"Unfortunately not."

"Treatable?"

"Mr. Delaney can take prescribed medications for anxiety, say, antidepressants or similar, but the best course of action is psychotherapy."

"You mean I have to see a shrink?" Delaney growls. I'm only glad he's not in front of the doc. Razr may have cut his throat by now.

"Yes. It's the best course of action, I'm afraid. You have to talk in order to heal and to keep on top of things mentally. This route is a lifetime commitment."

"What if I don't want to talk about shit?"

"Then your condition may stay the same, or it may deteriorate further. If you do decide to go down this path, alongside the psychotherapy, you'll also need the support of your family and friends."

"He has that already."

"According to my notes, Miss Jones, Mr. Delaney spends a considerable amount of his time on his own. From experience, it's at times like these where people with DID can withdraw into themselves and spend too much time reflecting and focusing on their initial triggering events. He needs to be helped to look forward to the future and to stop living in the past."

"Do you have any recommendations for us? Suitable specialists, etc.?"

"I'll email a list of qualified doctors to you all after we've ended the call."

I switch off after that and let them finish. I feel sick with guilt that Delaney spends so much time alone. I'm also worried that he's spending so much time living in the past he's struggling to see his future, more so when it comes down to who he should or shouldn't be spending it with.

Jaine: *How did things go with the O'Connells?*

Jessie: *Well, hello, boys!*

Jaine: *Yes, they're all very handsome.*

Jessie: *As we suspected it was the four sons and the da. Cillian's wife was also there.*

Jaine: *Sarah was there? I'm surprised they allowed a woman to be present at their reservoir dogs-style meeting.*

Jessie: *Yes, the eldest is a chauvinist for sure.*

Jaine: *What did you think of the future Irish king?*

Jessie: *If mobsters rolled their eyes, that's what he would* *have been doing. He's a handsome brute for sure, but I could tell he didn't like me straight off the bat.*

Jaine: *Why?*

Jessie: *I had a run-in with his employee with benefits.*

Jaine: *Ah, the delectable Candice.*

Jessie: *Yes. My relationship with Eoin went rapidly downhill from there.*

Jaine: *And Irish?*

Jessie: *I didn't look at him or talk to him in case you had a fly on the wall. I value my life.*

Jaine: *Goddamn liar.*

Jessie: *Well, he is by far the most personable and definitely the best-looking. So, I only looked once. Okay, maybe I looked twice, but… I really liked Dylan. I took a photo of him and everything. I'm going to print it and stick it on my ceiling so I can get off to it every night. Even better, I may get one of those pillowcases made. You know, the ones where you can have a face printed on. Do you think they print images onto vibrators or sex dolls?*

Jaine: *You didn't really take a photo of him, did you?*

Jessie: *No. I white lied about that part. But now I wish I had. Damn. Opportunity missed. Do you think he'll mind if I message him and ask for one? Or is that too much?*

Jaine: *What, so, he made that much of an impression?*

Jessie: *I know, right? You'd be forgiven for thinking, given how quiet and introverted he is, that it would be impossible. It wasn't. If that cute little Duster wall-flower was prepared to stick his dick in me, I'd offer to have his babies.*

Jaine: *There's such a thing as too much information. Now I can't get that visual out of my head.*

Jessie: *I know. I did warn you that my brain doesn't engage* *with my mouth half the time, didn't I? But then again, I'm not sure it would make much difference even if it did.*

Jaine: *And Da Duster?*

Jessie: *I'm Irish Catholic. What's not to love? Like putty in my hands. Do you think he'd enter me into an arranged marriage with Dylan?*

Jaine: *LOL. I hear you, Jessie, But I'm sorry to be the bearer of bad news. By all accounts, Dyl's hung up on a cliché blonde ex of his.*

Jessie: *How hung up?*

Jaine: *Really badly.*

Jessie: *Shit. No way! So, there's like no chance?*

Jaine: *Never say never, but I wouldn't get my hopes up if I were you*

Jessie: *Damn. I was so sure I felt a connection, you know?*

Jaine: *Sorry to rain on your parade. Anyway, being dicked by Dylan aside, how did you get on workwise?*

Jessie: *I've already started. I took my jacket off and got stuck straight in. Shit, I thought all my dreams were coming true. I was due to move into Dylan's apartment. Well, the adjoining annex. As you know, mine won't be ready for months. I think I should delay that for the time being, given he's pining over an ex. In fact, I really should find an alternative solution, although I'm not sure how easy that will be. I do need a home-based permanent fix asap, though. I have a lot of stuff—lots of screens. You know? Like Tom Cruise in that ancient Minority Report movie.*

Jaine: *Really?*

Jessie: *Really. I kid you not. I run most of my data in real-time, so I can't just set up anywhere. I'd need to be away from prying eyes and in a place I can lockdown at a*

moment's notice if I need to, hence why I always work from home.
Jaine: *Shit, you and Dyl really are a match made in outlaw heaven.*
Jessie: *I know, right? Typical. I guess the only silver cloud is that at least he likes blondes. Maybe I can sway him with my cooking. I make a mean lasagna.*
Jaine: *Well, you can but try, Jessie. Anyway, Dusters aside. Documentation. As much as your recommendation came in the form of a signed-in-blood, full money-back guarantee from Rodolfo, and I trust his word implicitly, I still need your full details before we can formally sign on the joint company dotted line.*
Jessie: *I'm on it. It's all completed. I just need my passport, which is at home. I'll ask my sister to find it and scan it in.*
Jaine: *Perfect.*

For some reason, I'm nervous about calling Eoin.

I know Jessie is her own person, but as she's now also officially under the JAL banner, I'll be judged. And harshly if he thinks it's deserved. She's representative of who I employ and choose to work with, so he won't pull his punches. On the contrary, if he has something adverse to say, he'll take great pleasure in doing so.

Asshole.

Then again, why does it bother me so much what he thinks? There's no time like the present. I dial his number and he answers straight away.

"So, what did you think of her?"

"Well, she's very annoying." He sounds pompous.

"Is that it?"

"She almost started a fight with Candice because she was being deliberately obtuse."

I roll my eyes and exhale loudly enough to make sure he can hear. "So, she's annoying and can be deliberately awkward, anything else?

"She's extremely loud and very forward."

"Anything positive?"

"At least she didn't cuss."

"It's not a prerequisite that to be employed by me you need to be able to turn the goddamn air blue. From a professional point of view?"

"She's perfect. Intelligent, determined, articulate when she wants to be and knows her craft inside out."

"So…?"

"The Dusters will be pleased to have her on board. Via you, of course."

"Good to know."

"Now, on a different matter, any order book changes from the Mexicans?"

"Nope. Still only one with the shortfall. Maybe the MC supplying them needs more time. Or maybe the price didn't match the quality. Who knows? I spoke with Delaney on the matter this morning, and the next order is due to be placed tomorrow. If there's a shortfall, then he's going to make the trip to Nevada personally."

"Keep me abreast of the situation."

"Of course."

"It's important we nip this in the bud, Jaine. My over-riding concern is it won't stop there. First La eMe. Which of our other clients will this MC target next."

"I assure you it will be handled, Eoin."

CHAPTER TWENTY-TWO

RAZR

The Iron Scorpions' Clubhouse, Brightling, New York

"By how much this time?" As soon as Knight called the meeting, I knew the Mexicans' order was short.

"Same. Around twenty-five percent."

"Shit."

"I've told Ace and Cillian."

"And?"

"The Irish are leaving it for the Scorpions to deal with. They think it's best-handled biker to biker, which is exactly how we thought they'd approach it. The Angels would prefer to get involved only as a last resort. It's too close to home for Ace. With Jaine so close to giving birth, he doesn't want any unrest or trouble on his doorstep."

"That's understandable." I exhale loudly. I was hoping the

problem had gone away and that the previous shortfall was a one-off. No such goddamn luck.

There's a prolonged silence in the council meeting room. No one dares speak. Instead, they all watch as I struggle to retain control over my rapidly dwindling sanity while thinking about how best to handle this.

"Fuck!" In a fit of rage, I throw my blade and watch as it sinks into the wall at the far end, narrowly missing Ripper's head.

"Sort out flights for me, you, and Blaze." I point at Knight.

"Shall we fly into LA or Vegas, Prez? If we fly into LA, maybe we can ask the Angels to line us up with some hogs."

"You will do no such fucking thing. Haven't we just said we don't want to involve them? Jesus Christ." I run my hands up the side of my shaved head in frustration. "No, we fly into Vegas. Speak to one of the local charters there and round up some rides. We can buy outright for top dollar or borrow and return. It's their call."

"You." I point at Blaze. "Contact the prez of the Undertakers and the prez of the Sons of Satan and let them both know I'll be paying them a visit."

If either of those fuckers has been deliberately disrespecting the Scorpions, the Angels, or the Dusters by stealing our trade, then they'll feel the wrath of my blade.

My chair topples to the floor as I stand, then storm out of the room.

"YOU MISSING HER?"

I know exactly who Mojo's talking about. I don't reply. She won't take it personally. She's known me for years. Instead, I motion for Flame to pass me another beer from behind the bar.

"She's back home now. Just so you know."

She continues regardless. She realizes I want to know almost as much as I don't.

"Is that right? And where might home be?" I turn to stare at her now. She's wearing jeans and a tank top today. It's quite a conservative outfit for her. Then again, she's due to hang up her cum slut badge in just over two months, so I guess it's time for her to start dressing so she can fit in in the outside world with normal people.

"I'm not allowed to say, but I've got her number if you want it?"

"So, you're not allowed to say where home is for her, but she said you can give out her number?"

She bites on her bottom lip, her forehead creasing into a frown. "Well, I'm not *supposed* to give it out."

"You're offering to."

"Only to you. No one else."

"Why me?"

"Because you care about her."

"And you figure that out how?"

"I've known you eleven years, Prez. Trust me, I know."

"You're mistaken."

"Who are you trying to convince, you or me? And she says she'll pay for the hog she borrowed."

I laugh dryly. "That she damn well stole, you mean. And with what? That ride's worth around twenty grand."

"Bailey has money. She bought me this for my birthday. I had it valued. Apparently, it's worth around five thousand dollars." She lifts the necklace she's wearing.

I glance at it. It looks like a quality piece on the surface, but it's my thinking that the stone is just a good fake.

"My guess is you've been lied to, Mo."

"Nope. I haven't. I had it valued by the designer who handmade it."

My ears prick up at this reveal. How the hell did Bailey manage to get her hands on that sort of money? We pay the cum sluts a small weekly allowance to enable them to buy the basics, but nowhere near enough for her to save that sort of surplus. Was she hiding something?

My demon is instantly alert. He can already smell the stench of disloyalty, and my mouth floods with the bitter taste of betrayal.

Drugs? Prostitution? How did she come by five grand? Is she involved with the fuckers who are trying to steal our business? Rage floods my veins as I put two and two together. Her disappearing at the same time as all this shit started to kick off. That's just too much of a coincidence. The answer to my own question is staring me straight in the goddamn face. Why else would she have run without a word to anyone?

There's only one reason.

Guilt.

I grab Mojo's arm, my fingers digging in and bruising her flesh. "What in the hell, Paul?"

She tries to yank it away, but I hold firm. "You give me that traitorous little fucker's number right now, Mo." I motion my head towards the bedroom area.

"She would never betray you, Prez."

Mo shakes her head slowly in disbelief as she stumbles forward. She's still determined to defend her two-faced best friend.

"How do you know that?" I'm aware I'm growling. My head is pounding with the blatant fucking deceit of it all as we enter Bailey's room at the clubhouse. It's the same as all the others except for some personal soft furnishings she added.

"I just know."

She watches as I open the unlocked tallboy and take out the suitcases Bailey left behind. She left in a hurry. There's no way she'd have been able to transport these on the stolen hog. She only took what she needed. Then she ran before the shit hit the fan. Before it was discovered what she'd been up to. Spying for another MC.

Disloyalty.

I run my hand over the surface of the luggage. They're subtle, I'll give her that. But they still scream money. And money that doesn't feel the need to flaunt itself either.

"No disrespect, Mo, but you don't know shit. See, it would appear that Bailey's pulled the wool over everyone's eyes, mine included."

Using my blade, I force open the first suitcase. I close my eyes as my fingers caress the clothing inside, its quality slipping through my fingers. The scent of her reaches out. The expensive citrus notes that replaced the cheap perfume she used in the beginning to hide what she was.

A liar.

Pulling the garments free, I roar as I rip them to shreds with my bare hands.

Deceit.

"Her number." I demand.

Mo watches me like she's frozen, her mouth agape. Why the fuck is she surprised? I've been betrayed by the woman I'd been fucking for months.

Have I lost it? The ability to smell a traitorous fucking rat? My guts have never let me down before, and yet here we are. Then again, my headspace seldom belongs to me these days.

"I want her goddamn number, Mo. Now!" I hiss, barely able to contain my fury and keep *him* at bay.

She turns and leaves the room, and I follow.

I look around her space when we get there. It's the same as all the others, apart from she's added wall hangings and other stuff to personalize the place through the years. There's a lot of it, but then she has been here for over a decade. I pick up the framed photo of her and Bailey from the bedside cabinet. They look just like any regular best friends smiling for a selfie.

They're not normal, though. Not really. They've been tarnished by what they've witnessed and by what they've done. The stench of the MC life will never wash off.

I put the picture back down.

"It's in my phone." Her hands are shaky as she reaches for the handset. She's terrified. I'm sorry I'm frightening her, but I make no outward apology for it.

My gaze continues to drift around the room as I wait for her to unlock her phone and get me the number. It's then I see the map.

"What the fuck's this?" I hiss.

If Mo could sink to the ground and disappear right now, she would.

"It was me tracking which towns Bailey was traveling through." She answers quietly, shuffling from foot to foot and looking at the floor. She knows better than to make eye contact with the monster who's surfacing.

"And this here?"

She looks up, and I stab my finger at the last pin on the map.

"It's where she lives, Paul," she whispers.

"Nevada," I say quietly.

If I needed any more proof of her guilt, then I now fucking have it.

Betrayal.

Picking up the framed image once more, I drop it to the floor, and I crush it under my foot. Bailey will pay for being dishonorable.

She'll pay with her goddamn throat.

CHAPTER TWENTY-THREE

LAILA

The Iron Scorpions' Clubhouse, Brightling, New York

"When do you need to leave?" I realize I sound clingy, but I heard, among other things, that he's chasing down Bailey, and I don't like it.

"Day after tomorrow."

He's not really looking at me. He's distracted. I'm also aware Sarah's watching us closely.

"Can't someone else go?"

I grimace. God, even to myself, I sound desperate and needy. Way to go, Laila. I watch as he runs his hand down the side of his head, then signals for Flame to pass him another beer from behind the bar.

"Nope."

"It's just, my parents are both at home, which doesn't happen that often, and I was kind of hoping we could go out for dinner, so you can meet them."

I feel my cheeks redden when Flame snickers. Paul shoots him a warning look, and Flame walks off to busy himself behind the bar.

Paul turns his attention back to me. "I've met your parents, Laila. Known them most of my life."

"Yes, but things are different now," I mumble.

"In what way?"

"I thought maybe that we were… you know."

"Nope, I don't know, Laila. Why don't you tell me exactly what's on your mind?" He's being deliberately confrontational to make me feel awkward.

I cringe. I don't want to have to say what's on my mind. I'm well aware I'll sound like a high schooler with her first boyfriend.

"That maybe we could be exclusive. You know. Now Bailey's gone?"

I swear I can hear a snigger coming from Sarah, but when I turn to look at her, she's staring in the opposite direction.

Paul looks at me with a mixture of sympathy and disbelief on his face. He's not even attempting to hide it like he usually does. I'm making a fool of myself. I know I am. Just because I want normal.

"I don't date, Laila."

"You dated Jaine." My response is immediate and sounds pre-prepared. It's because it is. She had his undivided attention for four years. So, why can't I have it now?

"Jaine and I didn't date. We spent time together, and we fucked for four years." He narrows his eyes at me. For some reason, he's not playing nicely today. No one knows why he's going after Bailey. My guess is she's the reason behind this foul mood of his. There's more to it than he's letting on.

He turns around to face me. "You want this, Laila? This lifestyle? You've witnessed first-hand what this world can be like, and it can be like that day in day out at any moment. A life with me means that's what you're signing up for. You ready for that?"

I know he's referring to what happened with the Colombian. To what Sarah did. To what I witnessed. I feel faint at the memory. Sick too. I can still smell the blood. The bodily fluids. Am I ready for that?

Death. Destruction. Cold-blooded murder.

He pulls me towards him, one arm snaking around my waist and the other fisting my hair and pulling my head back. I grimace at the rough handling.

"You want this?" His voice is low as he whispers in my ear. "Then you give me every part of you, sweet Laila. See, this isn't a relationship you can walk into and then leave. You want to suck it and see? You start with my dick. Then, once I'm hard, I'm going to fuck you into next week. If you're good with that, then we can talk when I get back."

His mouth drops to mine, his tongue pushing past my hesitant lips. My hands cling to his shoulders as he tastes every part of me. His mouth is ruthless, punishing.

Warning me. Telling me to run while I still can.

"You think long and hard about what and who you want, baby girl." His mouth hovers over my swollen lips.

"And if I agree to your… demands?" I whisper, the scent of his sandalwood cologne making me feel almost dizzy with desire.

"Then I'll offer to make you my old lady. And if you accept? Then not even that God of yours will be able to do anything to save your soul. You'll have signed a deal with the devil himself."

Have I got what it takes to be an old lady? *The* old lady?

There's only one way to find out.

"You've got yourself a deal… old man."

RAZR

I stare out my bedroom window and take in the single oak tree that stands at the compound's rear. It doesn't seem like five minutes since there was a group of us back there watching Bailey throw her stars. The taste of bitterness fills my mouth once more.

Anger. Hate.

The need for revenge floods my veins, and my alter-ego rises to the surface like some sort of junkie seeking a fix.

He wants to spill blood. *Her* blood.

She betrayed me. Betrayed the Scorpions. There's only one payment method acceptable for those sorts of purchases.

Closing my eyes, I rub my hands up the side of my head. I was thinking, hoping even, that I'd meant something to her. Not sure why. It's not like I ever showed her any care. Anyway, it turns out I was wrong.

She's left me no choice. Now I need to find her and personally serve her with her well-deserved penance. She's from the life. She knows the score. She knows there's no other outcome for the crimes she's committed.

I dial the number. It answers within three rings.

No words are spoken. She's waiting for me to talk first. She knows the rules. Just who the fuck is she? Is Bailey even her real name? I need answers, and I'll get them. Then I'll slice her throat.

"You betrayed me." My tone is low and laced with menace.

"Over what?" She recognizes my voice immediately. She doesn't question where I got her number. She'll know it was from Mo.

"The shit going down with the weapons."

"What the fuck are you talking about?"

"Don't fucking pretend like you don't know. You've betrayed the Scorpions and me."

"Bullshit, Razr."

"Don't lie to me."

"I'm not."

"DON'T FUCKING LIE TO ME, BAILEY!"

"I'M NOT LYING! I'M THE ONE WHO WAS BETRAYED! YOU HAVE NO RIGHT FUCKING CALLING ME! FUCK. YOU!"

"I'm coming for you."

"You don't know where I am."

I laugh sarcastically. In some ways, I'm surprised by this unexpected level of naivety from her.

"No? Well, Mo's tracked her best friend's movements on a fucking map that she has pinned on her bedroom wall. So, I know exactly where you are."

"Shit," she hisses.

"Didn't take you as being a Nevada girl."

"Shows how little you know about me. But, then again, I was just useful for dicking."

"You were a cum slut."

"I'm a fucking person, asshole! Always was."

There's a silence. She's right. I never saw her as a person. Not once. Well, at least not until it was too late.

Too late for what? I push the unwanted thoughts from my mind.

"Anyway, Nevada's a big state."

"I'll find you. If it's the last thing I do in this life, I'll fucking find you."

"Good luck with that."

She hangs up.

I rest my head against the window. The rage is almost overwhelming. I breathe deeply. In. Out. In. Out. Trying to lessen the drowning feeling. Taking my blade from my pocket, I slice it into the tip of my finger. My hand clenches around the flow of blood that instantly pools in my fist before it drips to the floor.

A temporary respite from my own madness flows through me.

The next thing my blade will cut into?

Her deceitful little fucking throat.

CHAPTER TWENTY-FOUR

JAINE

Jaine's House, Rising, California

I'm starting to wish I'd never answered my phone to Delaney. Or should I say Razr. The conversation so far has been one-sided, and its extent consists of the madman accusing Bailey of all sorts.

"What the fuck do you mean Bailey betrayed you?"

"Like I just fucking said, she betrayed the Scorpions and me. Then she ran. When the shit was about to hit the fan, and before she got found out, she went AWOL on a stolen twenty grand fucking hog."

"From what I hear from Sarah, she rode off into the sunset because you humiliated her."

"I've been through this with my sister. I had no choice."

"We always have choices, Delaney. If you cared anything at all about the girl's feelings, you wouldn't have done that."

"What the fuck does it matter?"

"Because that's the reason she ran, asshole. It's got nothing to do with the guns. Open your eyes. Can you not see what's staring you in the goddamn face?"

He ignores my question.

"Did you know she was from Nevada?"

"Of course I did. I prepared her contract."

"You're not telling me that shit's a coincidence?"

"That's exactly what I *am* telling you."

"Bullshit. She's guilty as sin, and she's going to pay with her throat."

"So, you're going to cut first, ask questions later?"

"I'll ask questions."

"And how do you plan on finding her? The address she gave was for a rental. She won't have gone back there."

"The Fat Boy has a tracker fitted, and I bet it's sitting right outside where the traitorous bitch is hiding out."

"Delaney, don't do anything you'll regret."

"I won't have any regrets, Jaine. Trust me on that."

It's clear he's made up his mind. No proof necessary. I'm frustrated by his insistence but I keep it to myself. Now is not the time. I'd just be wasting my breath.

"When are you flying out?"

"Tomorrow."

"You want Ace to meet you there?"

"Nope. We agreed this was too close to home for the Angels. The Scorpions will handle it."

"I appreciate that."

"You'll keep the Irish informed?"

"I will. I won't mention to anyone your thoughts on Bailey. We'll keep that between ourselves, and we'll see what comes to light. If she's guilty, you have my blessing to do what needs doing. If she's guilty, I'll gladly do the honors myself."

"The only person getting their hands on that pretty little throat of hers is me."

I pause before I carry on. "I hear congratulations are in order. Sarah said she overheard your whispered conversations with Laila. Your offer to make her the old lady of the Scorpions."

"I'm thinking about it."

"From what I heard, it's almost a done deal provided she puts out."

"We need to be compatible in every way, Jaine. You know that."

"Of course. Intimacy is a huge part of any relationship, so I get that. But she was saving that purity of hers for marriage. Are you going to wed her, Delaney? Not that it's any of my business, but if that thought hasn't even crossed your mind, then don't go there. Don't take something from her that you can't give back. As much as I'm not her greatest fan, the girl deserves better than that."

"Listen, I'm thirty-two years old, Jaine. I'm not getting any younger. Of course I've thought about marriage. Kids."

"With Laila?"

"Sure, why not? I care about her."

"Love?"

"You and Sarah are obsessed with that damn word."

"Marriage is a lifetime commitment, Delaney. Don't sell Laila or yourself short."

"Yes. I love her. Happy now?"

I END THE CALL WITH DELANEY. BAILEY'S NOT STUPID ENOUGH TO do what he's suggesting. She's run because of him. He's the only fool who doesn't see that. Still, there's only one way to find out for sure. I dial her number

"Now, I'm willing to give you the benefit of the doubt."

"Well, that's good of you because Razr sure as hell didn't."

"You can understand why."

"Because he's an insane asshole?"

"Listen, Bailey. I had a friend who used to say something that's stuck with me. If you don't have anything nice to say, it's best to say nothing at all."

"What the fuck does that even mean?"

"It means I'm happy for you to criticize Delaney's decisions and his actions, but we're not dissecting the man himself. He's not in a good place right now. You know that."

"And I am? He thinks I've betrayed him. That I ran because of something to do with guns."

"And you didn't?"

"No! I didn't know what the hell he was talking about. You know why I ran. Everyone does. Apart from him, obviously."

I exhale. Her pain is almost audible, and it makes me think of my own. Unfortunately, I'm thinking about *him* way too much these days.

"Tell me what the hell is going on, Jaine. If I'm going to lose my throat over something, I at least deserve to know what the fuck that something is."

"If I tell you, it goes no further. If it does, then I'll kill you myself. You got that? Then again, it's not that it won't already be common knowledge among the MCs around your parts. I'm sure the guilty party is already boasting about how he's undercutting the Irish and stealing their trade."

"Shit. No way?"

"Yes, way. The orders are down roughly twenty-five percent. We believe some Nevada MC has been getting their hands on weapons and selling them cheap to the Mexicans. Handguns in the main, but who knows where it will end up? They may have plans to grow to a larger scale and offer weaponry to others. We can't rule anything out at this stage."

"So, let me get this straight. There's a Nevada-based charter undercutting the Irish and selling weapons to La eMe?"

"In a nutshell, yes. And if they're selling to them, who will they approach next? Other Duster customers? It needs nipping in the bud now. If the Irish get involved, they'll simply arrange to have every single charter in the area razed to the ground. Trust me, no one in their right mind wants to make an enemy of Fergal O'Connell."

"You've met him? The Irish king?"

"Almost, but no. I do deal with his boys most days, though. Anyway, now that's out in the open, why don't you tell me who the fuck you are?"

"What do you want to know?"

"It says on your paperwork that you were with the Punishers previously. Is that true?"

"No."

"What the fuck do you mean, no?"

"I lied."

"But you have a reference from them."

"I forged it."

"Jesus fucking Christ."

"I'm from Sons of Satan."

"Jesus Christ. Lucifer's charter?"

"You know him?"

"Never met him, but I've heard of him. And what exactly were your duties for the Sons?"

"I didn't have any duties."

"So, you weren't a cum slut. You lied about that too?"

"Yes."

"So, what were you? Better still, who are you?"

There's a long pause.

"Bailey, if you don't tell me, I'll give Razr my blessing to open your goddamn throat. Now, tell me who the fuck you are." My tone is threatening and low because I mean every word.

"He's my daddy."

"Who?"

"Lucifer."

"You serious?"

"Totally."

"You stupid girl!" I hiss.

"I know… I…"

"You entered the clubhouse of one of the largest charters in the US without revealing that you're the daughter of the prez of another charter. That's disrespectful and deceitful. Razr has every right to cut your throat just for that reason, and frankly, he has my goddamn blessing right now. Jesus Christ, Bailey! What were you thinking?"

"I needed to get away from this place, and the life is all I know. I'd heard of the Scorpions. Who hasn't? And, well, they were on the opposite coast."

"So, you went in under the pretense of being a former cum slut. Who completed your online paperwork?"

"I can't tell you that. Anyway, it's not important."

"I want their name and their number. You send both to me after this call."

"It's not important, I said."

"It is to me, goddamn it, Bailey! This is my reputation. You've gotten in, and you shouldn't have. JAL's screening measures are second to none…."

"I did it myself," she interrupts.

"You what?"

"My sister. She has systems. Coded stuff that can do pretty

much anything. Break into the Pentagon and shit like that. I know my way around it enough, so I falsified all the paperwork. I'm sorry, but your JAL system was no match."

"You falsified the paperwork? That's a criminal offense."

"I'm already an outlaw. Last I heard, you are too, no matter how much you try to beautify that shit by wearing a professional badge."

I smile inwardly at that response. She sure is a ballsy little fucker.

"Listen, when this is all over, you, me, and that sister of yours are going to sit around a table, and you're going to explain to me exactly what you did."

"My sister doesn't know."

"Even better. You reap what you sow, Bailey."

"So which MCs are under investigation over the gun business?"

"The Sons and the Undertakers."

"The Sons have nothing to do with it. I can guarantee you that."

"How? You've been gone for quite some time. A lot could have changed since. It's been noticed that they've recently had a drive to increase numbers."

"Because they'll be doing a lot of transporting for La eMe."

"I didn't know La eMe were working hand in hand with an MC?"

"They are, and they will continue to work with the Sons moving forward. We have an alliance."

"Rodolfo hasn't mentioned anything."

"You know him?" She sounds surprised.

"Yes. I went to school with him. He's also a client."

"Well, the alliance isn't set in stone yet."

"Jesus Christ, Bailey. What are you telling me?"

My blood runs cold at what this stupid girl has been up to. I know exactly what she's about to say.

"It will only be formalized once my arranged marriage goes ahead."

"To?"

"Raf Flores. Rodolfo's younger brother."

"Shit. You know Delaney will definitely kill you for that. In his mind you've used him to cheat on someone else."

"I realize that."

I exhale loud and slow. "Word of advice?"

"I'm listening."

"Stay away from Delaney when he comes calling, which he will. Also, get rid of the Fat Boy. It's wearing a tracker."

"Jesus Christ, thank you." Her gratitude is evident. "Tell me what I owe, and I'll wire it across now. In the next hour, that hog will be untraceable."

"Twenty grand. I'll send the details across, and Bailey?"

"Yes."

"If any of this turns out to be another lie, then I won't need a tracker to find you. And I won't hesitate in sending you to meet your maker personally. You got me?"

"Understood."

CHAPTER TWENTY-FIVE

BAILEY

Bailey's Family Home, Colton, Nevada

"Who are you on the phone to, Bee? Raf will be here soon."

"Yes, Daddy. No one, Daddy." *Three bags full, Daddy.*

I pray to The Almighty he wasn't eavesdropping on my conversation with Jaine. Then again, my life will be over soon anyway, so what the fuck does it matter? I've texted my brother Conor. Someone will be here to collect the borrowed hog within the next half hour, and then it will be torched. He didn't ask any questions. He likely figured it was related to my vanishing act, so the less said, the better. That way, he can avoid being on the receiving end of an ear-clipping from Daddy if he says something he shouldn't on account of knowing too much.

Having wired the money across to one of JAL's business accounts, I toss my phone on my bed. I watch as it bounces off the quilted surface and lands on the floor.

It sums up the day from hell I'm having.

I glance around the room. It's all Venetian glass furniture on a grey background and with very few personal items on display. The color reflects my mood.

I leave my phone on the floor, deciding instead to stare out my bedroom window at the familiar mountainscape behind me.

I bite at my bottom lip to stop the tears from pricking my eyes. Some girls cry a lot. Me? Not ever. These past days, though, it's like I can't stop. Even more so when Jaine then went on to tell me the unwelcome news. She didn't have to tell me, but she thought I should know before it became public knowledge.

That Razr's making Strawberry Shortcake his old lady.

I'm grateful she did. I'd have found out sooner rather than later anyway, and I'd rather have heard the not entirely unexpected news from her as opposed to anyone else.

I didn't ask any questions, even though there were a million on the tip of my tongue. There were likely a million answers on the tip of hers too, but we left them as they should be. Unspoken. We're both realists. There's no point dissecting shit. No point questioning something when it's signed and the ink's already dried.

Razr's made his choice. That choice wasn't me. Suck it up, Bailey.

But see shit like this doesn't stack up for me. How can I love him as much as I do when he doesn't even care about me in the slightest? Surely the universe has to balance the scales somehow. Then again, maybe Razr loves Laila as much as I love him. Maybe that's the balance. All in her favor. The positive to my negative.

I'll get over it. What other choice do I have? My future is now mapped. Then again, wasn't it always? If Razr had declared his undying love for me, would I have been able to alter my destiny? Probably not.

After today, I'll be Rafael Flores's girlfriend, then fiancée, then wife, and finally, the mother of his children.

I stand up from where I'm leaning against the window ledge, then run my hands down the ass of my white jeans. Raf's a butt man, and he also likes blondes, unlike his brother, Rodolfo.

Today, he'll want to see just what he's purchasing, I'm sure. Not that he hasn't seen me a million times before now. But our relationship will change forever today, and neither of us has any say in the matter.

Two unwilling pieces in the outlaw game of chess moved to stand side by side, all to form an alliance perceived to be for the greater good.

Check and mate.

Happy that my figure is displayed to its full potential, I leave the security of my room to go seal my fate once and for all.

"Raf, it's good to see you."

"Liam, it's been a while."

Is that a subtle dig? I know my vanishing act is the reason it's been a while. I stand on the sidelines and watch as they share a man hug before they both turn their attention to me. The annoying little human sacrifice that went AWOL and caused a delay to the proceedings.

Why so urgent? Rumor has it Rodolfo has been singled out to become the next silent leader of La eMe, and he wants Raf as his number two. The other high rankers feel that as married men, they'll be perceived as offering more stability. Family is important to the Mexicans. It comes before everything.

Well, apart from La eMe itself.

"No Rodolfo today?" I look around, but the elder Flores is nowhere to be seen.

"Ah, no. He's on a date."

I snort-laugh. "With a non-blonde?"

"Yes." Raf grins at me from across the room. I mean, I should be delighted with my future husband. He's tall and lean, tanned, and handsome, and his too-long black hair is tied at the nape of his neck and perfectly set off by his designer stubble. Silver spacers adorn his ears. By all accounts, that's not the only piercing he has. He has several, and most of them all for the ladies' pleasure.

Not that I'd know firsthand. But many women do. Raf has played the field. The whole field. Perhaps that's why he's accepted me as his future bride. I'm the last female standing on the west coast that he hasn't dicked.

I'm sure once he's fucked me, he'll go back to his rumored philandering ways while I'll be expected to stay home, chained to the kitchen sink, my belly filled with his offspring.

The future La eMe heirs.

"I'll leave you two young ones to it."

My daddy makes himself scarce—no need to chaperone. We're a done deal. Raf and I both know it. We could fuck right here, right now and no one would even care.

"So how have you been, Bee? More importantly, where have you been?" His tone is playful with an underlying hint of dark menace.

I watch as he pours himself a whiskey. He knows where everything is. He's been here countless times over the years. We've known each other since we were kids. He's almost part of the family. He's also my brother Conor's best friend.

"Not sure that's any of your business, Raf."

My eyes glance around the room. It's ostentatious. All cream leather and dark walnut floors, with an over-the-top chandelier taking center stage. My daddy likes to flaunt our wealth—something he and Razr have in common.

I pick up a family photo of Conor and me and pretend to look at it. I'm not, though. I'm biding my time. See, I know I'll get into trouble for that response.

Raf walks over in deathly silence, grips my arm, and spins me around. I stare up at him defiantly. He's a handsome brute. Dark eyes sparkle menacingly, but I stand my ground. He forgets I grew up with him. I've seen all these looks that are meant to be threatening. I've witnessed him practicing them over and over again from boy to man. They don't work on me.

"You're going to be my fiancée, Bee. My wife. I won't tolerate this behavior. As your future husband, you will show me respect, and in return, I will show you the same. Now tell me where you've been."

"On the east coast."

"And who have you been fucking?"

I smirk at him. "If I tell you, will you afford me the same courtesy, Raf? Will you tell me who you've dicked in my absence? Oh, wait. You can't remember all the names because there have been so many."

He smirks in response. He knows I'm right. Everyone knows his reputation precedes him.

"Are you jealous, querida?" His voice is soft. He strokes his hand down my cheek as his musky cologne envelopes me.

I close my eyes and lean against his palm, pretending that I'm falling for his charms.

I smirk at him before pushing his hand away. "Nice touch, Raf. It might work on your numerous female conquests, but it doesn't work on me."

"Ah, but you will be my conquest too, Bee. You have no choice.

And I am looking forward to fucking that sass out of you once and for all." His eyes are laughing at me.

"Fuck you."

"On the contrary. It will be you that I'm fucking. So, give me his name."

"You're not getting it."

"His name, Bee." Again, he follows me, and again, he grips my wrist, this time painfully. I try to yank it away, but he holds fast, his eyes now dark and spitting fury.

Is he jealous? He can't be surely?

I frown at him. "Why do you care? This will be an arranged marriage. Neither of us wants to marry the other, so why the fuck are you getting possessive?"

His eyes narrow. "Who says I don't want this marriage?"

I stare at him, my frown deepening in confusion. "It's just for convenience, isn't it?"

"In part, yes, but if I was marrying purely for convenience, I could choose from any number of women."

"But you want to ally with the Sons?"

He smiles at what can only be my naivety. "We could have that without you and me having to marry, querida."

"So, you actually want to marry me?" I whisper, shocked at the reveal.

"Yes. As part of the deal, I've hand-picked you as my wife."

"But why?"

"I love you, Bee. Your untamable spirit. The fact that you stand up to me. Your beauty." He pushes my hair behind my ear as his eyes graze over my face. "I've known since I was a young boy that I would take you as my wife."

I shake my head slowly from side to side. I didn't expect this. I didn't realize this. When the arrangement was put to us both, I ran. I thought Raf would be glad I had. That my doing so would save us both from being part of a forced union. That everyone would realize the error of their ways and call the whole thing off.

"But I'm in love with someone else, Raf."

He frowns, but only briefly. It's not something he wants to hear. Unfortunately, I understand exactly how he feels.

Leaning forward, he inhales the scent of my hair before he fists it in his hand. Pulling my head back, his breath is hot against my lips. "Then I suggest you forget about him," he says quietly as his eyes roam my face.

He presses his mouth to mine, his experienced lips warm and coaxing. He's a master at his craft, that's for sure, as his tongue wraps expertly around mine. But there's no flood of desire to my core. I don't instantly feel wet. I don't moan against his lips because I just can't help myself.

That only happens when I kiss Razr.

I'm not sure if Raf notices my lack of response. Probably not, as when his mouth moves from mine, his eyes are dark with desire.

"I have discussed matters with my brother and your father. Two weeks from today, our engagement will be announced." His lips trail up my neck, causing me to shiver. "Would you like me to fuck you the night of our engagement, or would you prefer to wait until our wedding night? I'll leave that decision up to you."

I ignore the question.

"What happens after we're married?"

He smiles gently down at me. "Are you asking if I will be faithful to you?"

I nod.

"Yes, I will be faithful, Bee. I've well and truly sown my wild oats, as you've already pointed out." He chuckles heartily. "And when I'm married to the most beautiful woman in the state, why would I want anyone else?"

"I'm not…" I shake my head.

He presses his lips to mine, but only briefly this time. Our eyes connect, his full of warmth, mine no doubt full of confusion.

"You are to me," he whispers as he tucks my hair behind my ear.

And he means it. Guilt floods me. Raf's in love with me? Has he always been? Why have I never noticed? I thought neither of us had a choice in this marriage, but it turns out it's only me who has no choice.

I look at him. This young man of twenty-three, who I've grown up with and known most of my life. A man most women would climb over each other to claim as their spouse, and it makes me sad because I know he's being short-changed. Because I don't love him. Because I love someone else. Because he deserves true love. Raf deserves the best, and that's not me.

"I will do my best to make you a good wife, Raf."

And I mean it. I will. Pretty soon, my bed will be made, and I'll have to lie in it for the rest of my life. If I can't have Paul Delaney, then it may as well be with Raf as with anyone else.

At least he loves me. At least one of us can be happy.

CHAPTER TWENTY-SIX

RAZR

Bailey's Family Home, Colton, Nevada

THE DOOR OPENS AS WE APPROACH THE EXTENSIVE PROPERTY, AND I take in the prez of the Sons of Satan. For a man in his fifties, he's kept himself in pretty good shape.

"Lucifer."

"It's good to meet you at long last, Razr."

His handshake is firm, as is to be expected.

"These are my boys, Tadgh and Conor."

My eyes scan over his sons, both of whom are flanking him. Tadgh looks the spitting image of his old man. Apparently, he's my age, and he's earmarked to take over as prez when Lucifer decides to step down. Conor, in direct contrast, is dark, I'm guessing like his momma. Rumor has it she left town as Lucifer was still hung up on the ex who left him for another man.

"I've heard a lot about you, Razr." Conor smiles at me, and I nod in response.

"All good, I hope."

"Well, if it were all good, you wouldn't be doing your job properly now, would you?"

His smile widens. It's clear he's still wet behind the ears. A couple more years and that smile will be wiped clean off and replaced by lines.

"These are my men, Blaze and Knight," I reply, my attention back on Lucifer.

"Good to meet you, fellas."

He motions his head for us to step inside.

Internally, the house is luxurious. There will be no expense spared because there's no need. Lucifer will have limitless funds available. He has his fingers in a lot of pies. Not that I give a shit. There's only one pie I'm interested in, and he'd better not have his finger in that motherfucker.

The room we're shown into is all cream leather and dark wood, the chandelier hanging from the ceiling so large we have to walk around it to avoid banging our heads.

"Drink?" Tadgh offers.

"No, thank you." I decline, as do my brothers. We need to keep a clear head at all times. We're led to believe that the Sons of Satan is a decent charter. Highly respected. Still, it pays to be vigilant and form your own judgment on shit like that.

"I'll get straight to the point. As you know, we're here to ask..."

"The Sons don't supply guns. Not to anyone. We don't buy them in then sell them on, and we don't manufacture them either. You're barking up the wrong tree," Tadgh interrupts, his face impassive

I nod at him. I can feel my blood start to boil. My hand is itching for my blade, but I know present company won't be receptive to that sight, even if it represents no threat. Even if it's solely to preserve the remnants of my rapidly dwindling sanity, they won't see it that way.

"You've had a recent drive to increase your numbers. Why is that?" I narrow my eyes at him.

"We're in an alliance with the Mexicans. Transporting on their behalf. That's it."

"An alliance?" I raise an eyebrow at Tadgh. "How come no one's heard of this alleged alliance."

"Listen, son," Lucifer interrupts. "As Tadgh's rightly said, you're barking up the wrong tree. The alliance is just being finalized. We're joining ranks to strengthen both of our positions. As you know, the Sons is a fairly big charter around these parts. We're not as big as the Scorpions, but we're still top ten."

"And what exactly are you having to do to finalize this… alliance?"

I watch as he pours himself a whiskey. He throws it back in one then stares at me. I'm sure he realizes that if I don't get answers or I don't like what I'm hearing, one of us is going to die today, and it sure as hell isn't going to be me.

"Now, you see, son, that's not really any of your business. But I'll tell you as me and my boys here have nothing to hide. My youngest daughter is marrying one of their high rankers at his request. The young lad has offered, and she's accepted. Once they're married, the Sons will be handling all transport matters for the Mexicans."

"Transport?"

"Yes, transport. Nothing else. So we're not stepping on any toes."

"You're sure about that?" My tone's accusing.

He slams the whiskey glass down, the crystal shattering in his hand and cutting through his flesh. I watch as he closes his eyes then runs his bloody hand through his hair.

"Whatever you've heard about me, whatever's been said, you ignore that shit, you hear me? Now you're standing in my home, and I'm telling you the goddamn truth. I may be a murderer, but I'm as honest as the day is long. I'm no liar. My boys are no liars. My two girls are no liars. The truth will always come out. Anyone who thinks it won't is a fool. Now, don't disrespect and insult me in my own home by suggesting that I'm a liar."

I stare at him for a time. Our impenetrable gazes connect as we try to read each other. Neither of us can. I nod slowly. I believe him. My gut's saying he's telling me the truth.

"My contact got it down to two clubs."

"Who's your contact?"

"That's Scorpion's intel I don't ever intend to share."

"Mind telling me who the other club is?"

"You know I can't do that, Lucifer."

"You going after them tonight?"

"Why put off until tomorrow what you can do today?"

"You need some of my men to go with you?"

"Nope."

"Listen, son. From what I've heard it's the Undertakers, and if it is, you'll need all the help you can get."

"We can manage just fine. We're just here to have a civilized conversation like adults. We're not here to start a war."

I'm lying. The person responsible for trampling on my goddamn toes is a dead man walking.

"You may not want to start a war, but Reaper will. Stay for now. Let's you and I break the bread tonight and talk business. Now the Scorpions know the Sons aren't touching what's theirs, maybe there's an opportunity for us to work together. Confront Reaper tomorrow. It's Friday. The likelihood is, if you go tomorrow, his brothers will be compromised as they'll all be worse for wear. Come, sit."

Razr: *Folks are very hospitable here in Nevada.*
Bailey: *Is that so?*
Razr: *You've got twenty-four hours to run.*
Bailey: *Shows how little you know me. I'm not going anywhere.*
Razr: *Where's the hog?*
Bailey: *You mean the ride wearing the tracker?*
Razr: *How did you find out about that?*
Bailey: *I'm not stupid.*
Razr: *I'll still find you. I'm sure there aren't many girls who look like you living around these parts.*
Bailey: *Good luck with that. It's blonde city. It'll be like looking for a needle in a haystack. Why do you want to waste your precious time looking for me anyway?*
Razr: *You betrayed me.*
Bailey: *You still believe that shit?*
Razr: *It depends on what I find at my next stop.*
Bailey: *Which is?*
Razr: *None of your damn business, sweetheart.*
Bailey: *I'm not your sweetheart. I'm not your anything.*
Razr: *No, I guess you're right about that. I'll be seeing you tomorrow. Wear something nice around that pretty little throat of yours.*
Bailey: *Fuck you.*
Razr: *I'm game for one last fuck if you are.*
Bailey: *I'm sure your old lady wouldn't appreciate you cheating on her.*

Razr: *Tomorrow.*

CHAPTER TWENTY-SEVEN

BAILEY

Las Vegas, Nevada

"CHOOSE WHICHEVER ONE YOU WANT, BEE."

The back of Raf's hand caresses my cheek as he gazes into my eyes. He's become extremely tactile since I've accepted my fate and agreed to be the best wife I can for him. It's like he can't believe I'm going to be his.

I'm sure I'll grow to love him through time. It won't be the intense, all-consuming kind of love I feel for Razr. But it will be a love that's solely for Raf. I mean, it's not like I don't find him physically attractive. On the contrary. Visually, he's beautiful. It's just that my heart prefers strawberry blonde bikers with an attitude problem and a fetish for switchblades. Hopefully, one day that will all change. It's unlikely, though. It's just wishful thinking on my part.

"They're all way too expensive, Raf."

We're sitting side by side, his arm draped across my shoulder. Picking a diamond up, he studies it distractedly before tossing it back on the display cloth like it's made of paste and not worth millions of dollars.

"Nonsense. My family is extremely wealthy, as am I in my own right. Money is no object. You need an engagement ring that's as beautiful as you are, querida. And one that's fitting of a future heiress of La eMe."

I bite on my bottom lip and look around. It's not a shop. It's a room in a private house. There are a couple of chocolate-colored leather sectionals, one of which we're sitting on, on a grey marble floor. The pristine white walls are heavily adorned with contrasting colorful works of modern art. Immediately in front of us is an all-glass table covered in display cloths, each nestling a diamond of every size, color, and cut within their black velvet grasp. Each stone sparkles at us, each trying to entice us with its ostentatious extravagant beauty.

We're in the home of the designer himself. A craftsman who will make my engagement ring personally using whichever stone we wish before placing it in whatever setting we want. The price of him having to accommodate us in his private dwelling will no doubt be reflected in the exorbitant cost we'll be charged. Each diamond displayed in front of us is upwards of one million dollars.

"Don't you have a family heirloom or something?"

He frowns at me. Is he surprised by my question?

"We have my grandma's engagement ring, but it's old and with a sapphire at its center. Most women prefer single diamond stones, no? Expensive rings to show you how much you mean to us and how much we love you."

I turn to look at him, and his dark expressive eyes scan my face once more.

"Raf, I'd rather have something old and sentimental than something new. A ring that means something to us both."

His eyes glimmer with emotion. For the first time in his adult life, I'm finally seeing all of Rafael Flores. He's a murderer; of course he is. They surround me in my walk of life, and I was always destined to end up with one. But he's also a man with a beautiful heart. A man whose family means everything to him. A man who is my future husband and future father of my children.

A man who sees me.

A man who loves me just as I am.

"As you wish, Bee. My family, my father especially, will be delighted by this news."

"Then it's decided."

I smile at him, and his eyes drop to my lips, instantly darkening. I lick the bottom one, suggestively smirking as I do.

"You're a temptress." He chuckles at my deliberately leading him on, nuzzling his nose against my neck.

"Aren't you going to take me up on my offer?"

Growling, he fists my hair, then pulls my face towards his as his other hand drags me across to straddle him.

Devouring my mouth, his hands search my body before dropping down to cup my ass. I groan against his lips, and he thrusts his slim hips upwards, his noticeable erection pressing against me.

"I can't wait to make you mine, querida. To have that little pussy of yours clenching tightly around my cock countless times a day. The very thought of it is driving me insane."

I press down against his hard-on, and he growls loudly, his hips jerking against my hot center.

"Our wedding night," I whisper against his lips, a smirk on my face.

"We have to wait until then? Fuck, no, Bee," he groans, his expression pained.

"Fuck, yes, Raf." I chuckle.

"Then we must get married immediately after the engagement has been announced. I cannot wait to be inside you. Filling your sweet little pussy with my seed and your belly with my offspring."

His hand reaches inside my tank top before pulling my bra down and cupping my bare flesh. The tip pebbles immediately, and his dick hardens further in lustful response. Lifting my top, his mouth drops to suck hard on the tip, and I groan against his hair, fisting it in both hands. Arousal flows through me. We've spent a lot of time kissing and fooling around, and more and more, my body is starting to react to his. Frustratingly for both of us right now, it's not leading anywhere. When it does, I'm sure it will be extremely satisfying.

I want to do things right with Raf, though. Everything in the right order.

"I love you so fucking much, Bee."

Dropping my mouth to his, I silence him. Why? Because I can't say the same back.

Guilt floods me once more, and I whisper a silent prayer to The Almighty that one day I can. Because a man like Raf? Well, he deserves nothing less.

RAF SMILES AT ME WHEN MY PHONE VIBRATES, AND I USE MY FREE hand to pull it from my pocket, my other wrapped in his much larger one as he drives me home.

Conor: *Did you pick a ring?*
Bailey: *Yes and no. We decided to go with something old—Raf's grandma's ring.*
Conor: *I'll bet he's delighted you're such a cheap date.*

Bee: *Well, family's important to him.*
Conor: *Are you finally catching the feels for our childhood friend?*
Bailey: *Shut up, asshole.*
Conor: *Well, you've got my blessing. He's a great guy—the best. I'm glad you're finally seeing it too. Anyway, we have company at home.*
Bailey: *Anyone I know?*
Conor: *Nope. It's the prez of the Iron Scorpions and two of his brothers.*

My blood runs cold in my veins. Fuck. Razr's in my house? The asshole found me, and he doesn't even realize.

Bailey: *Will our guests be leaving soon?*
Conor: *They're talking business. Future alliances. You know how the old man is. He always wants more of everything. Importance. Wealth. Power. What he's already got is never enough. I think he's found his presidential soul mate in Razr.*
Bailey: *Think I can sneak in without being seen?*
Conor: *You don't want to meet them? Paul Delaney looks like he might be your type if you're into older men.*

How little does he fucking know.

Bailey: *I've got a headache, Conor. Plus, I'm as good as married, remember?*
Conor: *True. I guess I'll be asked to be best man now the show's finally on the road. Anyway, I'll unlock the back gates and switch off the security lighting. Message me when you're inside, and I'll reset everything.*

Bailey: *Will do. You're the best brother in the world. Do you know that?*
Conor: *Yes.*
Bailey: *Yes, what?*
Conor: *I know what you're angling for. And yes, I'll leave snacks in your room.*
Bailey: *I love you.*
Conor: *Just as well.*

Bailey's Family Home, Colton, Nevada

I can hear the mumbling of conversation the moment I open the door.

Paul "Razr" Delaney is only feet away from me, and he doesn't even know it. The biker I'm in love with—the one who's in love with someone else. The insane murderer who wants to serve me my throat on a plate for apparently betraying him is in the building.

My fucking building.

When I reach the safety of my bedroom, I lie back on my bed and pull out my phone. Then, smirking, I send a message.

Bailey: *Found me yet, or do you need some clues? A map, maybe?*
Razr: *Tomorrow, I said.*
Bailey: *I'm not a beck and call girl. I'm way too busy tomorrow.*
Razr: *You'll do as you're told.*
Bailey: *Or what? Are you going to put me over your knee and spank me for being a naughty girl, big bad prez?*
Razr: *Bailey.*
Bailey: *Made you hard yet, Razr?*
Razr: *Before I cut your throat, I'm going to fuck you.*

Bailey: *What if I don't want you to fuck me?*
Razr: *Quit lying to yourself.*
Bailey: *You can't fuck me anyway. I was told you've made Laila your old lady. I'm not sure she'd approve.*

I stare at my phone, but no more messages come through. Why? Because it's all fucking true. Then again, what does any of it matter? I'm getting engaged imminently, married not long after. That's if Razr doesn't cut my throat first for something I didn't even do.

There's a knock on my bedroom door. I freeze.

"You home, Bee?" I squeeze my eyes closed and swear silently. How can I deny it? The bedroom light is on.

"Yeah. Got a headache, though, Tadgh."

"You don't want to come and greet our guests? They've come all the way from New York."

"No, thank you."

"Can I come in?"

I open the door a fraction, making sure there's no one behind him before opening it wider and letting him through. I take in my eldest brother, who is the carbon copy of our daddy, right down to his piercing pale blue gaze.

He's the same age as Razr, and in many ways, they're very similar, although Tadgh doesn't have a crazy alter-ego. Neither of them suffers fools and will kill anyone who betrays them, blood or not. They would work well in an alliance together.

"You have a good time with Raf?" He snickers as he ruffles my hair. I shove his hand away. The asshole knows I hate that.

"Yeah." I nod.

"He's a good kid."

"He's not a kid. I'm not a kid either, Tadgh. Just because you're as old as Methuselah himself doesn't mean the rest of us are kids."

He nods, his eyes narrowing as he takes me in. "Where did you go, Bee? When you ran."

For some reason, I've always felt able to talk to Tadgh. He'd never betray me, I'm sure. Not even to the other members of our family.

"Another MC on the east coast. I wasn't ready to just settle. All I'd ever seen was Nevada. Same places. Same people. I needed to see some of the world. Experience a bit of life, you know? Before I have to get married and knocked up."

"You didn't bring any trouble back with you, did you? I heard about the hog we had to burn."

I shake my head to deny it, knowing full well the trouble I brought back is sitting just a few feet away in the other room.

"It's nothing I can't handle. So, what's happening with the Scorpions? Are we allying with them or not?"

"You know that's not a topic of conversation for womenfolk."

"I'm not any woman. I'm your sister."

He sighs, running his hand through his long blonde hair. "There's scope for us to do several things together, most likely using the Angels as an intermediary for some."

"They're based in California, right?"

"How'd you know that, Little Bee? Have you been doing your MC homework while you've been gone?" He ruffles my hair again, and I bat his hand away.

"I'm not clueless, you know." I huff.

"I know. I'm just being an annoying older brother." He sighs again. "I'd prefer Razr to accept our offer of help when he goes to meet the Undertakers tomorrow, though, or we might never form that alliance. It's like he's got some sort of death wish."

"He won't accept our help?"

Worry flows through me. Most of the Undertakers show no loyalty to other brothers whatsoever.

“Nope. He says he’s got it all under control. The man’s going to get himself killed. Anyway, I’d better get back, Bee.” He picks up a handful of my potato chips and crams them into his mouth.

“Hey!” I bat his hand away again.

“Later, baby sis.” Placing a crumby kiss to the top of my head, which I then dust off exaggeratedly, he leaves and closes the door quietly behind him.

I need to make a phone call.

Jaine answers straight away. I ignore niceties. I just get straight to the point.

“He’s here. Razr. He’s sitting in my front room.”

“Well, that’s a bit too close for comfort.”

“You’re telling me. I keep rubbing my hand across my throat. Anyway, from what I hear, the Sons may be allying with the Scorpions, using the Angels as an intermediary.”

“Nice of Delaney to ask for our permission beforehand,” Jaine grumbles.

“I’m sure he will. He’d never disrespect you. But, anyway, that’s not the reason for my call.”

“What is?”

“Razr and his two brothers are heading into Undertakers’ territory tomorrow. The Sons have offered them back-up, but it’s been declined. I don’t know if you’ve heard of the Undertakers before now, but they’re a charter who show no loyalty or respect to other MCs. If Razr was just going in there to have a friendly discussion, then just maybe he might walk away unscathed. My concern is, given how volatile his state of mind’s been lately, that he’ll go in their accusing Reaper of all sorts while swinging that switchblade of his around, and blood’s going to be spilled. Probably Razr’s.”

There's a pause while she digests what I've said.

"What do you need me to do, Bailey? If I tell him what I know, he'll wonder how. There's also every chance he won't listen to me anyway."

"You got any brothers in the area?"

She sighs. She has, and she doesn't want to use them, but she knows she may have no choice.

"Ace and Clay are in Vegas overnight collecting some overdue cash."

What she means is they're slicing and dicing someone who's deemed as having stolen from the MC by not paying their dues. They'll then take the deceitful fucker for everything they've got.

"You reckon they could swing by, or at least be in the area? I know precisely where the Undertakers' clubhouse is. I've been there a lot of times over the years as my daddy and Reaper used to be good friends. That was before Reaper got himself involved in trafficking. Word is he has a bit of a fetish for young flesh."

"Yeah, I have heard about that. He needs a bullet in his pedo skull."

"Hey, maybe we can hire The Exterminator." I laugh. "I mean, does that guy actually exist?"

"He exists alright. From what I hear, he's just taking some well-deserved time off. I'm sure a bullet in Reaper's skull can be arranged in due course if karma doesn't get the fucker beforehand. Listen, I'll speak to Ace about the Undertakers and gauge how big a threat he sees this situation. If there's a high risk, then we'll figure something out covertly, so Delaney doesn't know. The Angels were trying to avoid this battle as it's too close to home for us. That and the fact that I'm about to give birth. But I won't let any harm come to Delaney."

"You really care about him, don't you?"

"I love him, Bailey. I spent four years of my life with the

madman, and I can't say I regret any of them. He'll always hold a special place in my heart."

"Mine too."

There's a pause.

"Your engagement being announced soon?"

"Yup. Picked the ring today."

"You know…"

"Don't, Jaine. I don't want to hear it. If you're going to tell me Razr made the wrong decision and that he should have chosen me, or that Laila's no good for him, just don't. I know the answer to all that already. It doesn't change anything. He's a grown man. He made his choices. It doesn't mean I can just sit back and watch him get himself killed, though, even if he wants to slit my throat for shit I haven't done."

"Listen, Bailey. If Ace thinks there's a serious threat, he'll handle it. You keep out of it. It's no place for you."

"Why? Because I'm a girl? Because I'm only twenty-one?"

"Yes, on both counts."

"And what would you do, Jaine? Ask your twenty-one-year-old self that same question. What would you do if it were Ace?"

"I'd fight and die for the man I love, but Bailey…"

"Thank you."

"You're so manipulative. Goddamn it."

CHAPTER TWENTY-EIGHT

JAINE

Jaine's House, Rising, California

ROLLING MY EYES, I ANSWER HIS CALL.

"Eoin."

"Jaine. Has the situation in Nevada been resolved?"

"Delaney's there and dealing with the issue now. It's been whittled down to one MC, the Undertakers. By all accounts, they're not people who should be messed with."

"And you know that how?"

"I have a contact."

"You seem to have contacts all over the US, Jaine."

"What if I do?" I snap.

"Temper temper, Miss Jones."

"Sorry."

"Is there a problem?"

"Nothing I can't handle."

"If you need help with anything, you just need to ask."

I laugh dryly. "What and create an owing? No, thank you."

"You're the one who feels the need to create an owing, Jaine."

"Oh right. So, helping with the trafficking kids didn't, in turn, mean I had to furnish you with information on my goddamn clients."

"Only two."

"Two high-rankers, Eoin. And I had to introduce you to several others. And I had to dance with you. So, no, I'm not getting myself into any more personal debt with the Dusters."

"What's the alternative?"

"I'll deal with matters myself."

"As you wish. So, on the order shortage?"

"I'll come back to you once I hear from Delaney."

"Thank you."

"Now, about Jessie. I hear you've put her up in one of your unopened hotels for now."

"Yes. We're aware she needs to be able to go into lockdown at a moment's notice."

"Well, to make matters worse, her apartment contract has now been canceled by the realtor for reasons unknown. She's actively searching for something else suitable. As you'll appreciate, the content she's working on is extremely confidential. She's looking at several systems that she doesn't have permission to access. Caught looking at even one would carry a lengthy prison sentence."

"I realize that. I'll broach the matter again with her and Dyl. He has ample space, and his place is already set up to provide exactly what she needs. Leave it with me. I'll get it sorted."

"Thank you."

There's a pause.

"Jaine, what's wrong?"

His voice is gentle. Kind even. Tears of self-pity prick my eyes, and I curse myself silently. I don't want this fucker's kindness, his pity, or anything else.

"Nothing."

"It's not nothing."

"I said it's nothing!" I snap again before hanging up.

EOIN

Eoin's Apartment, Hudson Yards, New York

"Dylan." He answers immediately.

"Yes, Eoin."

"Something's going on with Jaine. She's short-fused. Temperamental."

"That doesn't sound so unusual for Jaine."

"Even more so than normal."

"She's getting pretty far along with the pregnancy now. Maybe it's hormonal."

"No, it's not that. Call it gut instinct, but something's bothering her. I want to know what it is."

"Are you worried about her?"

"Why would I be worried?" I sound defensive. I know I do. And it's because I am worried.

"You sound worried."

"Just find out what the issue is, Dylan. She talks to you." My response is more brusque than it needs to be.

"I'll do my best."

"Thank you."

"Is that all?"

'No. This Jessie situation. She won't move into your apartment? Her reluctance to do so could throw a spanner in the works."

"Apparently, she'd rather not."

"I thought she liked you?"

"Apparently, she does."

"What's the problem, then?"

"For some reason, she thinks I'm pining over someone, and she doesn't want to get in the way."

"There's not much chance of that. How would you meet anyone when you seldom leave your apartment?"

"Well, that's what she's gotten into her head. We're dealing with it."

"We?"

"Paddy and me."

"Why is he involved?"

"He knows more about these matters than I do. He knows his way around women's minds."

"Yes, you're right. He does. It's a shame I can't ask him to find out what the issue is with Jaine. Anyway, speak to Jaine. Find out and let me know, Dyl."

"I'll do my best, Eoin."

DYLAN

Dylan's Apartment, Hudson Yards, New York

"Paddy."

"How's it hanging, brother?"

"Just fine. Listen. Eoin says there's something wrong with Jaine. He's asked her what it is, and she won't tell him."

"And you want me to message her as your Batman to her Robin?"

"Yes. You have more chance of prizing it out of her that way than I have over the phone. Plus, she may ask questions about things I won't be able to provide answers to. Things that you talk to her about when you pretend to be me."

"You've become her best friend, Dyl."

"No, you have, Paddy. Again."

"True."

"You do know if she ever finds out about any of this, she'll probably never speak to either of us again."

"She doesn't want to speak to me ever again anyway, Dyl."

"She may also shoot us both in the head."

"Well, at least I'd be put out of my misery."

"Your life's not that bad, surely?"

"You're not having to marry Sophia while pining for the woman of your dreams as she carries another man's child and prepares to take the vows with him. Apart from that everything's just fucking peachy with my life."

"Eoin's also asking about Jessie. Why she won't move into my apartment."

"What did you say?"

"That we're getting it sorted. No doubt Jaine's putting him under pressure. She can't stay holed up in a hotel forever, plus, it's due to open soon. And it's not like Jaine can put her up in her apartment. Not with all the sniper gear hidden there."

"Leave it with me. I'll sweet-talk her and tell her things that will make her feel sorry for you."

"So, you'll make me out to be a loser."

"Brother, you do a good enough job of that for yourself," he quips.

"Very funny." Thinks he's hilarious does our Paddy. "So, you'll message Jaine?"

"Any excuse I get. You don't even need to ask."

PADRAIG

Padraig's Apartment, Hudson Yards, New York

Padraig: *You there, darlin'?*
Jaine: *Thought you'd forgotten about me. You haven't messaged me for at least twelve hours.*
Padraig: *Sorry for neglecting my duties. Is everything okay?*
Jaine: *Not really.*
Padraig: *A problem shared is a problem halved?*
Jaine: *It's this gun business. I've been speaking to a contact who's close to the problem, and she doesn't feel Delaney's equipped to handle the situation.*
Padraig: *I think we all know Razr's more than equipped.*
Jaine: *One-on-one, definitely. Anyone with half a brain wouldn't want to take him on. But my contact doesn't think he's got enough manpower with him to tackle the MC behind the problem. And because of that, he may be at risk. I don't want anything to happen to him, Dyl. He hasn't been himself lately, so he may not be thinking straight. In fact, I know he isn't.*
Padraig: *Okay, so let's look at this sensibly. In your opinion, what's the solution?*
Jaine: *That the Angels go in as back-up.*
Padraig: *I thought we'd all already agreed that option wasn't on the table.*
Jaine: *But what if it's the only option now due to timing and proximity?*
Padraig: *If it's the only option, what do you suggest?*
Jaine: *Ace and Clay are in Vegas. Scheduled to come back tomorrow.*
Padraig: *And it's on route.*
Jaine: *Exactly.*

Padraig: *Best case?*

Jaine: *Nothing happens, and everything goes according to Delaney's unshared plan.*

Padraig: *Worst case?*

Jaine: *Something happens to Ace and Delaney, and I can't let that happen.*

Padraig: *I don't like the sound of this. What's going through that head of yours, Jaine?*

Jaine: *That I should get my weapon, get in a cage, and head for Nevada.*

Padraig: *I can't allow you to do that. You're seven weeks away from giving birth.*

Jaine: *You do realize you're too far away to stop me?*

Padraig: *Please, Jaine. I'm begging you. Don't even think about it.*

Jaine: *I'm not sure what I'm doing yet. It depends on how much of a threat Ace deems the Undertakers to be.*

Padraig: *So, you'll talk to him first?*

Jaine: *Of course I will.*

Padraig: *Phew. Crisis averted. You'll tell me if you're thinking of driving to Nevada, won't you?*

Jaine: *Yes.*

Padraig: *Pinkie promise?*

Jaine: *Pinkie promise.*

CHAPTER TWENTY-NINE

RAZR

Motel, Colton, Nevada

WE DECLINED LUCIFER'S OFFER TO PUT US UP FOR THE NIGHT. Sharing an evening meal while discussing business is one thing, but making small talk over breakfast like we're one big happy family? I'll take a hard pass. I glance around the motel room. It was all we could access last minute. A single bed and a unit holding up a TV that only works intermittently. That's it aside from some basic wash facilities. Still, it's clean if the smell of Lysol is anything to go by. Even if the wallpaper is peeling in places, and the carpet's almost threadbare.

"You'll be careful, won't you, Paul?"

"Of course I will, baby girl."

"So, next weekend?"

"Yes, Laila. Next weekend, we can have dinner with your folks. Book somewhere expensive. My treat."

"They'll appreciate that."

"Good to know."

There's a pause while she considers how to phrase whatever she's about to say or ask. That means it's going to be something she knows I either won't like or appreciate.

"Do you think you'll ever want to give this up? You know. This other life."

"Nope." There's no hesitation with my response.

"Not even for me?"

"I'm a biker. I was born a biker. I'll die a biker."

"You're also a highly successful businessman."

"It's common for the two to go hand in hand, sweetheart. Many of the people I deal with fall into the same category as me. We like to deal with our own kind."

"Well, I still don't have to like it."

"You don't. But you do have to accept that it's who I am. And if you want to be with me, then this life is your future too."

"Okay." She huffs.

"Look, we spoke about this. You know what you agreed to. Are you changing your mind, baby girl? Because there's still time for you to run. You haven't gotten into bed with the devil just yet."

"No. I haven't changed my mind."

She sounds hesitant. It's because she's lying to me, and it's making my blade hand twitch. She doesn't accept who and what I am, no matter how much she insists that she does. And that's a problem. She wants to change me but I'm too set in my ways to be changed, plus, hand on heart, I don't want to. My daddy was a biker. And his daddy before him. I'm not sure how long it goes back for us Delaneys, but it's MC blood that flows through our veins.

It's then I realize I'm flicking my blade defensively, and I'm not even sure how it got in my hand. Dr. Matthews wouldn't be too pleased. My condition's deteriorating. I know it is. Those around me are meant to keep me calm. Sometimes. Most of the time. Laila has the opposite effect.

I'm feeling way too reactive to be dealing with this Nevada shit right now. I'm tired of fighting the demon in my head. It's easier at times just to give in. To let him win and take over. At least the normal part of me then gets some temporary respite. A chance to recuperate while he purges.

Sleep is a distant memory these days.

Being reactive also means making bad decisions. Should I have accepted the Sons' offer of back-up? Probably. We're walking into the unknown.

But I didn't. I can't go back on that now. And I have a very bad feeling about all this.

Bailey: *What time am I to expect you, Razr? I've selected a really nice necklace that displays my throat perfectly.*

Razr: *I might have to delay until tomorrow*

Bailey: *Why?*

Razr: *Got to pay someone else a visit today.*

Bailey: *Who?*

Razr: *Now that's not really got anything to do with you, has it, sweetheart?*

Bailey: *What time is this other calling? Why can't you come and find me afterward?*

Razr: *Are you so desperate for me to cut your throat, Bailey?*

Bailey: *Might as well get it over with. I told you already. I'm not running anywhere, Razr.*

Razr: *My meeting's at seven this evening. I can come find you afterward, all being well.*

Bailey: *What do you mean all being well?*
Razr: *Sometimes things don't go according to plan.*
Bailey: *Is your gut telling you that?*
Bailey: *Razr, is your gut telling you that?*
Razr: *I'll come find you when I'm done.*

Jaine: *How did things go with the Sons?*
Delaney: *It's not them. They want us to ally with them. I told them I'd need to discuss that with the Angels first and foremost.*
Jaine: *Nice of you to consider us.*
Delaney: *You're both, Jaine. You're an Angel, and The Exterminator is a Scorpion.*
Jaine: *True. Where and when are you meeting with Reaper?*
Delaney: *Why do you ask?*
Jaine: *I just want to keep the Irish informed on what's happening.*
Delaney: *Is that all?*
Jaine: *Why else would I be asking?*
Delaney: *Seven p.m. at their clubhouse.*
Jaine: *You'll let me know when you're done?*
Delaney: *Sure thing.*
Jaine: *Have you seen Bailey yet?*
Delaney: *Hopefully afterward.*
Jaine: *What do you mean hopefully?*
Jaine: *Delaney?*

I DON'T REPLY. I'M DONE TALKING. I TOSS THE PHONE DOWN ON THE bed and stare out the hotel room window at the three hogs parked up in the almost derelict car park. Yup. I've got a feeling tonight is not going to go as planned.

Not that I ever had a firm plan in the first place.

CHAPTER THIRTY

BAILEY

Bailey's Home, Colton, Nevada

I SHIELD MY EYES AS I STARE UP INTO THE CLOUDLESS BLUE SKY. The sun is sure as hell beating down today, and there isn't even a sniff of a breeze to offset this sweltering heat.

Lifting my tank top, I use its black surface to wipe the sweat off my face before massaging the top of my right arm. The dull ache makes it feel like it's about to drop off. I'm so out of practice. The last time I threw my stars was when I was in New York with a full audience and with Razr holding the target personally.

It feels like a lifetime ago now.

I'm worried, so I'm trying to burn off some nervous energy. The brief exchange with Razr has seen his unspoken bad gut feeling pass straight on to me.

"Nothing." I throw a shuriken.

"Must." I throw another.

"Happen." And another

"To." One more

"Him." My last one.

I jog across and pull them from the target that's been specially created to cater to my craft. There are two at the rear of the house, and both enable the wood to be slid out and replaced once the stars have reduced it to a pulp. It doesn't take long for that to happen. We then use the broken pieces for kindling for the fire in the sitting room inside.

I'm even more nervous as Jaine's not picking up her phone. Where is she? What has Ace said about the risks? It's not like I can phone him to find out. I don't have his number. And it's not like the contact details for the Angels' clubhouse will be listed on the internet.

They're leaving me with no choice. If no one's going to tell me what the hell is going on, then I'm going to have to go see for myself.

Guilt flows through me that I'm thinking of one man when I'm pretty much engaged to another. A good man. Well, if you can describe a murderer as being good.

I tell myself that it's human nature not to want someone to be killed in cold blood. But if it were anyone else, would I even care when it's pretty much an everyday occurrence in this life? I'm lying to myself. I know I am.

Still, rightly or wrongly, Paul Delaney is not going to die today.

Not on my watch.

"Where are you sneaking off to, Little Bee?"

Shit. My hand was just reaching for the front door. I squeeze my eyes shut, swearing silently to myself at having been caught. I'm going to have to tell a white lie. I just hope he doesn't see straight through it.

I turn around and stare at my daddy. The truth is, I thought he'd be gone. It's Saturday, and it's after six p.m. The clubhouse will be busy. Conor mentioned they've had some new cum sluts sign up. Fresh pussy, all eager to please. I'm sure my daddy still likes to get his dick wet from time to time.

I'm wearing my black leather pants and an unpatched leather jacket. My boots are the monstrosities that are good for riding a hog and for kicking the shit out of people. I figured I might need them instead of the heeled ones I usually wear in case I need to start running.

My stars are shoved down the inside of one, my phone down the other.

"I'm just going for a ride, Daddy. To blow the cobwebs away. See what's changed in the time I've been gone."

He frowns at me. He's looking for a chink in my armor. Something to let him know I'm actually a lying, two-faced scheming bitch. I do my best to give nothing away. I've learned from the master. He's got way more experience under his belt than me, though.

He nods slowly as he takes in my poker face. "Nothing's changed, Bee. You know things seldom ever do around here."

We stare at each other. He knows I'm hiding something. He just doesn't know what.

"Then I was going to see Raf. To talk about our engagement and our plans for the future."

I throw in that curveball.

His face immediately brightens at the mention of his future son-in-law. If my daddy could have been blessed with another son, he would have asked The Almighty for Raf. He's going to get his wish in a roundabout, second-hand kind of way.

"You two going to be dropping by the clubhouse? The brothers haven't seen you for a while, so I'd appreciate you showing your face down there soon."

"We'll see, Daddy. Anyway, I need to go." I lean over and kiss him on the cheek before turning and opening the front door. Once outside, I close it behind me. Leaning my back against the dark wood, I close my eyes and wait while my heart returns to a normal speed.

Daddy's right.

Nothing's changed in Colton. There's still just the same little row of shops that include a filling station, a post office, and a diner. It's more of a dispersed town than a buzzing, vibrant one. The properties are all spread out.

If people want to purchase anything of any consequence or go on a shopping spree, they simply head into Vegas. Around town, it's usually just kids that you see hanging around the diner, the older teens using the opportunity away from home and from under the watchful eyes of their folks to make out in the back seat of their cars. I'm guessing half the population of Colton was conceived in the back seat of one vehicle or another.

If you don't drive or ride, there's no point leaving your house. You can't get anywhere on foot. Everything's too far to walk.

My gaze drifts to the town church, which is painted white and stands tall. Its proud steeple stretches into the sky like an antenna that allows direct contact with The Almighty himself. It seems it's had a new coat of paint thrown over it in the time I've been gone, and there are a few more gravestones dotted around. A visual reminder that things have changed, and that, even in Colton, time does march on. That it doesn't stand still. Not for any of us.

And that, eventually, it runs out.

Father Murphy controls his flock from behind the raised pew inside those newly painted walls, handing out penances as he sees fit. Daddy attends every Sunday, but he doesn't insist the rest of us do, even though we're all born and raised Irish Catholic.

The only other building of any significance is the school located right beside the church. It's wearing the same fresh coat of paint. It must have been a two-for-one deal. It only caters to around fifty or so. More than enough seats for the youth population of Colton. Unlike Conor and me, Tadgh and Jay schooled in Vegas at a regular-sized school.

Colton itself is a biker town. Home to the Undertakers and the Sons. An invisible line has been drawn up this single street that separates both clubs. One MC controls one side and everything for miles beyond. The other MC controls the other. It's how it's always been for as far back as I can remember.

Reaper and my daddy used to be friends. Now they simply tolerate each other. My guess is they don't get into a fight because there's no point in rocking the boat. It's better the devil you know. Well, at least in Reaper's case.

In truth, both MC's illegal business ventures go way beyond Nevada. They've both had to expand and form alliances with other MCs and factions to survive and thrive. It's the way of the world these days, especially in remote areas like ours.

The townsfolk typically socialize at their respective clubhouses. Most men and boys of age are either a brother or friend of one of the two MCs.

A year or so back, the Undertakers started getting involved in trafficking. That's what caused the rift between Reaper and my daddy. From what I can gather, it's only gotten worse. Then again, Reaper is one mean motherfucker. Rumor has it he likes to fuck underage girls and boys. By all accounts, he's not fussy which. A hole's a hole. And he doesn't care if it's a willing one or not, either. Still. It's not going to stop me from paying his clubhouse an uninvited visit this evening. It's not like I have any real choice.

My hog kicks up dust into the desert air as I turn off the main drag and head in the direction of the Undertakers' clubhouse.

The Undertakers' Clubhouse, Colton, Nevada

"Abel. It's good to see you."

I take in one of the Undertakers' prospects as he walks across to the gated entrance of the clubhouse compound. Like most others, the external walls are grey, and the windows are sealed with metal and fitted with bars over the top. It's like these buildings have their own dress code.

Security cameras align with my bike. No doubt dozens of eyes on the inside are observing what's going on in real time on the outside. They're all watching with interest as the youngest daughter of the prez of the Sons of Satan stands just outside their hallowed ground.

"Good to see you too, Bee. What brings you out here?"

"I was just out for a ride and my hog started making a noise. I didn't want to go any farther in case it broke down. Yours was the closest place to pull over. You got someone who can take a look at her for me?"

Abel and I went to the town school together. Even though he's a few years younger than me, we always got along well enough. He's grown since, but he's still gangly and not entirely filled out yet. I watch as he runs his hand over his blonde buzzcut.

"The thing is, we're expecting company this evening, Bee." He frowns, looking thoughtful. He knows he can't really turn me away. If my bike breaks down, I'll be stranded. And the desert's not a kind place when you're stuck in the middle of nowhere. He knows that shit won't sit well with my daddy regardless of whether the clubs are allies these days or not. And he won't want to suffer his wrath.

"I don't need to come inside the clubhouse, Abel. I can wait in the garage while one of the brothers has a look at her for me."

I try my best to look like a useless female. I know my way around a hog, but he doesn't need to know that. Neither does he need to know that I've just loosened a couple of nuts on the back wheel.

He nods slowly, then turns to the building and lifts his hand to indicate to the watchers inside that the gates can be opened.

I listen as they clunk in response.

"Drive your hog around the side and into one of the bays. I'll get one of the brothers to take a look at her for you. If we can't get her fixed up tonight, you can borrow one of ours."

I smile gratefully at him. "I appreciate that, Abel. And I'm sure my daddy will too."

Driving into a bay, I kick down the stand. Switching off the engine, I inhale the familiar smell of fuel and grease.

I hear the other hogs approach the compound as I dismount. I've got here just in time. Leaving my full helmet in place, I turn to take in the riders as they approach.

I can't even begin to describe the feeling as I watch Paul Delaney ride the custom hog he's gotten himself a hold of up to the gates. He's not wearing a helmet, and his shortened strawberry blonde hair is tied back, displaying those perfect features of his.

A beautiful man on a beautiful machine.

My heart pounds in my chest. Even more so when his eyes connect with mine. Will he recognize me? Call me out? Walk over and slit my throat? It's worth it just to be able to see him again one last time.

His eyes drift over me slowly from top to bottom before connecting with mine once more. I'm wet. Soaked in fact. My nipples react under his silent scrutiny, crying out for his attention and pressing painfully against the fabric of my tank top. I close my eyes, imagining the smell of his sandalwood cologne and the salty taste of his skin.

When I open them, he's still staring at me. It's like he can read my mind and see all my smutty thoughts.

Turning away, I lean over deliberately and pretend to tuck my leather pants into my boots. I know he's watching. I can feel the heat of his stare on my ass.

What the fuck are you doing, Bee?

Wrong time. Wrong place. Wrong man.

I turn around just in time to catch his smirk before he rides into the compound and parks up at the entrance. It's impossible to look away as he dismounts the hog. The white Henley he's wearing emphasizes that unforgettable masculine form of his which is topped off by his leather cut. With his back to me, my eyes immediately drop to his ass, which is perfectly displayed in snug dark blue denim. Jesus Christ, has any man ever looked as good as Razr?

He knows I'm watching. That I'm transfixed. Like I could feel his stare, I'm sure he can feel mine. He starts walking, then pauses. Is he going to turn back around? It's as though the idea fleetingly crosses his mind. But he doesn't. I stare after his lean form as he continues walking before vanishing inside the clubhouse, flanked by Blaze and Knight.

CHAPTER THIRTY-ONE

RAZR

The Undertakers' Clubhouse, Colton, Nevada

I PUSH THE IMAGES OUT OF MY MIND. THE ONES DETAILING EXACTLY what I want to do to the girl in the leathers standing beside that custom hog of hers.

It's neither the time nor the place.

She seemed familiar, even though there's no way she can be. That perfect ass of hers as she put on that little show entirely for my benefit. I'm not too sure I'll ever get the visual of her bending over out of my goddamn head. At least not anytime soon. I've obviously gone way too long without pussy. Not even the new cum sluts in New York are piquing my dick's interest these days.

The sooner I cut Bailey's throat, the better. Once my brain transmits to my dick that she's no longer available, then maybe it'll show some interest in another female.

The trouble is, I'm not too sure she's guilty. So, the end result I had planned with her name on may no longer be on the cards. She's standing her ground way too determinedly. She's also refusing to run.

There's a reason for that.

I've got to admire her grit. She's got balls bigger than most men. And she's close. I can almost smell her. Almost taste her.

My dick twitches in my jeans at the thought of sinking into her warm wetness and feeling that perfect little pussy of hers clench around my dick as she screams out my name for the entire clubhouse to hear.

Once I'm done here, I'm going to find her. If she's not running, it's my thinking that she won't hide either. This defiance isn't bravado on her part.

I walk into the Undertaker's clubhouse. It's the same as any other.

Grey. Bare. Basic. Wipe clean. Bulletproof where it needs to be and with furniture that's disposable and easy to replace.

It's early Saturday night, and the air's already laced with the smell of pussy and tequila. The atmosphere is frigid. It turned that way the moment we walked in. It's the opposite of the receptive and hospitable welcome we received from the Sons. And there's a reason for that too.

These fuckers are as guilty as sin.

My gut's telling me everything about this place is all wrong. There's a thick tension. On the surface, they're all trying to portray a brotherhood where there is none. It's a forced camaraderie—an act. A display likely for our benefit.

"Razr."

He approaches me from behind. I immediately tense before slowly turning around. He's a backstabber, that's for sure. You should never approach a brother you've never met silently and from behind unless you mean to do them harm. Or unless you have a death wish.

"Reaper."

I take in the prez of the Undertakers. Like Lucifer, he's in his fifties. But unlike him, he's not quite so well-preserved. His short, dark hair is thinning, his torso is thick and stocky, and his skin wears a sallow complexion with a noticeable tinge of yellow that portrays ill-health and liver issues.

By all accounts, Reaper has no old lady or kids. I heard he prefers to stick to the cum sluts. The younger, the better. Some even suggest that he helps himself regularly to the kids he supposedly helps traffick these days.

Sounds about right. He has that look about him.

"At your service."

He smiles. It doesn't reach his eyes. It also adds nothing complimentary to his overall look. His teeth are yellower than his skin, and his eyes are a watery blue. The right one twitches as he attempts to stare me down. Many have tried. None have succeeded.

No one ever will.

"It's loud in here. Let's you and I find someplace we can have a chat in private." His fake smile widens. Even though half a dozen goons flank him, I realize he's talking about just me and him. Well, I didn't refuse a dance with the devil. I'm not about to refuse a dance with the grim reaper either.

The clubhouse falls eerily silent. The calm before the storm? Aside from the men at his side, the rest of the brothers look unsure of themselves, glancing awkwardly at each other and shuffling from foot to foot. It's my guess they don't get a vote here. Not on anything. They're simply told what to do by the man in front of me. It's also my guess that they're not entirely in agreement with what's about to go down.

Because mark my words something is about to go down.

I nod at Blaze and Knight to let them know that I agree to what Reaper wants. Just so they know not to react.

"Sure thing, Reaper. Lead the way."

He nods towards the door at the rear of the room. He walks. I follow. I'm not taking my eyes off this shifty motherfucker unless I'm given no choice.

THEIR COUNCIL OFFICE IS CLUTTERED AND UNTIDY, THE WOODEN table displaying their club logo—the grim reaper carrying a scythe—is covered in dust and grime. Figures. It's clear he takes care of his club as well as he does his health.

"Take a seat."

He watches as I do just that, sitting down on the one facing him.

"So, I hear you're visiting Colton over some gun issue."

"You want to admit you're selling to the Mexicans?" I just come right out with it.

"I'm not confirming or denying anything at this stage." He leans back in his chair wearing an arrogant smirk.

"You either are or you aren't, Reaper. On the basis that my suspicions are correct, let me just be clear on one thing. The Irishmen are businesspeople. Regardless of what you may or may not have heard about them, they're also fair. They aren't saying you can't sell your weapons. They're saying you can't sell to their existing customer base. Anything over and above that is fair game."

He laughs out loud, and I try not to grimace when the smell of his breath reaches my nose. Going by the rancid stench, it's obvious his insides are rotten to the core, just like his soul.

"Well, you see, Razr, our products are almost as good as theirs, and they're way cheaper. The customers around here? Well, they like a bargain, and who can blame them?"

"We both know it doesn't work like that, Reaper. A lot of investment goes into building these relationships at the front end. The Dusters don't give their time freely. That shit comes with a hefty price tag attached, and you know it. Do you want to pay personally for them having wasted their valuable time by treading on their toes and selling guns to their customers?"

He slams his fist down on the table, causing dust mites to launch into the air. "Now, you listen here, Razr. The Undertakers are just transporting. We don't manufacture nothing. This isn't our war."

I lean back on my chair. My demon is now screaming either for my blade or for his throat—ideally both.

"So, you're in an alliance with someone? Someone with a death wish who wants to take on the Irish mob?"

He shrugs. "We all have to earn a living somehow. Most other factions use the MCs for transporting. That's all we're doing. Nothing more."

"You on a percent? Of the gun sales?"

"Twenty-five."

"Then you can't class that as transport."

"The Scorpions and the Angels are on a percent of the Irish gun sales."

"Correct, but we're not treading on any toes. We've built our customer base from scratch. The right way. Honorably. We haven't stolen it from a brother by under-cutting them with lower price, lower-quality weapons."

There's a pause. He's going to say something I'm not going to like. He shuffles on his chair uncomfortably.

"Here's the thing, Razr. My supplier doesn't want to pull out. The sales are way too lucrative."

"And let me guess, your supplier is also working on increasing their range. So they offer exactly what we're doing."

"They're looking into it, yes."

"They can't sell without transport."

"Nope."

"And you realize that the sole reason your supplier is giving you such a high percentage is because you're the ones putting your neck on the line with the Irish by fronting this shitshow?"

"That may well be the case, but we need the revenue. The Undertakers is a large club. We have a lot of hungry mouths to feed."

"Then you find ways to earn a living without making enemies like the rest of us have to."

"Are you saying the Scorpions are an enemy of the Undertakers?" He narrows his eyes at me.

"I'm saying that if you don't quit what you're doing, the Undertakers will make an enemy of the Angels, the Irish mob, and the Scorpions." I just say it how it is.

He shakes his head. I know what's coming.

"Well, I'm sorry to have to tell you this, but we're not pulling out. We're widening our range and increasing our coverage. The reason for this private discussion of ours is that my supplier has asked me to make a verbal offer to the Scorpions. For you to join our alliance and distribute for us on the east coast."

I decide to play his game for now.

"Who's your supplier?"

"I can't tell you."

"How can I make an informed decision on behalf of my club if I don't know who they are?"

"All in good time."

"What would be involved in this alliance? What would you expect from the Scorpions?"

"Transport."

"Of?"

"Weapons."

"Is that all?"

"And people."

"What type of people?"

"Women and children." He smiles at me and licks his lips, his thoughts no doubt drifting to what he'd like to do with the latter.

"Sorry. We're not getting involved in trafficking."

"Shame. There's nothing tastier than a piece of innocent young flesh."

"You sick fuck," I hiss. My chair falls to the floor as I stand, my hand automatically reaching for my blade so I can slice and dice this twisted asshole. The problem is, he's already prepared for this reaction. He fully expected it. He pulls a Glock from the back of his pants and points it at me.

"Now, now, Razr. You need to calm down."

"My sister was trafficked, you sick motherfucker." I point my blade at him, but I don't make any attempt to move forward. He'll just blow my brains out, and that isn't going to help anyone. Least of all me. I'll have to bide my time. Be patient. Something my alter ego is no good at.

He nods.

"I heard all about that, and I'm sorry, Razr. I truly am." The asshole doesn't mean a word of that apology. He's not fucking sorry at all. It was probably his supplier behind the whole damn thing.

"Boys. Take his weapon, bind him, and then show our friend Razr here down to the cooler."

Two of his men have entered the room. I can almost smell the shit in their pants as they look at me. To bind me, they have to touch me. I can tell this yellow-bellied pair don't want to do that.

"NOW!" Reaper yells. They do as they're told, almost apologetically.

"What happens now?"

"Now I have to convince you to join us."

"And if I refuse?"

"You then become an obstacle." He shrugs.

"And as part of your twenty five percent cut your backer's instructed you to permanently remove anyone who gets in their way. Is that it?"

"Something like that."

"My men?"

"They'll be released without harm. You have my word on that."

I nod. It looks like I'm not getting out of here alive. My gut was right after all. It's game over.

THE COOLER IS NOTHING MORE THAN AN OVERSIZED CELLAR located down a flight of stairs underneath their clubhouse. It's a dark, windowless concrete prison and easy to hose down. There's a trough built into the floor, which leads to a drain to deal with blood and any other bodily fluids. On the far wall is a door that I'm guessing leads to the outside for the evidence to be disposed of covertly. Why make a mess dragging shit like that across the clubhouse floor?

There are no wash or toilet facilities, which means anyone who comes down here won't ever see the light of day again.

Riggings are fitted to the walls in various locations so shackles can be attached. That's precisely what they do to me.

I'm forced to sit. The floor is damp, and its coldness immediately starts to sink into my bones. It's like death itself is wrapping me in his icy grip in preparation for what's about to take place.

Still, today's as good a day as any to die.

No words are spoken until both his men leave the dank space. It's clear the fucker works alone and only uses the men as heavies.

I inhale deeply. It smells of death—a combination of copper, shit, and piss. The only sound is the slow, steady drip of the water coming down from the kitchen space overhead.

"I won't ally with you, Reaper, so you'll have to do what you need to."

He forces a snicker as he slowly paces the floor, his weapon clenched in his hand. He's obviously not thrilled at having to do what needs to be done today. His supplier is probably leaving him with no option. He has to deal with anyone who stands in their way. To pick them off one by one. It's easy for them to dictate from the comfort of their executive chairs.

"You don't even want to discuss it?"

"The Scorpions will never get involved in trafficking."

He sighs before running a frustrated hand through his greasy hair. Did he really expect me to agree to our involvement? Maybe he thought I'd do anything to save my neck, same as he obviously would.

I won't.

I'd also never betray the Angels or the Irish, just as they'd never cross the Scorpions.

Regret flows through me fleetingly, knowing that the Delaney line will die with me. My sister's kids will be O'Connells. Dusters.

The Iron Scorpions has had a Delaney at its helm for generations. Now it will pass to Blaze. My VP. Its future will be in his hands and pass down through his kin.

It's my only regret. A wife. A family.

As much as I can feel the cold sinking into my bones, there's also a realization. If I get out of here alive, I know exactly what I need to do.

It's when you realize you have no future, it then dawns on you what you want.

Who you want.

CHAPTER THIRTY-TWO

BAILEY

The Undertakers' Clubhouse, Colton, Nevada

"TAKE MY HOG AND JUST BRING HER BACK TOMORROW, BEE. I'M sorry none of the brothers can look at yours until then. But it's Saturday night. Most of them are already worse for wear and have their hands kind of full."

He snickers. By hands full, he means with cum sluts, as no doubt the debauchery is already well underway inside.

"It's no problem, Abel. You mind if I get myself a drink before I head back on the road?"

"Sure thing. Reaper's otherwise engaged at the moment as far as I know."

"Yeah? What's he been up to these days?"

We leave the bay and stroll towards the clubhouse entrance.

He shrugs. "Who knows? He never tells anyone anything

anymore. He's always shut away in that office of his making secret calls."

I stop and frown at him before resuming walking. "So, there's no council voting? No church?"

He shakes his head as we open the door, then make our way through the throng of people towards the bar. Some look surprised to see me in here. There isn't one person who won't know exactly who I am, that's for sure. They stare briefly, then just get back on with whatever they were doing. I'm one of them. Family. Closer than blood in most cases.

Even if I am from a different club.

"It's more of a dictatorship these days. Everyone's just expected to do as they're told. No questions asked. The handful who back Reaper are only doing so because they're being handsomely rewarded. He's buying their loyalty. From what I hear, most of the council members aren't happy at the road the club's being taken down."

"I've heard some rumors. I wasn't sure how true any of them were."

"If they're bad, then they're true. And that's the problem. A lot of the brothers are family men. It doesn't sit right with them some of the shit that's been going down."

"So why don't they do something about it?"

"No one will stand up to the prez. And apparently, he's also now got the backing of this new organization. No one wants to risk their lives or those of their family and friends by standing up to them both. Rumor has it anyone who does is signing themselves up for an automatic death sentence."

I take a seat at the bar.

"Two bottles of water, please." Abel orders on our behalf from the heavily-inked biker who's drawn the short straw and is having to play barman on a Saturday night.

"Sounds like you need a new prez."

He nods as he takes a long drink of water. "Yup. Folks here want exactly what the Sons offer. Loyalty. Trust. A proper brotherhood. The opportunity to have a say in how the club operates and the direction it's heading. I'm sure many would be tempted to jump ship, but no one wants to feel the wrath of Reaper."

"Yeah, he sure does hate my daddy."

He shakes his head. "Not sure it's that, Bee. I think he's just jealous. He wants to be like Lucifer. Have respect and loyalty from his men. But he's too self-centered and controlling. He's also too greedy for power and money."

"Well, my daddy likes power and money just as much as the next man." I chuckle.

"Yeah, but he distributes the rewards fairly and evenly. Reaper keeps the big bucks for himself and his right-hand men. The rest of us just get tossed the loose shrapnel."

As much as this information has been beneficial, my gut is telling me something's not right. I need to find Razr.

And fast.

"So, who were the visitors?" I try to come across as though I'm just making small talk.

"Some prez from a New York charter."

"They off talking somewhere?"

"As far as I know, Reaper was planning on encouraging them to ally with the Undertakers and our new supplier."

My blood runs cold. Is Reaper trying to convince Razr to get involved in trafficking? Does he not know what happened to Sarah? There's no way Razr would ever allow the Scorpions to become involved in that sort of wrongdoing, no matter how lucrative.

"And what if he doesn't agree?"

Abel shrugs then drags his finger across his throat.

"You mind if I use the restroom, Abel?"

"Sure thing, Bee."

He's now distracted by a pretty young cum slut. He's not patched in yet, so he's not allowed to fuck them, but it won't stop him from lining them up in readiness for when he can dick them all one after the other then start all over again.

FINALLY, SHE ANSWERS HER PHONE.

"Jaine?"

"Where are you?"

"In the disgusting ladies restroom in the Undertakers' clubhouse."

I wrinkle my nose at the smell of urine. Guessing the cum sluts don't do much cleaning around here. Then again, most are at the age where they've only just learned how to tie their shoelaces.

"Jesus Christ, Bailey. What the hell are you thinking?"

"I'm not in any danger, Jaine. They know me here, and they know my daddy. They wouldn't dare lay a finger on me. I pretended my hog had issues and that here was the closest port of call. They bought it. Dumb fucks."

"It was a stupid move to make on your own."

"Well, I had to take matters into my own hands. I haven't been able to get a hold of you, and there was no one else for me to call to let me know what was happening. Are you driving?"

"Yes. I'm in the cage."

"It's a bit late at night for you to be out on the road given your condition."

"I'm pregnant, Bailey. I'm not a goddamn invalid."

"Still, you've only got a few weeks left."

"I've got seven. Anyway, Ace is on his way."

"He's your boyfriend, right?"

"Yes."

"I'm looking forward to meeting him."

"I was hoping you never would."

"Why? It's not like I'm going to make a play for him like I did with Razr." I snicker.

"Not like that. I was just hoping you wouldn't be dumb enough to seek out trouble deliberately. It turns out I was wrong. You are dumb enough."

"Unrequited love," I whisper.

"What?"

"I'd do anything for my unrequited love."

She sighs. "I understand, and I have to respect you for that. Delaney doesn't deserve that sort of commitment from you. Not after what he did."

"You're right. He doesn't, but I'm here anyway."

"Did you see him?"

"Outside the clubhouse."

"Did he see you?"

"Yes, but I was wearing a full helmet, so he didn't recognize me. He's in a meeting with Reaper. According to one of the prospects, the Undertakers are making an offer to the Scorpions to ally."

"An alliance involving what exactly?"

"Weapons and trafficking."

"Delaney will never accept that offer."

"I know."

"So, Reaper will have shown his cards, Delaney will have turned him down, which may mean he's not getting out of there alive."

"That was my thinking. How long before Ace gets here?"

"One hour, tops."

"Where are you going?"

"I'm currently heading to Nevada. ETA one hour."

"Jaine, you shouldn't be coming here. It's way too dangerous."

"Love."

"What?"

"I may not love him the way you do, but I still love his troubled ass in my own way. I'm not about to stand back and watch Delaney get himself killed all because he's an idiot and he's not thinking with a sane head."

"So, you'd risk your life for him?"

"Of course I would, Bailey. He'd do the same for me."

"Listen, Jaine. I need to go. I have another call coming in."

I SWEAR SILENTLY TO MYSELF. TO ANSWER OR NOT TO ANSWER. I know he'll interrogate me. Then again if I don't take the call, he'll just hunt me down until he finds me.

"Bee, where are you?"

"Raf."

"Liam mentioned you were coming to see me, but you never showed up. He's worried. I'm worried. What the hell is going on, querida?"

"Nothing's going on."

"Bee, what are you hiding from me?"

"Nothing."

"Don't lie to me, Bee. Please." His voice sounds pained.

"Noth…"

"TELL ME!"

I squeeze my eyes shut. This isn't turning out how I planned. I was supposed to just waltz in here, save Razr's insane ass, then head off into the sunset and get on with the rest of my life.

With Raf.

"Promise me you won't tell my daddy?"

"I can't do that."

"Promise me, Raf, or I won't tell you."

"You're asking me to betray a man I think of like a father."

"I'm asking you not to betray your future wife, Raf. Guess it kind of trumps that."

"Fine, I won't say anything. Now, where are you?"

"I'm at the Undertakers' clubhouse."

"What the hell are you doing there?"

"Helping a friend."

"What friend?"

"Someone I met in New York."

"What friend, Bee?"

"Raf. I don't…."

"I've heard the Iron Scorpions are in Colton. The prez, Razr. Is this the friend you're referring to, Bee?"

His voice is deadly quiet. Menacing. Most of the time, I forget that Raf is a high ranker in La eMe. That he's a lethal killer in his own right, just like Razr. To me, he's just always been Raf.

I don't reply.

"It's him, isn't it." It's not a question. It's a statement.

"I don't know what you mean." I'm fully aware I'm just digging myself into a deeper hole. Lying's a fool's game.

"DON'T FUCKING LIE TO ME, BEE!"

There's a pause. I squeeze my eyes shut again. Raf hardly ever swears at me. He's a gentleman like that. Always has been.

Until now, that is.

"You ran to the east coast. I guess you ended up in New York. Am I right?

Guilt flows through me. I can hear the raw pain in his voice at the realization. Right now? I fucking hate myself for hurting him.

"AM. I. RIGHT. BEE?"

"I just don't want anything to happen to him, Raf. That's all. I swear that's all," I whisper.

"So, we save his neck, we sort out this gun issue, and then he goes back to New York."

"Yes."

"And you stay here. With me."

"Yes."

"And you'll forget all about him."

"Yes. That's exactly what I want. More than anything."

There's a pause.

"I'm on my way. Stay where you are and don't move."

"You can't just show up here, Raf."

"Watch me."

CHAPTER THIRTY-THREE

JAINE

On route to Colton, Nevada

HAVING BEEN ON THE RECEIVING END OF A LECTURE FOR THE PAST five or so minutes I finally butt in.

"Well, what was I supposed to do? Just sit back and do nothing, Ace?"

"That's exactly what you were supposed to do, PJ. Me and Clay have got this covered. You don't need to be trying to save the damn world when you're about to give birth."

"I've still got a week to go," I mumble. I have to keep remembering to tell other people I still have seven weeks to go. Only me and Ace can ever know that truth.

"A week."

"Maybe longer. Most women go over their due date in their first pregnancy."

"You're not most women, plus, you've been in pain, and the doctor said…"

"I know what she said, Ace. I was there. I'm pregnant, not hard of hearing. Anyway, I'm on my way now. I'm closer to Colton than Rising, so there's no point in me turning around."

"You deliberately didn't call me until it was too late to do that."

"Yup. You know me."

"Yes, I do know you. My frustrating as hell woman."

"Your frustrating as hell round woman. You still love me, though, right? Even though I'm the size of a whale?"

"There's just more of you to love, sweetheart. Anyway, you're the same as you always were. You just look like you're trying to smuggle a basketball up your tank top these days."

We both snicker. It's true. I'm still thin. Too thin, some might say. From behind, no one would even know I was pregnant.

"Well, at least I have tits for once."

"Yup, you do." He laughs out loud causing me to laugh in response.

"Make the most of them, Ace, as once this baby's born, they'll be back to being pretty much non-existent."

"It's what I love about you most, PJ. Your non-existent ass and tits."

"You're an asshole."

"An asshole who loves you, sweetheart."

"I love you too, Ace."

"And, PJ?"

"Yup."

"Do not under any circumstances go near the Undertakers' clubhouse. You hear me?"

"Hearing you loud and clear, Prez."

I PULL OVER, HAVING JUST WATCHED MY PHONE FALL INTO THE footwell because it vibrated so many times. Who and what now?

Padraig: *Jaine?*
Jaine: *Jesus Christ. Dylan. You've messaged me thirteen times in a row!*
Padraig: *Yes, because you weren't answering, and I know Ace isn't home. I was worried about you, darlin'.*
Jaine: *I'm fine. I'm in the cage. I pulled over as I could smell burning. It turns out my phone's set on fire due to the number of times you've tried contacting me.*
Padraig: *Very funny. Where exactly are you heading on a Saturday evening?*

I don't answer, hoping he'll move on to something else. Then I won't have to admit where I'm going.

Padraig: *Jaine? Answer me.*

This time I don't even get a chance to respond.

Padraig: *Jesus Christ, Jaine. Please tell me you're not heading where I think you are?*
Jaine: *I'm around one hour away.*
Padraig: *Jaine, you promised me.*
Jaine: *And I'm sorry for breaking that promise, but I can't let anything happen to either of them, Dyl.*
Padraig: *And I can't let anything happen to you. Don't you fucking understand that?*
Jaine: *I'm sorry. I didn't tell you as I knew you'd try to talk me out of it. You'd tell me I was being reckless and stupid.*
Padraig: *You are being reckless and stupid. I'm so fucking*

angry right now. You have no idea just how much. You're pregnant. You've only got seven weeks to go.

Jaine: *I'm still able to handle a gun, Dyl.*

Padraig: *And what if you have to run? What if you've no choice but to run, Jaine? What if you trip? Fall over? Hurt yourself? Hurt your baby? I need to speak to Eoin.*

Jaine: *Why?*

Padraig: *Because this is Duster business too, darlin'. We should never have let the MCs handle this on their own. I'm taking the next flight to Vegas. I'll see you when I get there.*

Jaine: *Don't you dare come here.*

Padraig: *I said I'll see you when I get there.*

Jaine: *Jesus Christ.*

Padraig's Apartment, Hudson Yards, New York

"Paddy? Is everything okay? It's almost midnight."

"Eoin, I've done something. Two things before I go on. I need you to promise me two things. The first one is, please just *try* to understand why I did what I did. The second one is, please don't tell Ma or Da."

"I can't promise you either."

"Then I'm not telling you."

"Paddy, we're not children anymore. If this is Duster-related business, you can't simply refuse to tell me."

"I can, and I am."

"Paddy…"

"Promise me, Eoin."

"Fine. I promise."

"I've been in contact with Jaine."

There's a pause. Is he upset? Disappointed? Angry?

"How long?" His voice is calm. Way too calm.

Shite. It's the latter.

Do I admit the truth? That it's been since just after she moved back to Rising? That by playing the victim card and waving an empty whiskey bottle in his face, I coerced our Dyl into letting me message her while pretending to be him?

Or do I lie and say it's only been a recent thing? See, it's my thinking that won't wash. Eoin may ask to see the message exchanges. He'd then know straight away that our Dyl would have needed to have undergone a personality transplant several months ago for him to have taken part.

I'm praying Eoin doesn't ask to see them. It may unearth a secret I'm not sure Jaine would want him to know about. In fact, there's no may about it. It definitely would and I'm not sure she'd take kindly to him knowing about her extra-curricular activities.

"Six months, give or take."

"So, the whole time she's been away?"

"Pretty much."

There's a loud clatter in the background. He's just thrown something or cleared the surface of something in a fit of rage. He's just like Da in that respect.

"Why, Paddy?"

"Why ask a question when you already know the answer? Because I love her."

"But you're engaged to someone else."

"I realize that. And I've accepted my fate like the good little Duster that I am, but I still need Jaine in my life. I will not do without her."

"You have to."

"Why? I've agreed to marry the Sicilian. Jaine's my condition."

"What do you mean your condition?"

"I will not give her up. If you attempt to force the issue, I'll call off the engagement to Sophia."

"Da would kill you with his bare hands."

"And I'd embrace it, brother. If I can't have Jaine in my life, then I'll welcome death into it with open fucking arms."

"Paddy…"

"That's my condition. Take it or leave it. I message her. Nothing more. She thinks I'm Dylan. I can't let her go. I won't let her go. She's my normal. She's my daily fucking bread. My sunshine on a rainy day. She holds my heart in her fucking hands, Eoin, and she always will. I will never let go of her completely, so don't ask me to. Do not push me to decide between Jaine and the family as you may be surprised by my decision."

I'm breathing hard. I'm not letting her go. I'm not going back to drowning my sorrows in countless bottles of whiskey. She keeps me sane. I need her in my life. She is my fucking life.

Even if I'm not hers.

"But she doesn't even know it's you."

"It's still better than nothing."

"She'll never speak to you again if she finds out, Paddy."

"She doesn't want to speak to me ever again anyway. It's not like I stand to lose anything. She doesn't love me back, remember?"

There's another pause. Has he hung up?

"Moving forward, I'll have it set up so I see everything. And I mean everything."

"Agreed."

"By telling me, you've made me complicit in all of this deceit of yours, Paddy."

"And what do you care? In your mind, Jaine is nothing but a biker chick with the mouth of a sailor. You don't even like her. Who knew, given we look so alike, that the type of women we go for would be completely opposite? Me. Jaine. You. Candice. Anyway, what do you care if, when she finds out, which we both know she inevitably will, that she'll just hate you more than she already does?"

"She hates me?"

"Yes. I'm not sure why. Does it matter?"

"I guess not."

"Anyway, she's in trouble. I want to go to her, Eoin."

"What sort of trouble? Paddy, given what we've just discussed, you're not going anywhere near her. Messages only. We've just agreed."

"Will you go, then?"

"Explain."

JAINE

On route to Colton, Nevada

"Jesus Christ, here we go."

I mumble it to myself as I roll my eyes. I'm about to answer on handsfree but decide against it. From experience, conversations with this asshole only ever make my blood pressure spike. It's safer to pull over.

"Eoin."

"Jaine, what's going on?"

"Quit hissing at me."

"TELL ME."

"And quit yelling. You hiss, you yell, I hang up. You got me?"

There's a pause, no doubt while he tries to rein himself the fuck in.

"Jaine, what's going on?"

"That's better. So Dyl's told you?"

"Dyl? Yes. Of course. Dyl's told me."

"You sound unsure. Forgotten your own brother's name? Heavy night?"

"Jaine, what the fuck is going on?"

"Did you just swear, Mr. O'Connell? Are my bad habits rubbing off on you? Maybe we should stop speaking so much. Better still, maybe we should stop speaking completely."

"Do you really hate me that much, Jaine?"

"I don't hate you."

"Dyl said you do."

"Well, I don't. To hate someone requires a lot of effort. You're not worth that amount of effort."

"I see."

Those two words are spoken so quietly that suddenly I feel guilty. That was uncalled for. It's not like me to be such a nasty piece of work no matter what someone's done. I seldom, if ever, hold a grudge. Only ever this one. With him. For obvious and deserved reasons. But it's still no excuse to be so deliberately goddamn hurtful.

"Eoin…"

"It's fine, Jaine. I get it. I deserve it. What I did…"

"Didn't deserve that response. I'm pregnant. I'm tetchy. I'm worried and, well, it was uncalled for. I'm sorry."

There's a silence. It's not strained. It's like some sort of truce is reached. Well, at least for now, and at least for the duration of this conversation.

"Can you fill me in on what's happening, please?"

"Delaney may be in trouble. I think we've all underestimated the Undertakers, or at least their prez and the faction he has behind him."

"Who's the faction?"

"I'm not sure anyone knows the answer to that question at this stage."

"Was this the situation you were going to handle by yourself?"

"That very same one. And I am. Ace and Clay are on their way there, and I'm also on my way there. It was Dylan who got all worked up about it."

"You're pregnant."

"Go to the top of the class. Has anyone ever told you Dusters that you're very observant?"

He ignores my smart mouth.

"We agreed the Angels wouldn't get involved."

"We have no choice. The Dusters and the rest of the Scorpions are too far away. Plus, Ace was local."

"You weren't."

"Nope. Taken me six hours so far."

"Why?"

"It's what you do when you care about people, Eoin."

"So, you're doing all this for Paul Delaney?" He sounds surprised. He's probably wondering why I would go out of my way to help even though there's nothing in it for me.

"And for Ace."

"And what will you be able to do when you get there?"

"Shoot the goddamn fuckers in the head."

He laughs, and it grates on my last nerve. I nearly throw our short-term truce out the window.

"You're hardly The Exterminator, Jaine."

I'd give anything to be able to tell this asshole the role I play in my spare time. The admittance is on the very tip of my tongue. One day. I need to bide my time. Plus, I need to say it when I can see his reaction. Where's the fun otherwise?

"That may be so, but I can still handle a weapon."

"In your condition you may be more of a hindrance than a help."

"At least I'm here."

“You told me you could handle it.”

“Touché.”

“I’ll be there by morning.”

“There’s no need.”

“There’s every need, Jaine. We shouldn’t have left it to the MCs to deal with.”

“It may well be all over bar the shouting by then.”

“Maybe so, but I think the Dusters still need to make their presence known, even if it’s to make sure the situation is completely razed.”

“Make your presence felt, you mean.”

“That too. I’ll see you in the morning, Jaine.”

“With Dylan? He sounded pretty insistent.”

“I’ll be traveling alone.”

CHAPTER THIRTY-FOUR

BAILEY

The Undertakers Clubhouse, Colton, Nevada

I EXIT THE CLUBHOUSE VIA THE BACK ENTRANCE. MY PHONE immediately flashes.

Raf: *Where, Bee?*
Bailey: *Are you able to meet me at the containers?*
Raf: *The ones at the rear of the compound?*
Bailey: *Yes.*
Raf: *Okay. And is it just you and me against the whole MC?*
Bailey: *For now, yes.*
Raf: *Do you have a death wish or something?*
Bailey: *It's better than involving the Sons and having civil war break out in Colton as a result. Plus, no one's touched me or threatened me in any way. If the Sons come in here all*

guns blazing, they'll be seen as the ones starting whatever war it is we'll all inevitably end up in.

Raf: *Razr didn't bring any back-up with him?*

Bailey: *He asked his two men to stand down before leaving with Reaper. They're being held somewhere. They'll be being watched. If they make a move to leave, every brother in the clubhouse will follow them or face the wrath of Reaper if they don't. Either that or they'll just shoot them both in the head. Ace is on his way. And his VP.*

Raf: *Prez of the Angels?*

Bailey: *Yes. They form the third part of the alliance with the Scorpions and the Irish.*

Raf: *Should we wait for them? I don't want anything to happen to you, querida.*

Bailey: *We can at least get in position. Wait for them there. Only act beforehand if something kicks off.*

Raf: *You're sure Reaper will deal with your prez out there?*

Bailey: *He's not my prez, Raf. And yes. He won't deal with him in the cooler while the clubhouse is at full capacity. And he probably won't want to leave it until morning.*

Raf: *I've just parked up. It'll take me fifteen minutes to walk there. Don't move, Bee.*

THE ONLY LIGHT SOURCE COMES FROM A RUSTED METAL DRUM THAT holds the last dying flames of the fire that's been lit on top. The flickering blue and yellow embers throw just enough light for me to make out my breath in the frigid air. I inhale the smell of burning wood and gasoline. It's a comforting smell—a familiar one.

I can hear and also feel the steady hum of the music coming from the clubhouse beneath my feet. It's joined by the occasional holler coming from a brother and the loud, forced laughter of a cum slut as she pretends to find one of their unfunny stories funny.

No one noticed me walk out the door. Or if they did, they didn't pay me any attention. Most if not all of them are inebriated, and Abel was too busy flirting with a cum slut who looked underage.

I glance around. There are a dozen or so containers out back—a mixture of old and new and in varying sizes and colors. Most have been graffitied, likely by the teenage kids who hang around the clubhouse because there's not much else to do in Colton. And also because their folks are probably inside.

This will be a popular making-out spot during the day and into the early evening for sure. Young girls will be looking for their first kiss, and post-pubescent boys will be looking for their first lay.

The Undertaker brothers use these structures as temporary accommodation when they've drunk too much to ride home safely and when the clubhouse itself is at full capacity. It's the only area that hasn't got security cameras. I guess Reaper figured no one would be stupid enough to venture near them considering who they housed at various times of the day and night. Then again, there aren't many outsiders who would know that they don't fall under the club's top-of-the-range surveillance system.

That's why it's one of their favorite spots for dealing with any walking, talking problems. No cameras. No witnesses. No proof.

Me? Well, of course I'm stupid enough to go near them. Since it's still early and given the level of intoxication most of the brothers in the clubhouse seem to be aiming for this evening, it's unlikely they'll be venturing out here anytime soon.

Anyway, stupid or not, I don't really have any choice. Right now, I'm the only lifeline Razr's got. At least until the others get here. Blaze and Knight can't do anything. If they dare move, they'll be as good as dead.

Razr should have accepted the back-up from the Sons. Fool. Of course, he wasn't to know about Reaper. That he's a disloyal motherfucker who flicks the bird at the shared outlaw badge. Or that he's working for others who remain invisible.

My phone vibrates in my pocket—an unknown number. I answer, and I'm met with the sound of silence initially.

"Bailey." The voice is deep, dark, and dangerous.

"Who is this?"

"It's Ace."

"Did your insane old lady tell you she's on her way here?"

"She did, and she's been told to stand back."

"You think she'll listen?"

"Nope."

"Where are you?"

"Close. We parked the hogs. We're on our way on foot."

"You been here before?"

"Not personally, but I know someone who has. Where are we meeting?"

"At the containers towards the rear of the compound. Head for them."

He disconnects the call, and I've no sooner put my phone back in my pocket when I'm grabbed around the middle, a hand placed firmly over my mouth.

"Don't scream, querida," a familiar, soothing voice whispers in my ear.

Relief flows through me as I turn in Raf's arms. I try to speak, but his mouth instantly covers mine, his tongue stroking deep. Hot. Demanding. Groaning against his lips, I snake my arms around his neck as he fists my hair, tilting my head back so he can eat me alive.

Dropping his other hand, he cups my pussy through my leather pants. A surge of desire flows through me, and I instinctively grind against his possessive touch.

"What the fuck are you doing, Raf?" I whisper against his mouth between his hungry kisses.

"Touching what's mine. I so want to fuck you, Bee. You want that?"

"What, right here, right now?"

He chuckles. "When we get back to your place. Or we can go somewhere else. Tell me you want to feel my dick inside you, querida. Or are you still going to insist that we wait until our wedding night?"

He peppers kisses down my throat before the flat of his tongue trails its entire length. I cling to his shoulders. Maybe it's the life and death situation we find ourselves in that's caused this adrenaline spike. But I want him to fuck me. And I haven't wanted anyone to fuck me since Razr.

I gaze up into the dark, lust-filled eyes of my soon-to-be fiancé.

"Yes, I want that, Raf."

He growls as he pulls my front against his now prominent erection.

"If anything happens tonight, I need your mouth to be the last thing I taste and my thoughts to be consumed entirely with fucking you. Nothing else matters. No one else matters. Only you, Bee."

Our hearts are beating in a wild but synchronized rhythm.

"I love you so much," he whispers against my hair.

"Nothing will happen, Raf." I whisper my response as a feeling of intense guilt envelopes me.

This isn't his fight, but he's come here for me. Because he loves me. He's just told me I'm the most important person in his world, and I've used his love for me to drag him here, put him in danger, all to help me save the most important person in mine.

Selfish. Selfish. Selfish.

"Bee, we're in an MC compound. There are dozens of bikers

inside, each one an armed killer. You can't say nothing will happen because neither of us knows that for sure."

Realization dawns on me. Anything could happen tonight. I don't care about myself. I'm not important in the grand scheme of things. I'm here to make sure nothing happens to Razr. But then, nothing must happen to Raf either. My beautiful Raf. The man who's been one of my constants my whole life. If anything happened to him due to my selfish actions, I'd never forgive myself.

We cling to each other as his lips claim mine once more.

"Sorry, don't mind us."

I swing my head in the direction of where the voice is coming from and immediately take in the two bikers. Raf and I were so lost in each other that we didn't even hear them approach. Both are tall and lean. One is blonde, the other dark.

The blonde smirks and winks, no doubt at having witnessed Raf and I eating each other's faces off. They stop when they reach us. The black-haired one looms over me, his blue eyes searching my very soul with his penetrating gaze. His hair hangs way down his back in inky waves, and his face wears a short beard which displays perfectly the chiseled features he has going on underneath. I don't need to look at his cut for the word *prez* to know that this is Ace. He has a distinct air about him—a presence.

"Ace." It comes out more whispered than I intended it to be, making me sound like I'm in awe of him or something. And who knows, maybe I am.

He smirks at me. "Bailey." His eyes turn to Raf, and they immediately harden. "Who's this?"

"This is Rafael Flores."

Ace's expression softens in recognition, and he holds out his hand. "It's good to meet you, Rafael. I went to school with your brother, Rodolfo."

"It's good to meet you too, Ace."

Unlike Raf, Rodolfo spent most of his childhood in California. His grandparents didn't keep good health, and after the death of his granddaddy, his grandma was on her own. She didn't want to leave the home she'd lived in with her husband her whole life, so Rodolfo moved there. When she passed, he returned to Nevada. It means a lot to me that it'll be her ring I'm wearing soon. I know it means a lot to Raf and his family too.

"This here's my VP, Clay."

Clay smirks again. He carries the air of a joker about him. I'm not too sure there's much about this situation to joke about.

Ace turns his expression back to me. "Have we got back-up coming?"

I shake my head. "Nope."

"Razr got any men with him?"

"Blaze and Knight are inside, no doubt being watched."

"We've got no plan?"

"No."

"So, let me get this straight. We have to take on an entire MC? Have you got a death wish or something?"

Suddenly, I feel foolish. Ace is pretty much repeating what Raf said. Of course we stand no chance against the Undertakers.

"I guess I was hoping that the brothers would turn against their prez since they don't hold him in any high regard."

"It's a bit of a risky strategy, Bailey, and I'm a little risk-averse these days, as I'm sure you'll appreciate. As you know, my old lady is about to have a baby. I'd sure like to be there to see that happen. I'm pretty sure she'd like me to be there to witness it too."

"What do you suggest I do? If I contact the Sons, they'll come immediately."

He nods slowly as if remembering something. "Yeah, that's right. Your Lucifer's daughter."

I nod silently back in response.

"If we get into any trouble, how long will it take them to get here?"

"Thirty minutes if they're coming from the clubhouse, maybe slightly less."

His lips form a thin line as he thinks. "A lot can happen in that time, Bailey. As soon as they step outside with Razr, you let the Sons know what's happening. That way, when they get here, they can't be accused of starting anything, only finishing it. But hopefully, they'll still arrive in time to save our asses if they need to."

"Deal. And what about Jaine?"

"She'll stand back. She just wants to be close by in case anything happens."

"You sure?"

"Nope. Never sure how her mind works. She does what she wants when she wants." His voice is soft as he talks about her, the depth of his love audible in his tone.

I want that for me. From Razr? From Raf? Then I feel guilty for even thinking about Razr, no matter how fleetingly. My hand reaches for Raf's. He covers it with his own, squeezing gently.

"Well, it seems we're in business."

I turn my attention to where Ace is looking. I know it must be the door at the rear of the clubhouse. There are only two ways out of the cooler. One is through the building itself, and the other is where we're all now currently staring.

Taking my phone from my pocket, I turn on the location finder, then message Conor.

Bailey: *SOS.*

CHAPTER THIRTY-FIVE

RAZR

The Undertakers' Clubhouse, Colton, Nevada

I'M NOT SURE WHETHER IT'S THE CHILL FROM THE NIGHT AIR OR THE fact that I've been sitting on cold, hard concrete for so long, but an involuntary shiver runs through me as we step outside. Or maybe it's a premonition. Because the way things are shaping up, it's not looking too promising that I'll be leaving Nevada anytime soon.

If ever.

Not sure why it takes six of them to lead me outside, since my hands are tied. Maybe they all want a souvenir. Maybe they all want the opportunity to brag that they took part in killing the prez of the Iron Scorpions.

I'm pretty sure that's what's about to go down.

I look around at my final destination. Containers. All different sizes and colors. The only light is from the glow of the last burning embers of a fire that's been lit in a rusty old metal drum. It flickers as it clutches onto the last remnants of its life—a bit like what I'm doing.

I haven't done too badly. I made it to thirty-two. My regrets from earlier resurface, and I swallow them down. They taste bitter on my tongue and acidic in my gut. Still, there's no point dwelling on what might have been. It won't be. It's done now. It's over.

I am the last in the Delaney line.

My will's written. My baby sister will never want for anything. Not that she ever would now she's part of the Duster family. The club will have enough funds to run for years with no additional income needed. I may not have achieved everything I wanted to in my life, but I'm a very wealthy man.

My thoughts then drift to *her*.

Regret surfaces again. But I can't change anything now. The devil's got his plans for me, and the grim reaper is here to collect me in person.

They lead me to the side of the central container. I can already see the bullet holes scattered across the side of its heavily graffitied surface. Death by firing squad, I guess.

So be it.

I face the metal wall, taking in the indentations along with the paint that's been cracked open by the sun through the years. It'll be the last thing I see before I turn and stare down the barrels of several loaded guns.

"What in God's name are you doing here?" It's Reaper.

"I was having some trouble with my hog. I was just about to set off. Abel's letting me borrow his until tomorrow."

My heart pounds in my chest at the sound of the familiar voice. It can't fucking be. Not here. Not now. I turn around to take her in, and my eyes scan over her in disbelief. It's the girl from outside. The one I couldn't drag my eyes off. The one who made my dick hard when it hasn't been hard in weeks. Not since her.

Bailey.

I stare at her, and she gives her head a subtle shake. She doesn't want me to let on that we know each other. But then again, we don't.

Because I never bothered to take the goddamn time.

"Little Bee, you shouldn't be here. You can't witness this, princess."

"What exactly can't I witness, Reaper? All I'm seeing right now is a bound biker being led out of the cooler. What do you intend to do to him?"

She nods her head in my direction, and I watch as the other goons back off. Her presence scares them.

With his back to me, Reaper runs his hands through his hair in frustration. "You don't need to know anything about that, Bee."

"You going to shoot him? Is that what you're planning to do?"

"I can't answer that, sweetheart."

"Yes, you damn well can."

"Bee, if you're going to force me to tell you, then I'm going to need to bury you in the same hole in the ground he's going in."

"So, what? You're planning on shooting him. All of you. Like an execution?"

Why does he keep calling her Bee like he knows her well?

I watch as she looks between Reaper's men. All of them lower their heads. Guilt? Embarrassment that they're each too lily-livered to take care of business personally? That they need to hold each other's fucking hands in order to do so?

They sure as hell don't like that she's seeing this. They mumble to each other and shuffle from foot to foot. Her being here means trouble. Potential big trouble for them. But why?

Just who the hell is she?

I don't know. What I do know is this is proof paramount that she's not involved in the gun business and never has been.

She never betrayed me. She never betrayed my club.

She nods her head towards me like she's never seen me before in her life. "What's he done that you need to pass him your calling card, Reaper?"

"He's just a problem that needs to be dealt with."

"So, you're just going to shoot another biker? An unarmed biker at that. In cold blood. All of you. You're going to use another brother for target practice?"

Again, she looks between his men. They now have two options available to them on how they deal with her. She either suffers the same fate as me, or they let us both walk. I doubt very much that it will be the latter.

Reaper raises his weapon and points it at her, which is what I suspected would happen. The stupid girl is going to get herself killed.

She's in the wrong place. At exactly the wrong time.

"Don't you fucking dare," I growl at him. "This has nothing to do with her. She's just a young girl. Don't you dare lay a goddamn finger on her, you motherfucker."

He and his men turn to look at me. With their attention diverted, I watch as she leans down and reaches inside her boot. What the hell is she doing now?

"And what exactly are you going to do to stop me, Razr? Head-butt me?" The fucker snickers. I can see his yellow teeth even from here, but thankfully, I can't smell his rancid breath.

I struggle against the bindings to distract them from Bailey more than anything else. She's obviously up to something, and whatever it is, she needs an opportunity to carry it through.

It's then I see the glint of metal. She's brought her stars with her.

She came here intentionally. She came here for me.

I watch as she readies one in each hand.

"Mac! Dagger! Look at what I've got for each of you boys." Both goons turn at the mention of their names, and I watch as Bailey throws both shurikens in quick succession. They cry out in pain, their hands clutching their faces. Blood quickly spills from between their fingers as they try to pull at the lethal piece of metal now lodged firmly before both fall to the ground. They're dead. The shiny silver blades jut out of their skulls from between glassy eyes still wide-open in shock.

She's killed. For me.

It's then I see the others appear silently from the darkness of the night. Ace, Clay, and someone else I don't recognize. Ace immediately slits the throat of one of the fuckers. I watch as he clutches at his neck, trying to stop his lifeblood from squirting all over the desert floor. It doesn't work. He drops to the ground, dead before he reaches the surface. Clay snaps the neck of another, smiling as he does.

The dark-haired man with them isn't a biker, but it's clear he's from the life. I watch as he sticks his blade low in the stomach of his chosen victim and proceeds to gut the fucker. Intestines spill to the floor moments before the asshole drops down dead, landing in the sea of his own guts.

The final one is a goddamn coward. He holds his hands up in the air in surrender. Does the fool think he won't die today by doing so? If we don't kill him, he'll be killed by his own brothers for betraying his club. Death by our hands would be quicker and far less painful, but he's made his choice by surrendering.

Bailey tries to run past Reaper to get to me, and as she does, he yanks her back by the hair. She yelps out in pain as he grabs her, wrapping his arm firmly around her waist from behind.

I instantly realize what this is. She's his get out of jail free card. His meal ticket. For some reason, she's important in all of this.

Ace runs over to me, cutting through my bindings with his

blade. I take the hand he's offering, and he pulls me off the ground, slapping my back as he does.

"You okay?"

I nod. I can thank him later. Then again, it's not likely that I will. Our gratitude remains unspoken most of the time. Saving a brother is pretty much a daily occurrence in this life.

"Bailey."

He nods. He knows that nothing matters right now but her.

I stride over to where Reaper is standing, the barrel of his gun pressed upward under Bailey's chin, his back against the container. Meanwhile, Clay has his Glock aimed at Reaper's head. Whatever the outcome today, surely Reaper knows he's a dead man walking.

"You let her the fuck go, old man," I growl at him as I pace the floor directly in front of them. My hand is itching for my blade. Ace recognizes my need and passes me his.

"You know I can't do that, Razr."

"She's just a girl. What the fuck has she got to do with any of this?" I hiss.

"She just killed two of my best men."

"Those assholes deserved everything they got. And you deserve the same ending, you fucker."

He snickers. "That may be the case, but while I have Little Bee here, no one will lay a finger on me."

"What the hell do you mean?" I stop still and stare at him.

He wraps her hair around his hand almost possessively. I immediately want to kill the pedo fucker for laying a finger on her.

"What the fuck does he mean by that, Bailey?" I stare at her. I know I'm finally about to hear what she's been hiding all these damn months.

"He means my daddy won't want anything to happen to me, so he'll let him walk. Well, at least that's what the asshole's hoping." She glares up at him.

"You got that exactly right, princess." He smiles down at her. "Who's your daddy, Bailey?"

She lifts her chin defiantly. Anger surges through me in preparation for her spilling her guts.

"I SAID WHO'S YOUR GODDAMN DADDY, BAILEY."

I watch as she opens her mouth, then closes it again as she glances past me.

"I'm her daddy. Bee's my youngest."

I turn around and glare at Lucifer.

CHAPTER THIRTY-SIX

BAILEY

The Undertakers' Clubhouse, Colton, Nevada

THE COLD METAL OF THE GUN PRESSED UNDER MY CHIN IS NOTHING compared with witnessing the frigid look of utter betrayal that fleetingly crosses Razr's face when he realizes who I am. It's so raw and undiluted. I can almost taste his pain and anger.

Stupid Bailey. Silly girl.

I thought I could play with the big boys and that no one would get hurt. But they did get hurt. They are being hurt.

I hurt myself by falling in love with a man who could never be mine. I hurt the man I love by betraying and lying to him for months. Worst of all, I hurt a man who loves me. Raf. A man I didn't even know loved me until recently. A man who's just witnessed me risking life and limb to save another.

"I'm sorry." I try to speak, but no words come out. Or at least, I can't hear them. I'm not even sure who I'm directing my apology to. All three of us, maybe.

"You will be, bitch."

Everyone turns to look at the sixth and final goon—the one no one's been paying any attention to. The one everyone had written off as yellow-bellied as he was too scared to die with his brothers. I stare at him. Well, I stare down the barrel of his loaded gun, which is pointed at my head from ten feet away.

I swallow. Hard.

Reaper needs me alive, so the odds were kind of stacked in my favor of me walking away from this shit show alive. But this brother who I don't know who looks to be no more than my age, well, he has a look about him. One that confirms he has nothing to live for, so nothing to lose. One that's suddenly reduced my odds of survival to single figures. Maybe even a negative.

"That there." He motions his head towards one of the stiffs on the ground. It's Mac, the first one I sent to the bowels of hell with my star lodged in his skull. "Well, that there's my big brother. And you killed him."

We stare at each other. I've seen insanity. I mean, I spent all those months with Razr, so I know first-hand what a madman looks like. But this. This is insanity mixed with pain, mixed with the potent stench of desperation. It's on a totally different level.

I realize he wants me to see all of the above in his eyes. He wants me to witness his suffering so he doesn't feel guilty about the next step. When he does what he feels he has to do.

Seek redemption for his dead sibling.

He shoots me a twisted smile as he cocks the gun.

"And for that, Little Bee, you're going to have to pay with the very thing you took from him. Life."

I don't know what happens next. I think maybe Reaper pushes me flat to the ground as dirt immediately fills my mouth and my nostrils. He's not saving me for my benefit. He's only protecting me as he needs me as a hostage to save his own sorry ass.

The gun goes off, and then there's deathly silence. Dread fills me. I try to raise myself off the ground, but Reaper's still pinning me down. I need to get up. I need to know. Something bad's happened. Something terrible. Something life-changing.

And it's my life. I just fucking know it.

"Get the fuck off of me, you asshole." I yell. I need to see. I need to know.

I push myself up and wished I hadn't. Oh, God. What have I fucking done?

"Raf!" I'm screaming, wrestling as the man who loves me, my future, lies on the ground with his hands clutching his stomach, the crimson color of his blood soaking through the whiteness of his Henley.

"Raf!" I struggle against Reaper's hold, but he hangs on fast to his only hope of survival. He pulls my back tight against his front, allowing his rancid breath to reach my nostrils and make me gag.

"Stay still, Bee, or I'm going to have to shoot you."

No one really knows what happens next. Or at least, I don't. One minute Reaper's arms are pinning me so tightly I can barely breathe. The next moment, something whistles through the air. I feel it touch my hair. I'm sure I do. Something lethal. Something deadly. Something deliberate. The next thing, Reaper's arms go loose around me. I look up into his face in shock, trying to understand what the fuck is going on. He now has the perfect round hole between his eyes, and a small trickle of blood leaking down his forehead. He's wearing a look of surprise on his face, and his brains are splattered across the side of the container behind him, no doubt caused by the bullet exiting the back of his skull after turning his brain into a smoothie.

I watch as Ace and Razr look at each other. In that brief exchange, I know they both know exactly what's just gone down.

None of that matters. Not now. Only one person does.

"Raf." My voice is tortured, pained.

All that matters is Raf.

I run to him, kneeling on the dusty floor so I can cradle his head in my hands.

"Bee…" His voice is barely audible. He sounds like he's far away.

"I'm here, Raf. I'm here." I smooth his hair back from his brow. His skin feels cold and clammy.

"I love you, Bee. I need you to know that I love you, querida," he whispers with a small smile before losing consciousness. I cradle him in my arms as they bring a cage around. The hospital is an hour away.

Please, God, let him make it. Please, God, don't let anything bad happen to him. He's a good man with a good heart born in a fucked up life. He doesn't deserve to die like this.

Not at twenty-three fucking years old.

"Bailey."

I turn to look at Ace. His face is ashen.

"Listen, I'm sorry. I need to go. Jaine…" He runs his hands through his hair. "It's the baby. Bailey, she's in labor."

"Go. Go!" I motion for him to go, but he stands there like he's in some sort of trance. I understand. I think we all are. "Ace, go to her. She needs you!"

I watch as he and Clay leave on the back of two of the Undertaker brothers' bikes. A show of solidarity by the now leaderless club, as it should always have been. Brother to brother. Family

Once Raf is inside the back of the cage, his head nestled on my lap, they close the doors before we start on the long drive to the hospital. I pray he survives the journey. We have our whole lives ahead of us. To spend as man and wife. Together forever.

The last thing I see as we drive off is Razr standing on his own, running his hands up and down the sides of his head as he does in that familiar insane way of his as he stares after the retreating cage.

Private Hospital, Las Vegas

I already know.

Everything is a blur as they lift Raf from my lap, leaving me sitting in a pool of his blood. I shared trying to stem the flow with one of the brothers, one who's as good as being a qualified doctor. We tried as best we could, but it still found a way to seep past our desperate fingers no matter what we did. It still found a way to escape Raf's weakening body.

I follow inside in a daze.

"Bee." I take in his parents who've met us here. Two people I've known most of my life—both crying for their boy. My heart physically aches as I take in his father, who Raf's the double of. His mother who's as beautiful on the inside as she is out.

They don't deserve to lose their son today.

His brother Rodolfo pulls me against his chest as he continues a conversation with my daddy, who followed behind us on his hog. He'll be telling him what's gone down.

He's crying. My daddy's crying.

I already know.

"The gun was aimed at Bee, and Raf stepped in front of it. He saved her. He stopped my baby girl from getting hurt or worse."

Pain wracks me at those words. I shouldn't have been there. Raf shouldn't have been there. Razr made his stupid gung-ho decision, and now my beautiful Raf is paying the ultimate price.

Alarms go off. Doctors are running everywhere like soldier ants dressed in little white coats. I'm suffocated in Rodolfo's arms. It's like if he holds on to me, he still has hope. But I don't offer hope. I'm the reason for this. This is my doing. My responsibility. My fault.

I already know.

Seconds pass. Minutes. Hours. Who knows? Time moves forward. Time stands still. Maybe the latter is better. That we can just stay in this limbo forever. No matter how painful it is. Yes, it's torture, but then the inevitability of the situation will never happen.

Because the pain of the inevitability? Well, that will be incomparable.

We stay where we are. Motionless. The smell of Lysol fills my nostrils, and the sound of silent tears fills my ears. My brain is flooded with memories of Raf and me growing up. He was one of the only constants in life. I loved him. I hated him. But no matter what, he was always there for me.

He was playful to start with, like another brother. But then, as we got older, he began to make my life a misery. Now I know why. Boys always pick on the girls they like, don't they? Tears run down my face as the memories click through my head like a slideshow. The signs were all there. I did know subconsciously. I must have, surely.

That he wanted me. That he loved me. That he was waiting for me.

The doors at the end of the corridor open.

I already know.

The doctors' faces are wearing that look. The one they wear on TV when they're faced with telling parents the words they don't ever want to hear in their lifetime. Words they should never have to hear. Why? Because it ends for them too.

Life.

Even though they still have to go to sleep and wake up each day.

Go through the motions of living on the outside when they're dead inside.

"I'm so sorry. We did everything we could."

Do they practice saying those words while looking in the mirror? So, they can get the balance of caring and sympathy just right? Even though I expected them, I still didn't want to hear the finality of those fucking words. I'd secretly hoped I was wrong, even though I knew I wasn't.

I felt Raf slip away from me in the back of the cage when we were moments away from the hospital. He was unconscious the whole journey. He clung on. He almost made it. What if we'd driven faster? What if we'd taken a detour? What if I hadn't come up with such a brilliant idea to save the prez of the fucking Iron Scorpions?

What if. What if. What if.

"Can I see him?" My voice sounds like it doesn't belong to me. I feel like I'm floating somewhere outside my own headspace.

It suddenly feels like the most important thing in the world right now. To see him. I silently pray no one asks to join me. Is that selfish? That I need this for me? This moment. With him. No one asks to. I silently thank God for that one show of mercy. Then again, he owes me one after taking Raf. The doctor nods at me, then turns and walks away slowly. I follow. It's already like a funeral procession.

As I walk, I dry my tears. I don't want Raf to see me crying. Sounds dumb. I know he can't. I just want to be brave for him. Like he was for me.

The room is white, cold, and clinical. It's still and deathly quiet. All the machines that should have been buzzing and beeping, trying so hard to inject life back into him, are now quiet in their humiliating, united defeat.

He has a white sheet pulled over him right up to his neck, no doubt to hide the bloody mess underneath. A sight I witnessed first-hand as I tried so desperately to keep his beautiful soul inside his body. I gaze down at him. His face is pale, but apart from that, he looks like he's asleep.

Then again, he'll now be forever sleeping. Just like he'll forever be twenty-three.

I push his hair back from his forehead before pressing my warm lips against his cool ones.

"I'm so sorry, Raf."

And I am. I'm sorry that I dragged him into my mess. I'm sorry that he gave his life for mine. I'm sorry that he'll never get married and have kids.

Most of all, I'm sorry that he ever had the misfortune of meeting me. If he hadn't, he'd still be alive. I'm also sorry that I had the misfortune of meeting Razr. If I hadn't, Raf would still be alive.

We'd have had a future. A life. A wedding. A marriage. Children.

Now Raf has none of that to look forward to. Thanks to me. I have no control over having a future. I'm Irish Catholic. The alternative isn't an option for me, plus I could never do that to my family.

But I don't deserve the rest. I don't want them. Not if I can't have them with Raf.

"I love you."

I say the words out loud. Words I never told him when he was alive. I know in my aching heart it will be my biggest regret in this life. I pray he can hear them now in death.

I do love Raf. In my own way. We could have been happy. We *would* have been happy. Ours would have been a marriage built on a solid friendship.

I try to swallow down the pain, but it's lodged in my throat. It will always be lodged in my throat. I deserve to choke on it for what I've done.

I stand there. I'm not sure for how long. Just staring at him. I don't want to forget anything about him.

I glance at the clock when I finally leave the room. The doctors will have recorded an official time of death, but I know precisely when it was.

Three twenty-five a.m.

CHAPTER THIRTY-SEVEN

JAINE

Private Hospital, Las Vegas

THREE TWENTY-FIVE A.M.

The time my beautiful little boy was born. This precious soul I now hold in my arms that I refuse to let go of is the most perfect thing I have ever seen.

According to the midwife, the pains I'd been suffering recently were minor contractions, as my doctor had rightly pointed out. Twenty minutes after arriving at the hospital on the back of a hog and in so much pain I could barely sit still, baby Finian arrived.

With a mop of jet-black hair, a pair of bright blue eyes, and weighing a good seven pounds and five ounces, this little man came screaming into this outlaw world of ours. And I knew the moment I looked at him who his father was. I didn't even have to search for the birthmark.

Irish, you have a son.

I want to call him. Tell him. Show him his little face. Point out all the features that are already the double of his daddy's. I want to share everything with Irish as is his given right. But I can't, and it makes me hate Eoin O'Connell all the more. I don't want Irish to miss out on a precious second of his little boy's existence. I want my son to know his daddy. Because he has the best pop in the world, he really does.

But what choice do I have?

Irish would insist that we marry. And whether it be that day, or a week later, or a year later, the Sicilian mafia would come calling for him. Demanding their pound of flesh. The only acceptable method of payment.

His death.

Sophia and Irish's marriage must go ahead. There's no other acceptable outcome. So, for now, and until I can return to Manhattan, Finian is a Steele.

Finian Fergal Jeremiah O'Connell Steele. Or Fin as he will always be known. Named after his Irish great granddaddy. Fergal's da.

No one will know that he's not Ace's son. No one will understand the relevance of the lucky birthmark, except for Ace and me.

And he'll be adored just as much as a Steele. He's already so loved. Unconditionally. By me. So much I'm overwhelmed by the sheer force of it. My Irish has given me a gift so precious. Given *us* a gift so precious. And he doesn't even know.

And my heart weeps because of it. And it will always weep until I can see Fin in his arms.

"Can I hold him, PJ?"

I look up at Ace, into familiar eyes as blue as the bluest thing ever. Eyes that are always open and honest with me. And I can see the disappointment that he's not Fin's biological father. He's not hiding it. But I also saw my big tough biker as he wiped away tears when he first looked at my son.

His son. Our son. Irish's son.

I also know I now need to tell him everything about why I've had to banish my beautiful, wonderful Irish from my life.

I nod and watch as Ace gently lifts him from my embrace. I know I'm handing him over reluctantly. I'm not being selfish. I'm just scared that they'll have some sort of sixth sense. That the O'Connells will somehow know he's one of them. That they'll show up and see the male family birthmark then try to snatch him from me.

I watch as Ace looks down on him. I take in the size of the tiny little bundle held ever so gently in the arms of this muscular, heavily-inked biker. Tears prick my eyes as he presses a soft kiss to his tiny forehead. He loves him, despite everything.

Because he's part of me.

And then what do I do? Like every other proud new mom, I use my phone to take a picture, capturing in time two of the people I love most in the world. I just desperately wish that the third could be here with us to witness the miracle of life and to hold his newborn son.

Then everything really would be perfect.

I stare at my phone, then scroll through. When I reach it, my finger hovers over his number. Not that I needed to search for it. It's imprinted on my heart.

I stare and I stare. It would be so easy just to press it.

Would he answer now he's moved on so easily with his life without me in it?

I love you, my Irish. I miss you so much.

PADRAIG

Padraig's Apartment, Hudson Yards, New York

Jaine: *Sends pic.*

I stare at the image. It's a photo of Ace cradling his tiny infant son in his arms. A mop of black hair peeks out from the top of white swaddling. Jealousy flows through me, and I hate myself for it. More than anything, I just want to be happy for them. For him. Even though he has everything I've ever wanted.

Ace is a good man. He loves her. He would die for her. If she can't be with me, then there's no one else I'd rather she be with; be protected by.

Tears prick my eyes. Those pathetic fuckers of self-pity. I've lost everything and gained nothing.

At least after my confrontational conversation with Eoin, I can now message her, but what does that really achieve? She doesn't even know it's me. I have to be careful what I say in case I give the game away. Even more so now our messages are being monitored by my big fucking brother. I wonder what she'd do if I did contact her.

Right here. Right now.

As me. As Padraig. As her Irish. Like I used to do a million and one times a day.

Would she acknowledge it? Would she respond? Would she call? She's probably already blocked my number to ensure I can't contact her after it dawned on her that she didn't love me. That she never had. When she cut me loose and decided she didn't need me in her life anymore.

I stare around my apartment, at the navy and cream décor. It's nice. But it's material shite. Yes, it's the best money can buy, but when it boils down to it, what do I really have? Nothing. Okay, I have possessions and all the money I could ever need. I have friends and family. But I have no one that's mine. No one who loves me.

Not for being an O'Connell. Or for being a Duster. But just for being me.

What difference does that make when I'm in love with my cliché blonde? When I'm in love with Jaine fucking Jones, soon to be Steele. I know precisely what unrequited love feels like. So, why would I want to inflict the pain of that on someone else?

What exactly have I got to look forward to?

Sharing my life with Sophia? Sharing my bed? The latter will never happen. Hell will freeze over before I'll stick my dick in her. Hell will freeze over before I'll stick it in anyone who's not Jaine.

A sexless marriage with no children; that's what I've got to look forward to.

Lifting my hand to my face, I'm not surprised to find my cheeks wet. I've always been the emotional sibling. The one who wears his heart on his sleeve, especially when it comes to Jaine Jones.

The heart she took when offered then never gave back.

My hands instinctively reach for the sparkling decanter, the amber liquid inside singing its siren's song to me, reminding me of its potency and ability to make me forget.

Do I? Don't I?

It'll numb the pain, at least temporarily.

I drop my hand and close my eyes in frustration. I know it's not the answer. I know anyone with half a brain knows it's not the fucking answer. But when you're faced with going through life knowing the only thing you want you can't ever have? Well, that's a harsh reality to face every morning when you wake and every night before you try to sleep. She even haunts my fucking dreams.

There's no escape.

I love you, darlin'. I miss you so much.

Rather than reaching for the drink, instead, I pick up my phone.

CHAPTER THIRTY-EIGHT

PADRAIG

Padraig's Apartment, Hudson Yards, New York

Padraig: *I guess he couldn't wait to make his mark on the world then, arriving seven weeks early.*
Jaine: *Trust me, he's already made his mark.*
Padraig: *Too much information, darlin'.*
Jaine: *Will you be Fin's godfather, Dyl? When I return to Manhattan?*
Padraig: *You really want that?*
Jaine: *More than anything. Well, okay, not more than anything, but I want it a lot. You mean so much to me these days. More than you probably realize. You make coping easier.*
Padraig: *Don't go declaring you're undying love for me or anything like that now.*
Jaine: *LOL. I'm not sure how I'll be able to stop myself.*

Anyway, there's no point. Your heart belongs to a cliché blonde Disney princess who I'm still convinced is just a figment of your imagination. So, it seems like you're safe from my evil clutches, Batman. For now, at least.
Padraig: *Good to know, Robin. Nice name, by the way. Fin.*
Jaine: *Short for Finlay.*
Padraig: *Born in Nevada?*
Jaine: *Same hospital I was born in, strangely enough.*
Padraig: *History repeating?*
Jaine: *Hopefully not. He's already way too handsome to be an ugly duckling like I was. He looks just like his daddy.*
Padraig: *Poor kid.*
Jaine: *His daddy is handsome and has the most beautiful soul.*
Padraig: *Very poetic, but Ace isn't really my type.*
Jaine: *He'll be upset to hear that.*
Padraig: *I know you've had your mind on other things, Jaine, and will likely have had your phone switched off but did you hear about young Raf?*
Jaine: *What about him?*
Jaine: *Wait. Oh, God, no. Are you saying what I think you're saying? He was only twenty-three years old.*
Padraig: *I'm sorry, Jaine. About an hour ago, apparently. Complications due to extensive blood loss. To be honest, gunshot wounds in the stomach like that are typically fatal.*
Jaine: *I know they are. I need to call Rodolfo. Bailey. Shit.*
Padraig: *Calm down, Jaine. You've just given birth. You don't need to go making yourself ill. You'll just upset the wee fella if you get yourself all stressed out and upset. You know he'll pick up on it. Plus, you can't change what's already happened. He's gone.*

Jaine: *No, you're right. I'll leave it until morning. It's been a long night for everyone.*
Padraig: *One other thing. Rumor has it the bullet that took out the prez of the Undertakers was engraved with an X. It's become common knowledge, at least in our world, that it was The Exterminator who fired the fatal shot. As you know, the Dusters thought he was taking some well-deserved time off. My da will want to know if he's back up for hire. Can you find out from Razr for me?*

THERE'S A PAUSE. SHE'S DIGESTING WHAT I'VE JUST SAID. SHE'LL pick up on it, I'm sure—the warning.

Jaine: *Thanks for the heads up, Dyl. Perhaps he was just in the area, or maybe it was a favor for an old friend. It's my guess this was just a one-off. As far as I'm aware, The Exterminator's still on time out and will be for the foreseeable future.*

Yup. She's got the message. Loud and clear. That our exchange is now being monitored.

EOIN

On Route to Colton, Nevada

"Can I get you anything, Mr. O'Connell?"

I glance at the woman who's been hired to be at my beck and call during the flight from New York to Vegas. It's a Duster aircraft, and the pilot is on a retainer. He probably wanted to make sure it stayed that way given how much we pay him, so he's brought along a female friend as a sweetener to keep me company.

I lean back in my seat and take in my surroundings. It's spacious. All cream leather seating and a mini-bar area with drinks and snacks. The smell of new leather permeates the air, as does the savory aroma of the complementary nibbles. There's a bedroom too, with a king-sized bed. Nothing but the best for the Dusters.

My attention switches back to the woman. I allow my eyes to roam over her, taking in exactly what's on offer. I know she'll want to make full use of all the facilities, including the bed. She's my type too. Tall, slim, dark-haired. Or at least she's what my type used to be until Jaine Jones came along with her boyish figure, lack of curves, and hair the color of spun gold.

She places her hand on my thigh, and I immediately brush it off. As much as it would be a once-in-a-lifetime opportunity for this woman, I still have a reputation to maintain. If I take her up on her offer, I'd need to go out of my way to make it the best fuck of her life. Right now, it's too much of an effort, more so as I'm only partially interested. That's why it's simpler just to fuck Candice. I already know I'm the best fuck of her life.

"I'm fine, thank you." My tone is curt and dismissive.

Picking up my phone, I scroll through the earlier message exchange between our Paddy and Jaine. Then I look at the photo of Ace and their new baby.

It would be foolish of me to think Jaine would ever send me such an image. On the contrary, aside from her dalliances with my brother, she's never brought up her private life during any conversation with me. That's because she sees our relationship as purely professional. I've never met Ace. Then again, I've never paid much attention to who or what he was to her. Our Cillian tends to deal with the MCs. I look at him now with his long black hair and heavily tattooed arms. He's exactly the type I envisioned Jaine would be with.

As I look closer, it's then that I see the similarities between him and Paddy. The similarities between Ace and me. All three of us could be related. So, Jaine Jones definitely has a type, and I'm it, it seems. And while she may not have been my type, she is now, hence why I'm declining the advances of the flight attendant.

I read through the words once more. Jaine clearly cares a lot for Dylan. Or should I say Paddy? Even as an alias, she adores him.

I stare out the window at nothing. Just thinking.

It doesn't sit right with me, this deceit. Really, I should put a stop to it as no good will come of it. But if allowing Paddy this level of contact keeps my baby brother away from the demon drink, then it's a small price to pay. What alternative do I have? Although, now Paddy's agreed he'll marry the Sicilian even though he's in contact with Jaine, I could relent and let them talk directly.

Jaine would continue with the lie that she fell out of love with him, so he goes through with the wedding to Sophia. Paddy wouldn't mention it either. Neither would wish ill harm to come to the other, so they'd just accept their fate.

There's no real need for me to stop them from communicating anymore with that in mind—the only thing preventing me from doing so is selfishness.

If Jaine starts talking to Paddy, she'll stop talking to me, and I don't want that. I want her to contact me. I want her to come to me when she needs to ask the Dusters for assistance with something or to relay information. That would stop if I lifted their communication ban.

So, no. Unfortunately, the ban will remain in situ until Paddy's wedding has taken place. After that? I can't stop them from communicating. But I'm hoping before then I can convince her to ditch the biker boyfriend, move back to Manhattan, and take her rightful place at my side.

I realize I have my work cut out for me, but I never back down from a challenge, especially one I've set for myself.

I scroll through the messages once more, and then my curiosity is piqued. The number Jaine contacts Dylan on isn't her business one. Is it for the burner she carries? Maybe next time I'll call her on that.

She won't have my number saved.

Would she answer, I wonder?

CHAPTER THIRTY-NINE

RAZR

The Undertakers' Clubhouse, Colton, Nevada

I'M STARTING TO WISH I'D NEVER TAKEN THE CALL.

"But you could have died, Paul."

"There isn't a day goes by where I'm not staring death in the face. It's the life I lead, baby girl. The life I choose to lead."

"But how can you choose to live like that? Is that the life you want for me? For our children?"

My mind immediately drifts to the image of Ace and his infant son. The one Jaine sent through this morning. I'm happy for Ace. Jealous. But happy all the same. Not of him and Jaine, for once. I realize I'm finally able to let her go. It's because he has what I desperately crave—a family.

After cheating death last night, I realize it's what I want more than anything.

I'm guessing the need in Ace to protect them will take second place to nothing moving forward. It will be his priority in life now. To raise his offspring and watch them flourish into adulthood before leaving to take their place in this world of ours.

His boy was born a biker. He'll die one too.

Same as Ace. Same as me.

My thoughts then drift to Raf. Twenty-three years old. His future wiped out by a bullet with Bailey's name on it.

He died for her. Just like she was prepared to die for me.

It doesn't make any sense.

I haven't asked about their relationship. It's only been a few hours since he passed and since everyone returned from the hospital. We're expecting Eoin O'Connell to arrive in the next half hour, so there's no time to dissect anything or ask questions. It will have to wait. The Irishman will expect answers.

"Laila, you have to ask yourself if that's the future you want. I can't make that decision for you."

"And I suppose we have to cancel the dinner we had planned with my parents?"

She ignores the question. Instead, she changes the subject and responds sulkily with one of her own. I'm guessing she needs time to digest what's happened. To consider the kind of life she would willingly be tying herself into. The type of monster she'd be marrying.

"I suppose we do."

"When will you be back?"

"After the funeral."

"And when will that be?"

"I'm not too sure that they've figured that out yet since Raf's body will still be warm. They're a religious family, so it will probably be soon."

"What shall I do about the dinner?"

Fuck the dinner. "Push it back a week."

"Okay."

"I've got to go, Laila."

For the first time ever, she disconnects the call. Not me.

I'm in Reaper's office. Let's face it, he doesn't need it anymore. It's a mess and is as unclean as the rest of this place. Yellow curled papers cover the desk along with a layer of grime and God knows what else.

Those not from the life think running an MC is easy for a prez. It isn't. It's the same as running any other organization.

You buy. You sell. You get paid. You keep your records.

The only difference is that we have to create multiple businesses to launder the cash through because we can't declare the official source most of the time. Not without asking for a lengthy prison sentence.

We still pay our taxes all the same.

Two things are critical to success.

You need the best lawyer money can buy. That's where Jaine comes in. And you need the best accountant money can buy. Apparently, Jaine's sourced one of those for us too now.

On the surface, it looks like Reaper never even tried to run this club successfully. It's no wonder he was so desperate for cash.

So desperate, he got involved with the wrong crowd and wound up getting himself exterminated.

The trouble is, his poor choices have resulted in the death of a high-ranking member of La eMe. I'm guessing, seeing as Reaper's no longer around to pay the price for that, someone else will have to.

Most likely me.

Is it deserved? I also made poor choices. Decisions that I will now have to stand by.

I move across to look out the window, and that's when I see her.

She's staring at the bloodstains on the ground. At the spot where Raf became as good as dead. That shot was not survivable. Raf himself knew it was fatal. We all did. Apart from Bailey.

Then again, deep down, maybe she did too.

She's changed and recently showered as her long blonde hair hangs wet down her back. She looks broken. Hopeless. She must feel my gaze on her as she turns around, and our eyes connect.

Blue on green.

I feel it deep inside me, whatever it is. Something that wants me to take her in my arms and make it all better. Make all this shit go away.

Keep her safe.

We stare. I only look away when Abel enters the room.

"The Irishman's here."

I nod, and he takes that as his cue to leave.

Pulling my blade from my pocket, I start to flick it back and forth methodically.

It's showtime.

RODOLFO, EOIN, ACE, LUCIFER, AND ME.

That's who's present and we're all currently standing in the Undertakers' council office.

Rodolfo looks like shit. His dark hair looks like he's run his hands through it a million times. He's unshaven. His eyes are bloodshot.

Figures. He's just lost his baby brother.

As much are we're all killers, our families mean everything to us. Our mission in life is to keep them safe. And more importantly, to keep them alive. For most of us, family is all we have that's good in our lives.

The lines of grief and loss that weren't there yesterday are etched firmly on Rodolfo's face today. They won't be the last ones he'll ever acquire, I'm sure. But some will run deeper than others. All will remain visible until he takes his last breath. I know exactly what they look like. I've been wearing them and seeing them in the mirror for years.

Ace looks tired, but there's an air of something about him this morning. Contentment. He's a family man now. He has the woman. He has the son.

The first of many, I'm sure.

Lucifer looks as worse for wear as Rodolfo. But by all accounts, Raf was like another son to him.

As for Eoin O'Connell? Well, I've only met the mobster on a handful of occasions. It's typically Cillian who handles any dealings with the MCs on behalf of the Dusters. Up until now, Eoin has never wanted to get his hands dirty dealing with the lowest of the low in our world.

I wonder why the future Irish king has now decided to take over the reins.

Not that Cill is complaining. In his words, he has enough balls to juggle while my sister has a firm grip on the other two.

It's clear Eoin isn't used to interacting with the likes of us. He doesn't dress for the part. He looks out of place. He's dressed immaculately, unlike us bikers, who are all wearing jeans and leathers finished off in a fine film of road dust.

Then again maybe that's deliberate.

He uses the same tailor I do. I can tell by the cut of his suit. No expense spared. When it comes to bank balances, we're pretty much at the same level. Both of us with more money than we know what to do with, but both always hungry for more.

"I hear congratulations are in order."

Eoin stares at Ace as he speaks. A look of something crosses his face. Only briefly. If I'd blinked, I'd have missed it.

Resentment? Annoyance? Dislike? Jealousy?

If Ace notices, he doesn't let on. Eoin walks across and shakes him firmly by the hand.

"Thank you."

I watch as everyone congratulates him with handshakes and pats on the back for a job well done.

The circle of life has taken place overnight. One extinguished, another just starting.

"I'd like for Jaine to be part of this conversation, please."

We all turn to look at Rodolfo as he makes this request, taking our seats as we do. The Duster sits at the head of the table, which is only to be expected. He's an arrogant son of a bitch, that's for sure. But when it comes to hierarchy, they sit firmly at the top of this triangle. This is their gig. They call the shots.

Rodolfo's request isn't too surprising. He's known Ace and Jaine for years.

"Jaine who?" Lucifer looks at Rodolfo, then at the rest of us.

"Ace's old lady and the legal representation for the Scorpions. Jaine Jones," I reply.

Lucifer narrows his eyes suspiciously.

"You got a problem with that?" I immediately start flicking my blade, and his gaze drops as though the movement suddenly hypnotizes him. What's he thinking about? He knows I'm not going to cut him. "She's completely trustworthy. Everyone here has had dealings with her in some shape or form. Well, I'm guessing apart from the Sons."

"So, what is she? A bent lawyer?" He snickers.

"Jaine studied at Yale with my youngest brother, Paddy. She's not bent. She's a master of her craft. She knows how to play the legal game better than anyone I've ever met." Eoin interjects this time, looking pissed off on Jaine's behalf.

I glance at Ace. His expression remains impassive, but it's my guess he's as surprised as I am by this glowing compliment from the eldest O'Connell.

Lucifer nods slowly. He still doesn't appear convinced.

"I'll get her set up." Ace leaves the room to do just that.

CHAPTER FORTY

RAZR

The Undertakers' Clubhouse, Colton, Nevada

JAINE SMILES AT ME FROM THE SCREEN PLACED AT THE END OF THE table. She looks good. She's glowing despite putting an Exterminator bullet in the head of that piece of shit, Reaper, and then giving birth to a son.

She was there for me. I'll never forget that. But then, she always has been.

"You okay, Delaney?"

"I've had better days, Jaine."

"Haven't we all."

She turns her attention to the Mexican, her face falling as she does. "Rod, there are no words I can say…" She wipes away the tears that are making sad tracks down her face. Jaine seldom, if ever, shows emotion. She's cut from the same cloth as the rest of us sitting here.

"Listen, I'm in a safe house at present. Ace and I thought it best given the current situation. I'm going to come and see you and your family. It also goes without saying that we'll stay for Raf's funeral."

"I appreciate that, Jaine. My folks will too."

"Ace."

He smirks as she acknowledges him, and she smiles. We're all witnessing a smile that's reserved just for him. I want more than anything for someone to smile at me like that. Because sadly I now realize that Jaine never did.

"Eoin." Her tone has changed to one that's way cooler than she's used for the rest of us. He was singing her praises earlier, but it's clear the feeling's not mutual. She's acknowledging his presence because she has to, not because she wants to.

The Irishman nods in silent response.

"And you must be Lucifer." She looks at the man who's sitting beside me. The man who looks like he's about to throw up in his own damn mouth.

"Jaine Jones." There's a pause as he rolls her name around his tongue. "The fellas here have all been quick to tell me how good you are. So, tell me, are you accepting new customers?"

She shakes her head, switching her focus back to O'Connell, for some reason.

"No. I'm not living in Manhattan right now. I've got a colleague running things for me in my absence. It'll be another year or so before I'll be making the move back. Only then will I be considering taking on new clients."

"You not thinking about opening an office on the west coast?"

"Not at this time. Most of my contacts are all east coast based. I can't say I haven't been toying with the idea, though, as I'll live between New York and California. Maybe it's something I'll consider once I've had an opportunity to build up a suitable network of contacts to make it beneficial for all parties concerned."

"You mean to fill your back pockets with high-ranking people on both sides of the law?" He sniggers.

Fool.

The rest of us know that comment is the equivalent of waving a red rag in front of a raging bull.

"What I mean is being able to offer my clients a service that's going to cost them money. A lot of money. I would need to ensure them value for that money. If you're insinuating that I in any way break the law, Lucifer, then think again. I don't break the law. I don't break the rules. I merely bend them better than anyone else in the business."

She puts him in his place before smiling at him dismissively.

"Anyway, gentlemen, shall we proceed?"

She folds her hands in front of her. She's putting on her legal head now. This is where she'll play devil's advocate, judge, and jury. I've seen her at work so many times. She'll leave the execution part down to the rest of us.

That's if we see fit to take things that far.

"Now, let's all run through the events leading up to last night. We should keep anything personal out of this. If we all start fighting amongst ourselves, then we'll never get anything resolved."

She turns her attention to Rodolfo.

"Rodolfo, why the hell did La eMe decide to start purchasing weapons from the Undertakers? More so when the alliance had only just been entered into?"

He shrugs. "In a nutshell? It was a local supplier offering better pricing."

"You didn't think to approach the Irish to ask them to review their selling prices?"

"No, we didn't. We also didn't consider the implications of ordering from another source."

"We're talking millions of dollars worth of handgun sales over twelve months, Rodolfo. That's going to affect any business's bottom line. That will always cause questions to be asked and challenges to be made. First La eMe. Who next? The situation could easily have spiralled."

Rodolfo nods in silent response.

"That aside, the Undertakers should never have accepted the orders in the first place. They should have asked to be brought in on the alliance. There's room for everyone. We all need to earn a living. The key thing is that we're mindful and respectful of each other while we're doing so."

"It was only ever a trial run, Jaine. It turns out the feedback from our men was that the weapons weren't of a decent enough caliber to continue with anyway, so no future orders were ever going to be placed. Still, I appreciate what you're saying. There were errors of judgment on both sides. What I don't appreciate is how badly the situation was handled. My baby brother is currently laying on a mortuary slab."

Silence fills the room. We're all acutely aware of the fact that a young man lost his life over this. Several did, in fact.

"It was agreed on our end that the Scorpions would handle the discussions, Rodolfo."

"Then maybe Razr should have brought more men with him. Maybe then it wouldn't have ended up in a blood bath!"

"We turned down an offer of back-up from the Sons, and we shouldn't have," I interrupt. It's a decision I've been cursing myself over ever since.

"No, I guess you shouldn't have," Rodolfo hisses.

"Now, listen, I never asked for any goddamn assistance. I don't know how Bailey figured out where I was or why the hell she'd try to stage a rescue attempt. And I don't know why Rafael was there either," I hiss back. I'm well aware I'm flicking my blade again.

"Delaney's right," Jaine replies quietly, obviously trying to placate Rodolfo. "If his own poor choices meant Delaney lost his life, then that was his decision. He never asked for anyone to intervene. He would have accepted his fate."

"He didn't even ask for The Exterminator to intervene? I mean, it's common knowledge that the sniper works via the Scorpions."

Eoin throws that bomb in there, and everyone turns to stare at the Irishman. He reaches into his inside jacket pocket before placing the bullet on the table. It's the one that killed Reaper. He must have been passed it by one of the Undertaker brothers who took care of the clean-up. He's a Duster. It's not likely they'll refuse him anything. We all watch as it rolls into the center. Four of us already know it's engraved with an X.

I watch as the others pick it up to inspect it.

"Maybe the sniper was just in this area and decided to help out an old friend." Jaine holds Eoin's gaze. He has no clue who the sniper is, and it's clear this lack of knowledge is eating him alive.

"So, you expect us all to believe that he was just passing Colton, Nevada, in the middle of the night." Eoin laughs dryly.

"You can believe whatever the hell you like, Mr. O'Connell."

The rest of the room watches as they stare at each other in silence.

"I thought he was no longer for hire."

She turns her attention to Lucifer. "He isn't, as far as I'm aware. So, I guess he was just in the right place at the right time."

"He saved Bailey's life," I mutter. Everyone knows it's true.

"How the hell do you know my daughter anyway?" Lucifer interjects.

"Lucifer, you want that answer, then I suggest you speak to Bailey. This is neither the time nor the place for that conversation. Now from where I'm sitting, we've all been in the wrong here. No one is entirely blameless," Jaine continues. "Rodolfo, La eMe should have discussed the gun pricing with the Irish before downsizing the order and placing it elsewhere."

He nods silently in agreement once more.

"Eoin, the Irish should have gotten their hands dirty from the outset rather than insisting it be handled biker to biker."

"Agreed, Jaine. Rest assured, lessons have been learned from our side."

"Ace, we should have had the Angels provide the necessary back-up. Unfortunately, we have to realize we can't pick and choose where we involve ourselves. That's something you and I have to take responsibility for."

Ace nods.

"Razr, you should have accepted the offer of support from the Sons."

"I'm well aware of that."

"No-one here, except for Lucifer, would have known how underhand Reaper was. That aside no one would have known he was instructed by his backer to kill anyone who stood in their way. That proves none of us was prepared enough. That's a failing on all our parts."

"And it's that failing that saw my kid brother get shot," Rodolfo snaps back.

I can understand why. The rest of us have lost out financially. He's lost his own flesh and blood.

A moment passes before Jaine speaks.

"I'm going to have to disagree with you there, Rod. I'm sorry to have to say this, but Rafael was an adult. Young, yes, but a grown man all the same. He made his own decisions. He knew what he was doing, and he knew the risks involved. The loaded gun wasn't pointed at him. He made a split-second decision to take a bullet for Bailey. What he did, he did through choice. What he did, he did for love. Let's not forget that. Let's not belittle what he did and take that away from him. The ultimate sacrifice he chose willingly to make for her."

"What do you mean for love? Will someone please tell me what the fuck is going on here?"

Jaine turns her attention back to me. I immediately know I'm not going to like what I'm about to hear.

"Delaney, Raf and Bailey were as good as engaged. They were part of an arranged marriage to ally the Sons and La eMe."

Anger roars through me.

She may not have been involved in the gun business, but she still fucking deceived me. She'd been cheating on him. With me. Betrayal flows through me, so strong I can almost taste the acidic bitterness on my tongue.

I stand up, and my chair falls to the floor.

"Where the hell are you going, Delaney?"

"To find Bailey."

"Don't do anything stupid."

I ignore that comment. Right now, all I seem to be doing is stupid. I slam the door as I leave. I'm sure they can fill me in later on what's been agreed and decided.

"What the hell's going on, Jaine?" I can hear Lucifer's voice from behind the closed door as I storm off.

"It's not my place to say. You need to speak to your daughter."

CHAPTER FORTY-ONE

BAILEY

The Undertakers' Clubhouse, Colton, Nevada

I'M STANDING AT THE BAR WITH ABEL WHEN RAZR STRIDES OUT OF the office with a face like thunder.

"We need to talk." He looms over me, a wall of fury, standing so tall and so close my nose is almost touching the president label on his cut, the scent of leather so strong I can almost taste it. He's got his threatening Razr voice on, which immediately stuns Abel into silence. He might frighten him, but he sure as hell doesn't scare me.

Neither as Razr nor as Paul Delaney.

He grabs my arm painfully.

"Quit manhandling me, asshole." I try to yank myself free, but he holds on fast.

"Outside. Now." His hand slips to my wrist as he pulls me along behind him like a naughty child. People stare, mouths agape, as he drags me along, my heels digging into the ground, making no difference whatsoever to the speed we're traveling.

We walk behind the building to the scene of last night's shit show before he finally releases me, throwing my arm away from him in disgust.

"Why?" He immediately starts running his hands up and down the side of his shaved head as he tries to control his temper and keep his demon in check.

"Why what?" I fold my arms in front of me like a petulant child, rolling my eyes exaggeratedly. I'm well aware I'm behaving immaturely.

"Why did you lie to me, Bailey?"

"I didn't…"

"WHY THE FUCK DID YOU LIE!"

The force of his anger takes me by surprise. I expected him to be annoyed when the truth came out, but I never expected this. Then again, I've seen him almost kill a brother for way less than what I've done.

"I needed to get away. From Nevada."

"So, you thought you'd travel all the way to New York and worm your way into my club and into my fucking bed by pretending to be a cum slut."

"The MC life is all I know, and the opposite coast seemed like a good idea at the time. Your bed? Well, that just sort of happened." I tilt my chin defiantly. I mean, it's not like he had any complaints at the time.

"For all those months, you lied. To me. To Mojo. To all of us."

"I didn't lie. I said I came from an MC background, and I did. No one asked me a direct question about the role I played there."

"Don't goddamn lie, Bailey. Jaine will have asked that very question. Before you were accepted, she would have asked that question."

His voice is worryingly quiet now. He's right. I was asked. I said I was a cum slut for the Punishers. I blatantly lied.

See. This is the precise reason why my daddy says it's best never to lie.

"She did, didn't she?"

"Yes. She did."

"Meaning you lied to her too. You should have told her the goddamn truth. That you were the daughter of the prez of another charter."

"Then I wouldn't have been offered the role."

"Exactly. You wouldn't have been."

"I would never have betrayed you, Razr."

"That's not the point. You're the daughter of a high ranker from another club, and you were living within the confines of mine. You were party to a lot of our inner workings as a result."

"It was only meant to be for a month or so. I just needed a break. A chance to think and clear my head."

"So, you thought you'd do that in my club and in my bed and then extend this break to the best part of a year." He's flicking his blade now, clearly moments away from releasing that alter ego of his before proceeding to slit my throat like he's been threatening to do. I know I deserve it. I've lied. I've been deceitful.

"I'm sorry."

I'm not sure what else I can say. In his mind, I've betrayed him and his club. I've pretty much spat on the Iron Scorpions' badge.

"If you were anyone else. If…."

"I'd be dead. I know."

"Why'd you run anyway? From here? Why'd you feel the need to leave Nevada?"

"They haven't told you?"

"I want to hear it from you. I want the damn truth to come out of that deceitful little mouth of yours for once," he hisses.

"My daddy…"

"Lucifer." He laughs dryly.

"My daddy entered me into an arranged marriage with my childhood friend, Rafael Flores. His family members are high rankers in La eMe. Daddy thought we were the perfect match. He's always loved Raf like he was a son."

I can feel tears of self-pity fill my eyes as I talk about him, causing me to have to pause before I can continue. Razr knows why I've stopped. He's not stupid. But neither of us comment on my visual and audible displays of weakness.

"Anyway, I didn't want to get married. Not to Raf. Not to anyone. But I wasn't being given any choice. It was a done deal. Off the back of it, the Sons and La eMe would ally. It was a business decision—a good one for both parties. Call me old-fashioned, but I wanted to marry for love. I didn't want to be used as a pawn in some political game of outlaw chess. I couldn't see any way out, so I ran."

"You didn't love him? Raf."

"Yes and no."

"Meaning?"

"Raf is—or he was—one of the constants in my life. Someone who'd always been there for me. My mother skipped town when I was a baby leaving me and my brother Conor behind. It sort of fucks you up in the head. Knowing that your own mom cared so little that she could just stroll off into the sunset without a backward glance and leave you behind. Raf was our friend. Mine and Conor's. He's always been there for me. He's never let me down. So, yes, I loved him. But I wasn't in love with him."

"But you were going to go through with the engagement? The marriage?"

"Yes. Even though I wasn't in love with him, Raf was in love with me. I figured at least one of us could be happy, right? I mean, he was a great guy. The best. I would have been the envy of women from all over. We would have had a good life together. A strong marriage built on a foundation of friendship."

"But you didn't love him."

"I think I could have learned to love him. Anyway, what does that matter? I mean, isn't true love really just a figment of the imagination anyway? A rush of lust and pheromones between two willing parties that will just fizzle out over time?"

"Why'd you leave?"

"I just told you."

"New York. Why'd you leave New York?"

"I needed to come back home."

"Is that the only reason?"

"No."

I shuffle awkwardly from foot to foot. There's no way I'm admitting anything. Not when Strawberry Shortcake's as good as his old lady now.

"What were the other reasons?"

"I didn't want to pretend to be a cum slut anymore." His cum slut. He knows that's what I'm really saying.

"A role you shouldn't have been offered or taken up in the first place."

"I guess so."

He strides over to me. Tall. Menacing. Achingly familiar. He's so close his sandalwood cologne immediately wraps its invisible arms around me. Pulling me in. Drugging me. I close my eyes in an attempt to blank him out, but it doesn't work. It just heightens all of my other senses and makes me even more acutely aware of his presence. It takes everything not to inhale deeply. I want to breathe in Paul Delaney so he becomes part of the oxygen I need to keep me alive.

"Do I repulse you that much, Bailey?" His voice is barely a whisper.

I shake my head slowly from side to side. I still can't look at him. Why? Because I don't want those penetrating green eyes of his digging into mine, searching for truths I don't want to give up.

Does he already know how I feel about him? That I fucking love him. That I'm in love with him.

"No, of course not. It's not that. It was never that." I lick my lips nervously.

His gaze tracks the movement of my tongue, and he lowers his head, so his hot breath can mingle with mine. His lips are so tantalizingly close I can almost taste them. Is he going to kiss me? I want his mouth on mine—just one more time.

Before I do what I have to do. Before I say what I have to say.

I don't wait for him to decide. Instead, taking the demon by his horns, I snake my arms around his neck and press my mouth to his, pushing my tongue past his lips. My center immediately throbs as the familiar flavor of raw testosterone and everything else that makes up Paul Delaney explodes on the tip of my tongue.

He pulls me to him with one hand, fisting my hair and tilting my head with the other as his tongue strokes deep. Searching. Rediscovering. Remembering.

A groan passes my lips, and he responds with a growl of his own as our tongues collide, tangle, and taste.

His mouth leaves mine briefly to suck hard on my neck, the flat of his tongue running up the full length of my throat before he devours my mouth once more.

Why did we spend so many months not kissing? Such a fucking waste. His mouth is addictive. He's addictive.

He walks me backward until my back's pressed against the clubhouse wall before lifting me so I can wrap my legs around his waist and anchor myself to him. He growls his approval as his dick presses against my clit, its magnificent length hard, thick, and throbbing.

"You want my cock, sweetheart?"

He's grinding against me now, the friction so fucking good I'm almost crying with the need for release.

"Answer me."

"Yes. Fuck me, Razr. I need you to fuck me."

"You sure that's what you want?"

Just this once. Just this one last time. I need to feel his dick inside me. I don't get a chance to reply as he's kissing me again, his tongue filling my mouth as his slim hips pin me against the wall.

"Interrupting something, am I?"

My blood freezes in my veins at the sound of the familiar voice, and I squeeze my eyes shut in embarrassment that he's witnessed me in such a compromising position.

"Daddy," I whisper as I unravel myself from Razr's embrace and lower my feet to the ground.

I turn to face him, and he narrows his eyes at me before looking between us both.

"There's no need for me to ask where you've been all these months now is there, Bee?"

He nods at Razr before turning around and walking off.

"Shit," Razr hisses, running both hands up the side of his head.

I don't reply. I simply walk away, following my daddy. It's silently what he's ordered me to do. No questions asked. Right now, I'd give anything not to be in my own shoes as, going by my daddy's reaction, he's not thinking that Razr and I are a very good match.

CHAPTER FORTY-TWO

BAILEY

Bailey's Home, Colton, Nevada

"DADDY'S NOT BEST PLEASED WITH YOU, LITTLE BEE."

"You don't say, Jay."

"Can't say I am either."

"Why? It's not like Razr isn't a biker."

I throw myself on top of my bed. In the absence of a mother figure, my sister will have been called upon to lecture me and explain to me the error of my ways on behalf of my daddy. There really is no need.

I already know exactly where I fucked up.

"How the hell did you manage to worm your way into the hallowed ground that is the Iron Scorpions' compound anyway?"

I don't reply. I'm sure she'll figure it out by my silence.

"Bee, please tell me you didn't touch my stuff?"

"I'm sorry, Jay. In hindsight, I well and truly fucked up every single thing."

"Shit, Bee. At times you really do act your age."

"I said I'm sorry."

"I'm surprised Razr didn't cut your throat with that infamous blade of his when he found out who you really are."

"The only reason he didn't is because I led the hog cavalry to save his ass and because of what happened to Raf."

"He said that?"

"He didn't need to."

"I'm still kind of surprised. The man's got a reputation. He's also eleven years older than you. He's a grown-up. He should have known better."

"Than what? Than to get involved with a younger girl?"

"I never said that. Don't go putting words in my mouth."

"But it's what you were implying. What's his age got to do with anything?"

"Because he'll be at a different place in his life."

"What place?"

"Marriage. Kids. That sort of place."

"You forget that I was about to become engaged to Raf. To then get married and have kids."

"Okay, so it's also the reckless way he lives his life. As his old lady, he's liable to get you killed. Razr is a dangerous man. Daddy just doesn't want anything to happen to you, Bee. None of us do. I mean, you nearly got yourself killed last night. And Raf? Well, he did."

"Razr didn't ask us to help him. It was my choice."

"Yup. It was. But you wouldn't have had to make that choice if he hadn't made that stupid decision of his in the first place. He was offered back-up, Bee. He turned it down."

"He's not in a good place right now."

"From what I hear, Razr is never in a good place. Maybe he needs some professional help with that. I know, I know we're at risk every day living this life of ours, blah, blah, blah, but being with someone like Paul Delaney, you'd multiply the level of danger you face on each of those days by one hundred. He's a ruthless killer with a lot of enemies, and that list only grows longer each day."

"He's hot-headed."

"The word you're looking for is crazy, Bee. The man is insane. If it hadn't been for The Exterminator, you might well be dead right now. His bullet penetrating Reaper's skull is what kept you alive."

"Reaper wouldn't have killed me."

"You don't know that. He only needed you to help him escape. After that, what was he going to do with you? Take you with him?"

She's not saying anything I haven't already thought about several times since. No one needs to remind me of how dumb I acted and what the end result was.

Of what happened to Raf.

"Well, I'm sure you'll be pleased to know that I won't be seeing Razr again after tomorrow."

"Is that right? Because Daddy says you were almost fucking against the Undertakers' clubhouse wall."

"He said that?"

"Well, not in those exact words, but that's what he implied. What were you thinking? Raf's not even been laid to rest yet, Bee."

"I know how it looks, but please just let me handle things in my own way. After tomorrow, Razr and I are done. Don't worry."

"I'm relieved to hear that. And Daddy will be too. My only hope is that you know what the hell you're doing. We all want what's best for you. And that's not Paul Delaney. Well, at least not unless he has a head transplant to rid himself of that insanity he has going on in there, along with handing that death wish he's carrying around with him into lost and found. I mean, he's handsome and all, but what good is eye candy if you're stone-cold dead and can't appreciate it?"

"None of it matters, Jay. I've already told you. After tomorrow, we're done. Anyway, Razr already has someone lined up to be his old lady back in New York."

"Well, I wish her the best of luck. She's going to need it."

"Are you coming to the funeral tomorrow?" I change the subject.

"I can't get away. The timing couldn't have been worse. Not that Raf got to choose the timing, but you know what I mean. Anyway, I've already spoken to his folks and sent some flowers. I've told them I'll go pay my respects at the cemetery next time I'm in town."

"How's the job going?"

There's a long exhale. "Solve one problem, several more appear."

"Sounds fun. Will you be home soon?"

"For Daddy's birthday. But only for a fleeting visit. Then I need to get back. I have some new clients I need to meet." There's a pause. "I hope it all goes well tomorrow, Bee."

I laugh dryly. "What, when we bury the man who was meant to be my future?"

"I know I've said it a hundred times now, but I am sorry."

"I know you are. I am too."

"You're being so brave. If it were me, I'd be a mess. But then, I've never been as strong as you."

"I'm being brave because that's what Raf would have wanted me to be. That's the only reason."

"You make him proud tomorrow, you hear me?"

"I will."

"Bee, while I'm on the phone, I need you to go into my room and dig something out for me."

"Sure thing."

CHAPTER FORTY-THREE

BAILEY

Whispering Mountains Cemetery, Colton, Nevada

It's a surreal kind of a day. My first funeral. I guess I always expected my first to be for an older person. Someone who'd lived a long and full life. Like one of the older brothers or one of the ancient Colton townsfolk.

In this life, old age is never guaranteed. It's just something each of us aspires to achieve. Age as a number is irrelevant to us. No pun intended given his recent passing, but the Grim Reaper's not choosy. A soul is a soul.

Raf's life hadn't really begun before it was taken from him. He had his whole future mapped out—a future he wanted to share with me.

He died. For me.

And today, we'll lay him in the cold, hard ground.

Alone. Unmarried. Childless.

Tears prick my eyes, but I will not shed them. I will be brave for him today. As brave as he was for me when he stepped in front of that bullet with my name on to save my unworthy life.

I didn't deserve it. I didn't deserve him.

I look around the cemetery. It's beautiful, with an expanse of headstones all beautifully carved and with graves all well-tended. The Flores' have their own family plot. Many spaces filled. Most empty. I'm guessing each Flores knows which has their name on it. That each of them has chosen their own final resting place.

If we'd married, maybe I'd have been asked to choose my own too. I'll never know now.

I can't even begin to quantify how many mourners are here. How many people have shown up to pay their last respects. The cemetery is filled with males in suits and males in leathers, all adorned by pretty, perfumed females. The La eMe are suited, and the bikers are wearing cuts. Some things will never change.

It's the way of our world.

Most of the womenfolk are already in tears. No doubt, their minds are plagued with the prospect of losing their husband, siblings, or children to the same fate as Raf. Gone in the blink of an eye at twenty-three years old.

Conor squeezes my hand and looks down at me. In return, I stare up at him. We're both in full leathers today, and my jacket's patched to the Sons of Satan.

I never really had girlfriends growing up. The only female friend I ever had was Mo. It was always me, Conor, and Raf. If girls did befriend me, it was only because they wanted to hook up with one of them. Now, there's just the two of us. My brother looks tired. His eyes are haunted. Selfishly, until now, I'd forgotten just how much Raf meant to him too. He's lost his best friend. The boy turned man he shared all of his memories with, including the ones they never shared with me as they weren't for a young girl's ears.

I smile up at him, and he pulls me against his side, wrapping an arm around my shoulder. I almost lose it at this blatant show of tenderness, but I bite my lip and force the tears back.

"Bailey."

I recognize her voice immediately from behind me. I turn to look at her, my lip quivering.

"Jaine." The word is barely audible.

Pulling me to her, she holds me fast in a vicelike hug. She's trying to pass her strength on to me at the same time as absorbing my pain. I've seen her do it a million times with Razr. To calm him down. I close my eyes, and I accept the embrace.

"You got this. You hear me?"

I nod, not trusting myself to speak.

I turn to look at Ace, Blaze, and Knight, and we simply nod at each other. Everyone knows who I am now. Whose daughter I am. Then I turn to Razr. He looks like he's wrestled with his demon all night long then lost. I know better than most how much of an insomniac he is. He's never looked this bad, though. His eyes are bloodshot, and his face is gaunt like he's not been eating.

He's finally reached rock bottom.

I nod at him, as I did to the others. This isn't about Razr and me. We can cross that bridge later on today for the final time.

Right now, it's all about Raf.

"Bailey, it's time."

Conor takes my hand. He leads me until I'm standing in front of the walnut casket that contains the earthly remains of Raf. It's already positioned for lowering into the ground beneath. Is it wrong that I want to prize it open so I can see his beautiful face one more time? I want that so badly. But the time has passed. Just as his time in this world has come to an end.

He died. For me.

"Bailey."

I stare up at Rodolfo Flores. His dark hair is shorter, his body is broader, and he's wearing more of the life's lines on his face, but there's no mistaking he's Raf's brother. He passes me the compulsory St. Christopher.

"Will you?"

"I..." I stare at the neckpiece. I never expected to be part of their ceremony. I'm not even sure I should be. It's not that I don't want to be. I don't deserve to be.

Raf deserved way better than me.

Rodolfo knows what I'm thinking. My doubts. My reasons. Everyone knows I ran away to escape my fate. To escape my future with Raf.

"He'd want you to, Bee."

I nod. How can I refuse?

Father Rodriguez gives a sermon, but I hear none of it. Instead, I stare at the casket, my thoughts on Raf. I let the memories flow through my mind, and I place each precious one in a box before closing it to keep them safe. I'll carry them with me always.

As long as I still have them, he will never be truly gone.

The sermon ends, and I pull my Glock out from the back of my pants. We're all led by Raf's daddy as the congregation fires our three shots into the air as a mark of respect.

Rodolfo takes the gun from his daddy's hand and walks over to me. I'm conscious everyone's about to witness the exchange, and the knowledge almost causes me to break down. I need to cry so badly, but I don't. I can do that later in the privacy of my own home. Right now, I need to be strong.

Together, Rodolfo and I approach the casket. He hands me the weapon that's still warm to the touch, and I wrap the St. Christopher around it before placing it on top.

Both are to keep Raf safe and protected throughout his journey into the next life and beyond.

I walk back to Conor, keeping my eyes on the ground. I can't look at anyone. It's too much. Too raw. I feel too exposed.

"You did good, Little Bee."

My daddy wraps his arm around my shoulder, and I simply nod. I got Raf killed. I'm the reason he's dead. How did I do good?

We stand quietly as people start to disperse. Many to Raf's parents' house. Many to the clubhouse, where they'll all drink themselves into a stupor.

"I'll call you tomorrow." I nod at Jaine and watch as she walks away with Ace. Razr looks at me before lowering his head, turning to go with Blaze and Knight.

"Razr." He turns around when I say his name, then walks back and stands in front of me. "We need to talk."

He nods.

"Bee…"

I cut my daddy off. "Daddy, Razr, and I need to talk. You already know my mind's made up on this." My tone is harsh because he does know it.

It ends. Today.

"I'll head off to the clubhouse with the others," he says reluctantly, kissing me on the side of the head before shaking Razr's hand, then walking away.

I walk in the direction of my hog.

"Where are we going, Bailey?"

"To my house."

Bailey's Home, Colton, Nevada

He followed me home on his borrowed custom hog, and now he's followed me into my bedroom. We both know what this is.

Closure.

I remove my jacket, laying it on the chair in the corner of the room, then take off the rest of my clothing before walking back over to stand in front of him.

"Bailey…"

The hunger burning in his eyes as he takes in my naked flesh betrays the hesitancy in his voice. He wants this as much as I do. He needs it as much as I do. If he pretends otherwise, then he's a fucking liar.

"Actions speak louder than words." I drop my hand to rub his dick through his jeans. I'm not surprised to find that he's already rock hard after my strip show. We never had any issues when it came down to fucking compatibility.

It was everything else that was the problem.

"Show me what you got then, Prez." I smirk at him. It doesn't seem that long ago since he said those words to me back at the Scorpions' clubhouse.

Back when Raf was still alive. Back before I got him killed.

Given the green light, I watch as he strips to his jeans. His eyes darken with every item of clothing he loses. Fisting my hair, he tilts my head back and stares down at me, his eyes searching my face.

Then I realize. He knows. He's doing exactly what I'm doing. He's making memories of a time in his life. A person in his life. A person that, after today, will no longer be there.

"You just going to stare or what?"

His eyes connect with mine before his gaze drops to my lips.

My heart's pounding in my chest, and I'm pretty sure my arousal's now running down my thighs.

I. Want. Him.

Like I will never want anyone again in my life. Like I have never wanted anyone. My body's screaming out to be possessed by the demon that is Paul 'Razr' Delaney.

One. Final. Time.

His eyes bore into mine as he cups my face before pulling my bottom lip into his mouth and biting down. I whimper at the pain, gripping onto him as my legs start to shake. I'm going to come just thinking about what he's going to do to me next. He doesn't even need to lay a damn finger on me.

He knows how close I already am. It's only too evident when the smug bastard smirks down at me. His mouth covers mine in earnest this time, his lips hard and demanding as they move against my own, crushing them under his before his tongue strokes deep, filling my mouth.

All the blood in my body flows straight to my clit the moment he leans down and sucks my nipple into his mouth, causing the tip to tighten painfully. Fisting his hair in both hands, I press against him, my needy body begging for more from his hot, greedy mouth.

He lifts me and I wrap my legs around his waist, then he drops me backward on the bed before sucking hard on the other nipple.

"I need to taste you, Bailey." His hot breath whispers against my ear before his mouth drops to bite hard on my neck. To mark me like he did way back then.

It'll only be the second time he'll have ever gone down on me. Most bikers never eat cum slut pussy for obvious reasons. Not even with a dam.

He licks and bites his way down my body as his hand drops down to my already slick folds.

"You're so fucking wet, sweetheart."

Thrusting two fingers inside me, he starts to finger fuck me hard and fast, the sound of how wet I am filling the silence, along with my appreciative groans of sinful pleasure.

"Razr…"

His mouth covers my clit, and he sucks hard. The force of the unexpected orgasm rattles through me, causing me to clench my thighs tightly around his head.

"That's it, sweet Bailey. Let me taste every last fucking drop of you."

Pulling out his fingers, he forces my legs apart, then his mouth devours me, wrenching another orgasm from me. In the end, I have to push him away from my over-sensitized clit.

Lying there, I watch as he strips off the rest of his clothes, revealing that perfect male body of his that's bumped and ripped in all the right places. A body that displays perfectly the plethora of black ink he wears. It's the most beautiful artwork in the world. He watches me as I admire him, then he fists his dick in his hand and slowly pumps his shaft up and down.

"You like watching me fuck my hand, sweetheart?"

He's asking a question he already knows the answer to. He growls as he strokes himself faster and harder, his lips parting when the first licks of promised pleasure reach his brain, his pre-cum now running freely down his fist.

"Razr. I need you to fuck me, not your hand." Dropping my fingers to my pussy, I rub my clit in slow, steady circles. His show's done what it intended to. I'm already chasing my next orgasm.

He sheaths his erection, then drags me down the bed, thrusting inside me in one swift movement.

My eyes roll to the back of my head. I swear nothing will ever feel as good as Razr's dick inside me. Its thick, possessive length fills me completely, like God made it with my name invisibly inked on it. Resting my legs against his torso, he grips my hips and starts to fuck me hard and fast. Sweat sheens his body as he tilts my hips so he can reach my sweet spot and sink even deeper. Too deep. Painfully deep.

The combination of pleasure and pain pushes me over the edge, and my nails dig into his thighs as I claim my release once more.

My walls clench around him, and he deliberately slows his movements to let the flood of my wetness coat his shaft before fucking me hard into the bed, then, with a roar, claiming his own release.

We lie there afterward, his full weight on top of me. Smothered. Breathless. Satisfied.

"Can I ask you something?"

"Depends on what it is," I reply truthfully, praying he doesn't move. Praying this moment will never end.

But it will. It has to.

He lifts his head from the crook of my neck and looks down at me. I stare back, appreciating the greenness of his eyes with their scattering of gold flecks while searching for the monster that lurks just beneath the surface.

I can't see him, but I know he's there.

My eyes then take in the face and the achingly beautiful man that is Paul Delaney.

"Why did you risk your life for mine?"

My cheeks heat. "Because I didn't want anything bad to happen to you."

"Why, Bailey?"

"Because I care." It may be a complete understatement, but it's still true.

His eyes scan my face. Watching. Waiting. He suspects my feelings, I think, but he doesn't know for sure. And he never will. At least not from me.

"Care to expand on that?"

"Not really." I pause for a moment before I continue. "I know there are two sides to you. The one that's here now, Delaney. And the other one, Razr."

He frowns at me, likely wondering how or why I even noticed, so I answer his unspoken question.

"I spent most of my time in New York with Razr. I know him quite well. I've only met the other person a handful of times."

He nods. He gets it.

"I just didn't want anything to happen to the man because of the poor decisions made by his alter ego."

He moves off me, rolling onto his back and pulling me with him before tucking my head under his chin. He smells of clean sweat and sandalwood cologne. A scent I wish I could bottle. A scent I pray I never forget.

"What do you want from me, Bailey?"

"Nothing. Or at least, not yet."

"Meaning?"

"Meaning that, in around ten minutes, I'm going to have to ask you to leave."

"Then?"

"Then nothing. Then we'll never speak to each other again."

"And why is that?"

"For one, you sort of have a girlfriend, and you've told her you'll consider her as your old lady."

"I don't have a girlfriend. I only told her we'd discuss things when I get back."

"All subject to her letting you fuck her. I've already heard all about it."

There's a pause.

"And? You said for one, so I'm guessing there's a second reason."

"There is."

"What is it?"

"I'm the reason Raf got killed."

"Bullshit," he hisses.

He can argue all he wants, but I know it's true.

"If I wasn't there, he wouldn't have followed me." He attempts to interrupt again, but I stop him. "Let me finish." I pause. "I'm not the only reason Raf got killed. See, if Razr hadn't been so pigheaded and had accepted the offer of back-up from the Sons, there would have been no reason for me to be there."

"What are you getting at, Bailey?"

"That both me and Razr are responsible for Raf's death. I can never forgive him for the part he played, just as I will never be able to forgive myself. So, I've decided that I never want to see Razr again. Which means I can't ever see you again either."

CHAPTER FORTY-FOUR

JAINE

Jaine's House, Rising, California

"I APPRECIATE WHAT YOU'RE SAYING, EOIN, BUT DELANEY'S NOT IN a good place right now. Trust me, we're acutely aware of that and have the very best consultants handling his case with no expense spared. So, we will get on top of things."

"We could have ended up going to war with the Mexicans over this."

"But we didn't."

"Only because of your relationship with Raf's brother. Expertly handled, by the way."

"Thank you."

"But a young man still died."

"Delaney had nothing to do with that. Raf made that decision all on his own. If you step in front of a loaded gun, chances are, you're going to wind up dead."

"But if Razr had accepted the Sons' offer, it might never have come to that."

"If. It's a big word. If the Angels had backed the Scorpions. If the Dusters had gotten their manicured hands dirty. That's a lot of ifs right there. You appear determined to hold Delaney responsible, but in my opinion, we're all just as guilty. We're all responsible for Raf ending up in front of that weapon. But no one more so than Raf himself."

"Razr can't end up being a liability to the alliance, Jaine."

"He won't. Delaney has mental health issues. You can't penalize someone for that sort of shit these days. It's being handled. Leave it be now. Anyway, I'm carrying the can for it, isn't that enough? I'm the one who's had to agree to become the legal representation for La eMe so there can be no mixed lines of communication moving forward."

"You don't sound best pleased. I'm sure it will be a very lucrative deal for JAL."

"Given the frequency with which you have Dylan check my bank accounts, I'm sure you already know that I don't need the money. I'm spinning enough goddamn plates as it is. Rodolfo's been chasing to use my services for years for his illegal wrongdoings. I've always been able to decline due to location. Now I've been given no choice in the matter."

"Blame Razr," he retorts.

"You're starting to piss me the fuck off."

"At least we're not insisting you represent the Dusters. Yet."

"Not a chance."

"You wouldn't want to work side by side with me every day? I think we'd complement each other."

"If there's a fate worse than death, that's it right there."

"Charming."

"Thank you. I do try. Anyway, you have your own in-house legal representation."

We both know I'm talking about Irish.

"Paddy handles the internal contractual side only. But, like La eMe, we may need someone to handle our part in this alliance. We may also need someone to handle our external communications. Jessie seems to think that questions may still be asked on our new business ventures and…"

"And you can find someone else."

"What if we don't want to find someone else?"

"Tough shit."

"We're already using your services."

"For accountancy, that means Jessie. For legal, that means me. And as far as I'm aware, I haven't created an owing, so you can't railroad me this time."

"Haven't you? Why have you had to offer your services to La eMe, then? You obviously believed you'd created an owing to them. Why not to the Dusters?"

"Listen, Irish trained in the same field I did. I'm sure he can handle it. He'll be able to monopolize the IRS with ease. He's a people person. Unlike you."

"Did they unearth anything at the clubhouse? Find any indication of who the faction was behind the Undertakers?"

He ignores my barb and immediately changes the subject away from his brother. Figures. He wants to keep it on himself as he's so vain.

"Nothing. All clean. Reaper's gut must have warned him he was living on borrowed time, so the place was wiped. No phone found. No laptop. Zilch. His life went into lockdown, and all the wrongdoings he was involved in were expertly hidden. Perhaps by the faction in question, as soon as they heard the Scorpions were coming to town. Unfortunately, his right-hand men were dead long before we got there, and the final one was killed in the crosshairs."

"I don't think his backer will be happy."

"Agreed. And I worry that they'll bide their time before seeking revenge of some sort. Who will they target? It's my gut feeling that the gun business was just a cover-up for the much more lucrative trafficking system they were both heavily involved in. Most of the cum sluts at the Undertakers' clubhouse are underage for sure, although the paperwork they produced when questioned would deny that. It's been expertly produced, I have to say. I can tell the ink's still wet, but others could be forgiven for being fooled."

"Yes, you may well be right. Very observant of you."

"Full of compliments today. What are you after?"

"What are you offering?"

"To you? Nothing."

I know he's angling to use me for legal services now he's got it in his head. That much is obvious. Well, I'm not doing it.

"We have it on good authority that the Bratva's not involved this time around. Perhaps our new pakhan has some morals."

"Or maybe he's just finding his feet before joining the party. Anyway, that's both good and not-so-good news."

"In what way?"

"Better the devil you know. And also, the devil you know about. If it's not them, then it could be one of several."

"Well, we know it's not the Dusters or the Mexicans."

"And we know it's not the Bratva now. So, I guess taking out Lebedev was worthwhile after all."

"It was. And both Razr and Bailey were extremely lucky that The Exterminator put in an appearance on their behalf when he did. I wonder how he knew they would be there. I suspect luck had nothing to do with it."

"Surely, it's not that big of a surprise, Eoin? The Exterminator works via the Scorpions. Always has. It's my guess he simply showed up on the off chance that Delaney might need him. He'll have gone back to ground now."

"Pity."

"Sometimes folks just need a break."

"I noticed that Lucifer spent a long time talking to Ace. On the surface, the conversation looked quite tense. Anything we should be concerned about?"

"I noticed too and did ask. Nothing untoward, Ace assures me."

"Good to know."

"For the record, it's since been agreed that the Sons of Satans' council will also run the Undertakers. It makes complete sense given they operate in such close proximity. They've called church, and the brothers are in agreement. The vote was almost unanimous, although there's always the risk it may be a knee-jerk reaction to what's happened. Lucifer's highly respected as a prez. He's already allied with the Scorpions."

"That may all change now he knows Razr's been sleeping with his daughter."

"Lucifer's a businessman first and foremost. And a very successful one from what I can gather. You don't become so by allowing emotions to become involved. If he can form ties with a charter on the opposite coast, one as influential as the Scorpions, then he'd be a fool to turn that opportunity down just because Razr's been dicking Bailey."

"Maybe."

"Definitely. Anyway, what's happening with Jessie?"

"Dylan's meeting with her today."

"How's progress, Jessie?"

I'm trying not to touch base with her too often, but I'm conscious I need to keep abreast of the situation in case the eldest O'Connell puts me on the spot. I've no doubt the smug fucker would get off on me not being able to provide him with an immediate answer.

Asshole.

"I'm working my way through things as quickly as possible, partner, but it's a real mess. They should sue their previous accountant. But given how creative they were asking them to be, maybe they've only got themselves to blame."

"Let's try to formalize a contract duration for this one. I need a line in the sand date. I don't want to be dealing with them any longer than I have to. Eoin's already hinting that he wants access to JAL's services. I need to avoid that at all costs."

"They're never going to want to let me go, though, Jaine. Pretty soon I'm going to become indispensable to them."

"We have other customers we need to offer our services to."

"Once I'm on top of the backlog, I'm sure I can handle several others. In the meantime, maybe we need to start a recruitment drive."

"And how would you suggest we do that? Advertise in the outlaw press? Listen, I'll put out some feelers. In the meantime, let's focus on getting this current issue with the Dusters addressed, and then we can take it from there. How did it go today? Eoin told me you were meeting with Dyl."

"All good."

"Care to expand?"

"Well, as you know, there was talk of me temporarily moving into the annex attached to Delectable Dylan's apartment as he's currently rattling around in that huge place all on his lonesome.

"Delectable Dylan. I like it."

"Well, credit where credit's due. That silent Duster is pretty much edible in my humble opinion, or at least I'm pretty sure certain parts of him are deliciously tasty."

"I'm not sure humble's a word I'd use when it comes to you, Jessie. And please spare me any further Dylan-inspired thoughts, especially when it comes to eating, touching, or dicking."

She snickers. "Sure thing, partner. Anyhow, as you know, my apartment purchase fell through, and the Dusters put me up in an unopened hotel."

"Yup. I already know all this."

"Well, it turns out the hotel's opening soon. I then can't stay there because, once it's open to the general public, people can pretty much come and go as they please. Also, it will be a free for all when it comes to wi-fi. Potential security breaches right, left, and center.

"Solution?"

"Well, given Dylan's madly in love with this cliché blonde you've mentioned, I figured moving in with him wasn't the best idea, even if it is an annex and even if it is only temporary. I'm all for us bunking up together, but I don't want to have to wear earplugs further down the line if my landlord suddenly starts getting it on with his happily ever after two doors down."

"I can appreciate that."

"Anyway, it turns out the apartment directly below is empty. The boys use it for storage or something at present. Bodies, weapons… who knows?"

"Expensive storage?"

"They can afford it. Anyway, I'm buying it. They'll extend all the security that already covers Dylan's penthouse to cover the apartment below. They'll also set it up to go into immediate lock-down at the press of a button."

"Are they offering you a discount?"

"I don't want one. I'll owe them if I accept a discount, and I don't want to owe anyone. So, I'm paying full market price for the apartment along with all the mod cons."

"Best way. So, when are you moving?"

"Well, I need to go back home in the not-too-distant future. So, as soon as I return, hopefully. And even more good news… I finally have my passport. I'll drop everything into JAL later today."

"Good to know. So, are you going to be popping to Dyl's every day to borrow bread, sugar, and milk?

"See, that's why we work so well together, Jaine. You can read my mind."

"Later, Jessie."

I laugh as I hang up. I know she's being completely serious.

Poor Dylan.

I KNOW WHAT IT'S GOING TO BE ABOUT BEFORE I EVEN TAKE THE call.

"Jaine, Cillian won't go into details, and neither will Paul, so I need you to tell me. Be completely honest with me."

"Your brother dropped the ball. It started a domino effect that resulted in a high ranker from La eMe losing his life, Sarah."

"Oh my God. Tell me everything."

"Delaney refused assistance. He went in gung-ho style as Razr does. Twenty-three-year-old Rafael Flores ended up shot in the gut. He died a short time later, but it was fatal the moment it struck his body."

"You saw it happen?"

"No, I wasn't there. I was parked up waiting on an update from Ace."

I'm lying. I watched it happen in slow motion moments before I ended Reaper's fucked up life.

"They're all whispering about him at the Duster end."

"I'm aware of that."

"You spoke to Eoin?"

"Earlier today."

"They say you managed to stop war from breaking out by offering your services to the Mexicans."

"Something like that."

"How can Paul and I ever repay you?"

"You don't have to repay me. It's what we do. What I do. When it comes to Delaney, I will do anything. He has my full support always. He knows that."

"So, what do we do now?"

"Sarah, he's not going to like this, but it's now the only option available to us as far as I can see. We need to steer him down this path for his own sake and the safety of those around him."

"What path?"

"We need to encourage him to sign himself into rehab. I've found a sanctuary that caters specifically to folks with Delaney's mental health issues. He needs to open up to someone. Talk about his past. Let the fuck go of it. That's if he wants to have any future. Right now, he's a danger to himself and others. He needs to learn to cope, but not by using someone else as a crutch. Delaney needs to learn to be independent and stand on his own two feet. He needs to learn how to survive without relying on anyone else."

"You're right, Jaine."

"As VP, Blaze can run the club for a month while Delaney confronts his issues head-on. My concern is if he doesn't, and something else happens, then the Irish will want to remove the Scorpions from the alliance. Delaney must be made to see that his reckless behavior affects way more than just him. Rafael's death is concrete proof of that."

"You got the details?"

"I'll fire them across now."

CHAPTER FORTY-FIVE

RAZR

The Delaney Home, Brightling, New York

HE'S SCREAMING OUT FOR ATTENTION IN MY HEAD. MORE SO THAN usual. And nothing is silencing him. It's because he knows I'm weakening. All the events that took place recently in Nevada with Lucifer, with Reaper, and with her have pushed me to breaking point

"My parents really like you, Paul," Laila shouts through from the kitchen, but her tone doesn't sound half as convinced as her words.

"Your daddy spent the entire evening looking down his nose at me, Laila."

And I spent the same entire evening trying to stop myself from using my steak knife to cut open his damn throat as a result.

"You know that's not true."

But it is true. Why lie?

I'm standing in my childhood bedroom. Everything is in muted tones of grey. Framed images of custom hogs line the walls. It's sparse. I've never been one for clutter, even when growing up. It's always been quality, not quantity for me. Unless the latter is related to money or property, that is.

The only place that's crammed full of unnecessary shit is my fucking head.

I quickly remove the suit I'd been forced into wearing all so I could project the image of the perfect future son-in-law like Laila wanted. I'm not, though. I'm imperfect. Unlike her.

I quickly shed the professional image like a snake sheds skin to reveal the true inked me underneath.

The murderer. The madman. The biker.

My nail digs into my fingertip. Something it's been doing all evening.

Throwing on my jeans, I reach into the back pocket and pull out my blade. Flicking it open, I welcome the feeling of relief that flows through me the instant I slice that sharp piece of metal through my hardened skin.

The pressure in my brain immediately eases, the familiar sensation of blood gathering in my clenched fist offering me a temporary respite.

Warm. Sticky. Oozing.

The trouble is, the length of relief my fixes give me is getting shorter and shorter. And the highs are getting lower and lower. Soon, cutting won't even help. And my alter-ego knows it.

He's waiting. Impatiently.

I'm spiraling downwards. I know there'll be no rock bottom for me. It'll just be the gaping maw of hell itself, and there's no coming back from there.

I only pray to God I don't take anyone else with me when my

time comes. But then again, God doesn't give two fucks about my prayers. About our kind. The lowest of the low.

Biker trash.

"Are you okay, Paul? You're bleeding."

Her familiar voice breaks my trance. My demon almost purrs at the sound. He welcomes her.

Because she lets him get away with murder. Because she turns a blind eye to the death and destruction he causes.

Whereas the other part of me? The sane part? Well, he now hungers for someone else.

It's gone a full one-eighty.

She lifts then studies my bloodied hand. I'm surprised she remains upright and doesn't collapse in a heap on the floor.

"It's just a scratch, Laila."

Leading me to the ensuite bathroom, she turns on the faucet and holds my hand under the steady stream of water. It stings. It's a welcome feeling. A feeling that lets me know I'm still alive. Still in the present. But only just. And for how long? That's anyone's guess. God himself only knows that answer. But at the rate I'm going, it won't be for too much longer.

I stare at our shared reflection in the over-sink mirror. The inked biker with the partially shaved head and hair falling into his troubled eyes, leaning over the pocket-sized girl he's known pretty much his entire life.

Light and dark. Good and evil. Right and wrong.

Wrong. Wrong. Wrong.

The word is now stuck in my head.

She frowns at my cut. It's not a scratch. Together we watch as the blood runs freely into the sink.

Drip. Drip. Drip.

She knows I've just done it with my blade. Deliberately. But she ignores the fact. Even though it's staring her straight in the face, she doesn't want to see it. She just wants to patch me up. To stick a band-aid over the fact that I'm an insane fuck-up in the hope that it will all just go away.

It won't.

It'll just be hidden from view. Same as it's always been. But pretty soon, I won't be able to keep him hidden. Pretty soon, he'll win.

And I'm sure that fucker can already smell victory.

I know that what Laila wants from me will eventually lead to my downfall. In the end, my trying to be what she needs will lead to my self-destruction. Unlike everyone else, I've figured out that she wants me to remain two people.

Razr, the biker. Delaney, the businessman.

She wants me to live two separate lives. Here at home with her as Delaney. And at the clubhouse when I need to give into my demonic urges, I'll be the other.

It's not her fault. She just wants normal. And I completely understand that. But I'm not normal. I will never be fucking normal.

I watch as she fixes a band-aid over the cut, the beige fabric material instantly darkening as the blood desperately seeks a way out. It's the equivalent of sticking your finger in a dam. It won't hold back the impending flood. At some point, it will break through.

My head throbs as I stare at the restriction. The one that's trying to stop my release from flowing freely. The one that's blocking my pain from ebbing as it does. I stare at the band-aid. Then I stare at Laila. I then realize there are two restrictions, not just one.

Our eyes connect in the mirror.

"It's time for bed, Paul," she whispers, her gaze searching mine as she takes my hand in hers.

She tilts her head up to look at me, and I touch my hand to her face.

I frown when I leave a bloodied mark on her cheek before letting her lead me silently into the bedroom.

The Iron Scorpions' Clubhouse, Brightling, New York

"I'm not going into fucking rehab."

"You've got serious mental health issues, Paul, and they're getting worse. You need help. Expert help. What went down in Nevada is proof of that. These one-on-one sessions with Dr. Matthews are obviously not enough. But then again, you only turn up when you can be bothered. This shit has gotten out of control. Way out of control."

"Sarah…"

"I mean it, Paul. You get help. I don't want you anywhere near my baby unless you get yourself sorted out. I've only got a handful of months left to go. If you want me and my baby to be part of your life, then you prove it."

I can tell by her tone that she means it. She won't let me be part of her kid's life, which means I can't be part of her life either.

"Back me up here, Jaine." She's got her on hands free. Two against one so I'm out-numbered.

"She's right, Delaney. Enough's enough. It's time. You need to learn to live your life without relying on other people. Stand on your own two feet. You need to learn to love yourself as much as those around you love you."

Her voice breaks. I know it's probably just hormones. Still, I don't like the fact that I've almost reduced Jaine to tears. She deserves more from me. Way more. I've used her all these years. Stolen her energy and pulled at her strength for my own selfish needs and to prop up my undeserving self.

I've taken from so many people and given nothing back.

My thoughts drift to *her.*

I used her, humiliated her, took everything she had to give. In the end, I destroyed her life and her future to the extent that she never wants to see me again.

She saved my life. I gave her nothing in return. Just as I've done with Jaine countless times. My demon destroyed my relationship with my sister until she ran. And she didn't stop running for seven years.

Do I want that to turn into forever? Watch her and her kids live their lives from afar because I'm too fucked up to ever be part of them?

Cillian O'Connell won't let me anywhere near his kid if he thinks I pose a threat. He'd strike me down first. All of the Dusters would. No questions asked. I can't blame them.

With a sound mind, I'd do the same.

They all deserve more from me. So, it's time I gave them more. It's time I gave something back. Hopefully, it's better late than never. And hopefully, it's a battle I can win.

"Where and when?"

CHAPTER FORTY-SIX

BAILEY

Bailey's Home, Colton, Nevada

One month.

One month to the day since we laid Raf to rest. One month to the day since I last saw Paul Delaney. The absence of both hurts.

I'm surrounded by family. I'm surrounded by friends. But I've never felt so alone in my life.

Raf, my constant. Raf, who I took for granted. Raf, who I just assumed would always be there. Raf, who I'll never see again.

And I cry. Every day I cry. Because I miss him.

Razr, my nemesis. Razr, who took me for granted. Razr, who just assumed I would always be there. Razr, who I'll also never see again.

And I cry. Every day I cry. Because I miss him too.

I lie on my bed and stare at the ceiling like I do minute after minute, hour after hour, day after day. What else is there to do when my life stopped when Raf's ended?

Mo messages me several times a day. Jaine too. Both are careful never to mention *him,* though. They know they'd risk alienating me forever. It's too soon. Way too soon. Will it always be too soon?

Most definitely.

Through eavesdropping on whispered conversations between my daddy and Tadgh, all I know is that Paul Delaney has gone into rehab. He's been in there for almost as long as I've been staring at the ceiling.

It's all too little too late as far as I'm concerned. It won't bring Raf back. It won't change anything in my life. I'll still be lying here for all eternity, just existing. Pretending on the outside, purely to salve the conscience of others, that I'm still alive while being stone cold dead underneath.

It'll all still be my fault. And his.

I wonder if Razr is just lying on his bed in whatever facility he's in. Is he staring at the ceiling the same as me? Minute after minute, hour after hour, day after day, asking himself the same countless *what-if* questions over and over?

I envy him. He'll have a future after all this. Life after death. He'll dust himself down and move on with Strawberry Shortcake. Marriage. Kids. A future. They'll already have it all mapped out, I'm sure.

I have none. It's not that I can't have one. I don't deserve one. And who would I share it with anyway?

My phone vibrates.

Jay: *How are you bearing up?*
Bailey: *Same.*
Jay: *How was Daddy's birthday? I had to deal with pressing matters at work in the end. Speaking of which, I need to talk*

to you about that, but I guess now's not the best time. I'm sorry I couldn't make it back.
Bailey: *Life goes on, Jay. Anyway, it was just an excuse for people to visit, drop off casseroles, then fuss and pry.*
Jay: *People care and they're just trying to show it.*
Bailey: *I understand that. I appreciate it.*
Jay: *You been to see Raf yet?*
Bailey: *I'm working my way up to it.*
Jay: *He'll be missing you.*
Bailey: *He's dead.*
Jay: *He's moved on to the next life is all.*
Bailey: *I'd like to think that. I miss him.*
Jay: *I know you do.*
Bailey: *The guilt is crippling me, Jay.*
Jay: *He made his own choices.*
Bailey: *But if I hadn't gone.*
Jay: *You might as well say if you'd never been born.*
Bailey: *I've thought about that too.*
Jay: *Bee, those are dark thoughts.*
Bailey: *I know. I won't do anything stupid, don't worry.*
Jay: *Do you need to speak to someone? You know, like a professional person?*
Bailey: *No. I just need a bit more time.*
Jay: *You need to go see him. Speak to him.*
Bailey: *I will. Soon.*

CHAPTER FORTY-SEVEN

RAZR

Three Months Later
The Delaney Home, Brightling, New York

ONE MONTH TURNED INTO THREE.

In the end, I wanted to stay longer, but I needed to not turn the sanctuary into just another crutch—a place to hide.

I need to get on with my life. I need to start living.

Putting my bags down on the floor. I stare around my childhood home. It's the same, but somehow, it feels different. Just like me, I guess. I'm pretty much the same on the outside but different on the inside. The changes to me as a person can't really be seen by the naked eye. Only the physical changes that come with three months of good clean living.

I've finally made peace with the ghosts from my past. Maybe that's the reason it feels different.

Two of them used to live here.

Sarah sent me a message offering to pick me up from JFK, but instead, I caught a cab. It's been a long time since I've used any form of public transport. I'd usually have a driver or one of the brothers pick me up.

Traveling in a cab would have been way below the old me.

These past few months have taught me, though, that underneath it all, I'm just a man, the same as any other. Removing all the titles. Billionaire. Biker. Murderer. Sibling. Brother.

I'm just me. Paul Delaney.

I may have more material possessions than most, but I realize now that none of that shit matters. We live. We die. Same fate for all of us. We come into this life alone. We leave the same way.

And I realize now that alone doesn't have to be a place I need to avoid. I can be alone. I can survive alone. I can now even appreciate being alone. Having to spend time in my own thoughts and in my own head no longer sees me reaching for my blade, cutting myself, or pulling at my hair.

I've also had to accept death for what it is. An ending. Temporary or otherwise depending on your beliefs, but an ending all the same. I've been affected by several.

My parents. Raf.

I've learned that I need to accept every one of them, celebrate each life, and then move on and not look back. I can no longer dissect or dwell on the negative aspects of loss or the vacuum of my mental illness will just suck me straight back in.

I understand now that I don't have to shoulder any never-ending guilt because I've learned to forgive myself.

Don't get me wrong. I'm an outlaw, and I will always be an outlaw. I will always be a killer. But from now on, I'll kill where killing's due and deserved. No more recklessness. No more risking other people's lives by killing as a salve for my own sanity or just for vanity.

I know I have several apologies to make. As part of my treatment, I made a list, and I've written each individual concerned a letter, which I need to hand-deliver personally. It may not be what they want to hear or read, but it's what I think I have to tell them. Each one is written by my own hand and in my own words.

Each one is written from the heart.

I can ask for their understanding. I can seek their forgiveness. I appreciate that they don't have to give me either, and if they choose not to, then I'm okay with that.

I have to be.

There can be no going back to where I was three months ago. If I go back, there's no way out for me next time around.

There's no time like the present. It's been three months since I last spoke to anyone in my life.

I dial her number.

"Laila."

"Paul, you're back. It's so good to hear your voice."

"It's good to hear yours too, baby girl. I have to see you. There's something I need to give you."

Bailey's Home, Colton, Nevada

I dismount the custom hog I've borrowed and take in the white-painted property with its cream-tiled roof. It looks the same as it did last time I was here, with the same stunning mountain backdrop.

The air doesn't smell much of anything, and the stillness and silence of this place are so loud it's almost deafening. I could never live here. I'd go stir crazy. I'm a city boy. I always will be.

I stand and stare. It's been almost four months. I was expecting things to have changed because I have. But nothing has.

I find myself wondering if she has.

Lucifer knows I'm paying a visit today. It was only respectful to let him know in advance that I'd be turning up at his home to call on his youngest daughter. He's also aware of the reason. That I'm here to make amends.

Or at least to try to.

I'm also here to admit some truths. Stuff that needs saying regardless of whether I want to say it or whether she wants to hear it. Everything will be laid bare then. At least from my end. If she chooses to continue to self-flagellate over Raf's passing, then I guess that's her choice. We all cope in different ways. We all heal in different ways too. I just need to wipe the slate clean to finally move on. After Nevada, I'm heading back to California, where I'll then board a flight from LAX back to JFK.

Back home.

This is the last hand-written letter I need to deliver personally. It's also the most important one.

By all accounts, and from what I've heard, Bailey seldom leaves the house these days. Instead, she wallows in her guilt and self-pity all day long, wishing she had died with him.

Rafael Flores.

But she didn't. Folks keep telling her that. They keep telling her she needs to move on with her life. Start living again. But she doesn't want to hear them. She doesn't want to listen. Maybe like I did, she needs some professional help. Then again, when it comes to that shit, you have to be prepared to accept what you need and then be prepared to ask for it. I know better than most that, sometimes, when you face those sorts of confrontations or have to make those sorts of life-changing decisions, it's easier just to let yourself drown rather than try to fight your way back to the surface.

I walk towards the door, then pause. My first hesitant step. It'll be the first of many, I'm sure. I just need to keep on walking.

Always forward. Never backward.

The door opens before I reach it, and I take in Lucifer. He looks to have aged ten years since I last saw him. I know it'll be over the worry and concerns he has for his youngest.

"Razr." He holds out his hand, and I shake it. The alliance between the Sons and the Scorpions is now in place, set up in my absence but with my full agreement. Blaze has filled me in. He's still acting prez for the Scorpions while I close off these last few remaining personal matters.

"Lucifer."

"You're looking well."

"I feel well." And I do. I guess that may change when I take back the clubhouse reins, but for now, I'm embracing it. When I step back up to the plate, I'll just take things one day and one step at a time. It's all I can do.

"She's in her bedroom. I think you already know where that is."

It's a subtle dig. He knows where we went the day of Raf's funeral. He suspects what happened between us that day too. Still, there's no point either admitting or denying something that's not his business. Bailey and I are both adults, even if there is a substantial age difference between us.

Everyone accepts that age is irrelevant in this life. You have to be either skilled or lucky to reach a high number. So, until your number's called up, you have to grab hold of everything you can.

He steps aside to let me enter the house, and I follow him through the property. Nothing's changed inside either. Again, I'm not sure why I thought it would have. Perhaps because it feels longer than a few months since I was last here.

I approach the dark wood door. The only thing that's now standing between me and her. Adrenaline spikes through me, and for the first time in months, I suddenly want to reach for my blade.

I don't.

I need to face these emotional spikes head-on. Talk about them, depending on the willingness of the other party to do so. Regardless of how awkward or painful it may be. Then I need to move on. I can't force anyone to do anything. I can only say my piece and hopefully then be offered the opportunity to listen to theirs in return.

I knock on the door, and it creaks slowly open.

No words. No nothing. Just a silent invitation to enter.

She's standing facing the window with her back to me. Her blonde hair is longer than it was, her frame thinner.

"Bailey."

She turns to look at me, and my breath catches in my throat, my heart pounding in my chest.

She looks so fragile. So beautifully broken. Her eyes are so blue on her face I immediately lose myself in their depths.

"Razr." Her voice is barely a whisper as her eyes scan over me. There's a hunger there that's reflected by the one shining from my own. There never was any shortage of attraction between us. There's no point in trying to hide it.

I'm never hiding anything. Not ever again.

She's wearing a tank top and cargo pants. The tank girl look that Jaine typically wears. Maybe it's a west coast thing. I know Bailey's kept in contact with her the same as with Mojo.

"You're looking well."

"Thank you," I reply. What else is there to say? "You look…"

"Like shit," she butts in with a slight smile. "It's okay. You can say it."

"Beautiful, I was going to say." Because she does. I was just too damn stupid to see the beauty both on the surface and shining out of her before. I was too busy living in the past and too much under the influence of Razr.

"How have you been?"

"I've been out of action for a few months."

"In rehab. I heard. I'm glad you finally sought some help."

"Me too. Better late than never, I guess. How have you been?"

"You just have to look at me to know the answer to that." She laughs softly. "I've been… existing."

There's a pause.

"Thank you for letting me come here today."

She nods. "I figured you needed closure of a different kind than what we shared last time."

There's another pause.

"I wrote you a letter. It's something they… well, it's something the people at the sanctuary recommend doing. I can read it to you if you like or…."

I take it from my back pocket and start to walk across to pass it to her. She visibly tenses as she stares at the envelope in my outstretched hand, and I know she doesn't want me to come any closer. Turning her back on me, she switches her gaze out the window.

"You can just leave it on the bed, Razr."

I know that's my cue to leave. So, having delivered my very last hand-written letter, I turn and do just that.

Quietly closing the door behind me, I know I'll never forget the finality of the click it makes as I leave.

The truths I wanted to say? I realize now's not the time. I can speak, but I can only be heard if the other person is willing to listen. Bailey isn't. At least not yet. Maybe another opportunity will arise one day. Maybe it won't. Maybe my redemption from her will never be granted. And I'm okay with that. Because I have to be.

CHAPTER FORTY-EIGHT

BAILEY

Bailey's Home, Colton, Nevada

I HAD NO CHOICE BUT TO TURN AROUND, SILENTLY ASKING RAZR TO leave. The tears were pressing against the backs of my eyes, and I was struggling to hold them in.

I did it for his sake, not for mine.

He looked well. He's obviously been living a good life and working out. Health and vitality shone from his eyes, along with acceptance. He's ready to move on with his life. That much is clear. We're at opposite ends right now. Maybe we always were.

I needed him to go. I didn't want to undo all the good he's done for himself by making him feel guilty about my shitty state of mind. That's my problem, not his.

It's my guilt. My burden to bear.

He's accepted his part and paid his price.

I know he must have been out of his comfort zone today, and

that would have been a classic blade-flicking moment in the past. His demon is now clearly under control, and I'm happy for him. I really am.

I was desperate to grab the letter out of his hand and read it, but I knew I had to do that part alone. Hiding my emotions and my reactions from him would be impossible. I'm expecting it to be his confirmation and admittance that he's moving on with Laila. That they'll take the vows together. Prepare for their future. And that he's sorry. That he seeks my forgiveness. That he wants redemption for the part, he played in taking away mine.

Can I grant him that?

So, I wanted him to leave. I turned my back on him, giving him no choice. But why did his immediate acceptance feel like another death? I've lost the man who loved me and the man I love.

That's my penance. My price to pay.

I reach for the envelope lying on the bed. The last communication between us. The last unspoken words. It's plain white. Nothing fancy. Cheap, if I'm honest, which is not something I would have associated with Paul Delaney. Has he changed that much that appearances no longer mean anything to him?

There's no name on the front. Did other people receive one? Or was it only me? How did he differentiate between the envelopes if there were several recipients?

Not that it matters.

I turn it over and rip it open untidily, the jagged edges symbolizing the jagged pieces of my once again broken heart. I speak the words into the once more empty space.

Bailey,

I know it probably seems strange that I've come all this way to deliver a letter with so few words. But that's me. A man of few words. The words I do speak always come from the heart. I mean every single one of them.

I don't deserve your forgiveness, Bailey, so I'm not going to ask for it.

Instead, I just want to say that I'm sorry.

I'm sorry for being an asshole. I'm sorry for fucking everything up, but most of all, I'm sorry for not ever seeing you as a person.

I see you now.

I love you.

Paul.

I read it over and over and over again.

Thousands of miles to deliver a handful of words. Words that meant something to him. Words that should mean something to me.

They do. And they don't.

He's apologizing like it makes everything better. It doesn't. I guess he feels lighter now he's gotten all that off his chest.

Well, lucky him. I fucking don't.

I feel cheated. Then again, what was I expecting? I wanted more. I needed more. There's not enough here for me to use as a salve against my fragile state of mind. Not from that small smattering of words.

But that's my problem. No two guilty consciences will ever match. It doesn't stop me from wanting them to. It doesn't stop me from wanting to inflict my mental pain and anguish on him so he can fucking feel the depths of my despair.

Nope. It's not enough. This hand-written note that was meant to make everything better has made things worse.

I crumple it up and throw it across the room in disgust. Then I stare at it lying there on the floor in the exact spot where he was standing.

It's like the damn thing landed there on purpose.

Minutes pass before I walk across to pick back up this last piece of him, and when I do, my olfactory senses get accosted by the familiar scent of his sandalwood cologne.

I breathe it in, and tears prick my eyes.

I then realize my frustration was because I wanted more. But not more of his apologies. I wanted him to say that he'd missed me too. I wanted him to tell me that he was in love with me too. I wanted him to say that these past few months have been torture for him too.

Then I realize I'm a fuck-up who doesn't know what she wants. My brain is back and forth like a swinging pendulum, and I'm pushing and pulling at people.

I smooth out the crumpled piece of paper as best I can.

I love you.

What the fuck does that even mean anyway? Because the way it's written, it gives nothing away.

CHAPTER FORTY-NINE

BAILEY

Two Months Later
Whispering Mountains Cemetery, Colton, Nevada

I COME HERE EVERY DAY TO TEND TO HIS GRAVE AND TALK TO HIM. He answers me back in his own little ways.

The breeze in the trees causing the whisper of the leaves. The lone cry of a single blackbird. The familiar smell that seems to come from nowhere then vanishes the instant it's recognized and made itself known, leaving me to try to remember where and when. Because I already know who.

Raf surrounds me here.

In the end, I did seek professional help. My doctor says I have to work on forgiving myself. Maybe that's why Razr and I connected so well. Underneath it all, we're just a pair of fucked-up souls, each of us seeking redemption from our past.

"Bailey."

I lift my hand in a small wave as Rodolfo approaches his family plot. "Sorry. I can leave if you want to spend some time alone with him." I smile up at Raf's older brother from where I've been kneeling on the ground, trying to choose the perfect location for the new potted plant I've brought with me today to add to the already extensive collection that adorns his grave.

Raf's final resting place at the cemetery is now a vast array of colors. All beautiful. All vibrant. Just like he was.

My smile fades, and I bite my lip. I've only seen Rodolfo a handful of times since it all happened, and it was always as part of a group. My nervous hands start pulling at non-existent weeds, suddenly needing something to do.

"It was you I came to see, Little Bee." He smiles gently as he kneels beside me. My hands continue to grab at nothing, and he takes the one closest to him to stop me from losing myself to my guilt.

"Thank you."

"For?"

"Looking after his resting place so well."

"It's the least I can do."

There's a pause. So much to say, but how to say it? Shake the bottle and let it explode, or open the top gently and let it trickle out? None of them seem right, given the unfortunate circumstances. I'd rather keep it firmly closed, but I know I'm not going to be allowed to do that today.

I glance at the man who looks like his brother, and tears immediately prick my eyes as a familiar dark expressive gaze meets mine.

"I've wanted to speak to you for some time, Bee, but I know you haven't been in a good place."

I shrug. "We all needed our time to heal. Each of us in our own way."

He nods. I watch him swallow down the emotions that are building in his throat. “He loved you so much, Bee.”

“And I realized that way too late.”

There’s another pause. It’s not uncomfortable or awkward. It’s necessary. Each break is in preparation for the next stepping stone. To the next moment of reflection and acceptance.

“Razr stopped by to see us when he was in town.”

I’m surprised by that. I knew there may have been other letter recipients. I never expected Raf’s family to have been one of them.

I simply nod.

“What happened to Raf, Bee… it was an accident. Nothing more. It wasn’t anyone’s fault. It was just his time.”

Silent tears run down my cheeks. I only realize when one drips onto my denim shorts, turning the pale material dark.

“I want him to come back,” I sob.

“We all do, Bee. But he can’t ever come back. But we’ll see him again. You know that, right?”

I nod.

“I’m here because now’s the time to say what needs saying.” He’s trying to be firm but gentle at the same time.

“And what needs saying, Rodolfo?”

My voice is a whisper. My heart is aching so bad, and my throat has a lump so big I can’t even swallow it down.

“Well, now that you’ve started on your healing journey, it’s time for me to tell you that this isn’t what Raf would have wanted. To have you spend your time mourning him and letting life pass you by. He loved you more than anything in this world. It would break his heart to see you like this. All my baby brother ever wanted was your happiness.”

“I know.” The words are barely audible as the tears now fall freely.

"You need to start living your life again, Bee. Can you do that for me?"

I shake my head. "I'm not sure I can."

He takes my hands in his before pulling me gently around to face him. "Then do it for him. Live your life for both of you. For you and him."

I watch as he reaches into his front pocket and pulls out the small black velvet box. I immediately know what's inside even before Rod snaps it open.

"Rod, I can't…" I sob, shaking my head.

The sapphire in Raf's grandma's ring sparkles up at me. The piece of jewelry that should have symbolized our future together.

"It's yours, Bee. Raf was so happy you wanted to wear it. My folks want you to have it. See, you'll always be family to us. A sister. A daughter. No matter what." Rod slides it on the fourth finger of my right hand, and I gaze down at it.

He pulls me against him, and I rest my head on his shoulder.

"Live your life, Bee. Please. Do it for him. It's what he would have wanted."

I nod silently.

How can I refuse?

Bailey's Home, Colton, Nevada

It's been two weeks since I spoke to Rod. It's taken me that long to mentally prepare myself for what it is I need to do.

Move on with my life.

Before I can I know I need to find my own closure. I need to draw a line under the past.

Acceptance.

It took me a long time to find it, but I've finally reached that stage. Sure, if I could change things I would but I can't. We only get one shot. We don't get do-overs.

Raf doesn't have a future. He chose to give his up so I could have one. Rod's right. I need to live my life for me and for Raf.

Because if I don't then the ultimate sacrifice he made for me was for nothing.

And it has to mean something. Moving forward I need to make every day of my life count. To honor him. To thank him. Because he deserves nothing less from me.

I twist his Grandma's ring around my finger as I dial her number.

"Thank you."

"For?"

"Waiting until I was ready to talk about him."

She knows exactly who I mean.

"You and Delaney both needed time to heal. Everyone does that shit in their own goddamn time."

There's a pause. She's waiting for me to start peppering her with questions. Will I get any answers? I guess that depends on what I'm asking. I know better than most now just how protective Jaine Jones is over Paul Delaney.

"Did you get a hand-written letter?"

"I did."

"What was in it?"

"That's between Delaney and me." Typical Jaine giving nothing away.

"How did he sign your letter off. Can I ask that at least?"

"I love you."

"Same as mine."

"What's eating you up, Bailey?"

"Does it mean I love you, or does it mean *I love you*?" I know I sound frustrated and confused but that's because I am.

"You'll have to ask him that yourself."

"Do you know the answer?"

"I do."

"Did he move on with Laila?"

"That's something you'll also need to ask him yourself."

"You know that answer, too, though?"

"Yes."

"What are you saying?" I huff.

I know she'll be rolling her eyes at me. "I'm saying that if you want answers to those sorts of personal questions, you need to ask the man himself. He's ready to talk to you. He's been waiting for you to be ready to talk to him too."

"Are you saying I need to go to New York?"

"I'm saying nothing. That's a decision only you can make, Bailey."

"This conversation's not been in any way helpful."

She chuckles. "You're welcome."

"Anyone ever told you you're a pain in the ass?"

"Yup. Most days."

CHAPTER FIFTY

RAZR

Two Weeks Later
The Iron Scorpions' Clubhouse, Brightling, New York

I stare out the bedroom window at the single tree. It's open slightly, and the smell of petrichor hangs in the air after the recent shower. It's the only indication that it's been raining. Any other telltale sign has long since been stolen by the hot sun.

I feel content.

Turning thirty-three a week back was a milestone I sure as hell never thought I'd reach. Not living the life I lead and with the countless enemies I've made along the way.

I haven't heard from Bailey since I hand-delivered the letter.

Scratch that. She sent me a message on my birthday. No kisses or anything. Just those two words.

Happy Birthday.

Life's moved on. It had to. There's no reckless decision-making these days. Everything runs through the council members as it used to, rather than me making rash spur-of-the-moment choices that wind up getting people killed.

If I overstep the mark, which I typically always do, then Blaze reins me in. He's a good VP. He's much more suited to the role than the yellow-bellied Bomb ever was with his outdated views and opinions.

My phone vibrates, and I smile, knowing what it is even before looking at the screen. It's another picture from my sister, this time with Fergal O'Connell holding baby Caoimhe in his arms, a beaming smile on his face as he looks down at his little granddaughter with hair the same color as mine.

She was always destined to be a redhead with Sarah's strawberry blonde coloring and Cill's auburn.

I've only ever met the infamous Da Duster once at Cillian and Sarah's formal wedding, which was held purely as a Manhattan elite social event. An exclusive function that took place so that every high-ranking outlaw, politician, and bent pig could attend to witness the union between the Iron Scorpions MC in conjunction with Delaney Enterprises and the Irish kings, aka The Hudson Dusters.

His reputation does him no justice, and his eldest son is shaping up to be just like him. Any sane person wouldn't cross either of them. The youngest O'Connell looked out of place during the whole event. On the other hand, Padraig was the life and soul of the party. He joked and laughed, but it never once reached his eyes.

Jaine.

We didn't mention her, but he had that look about him. And he knew that I knew. I recognized it immediately because I wore it myself for a long time before realizing that I'd finally fallen in love with someone else.

I'm not sure fate will let him off quite so easily.

He had to escort Sophia Ruocco to the event. She looked like the cat who got the cream. Or should I say kitten, since she's only seventeen years old. Theirs is to be an arranged marriage. To join the Sicilian mafia and the Dusters together. Not sure why anyone would want to tie themselves to the Ruoccos. Why the Irish would willingly agree to taint and contaminate their bloodline with theirs is anyone's guess. They must have thought it a good idea at the time, and Padraig was the unfortunate O'Connell who drew the short straw.

I return my gaze to the tree. My gut's telling me something's going to happen today, and it seldom lets me down. Usually, that type of uncertainty would see me reaching for my blade, my fingers craving the familiar soothing motion of the repetitive back and forth, maybe with a little cut if my brain felt over-loaded.

I've learned to accept that what will be will be these days. To distract myself, I've learned to focus on the positive things in my life. I've also learned to appreciate what I've got rather than crave what I haven't or miss what I've lost. Yes, I'll still slice and dice a fucker. Yes, I'll still slit a throat. But these days, only when it's necessary and only when it's deserved. Not just as a form of release or simply because I can.

I answer the phone within three rings like I always do with her.

"Jaine."

"The accountant."

"What about her?"

"I've made the necessary arrangements for her to drop by the clubhouse. Sorry it's taken so long. The job she's been working on has been taxing. No pun intended."

I snicker at the unintentional joke. "You sent the contract?"

"Just done."

'How're things?"

"I'm pregnant."

Those two words leave me hollowed out for a split second. I

feel the familiar flicker of jealousy, but I douse those flames with a dose of cold, harsh reality.

If it's meant to happen for me, then it will happen.

She's married now. She and Ace kept it to locals only. Even my sister wasn't invited, and she and Jaine are as thick as thieves these days.

Sensible decision. You ask one high-ranker and you have to ask them all. Memories can be long in this life. If she'd asked Sarah, she'd have had to ask me, and given who my sister's married to, all the O'Connells would have expected to tag along.

She and Ace already have little Fin, who's seven months old now. It makes sense that they'd want to add another, so he has a sibling to grow up with. I don't think they'll stop there. Jaine doesn't have any brothers or sisters, and she didn't have many friends growing up. It's my guessing she'll want the opposite for her kids.

"When?"

"In around six months. We haven't told anyone else yet. We wanted you to be the first to know."

"Congratulations."

"Thank you."

"So, I'm guessing your return to New York's now delayed?"

"Yes. I think it'll be at least another twelve months."

"So long?" I let out a long, low whistle.

"I'm sorry, Delaney. I just need to get this little one safely in my arms before getting back on that legal treadmill. I know Cherry hasn't mapped out and you've had some close calls. I'll take the reins back as soon as I can. I'm conscious I also need to look for a legal brain with an MC background. More so now I have La eMe to contend with. I don't want to spread myself too thin. But it's like searching for rainbow-colored rocking horse shit. I'll need to hire a new recruit and train them up personally."

"Maybe you should start searching now."

She laughs. "Is Prescott that much of a headache?"

"Something like that."

"Is Sarah there today?"

"She's mentioned that she'll be dropping by."

"Give her and the baby a kiss from me."

"Will do."

I hang up. With one last look out the window, I turn and head for the shower.

THE BEST WAY TO DESCRIBE IT IS A VIBRATION OF AIR FOLLOWED by a thunk. You can tell it's metal, though. Metal cutting into wood.

Thunk. Thunk. Thunk

Am I hearing things? Are distant memories coming back to play tricks on me? I tighten the towel around my hips and walk to the window. I know before I look out what I'm going to see.

The sun glints off the mirrored surface of each shuriken as she throws it at the piece of wood that's now resting against the tree. She's slimmer. And she's even more beautiful if that's possible. She's also older and wiser. Not that you can see either of those things. But I can sense them in the way she moves, and in the determined set in that chin of hers.

Her mouth turns up into a smirk. She knows I'm watching. She knows she has my full attention. She knows I'm her very own captive audience.

She's gone through mental torment, and her beast has only just spat her back out.

She's ready to talk. I know that.

But just because she's reached that place doesn't mean she'll be saying anything I want to hear. Still, there's only one way to find out.

"Bailey. How did you get here?"

"I rode my hog, then Jamie let me in the gates."

"You rode? From Nevada to New York?"

"Did it the other way around the first time. Figured I'd see if things looked any different heading in the opposite direction."

She throws the last of her stars, then jogs off to claim them from the old piece of wood. When she turns around, she's staring straight at me. My heart leaps into my mouth, which now feels as dry as a bone.

Shit. All this time waiting, and now I have no idea what to say to her.

"Why did you come back?"

I watch as she places her stars back in their safety pouch. She starts walking towards me, her eyes full of hunger. She's hiding nothing. It's there for the world to see. How much she wants me. Even though my dick twitches in response, I know I don't want sex from her.

She stops right in front of me, the familiar citrus notes of her scent invading my senses.

"Figured we needed to do some talking."

I nod. "Shall we?" I motion my head towards the old bench.

"Sure thing, Prez."

I walk behind her, my eyes greedily drinking her in. Shit, she looks good. Damn good.

We sit side by side. The bench isn't large. I guess we could still avoid our legs touching if we tried, but she doesn't seem to mind the physical connection and doesn't attempt to distance herself.

"I wasn't expecting to see you again, Bailey."

"I know."

"For the record, Razr is under control these days, but he's still there. He'll always be there."

"I know that too."

"Anyway. You said we needed to do some talking, so I'm listening."

She stretches out her legs in front of her. My eyes skim over their slim leather-clad length, finished off with boots. It's the same get-up she was wearing that night in Nevada. When her life ended, and when mine reached rock bottom.

"I'm sorry I lied to you and Jaine about where I'm from. I am from the life, so, I didn't lie about that part. And like everyone else, I've stared death in the face on a few occasions and witnessed other people be served it more times than I can count. Raf's death hit me hard, though. I'm not looking for the gold medal for grieving the most. I'm pretty sure it hit his family even harder. I can only say how it affected me. I can accept now that it was just his time. None of us know when our number will be called in. It was the guilt. It swallowed me up whole. Raf loved me. I didn't know that. At least not until I went back home. I thought he was being forced into this marriage just as I was. But he wanted it. Wanted me.

"When he found out what you and I did all those months, it caused him so much pain, and it made me hate myself for hurting him. So, when he died, I imploded."

She pauses and paces herself, trying to stop the guilt from drowning her once more. I know all the signs.

"In the end, Raf died saving the person he loved most because I needed to save the person I love most."

There's a pause. She must realize what she's just admitted to.

"Are you saying what I think you're saying, Bailey?"

"I guess I am."

"Say it."

"I thought I just did."

"No. You intimated it. Say the damn words, sweetheart."

"I love you. I'm *in* love with you."

She leaves that out there. We both do. The only sound is the rustle of the leaves from the single tree watching over us both—the only witness to what she's traveled thousands of miles on a hog just to confess.

She smiles at the sound like she recognizes it. Like she's heard it before somehow.

"Laila?"

She's traveled the same distance to ask that question of me too. And it's a question I finally have the answer to.

Seven Months Earlier
The Delaney Home, Brightling, New York

Laila turns to face me, and I take in the blood drying on her cheek. It doesn't belong there. She doesn't belong here. This is all wrong. On every level. What the fuck was I even thinking?

Just because she's from my past, it doesn't mean she's my future.

My eyebrows furrow as I look down at her. She's still wearing the dress she had on when we met with her folks earlier. She looks cute. Not a word typically used to describe an old lady.

"Laila."

Her hands on my shoulders, she stands on her tiptoes to reach up to press her lips to mine. I know what's on offer. What she wants me to have. What she wants me to take.

Covering her hands with my own, I slide them away, then step back before our mouths can connect.

"Laila." My tone sounds sympathetic, and she immediately picks up on it.

"What is it, Paul?" She frowns and yanks her hands away. She's confused. Hurt. I hate myself for making her feel either of those things.

She also seems resigned. She already knows.

I tried to make it work, but we're from entirely different worlds. I've just witnessed Bailey fall apart, and she grew up in the life. How would Laila cope in a shit show like what went down in Nevada? She wouldn't. She couldn't.

I can't do that to her. To her folks. She deserves better than me. She deserves to live a happy life and a safe one. I can't offer her the latter. I'm not even sure I can offer her the first.

There's also the fact that I'm not in love with her.

I'm in love with the beautifully broken girl. The one who's sleeping under the stars of Nevada. The girl whose future I fucked up because of my reckless behavior and poor choices.

The one whose guilt is slowly tearing her apart and destroying her.

I watch as Laila walks towards the bedroom window. Her back is rigid, her arms folded.

"It's Bailey, isn't it? You're in love with her." Her words bite at me with bitterness and anger.

No matter what I say, it will hurt her, so I may as well just be honest. I only hope one day she'll forgive me for allowing anything to even start between us, knowing in my heart of hearts that it could never lead to anything. That it could only ever have ended like this.

One day, she'll thank me.

"Yes."

A single word answer.

And I realize I'm admitting it to myself as much as I am to Laila.

CHAPTER FIFTY-ONE

BAILEY

The Iron Scorpions' Clubhouse, Brightling, New York

Her name hangs in the air. Suspended and out in the open. I've just revealed my innermost secret then ended it with Strawberry Shortcake's name, followed by a question mark.

He doesn't answer straight away.

They're probably living together. Or engaged. Or she's pregnant. Or maybe they're even already married, although he's not wearing a wedding ring.

Still, I came here to bare my soul. To wipe the slate clean and start again. It's time to cleanse, no matter how awkward, painful, or embarrassing it is. I'm a big girl. I can handle it. Nothing can be worse than what I've already gone through.

So, what's a little humiliation sprinkled on top?

"What about her?"

He finally answers my question with a question. Great. "Are you and her…?"

"No."

"Why?" I turn to stare at him. His hair's growing back in at the sides. He'll be letting it as he'll no longer feel the need to yank it out. I've not seen sight of a blade yet, either. He really is healing himself.

"It would never have worked out between us. We're too different."

"Any other reason?"

"Are you sniffing for something, Bailey?"

"Might be."

He's playing with me, but then he can, as he has the upper hand now I've just declared my undying love for him. My currently unrequited undying love.

"I wasn't in love with her."

"Right. Any reason for that?"

"Say what's on your mind."

I feel tongue-tied all of a sudden. "The letter."

"The one I traveled thousands of miles to deliver personally? The one you had me leave on your bed?"

"That's the one."

"What about it?"

"The way you signed it off. You signed off Jaine's the same way. She told me."

"I love you."

"Yeah, that's it. I just…"

"I love you."

"I know what it…"

Realization finally dawns on me, but only when he grabs me around the waist, yanking me across to straddle his lap. "I fucking love you, Bailey."

He stares at me, and my eyes slowly graze over his perfect features. Well, at least to me they are. His green eyes are shining on his face.

Love. Contentment. Lust.

They radiate all three and more. And the latter is definitely the most prominent one right now, going by the bulge now pressed against me, which is growing thicker and harder with every beat of his heart.

He. Loves. Me.

"Has there been anyone else? Not that it's any of my business." My voice fades into a mumble when I realize I sound like a possessive freak.

"Not since you, sweetheart."

"Me neither."

I don't get a chance to say anything else as his mouth finds mine, his tongue stroking deep. Searching. Savoring. Remembering. I can feel the love on his lips. Asking questions and answering them at the same time. My tongue tangles with his, tasting the deliciously addictive adrenaline and testosterone flavors that make up Paul 'Razr' Delaney.

He stands, and I wrap my legs around his waist as he supports my ass with one hand and starts walking. I have no idea where we're going. I don't care.

I'd go anywhere with him. Anywhere at all. We've already been to hell and back.

The familiar smells of tequila and sex hit me, and I know we're inside the clubhouse. Hollers and wolf whistles sound out, and I can't help but smile against his mouth. He smiles back, our lips never parting.

"If you can't be good, be careful!"

Sarah snickers, her voice ringing out loud and clear.

He pushes the door leading to the bedrooms with his foot and strides forward. The heady combination of sandalwood and leather intensifies the moment we near his room, wrapping their familiar arms around me like an aphrodisiac.

Not that I need any where he's concerned.

He opens the door, then spins us around, using my back to close it. I place my feet on the floor, and he yanks my tank top over my head in one movement, then unclips my bra and tosses it to the side.

His mouth drops to my nipple, sucking on it hard, and my hands immediately fist his hair. Moaning my pleasure, I close my eyes and rest the back of my head against the door as he immediately unbuttons my leather pants and pulls them down my legs, along with my underwear. Stepping out of my boots, I kick them aside.

Typical biker. I'm naked, and he's still fully dressed, but right now, I don't care.

His hand drops to my pussy, thrusting two fingers inside me. I'm so wet. I should feel embarrassed by the sound of just how turned on I am, but I'm not.

He yanks his Henley over his head with one hand as I work on unbuttoning his jeans before grabbing hold of his velvet-covered steel shaft.

So long. So thick. So hard.

"Razr." It's a whisper. A need. A demand. I need him to fuck me.

"Patience, sweetheart. Let me get a condom."

"No condom." I shake my head.

He frowns.

"We've practiced long enough, Razr. And I'm also conscious of how old you're getting." I smirk.

He knows exactly what I'm offering him.

His nostrils flare as he takes on board what I'm saying. His eyes bore into mine, his expression changing to one of sheer possessiveness.

Lifting my legs around his waist, he thrusts his unsheathed cock into me in one movement, then starts to fuck me hard against the door.

My back hurts at the relentless pace, and my legs ache from trying to keep myself anchored around him as he pounds into me like a man possessed, but none of that matters. Tilting my hips, his cock connects with my sweet spot, and I scream out my pleasure so loud I'm undoubtedly sharing it with the rest of the clubhouse.

His dick sinks deeper as he claims his own release, his mouth sucking hard on my neck. He continues pumping into me as he empties himself, each thrust deeper and more determined than the last, knowing there's no barrier between us. Knowing what this could mean. He's coating my insides with his cum, making sure no part is missed, claiming every part of me as his.

And I am his.

Because from this day on, we will be beautifully broken together.

CHAPTER FIFTY-TWO

BAILEY

Two Weeks Later
The Iron Scorpions' Clubhouse, Brightling, New York

"Is it safe to sit here?"

I roll my eyes at Sarah as she snickers and points at the freshly made bed. I mean, I understand her concerns. Razr and I have been fucking so often I've felt like handing ear defenders out by way of an apology to the rest of the brothers and the other old ladies.

I'm Razr's old lady.

I smile inwardly at my new title—the old lady of the Iron Scorpions. And soon to be Mrs. Paul Delaney.

"I think I'll just use the chair." She takes a seat in front of the window. "You there, Jaine?"

We've got her on handsfree.

"I'm here. Where's baby Caoimhe?"

"She's with her grandma. I swear Roisin has her more than I do. She's obsessed with her first grandchild."

"Ma Duster's waited a long time to meet her first grandbaby, I guess. And Laila? Where's she at?"

Jaine changes the subject. She must be sick of talking about babies all the time or something.

Laila's become pretty much a regular at the clubhouse these days. There are no hard feelings between us. According to Sarah, in the end, she realized that she and Paul brought out the worst in each other. Both of them were trying to be the opposite of who they were to make the other person happy. It was never going to be sustainable in the long term.

"She'll be here in an hour or so. She's on a lunch date with that brain surgeon she's been seeing. She's currently playing the field. I've also noticed her giving young Jamie the eye on more than one occasion." She snort-laughs.

"But he's only nineteen."

"Maybe she wants to be a cougar. Who knows? Rumor has it his family are old money, so it's my guess her folks wouldn't discourage a match." Sarah shrugs.

"Really? I wonder what attracted him to this way of life."

"Rebellion, maybe? As far as I know, a lot of the brothers come from wealthy families." She shrugs again.

"I thought Laila's folks didn't want her getting with a biker?" I ask, confused.

"No, her folks didn't want her getting with Paul, and that was because of his very noticeable lack of sanity more than anything. Anyway, enough baby and Laila talk. Spill, Bailey."

I lie back on the bed. No matter how often the expensive sheets are washed, they still smell of his sandalwood cologne.

"Earth to Bailey. I know you're in love with Paul, but can we at least have a conversation without you drifting off with that dumb lovestruck expression on your face? You haven't been seen for the best part of two weeks, although by all accounts, the whole of New York has heard you screaming like a scalded cat every time you get dicked by my brother."

"I'm sure they can hear you too. You said you and Cillian are fucking like rabbits these days, chasing baby number two." I chuckle as I throw a cushion at her.

"That may be the case, but no one can hear us. Cill is all possessive about stuff like that. Our bedroom is sound-proofed. He won't even kiss me on the lips in front of anyone who's not immediate family, and even then, it's a peck. I'm his, and he's not one for sharing."

"Sounds about right." Jaine laughs out loud.

"So, spill, Bailey. Has my big brother told you he loves you yet?" Sarah asks.

I nod.

"For the benefit of Jaine, Bailey has just nodded. And?" she continues.

I mentally prepare for a Sarah peppering. I've already worked out that she thinks as we'll surely be sisters-in-law one day that there should be no secrets between us. My life will never be my own again. I've also learned that she's one hundred miles an hour, nosy as hell, and typically flies through life by the seat of her pants with no thoughts of the consequences.

"He had a video call with my daddy last night to ask for my hand."

"Jaine, do you remember when Cillian had to ask Paul for mine? The bloodbath?" Sarah laughs, finishing with another unladylike snort.

"How could I ever forget? It was my blood. If you recall, I got stabbed in the goddamn wrist, and you had to stitch me up."

I listen to them reminisce, knowing this will be me with them moving forward, and I kind of like that thought.

Girlfriends.

I never really had them before now, apart from Mo. Mo who starts a newly created cooking and cleaning job at the clubhouse next week.

"Anyway, my daddy must have said yes in the end as we're going ring shopping this weekend."

"And are you okay with another ring, Bailey? And with the speed of everything?"

I know Jaine's referring to the fact I'm wearing Raf's ring, which I won't ever take off.

"Yeah. I know Raf would just want me to be happy."

"Rodolfo said you and he had a long talk."

"Yes, we did, and it helped me so much."

"Well, Delaney is a good man. So, you make sure you look after him. If you don't, you'll answer to me personally."

"I will."

Sarah sighs, smiling fondly. "Who knew all my big brother ever wanted was a wife and kids of his own."

"Well, we've already started on the latter," I admit.

"What? You not even taking time to practice?" Sarah asks.

"We practiced for months before I moved back home. Plus, there's his age to consider. I know he doesn't want to be an old daddy."

"True." She snickers.

"Well, we can't say anything, Sarah. It's not like either of us hung about," Jaine adds.

"No, you're right." She looks thoughtful for a moment. "I mean, I was meeting up with Cill wearing a blindfold, and I had no idea who he was. I'll have to admit to my baby girl one day that she's only here because of a burst rubber and a failed morning after pill."

She shrugs, and we all laugh.

"Anyway, I've got some news too. I've already told Delaney, Cherry, and Sasha."

"I'm insulted I'm not on your top tier." Sarah huffs.

Jaine ignores her barb. "I'm pregnant."

"Again?"

"Again."

"I mean, my ovaries would be crying out too if I had to look at Ace every day."

"You've never even met him." Jaine snorts.

"I've seen pictures," Sarah argues.

"I've met him," I add, showing off.

Sarah rolls her eyes at me, and I smirk.

"Anyway, enough drooling over Ace. His head is big enough as it is. I'm just over three months."

"Is that going to delay your return to Manhattan?" Sarah asks.

"Yes, unfortunately. I need to get this baby out of me before I can pick up the reins of JAL."

"How long?"

"I'll be back in twelve months. Maybe slightly more, maybe slightly less."

"Let's hope your baby comes early again. Given Fin's size when he was born, you'd struggle if you went full term."

"He was just a big baby."

"Maybe. Anyway, congratulations. Hopefully, Cill and I will be celebrating soon too. It's not like we're not trying hard enough."

"We didn't need to know that part."

"I know, but you know me. Sharing's caring. So, Bailey. Have you given any thought to bridesmaids?"

"Well, I've got one sister, and then there's Mojo," I reply. I know where this is leading—Sarah's not one for beating about the bush.

"You need four."

"Why?"

"It's a lucky number."

"It's not my lucky number."

"It's Paul's. I'm sure of it."

"So, you and Jaine, right? Is that what you're angling for?"

"Me? Angle?"

Jaine bursts out laughing. "You should feel honored she's even bothering to ask, Bailey. Normally Sarah just bulldozes over everyone and everything to get her way. Anyway, not that you've even offered, but sorry. I have to decline. Next time I'm in Manhattan, it will be when I return for work."

"Jaine!" Sarah whines.

"Sarah." There's a warning in Jaine's tone. There's something they're not sharing with me.

"Got it. So, three bridesmaids. Now I'm sure that really is Paul's lucky number."

"He'll say it is even if it isn't."

"Well, that's what brothers are for. To do the bidding of their sisters, no?"

"All mine ever do is noogie me and get on my nerves."

"Well, there's that too."

"I'm just grateful I don't have any siblings," Jaine throws in.

We all laugh.

"So, you're meeting with the new accountant today. What's she like?"

We're standing in the bar area. Well, Sarah's standing. I've been dragged onto Razr's lap to be manhandled because he can't keep his wandering hands or mouth to himself.

"Since I'm meeting her for the first time today, I'm not sure how to answer that, Sarah."

"Oh, so it's a woman."

She winks at me, and I can't deny that there's a little flare of jealousy that runs straight through me. I don't need any more competition when I've only just got him back.

Then again, he loves me—no one else.

Razr tightens his hold around my waist as if he can read my fleeting insecure thoughts to let me know there's no need for any of them.

"Yup. Female. And she's due at two p.m., so any minute now."

As if on cue, Jamie gets up from where he's sitting and talking to a fully dressed cum slut the moment the security cameras show a black SUV approaching the compound.

"That's a Duster vehicle. I'd recognize it anywhere. So, are you guys going to be sharing the same accountant?" Sarah smiles widely.

I'm guessing she already knows the female in question and likes her.

Razr shrugs.

I step down from his lap, figuring it's not really an appropriate place for me to be sitting as he's about to go into a business meeting. He uses the opportunity to spin me around.

Every opportunity we get, we stare at each other and try to live in each other's thoughts. His eyes bore into mine, and they're full of love and emotion and all the reassurance in the world. He knows me. He knows what I need, when I need it, and I love him for it.

"I love you," I whisper in his ear.

"I love you too, sweetheart," he whispers against my mouth as his tongue traces along my bottom lip.

"Sorry to interrupt your little making-out session, but I'm here to talk numbers."

I recognize the voice immediately. Shit. What the hell is she doing here? What the fuck are the chances, and how do I handle this?

I spin around and take in the leggy blonde that would put most supermodels to shame.

"Paul, Bailey. This is Jessie." Sarah introduces the accountant, who it seems works for the Dusters also.

She holds her hand out professionally, and Razr shakes it firmly with his.

"It's nice to meet you, Mr. Delaney. I've heard a heck of a lot about you. Some might say in way too much detail." She winks at him cheekily. "And it's nice to see you too, Little Bee." She turns her attention to me and pinches my cheek, causing me to slap her hand away.

"Little Bee?" Sarah frowns.

I ignore the question.

"You work with Jaine?" I'm more whispering than talking.

"Yes siree."

She pulls me in close for a hug. She whispers, but loud enough for it to be heard. "I know. I know. We should have told you before now, but when it finally came to light, Jaine and I just figured the truth would eventually come out on its own. We didn't want to give you anything else to contend with. Not while you were still healing."

She steps back, keeping her hands on the tops of my arms while I stare at her in shocked disbelief.

"Wait. You guys know each other?" Sarah looks between us, her frown deepening as curiosity eats away at her,

"You could say that. Jessie's my sister."

EPILOGUE

PADRAIG

Four Months Later
Padraig's Apartment, Hudson Yards, New York

Jaine: *You there, Dyl?*
Jaine: *Dyl?*

I PULL OUT THE PHONE FROM UNDER MY PILLOW, THE PLACE I KEEP it so I can feel it vibrate, letting me reply straight away. Staring at the messages, I then look at the clock. It's four a.m. Shite. Something must be fucking wrong. Has she gone into labor? Jesus Christ, please let everything be okay.

Padraig: *It's the middle of the night, darlin'. Is Fin okay? The baby? You're not having any pains or contractions or anything like that, are you? You gave birth last time around now.*

Jaine: *Everything's fine. I can't sleep.*
Padraig: *So, you figured we'd make a fine pair of matching insomniacs?*
Jaine: *Something like that.*
Padraig: *Have you tried counting sheep?*
Jaine: *Does that actually work? I'll try anything. I haven't slept a wink in days.*
Padraig: *As far as I know, it's a tried and tested method, but it only works with sheep. You can't go substituting them with anything else. I tried it with cows once, and it was a no-go.*
Jaine: *You're not funny. I'm being serious.*
Padraig: *Not even a wee bit funny?*
Jaine: *No.*
Padraig: *Isn't Ace there?*
Jaine: *He's had to go to Vegas again and then detour back via Colton. Some of the ex-Undertaker brothers are still restless. Lucifer and Tadgh are worried that they may be in contact with Reaper's original backer. We're not even sure how they know who they are. Then again, maybe the backer contacted them. Anyway, they deny it, of course. They wanted Ace's involvement as he's good at diffusing these situations. We don't need them getting rebellious. We don't need a mutiny on our hands.*
Padraig: *It's that what's keeping you awake?*
Jaine: *No.*
Padraig: *So, what's on your mind? We'll be here all night if I have to drag it out of you one word at a time. What's keeping you awake? You can trust me with anything, you know that. I am Batman, after all.*
Jaine: *There's some family stuff that's come to light. I don't know how to deal with it. I'm not sure I even want to deal with it.*

Padraig: *A problem shared?*
Jaine: *It won't be halved this time, trust me.*
Padraig: *So, is that the only thing on your mind?*
Jaine: *No.*
Padraig: *I'm going to need more than that, darlin'.*

She's typing. Seconds pass. Minutes. Hours. It doesn't matter. Lying on my bed, I hold up my phone and stare at the screen. I know I'm wearing a contented smile. I'm taking whatever comfort I can from the fact that she's only talking to me right now—only relying on me.

Even if she doesn't know it's me.

Right now, it's just us. It's just like old times. I'm her confidant. But then again, I'm not.

Jaine: *I miss him, Dyl.*
Padraig: *When's he due back? Tomorrow?*
Jaine: *Not Ace.*
Padraig: *Who?*
Jaine: *Irish. I miss Irish.*

I feel like I've been sucker-punched, and a roller coaster of emotions barrels through me all at once.

Desperation. Resignation. Love.

Hope.

I stare at the message. She misses me. But why? She asked me never to contact her again. She told me she didn't love me anymore. That she never had. So why does she miss me? And why say it after all this time?

Tears prick my eyes. If she misses me, then surely there's still a chance.

I try to type a response, but I fumble with my phone, suddenly all thumbs. I swear silently in frustration as I start to panic that she'll disappear, and that this conversation will end. And that I'll never know. Because I need to know.

For the love of The Almighty, I need to know why.

Why the fuck is she admitting to missing me after all this time?

I know I should have forgotten her. She's married to Ace now. She has the most beautiful little boy and another one on the way. She's moved on and left me behind.

But I can't move the fuck on. I will never be able to move the fuck on.

Not from her. Not ever.

It's not her fault that she's my everything. It's not her fault that every day I silently weep that I'm not her everything too.

Since that fateful day almost two years ago, all I've done is stand here in the exact same spot like the dog pining for the owner who dumped him and then drove off. Praying she'll realize she made a mistake. Praying she'll come back.

For me.

Hope.

Padraig: *I'm sure he misses you too, Jaine.*

Jaine: *I need to hear his voice, Dyl.*

I wipe the tears that are now steadily falling. What the fuck is going on? What the fuck is she saying?

And why now?

I'm due to get married in a few months, for fuck's sake. The invitations have already been written and are ready to be sent out.

Padraig: *I'm not sure what we can do about that, darlin'.*

Jaine: *I know. It's stupid. I've tried to be strong, but it's driving me insane, you know? I can't remember what he sounds like. I've forgotten. Can you believe it? And I can't stop crying because of it. It's tearing me apart.*
Padraig: *Jaine.*
Padraig: *Jaine?*
Padraig: *Jaine!!*

I know when she doesn't reply that she's gotten emotional.

Is it wrong of me to want that? That I'm taking pleasure from her pain? That I want her to hurt like I've been hurting all this fucking time?

Tears mean hurt. Hurt means feelings. I want to know what those feelings are.

Hope.

Padraig: *Jaine, if you don't reply, I'm flying to California right fucking now.*
Jaine: *Can I call you?*

Fuck. Fuck. Fuck. Dyl won't be expecting a call from her, and even if he answers, he won't have time to read what's been said beforehand. So, he won't know what to say. Not that he would anyway. He won't know how to comfort her. How to reassure her. How to fucking love her the way she deserves to be loved.

No one does. Not like I can.

Padraig: *It's not a good time, Jaine. I'm sorry.*
Jaine: *You have company?*
Padraig: *Something like that.*

Fuck, now she's going to think Dyl's got someone with him. What a mess.

Jaine: *Dyl, I'm sorry. I should go. It's just no one else understands. You've been there from day one. You were the first person I spoke to.*

Day one of what? What the fuck happened on this day fucking one that I'm not party to because something obviously did.

Padraig: *I'm sure one other person does, Jaine.*
Jaine: *Does what?*
Padraig: *Understand.*
Jaine: *Who?*
Padraig: *Paddy.*

She's typing. Seconds pass. Minutes. It feels like fucking hours.

Jaine: *I can't.*
Padraig: *Why can't you?*
Jaine: *Are you telling me you think I should?*
Padraig: *I can't tell you what to do, darlin'.*
Jaine: *But even if I did, it's the middle of the night. Would he even be awake? Would he even answer?*
Padraig: *I'm sure when he sees your name, he'll answer straight away.*
Jaine: *What would I even say?*
Padraig: *Whatever's in your heart.*

Lying back, I stare at the ceiling.

I desperately want to hold her. Touch her. See her. I want everything from her. Always her. Only her. But I can't have that. I can never have that.

She can never be fucking mine.

Tears run down my face, soaking the pillow below.

My heart beats loudly in my chest at the thought of hearing her fucking voice. Just one more time. Is it selfish of me? It's not a lot to ask, is it? Her speaking to me as Irish.

Her Irish.

She won't call. She'll back out. She'll drift off to sleep now, and it will all be a distant memory tomorrow. We'll laugh and joke about her brief moment of reflection that fleetingly turned into an all-consuming split-second madness before it was gone again.

A madness that almost won. A madness I want to fucking win.

Is this all just wishful thinking on my part? Or am I dreaming?

Then I realize it's the latter. Not a dream, but a nightmare I'll never wake up from. I've been sleep-walking through life since she let me go almost two years ago.

And what if she calls?

What do I say? Do I just listen? Let her get it all off her chest while I imagine her in my arms, silently telling her how much I fucking love her?

Because I do. I will always love her until I take my last dying breath. She's it for me.

My end game that never will.

But what if she says things I don't want to hear? What if she confirms that she doesn't love me? Never had. Never will.

Holding my phone to my chest, I wait, and I wait, and I wait.

Nothing.

I switch on some music. Ed Sheeran springs into life.

Give Me Love.

How fucking fitting. I lose myself in the lyrics.

Praying. Asking. Begging.

It's then I hear the heart-wrenching sobs, and I realize they're my own. Jesus Christ. How would she react if she knew just how much I fucking love her? Please just once. I'll never ask for anything again, I swear, God.

My phone rings with an incoming call.

Jaine Jones.

Author's Note

I hope you enjoyed Razr's story.

RAZR is NOT standalone.
RAZR is BOOK 3 of a SERIES, which contains an ONGOING STORYLINE that CONCLUDES in BOOK 6, DIRTY PADRAIG.

These books contain MULTIPLE POVs from characters across the entire series.

Due to the nature of the CONTINUING STORYLINE, these books MUST be
READ IN ORDER.

The Outlaw Chess Reading Order

ACE

DIRTY CILLIAN

RAZR

DIRTY DYLAN

DIRTY EOIN

DIRTY PADRAIG

These books are NOT standalone.

Due to the nature of the CONTINUING STORYLINE

PLEASE READ IN ORDER.

Acknowledgements

For Reuben.

About the Author

Harley Diamond is a writer of romance novels with plot twists that will leave you begging for more. In every dirty story, an angsty bad boy and a badass queen lead the cast.

When Harley's not reading, she's writing. When not doing either, she's plotting to unleash her next novel on you from her non-working farm in West Yorkshire, England, surrounded by her faithful but very needy companions. Her seven rescue dogs.

Facebook Group: Harley’s Hangout
Facebook Group: Harley’s Spoilers

www.harleydiamond.com

Printed in Great Britain
by Amazon

60266918R00228